I0666220

THE LOST AND FOUND TRIO

Grif, Flynn & Max

By

J.M. Madden

Copyright © 2014 by J.M. Madden
Print Edition

This book is a work of fiction. Names, characters, places and incidents are either the product of the author's imagination or are used fictitiously, and any resemblance to actual persons living or dead, business establishments, events or locales is entirely coincidental.

Any logistical, technical, procedural or medical mistake in this book is truly my own.

Contents

HER FOREVER HERO

By

J.M. Madden

CHAPTER ONE

✦

S HE WAS ABOUT to spew.

Grif watched uptight and luscious Kendall Herrington try to control her nausea in the midst of the board meeting around her. She had done pretty well for the last few minutes, but he'd memorized every expression on her cool, smooth face, and knew she had about reached her breaking point.

Now, the conundrum was, did he help her out by interrupting this volatile meeting so that she didn't have to? He could slip up behind her, whisper into the delicate curve of her ear some falsely important message and escort her out of the room. It would look legitimate and would save her image. She could step into her office, use her private bathroom and these stuffed shirts would be none the wiser.

Her full lips compressed and her pale eyes glazed over as the man to her right tried to hammer home his point.

No more time.

Stepping forward, deliberately in front of the shark beside her, he leaned down into her space. Her wide green eyes fluttered shut as he whispered into her ear, "You should probably step out before you compromise yourself."

Her eyes opened and she gave him a sharp look, but nodded her head. Pushing to her feet, she addressed the table.

"Gentlemen, excuse me for a moment please. I have an issue I need to deal with."

A couple of them shook their heads, as if they couldn't believe there was anything of more importance than what they were talking about. Her father shot her a look, both concerned and aggravated, but nodded her away.

As she walked the length of the table to the opposite end of the room, Grif hoped he was the only one who noticed how shaky she was on her too-tall boots. As soon as the door closed behind them, he gripped her elbow in his hand to help her down the hallway, but she pulled away. "I'm fine, just a little nauseous. Must have been something I ate."

Right. Something you ate. Or was it something you screwed? The woman had to be delirious if she didn't realize she was pregnant.

The staff at Herrington Limited were bustling, knowing that every major stockholder in the company sat in the boardroom just a few feet away for the quarterly meeting. Nobody said a word to the boss's daughter as she headed purposefully down the hallway to her office. Grif fell in a step behind her, eyes roving over everything yet focused on her. Kendall's secretary was not at her desk when they walked in, so she crossed to her office. As soon as she made it inside, she all but ran to the private bathroom, slamming the heavy oak door shut behind her. Grif let her have her privacy, though it hurt him to hear her retching inside. Her phone started to ring, but he let voicemail grab it, moving to stand at the wide windows across the way.

Snow swirled outside, calling for him to come out and play. With the way things were going in the boardroom, though, he'd be here for several more hours before he would be able to relax.

And did he really have the right to play if Kendall was pregnant?

The toilet flushed in the bathroom and he heard water running into the sink. She would walk out of that bathroom beautiful and as put together as always, as if the last ten minutes had never happened. It was one of the things he admired about her, that iron spirit.

It was also one of the things he hated.

Vail was one of the most beautiful cities in the country, maybe even the world, and she wouldn't even look out the window. If it didn't have a spreadsheet or prospectus attached to it, she wouldn't give it a glance.

The door opened and she stepped out.

Grif couldn't even tell she'd been sick; the only indication a slight narrowing of her pale eyes. Her long, blond hair had been wrapped into a damn knot low on her neck, away from her face. He hated those things, because it was the only way he'd seen her wear her hair here. Only once had he ever seen it down. It had hung in a mess of unbelievable curls almost down to her waist.

The knots she tamed her hair into did highlight the perfection of her bone structure. Women spent millions chasing the high cheekboned, lean-jawed, full-lipped look Kendall had made her career from, but didn't appreciate. She had been a runway model in every country of the world, but her passion was the family business. Real estate. And timber.

He shook his head.

"Something wrong, Mr. Parks?"

Her cool whiskey voice broke into his thoughts and brought his gaze to hers. She stared at him, as if daring him to bring up the incident in the bathroom. "No, ma'am. Glad to see you looking more like yourself."

Her eyes flickered and looked away. She smoothed her elegant hands over the sleek column of her black slacks, adjusting the fit, and took a deep breath. "Well, then, we've wasted enough time. Let's get back to it."

Grif almost laughed out loud. The way she said the words it sounded like she'd left the meeting and puked her guts out to appease a whim of his.

Whatever.

When she re-entered the boardroom, all eyes lifted to her; some angry, some relieved, others ambivalent. Whether she took over the company for her ailing father or not was the hot topic right now and she couldn't appear weak in front of the nay-sayers. Kendall Herrington hadn't had the chance to be groomed for the company at her father's knee like some other men were, because of a nasty divorce when she'd been a child. Her mother had moved the two of them to New York, where she'd had the best of everything...schools, nannies. It was where she'd gotten into modeling.

It wasn't until Kendall was a teenager that her father started to be a more vital part of her life. Her passion for the family business had competed with her desire to please her mother by being one of the premiere models in the industry. Grif wasn't ashamed to admit he'd gazed at her magazine pictures a little longer than strictly needed.

But that successful modeling career made these men believe that she wouldn't be a good fit for the company. He hated the way they fought everything she said. She had legitimate, progressive, environmentally friendly ideas for taking over the company, but these old codgers didn't think she could do it. They were much more comfortable with her father. When old man Herrington manned the wheel with Kendall as his second, things flowed smoothly. But they didn't have the faith in her to navigate the Herrington ship through treacherous economical waters alone. She'd done a good job with her father backing her up. Now that he was almost completely out of the picture though, she struggled to maintain her course.

Because they refused to support her.

As he moved to stand against the wall, his eyes drifted down the length of the table to her primary competition, Hunter Groves. Hunter seemed concerned and solicitous until Kendall's back turned. Grif didn't miss the glint of enjoyment that flashed through his cunning eyes.

Now, if only Kendall would see it.

For some reason she had a glaring blind-spot where he was concerned. Grif knew they'd grown up together, almost as close as brother and sister. When he'd first scouted the job he discovered they had dated years ago, but both seemed to know it felt wrong. If they were at loose ends they escorted each other to parties, but the practice had begun to fall away. Hunter very rarely seemed to be without an escort.

Which made Grif happy. He didn't know if he could tolerate Hunter being near her.

KENDALL FORCED HER eyes away from her distracting bodyguard standing so stalwart against the wall. His hands were clasped in front of himself and for a minute she couldn't remember which one was the prosthetic. He wore black leather gloves to conceal both hands, she assumed for some tactical advantage.

His right hand was the fake one. She'd seen it a time or two when they were traveling. He'd worn a shirt the night they'd… No. Not thinking about that right now.

It was no surprise she couldn't tell his two hands apart. They behaved exactly the same way. The prosthetic was able to move like his good hand, and she'd never seen him fumble anything. To a regular bystander, he seemed normal.

When her father had contracted with Lost And Found Investigative Service to hire her a bodyguard team after a recent issue with an old stalker, she'd laughed in disbelief. The man had already been jailed, but her father had been adamant. "You never know what kind of crazies are out there. Besides, you're part of a well-known family."

She'd shaken her head. "They're disabled."

It was a good thing she wasn't actually in danger, otherwise she'd have been pissed that he hadn't hired her the best. But he'd promised her that the former Marines were more than good enough.

Kendall had fumed, but easing her father's mind right then was more important than anything she wanted to argue about. She'd given in, reluctantly.

The two former Marines had moved into the condo next door, rotating twelve hour shifts. If they weren't actually in the condo with her, they were watching the cameras that had been installed around her fifth floor unit. The scrutiny made her feel claustrophobic, but it seemed to take some of the worry from her father's eyes.

As she tried to concentrate on the business in front of her, she kept Parks in her peripheral vision. She had to acknowledge that he seemed more than qualified to her now. She'd had bodyguards before, many times, but none of them had inspired the same feeling of calm in every situation that Parks did. He wasn't hulking, like some of the men she'd used before, but solid. She stood six one with her heels on, and he was a little taller. Yes, he outweighed her by probably a hundred pounds, but the bulk seemed necessary for his frame.

Man, that suit fit him like it had been painted on.

She blinked, realizing she'd missed part of the conversation. This bug had gotten her down, and she needed to shake it off. Maybe she needed to take the time to go to the doctor.

The meeting continued on until her father pushed slowly to his feet. "Gentlemen, and Kendall, I believe we should break for now. We'll vote on my successor at the next quarterly meeting. You have the information you need to decide in front of you. Take the files with you and study them at home. We'll resume talks in April. Have a good weekend, gentlemen."

Hunter pushed away from the table. "Thank you, Frank. I have a date to get to."

He winked at the men around him, gathering chuckles. Kendall tried not to wince at the blatant double standard. If she'd said the same thing, they'd have all blustered and complained about her not being a positive representative for the company.

But no. Boys would be boys.

Hunter's father Roger sat at the opposite end of the table with a frown on his face. Didn't look like he liked the way his son left the meeting, either.

She pushed to her feet along with the others and circled the table to her father. Anxiety clutched at her insides as she took in the lines on his face. This had been a long meeting.

"Is Charles coming for you, Dad?"

He smiled at her and waved a hand. "Of course. I told him to just wait downstairs until I get there."

Kendall watched her father move, wishing she could give him twenty of her years. Frank Herrington had been a force to be reckoned with until a series of heart attacks earlier this year had set the timberman on his heels. After a triple bypass and rehab he'd bounced back, but the effort had cost him. When he'd called her three months ago to ask her if she wanted to be considered to take over the company, she'd been surprised that he would be handing over the reins so soon, but she'd understood. She'd accepted the challenge on the spot and moved from aquisitions to management, learning directly from him. Then she'd started to actively lobby for her position in the company.

Her father had other concerns, too. His current wife Deedra had proven just as high maintenance as Kendall had predicted. Sometimes she wondered if the woman was trying to put her father in the grave with her reckless activities. Flirting with men half her age, causing trouble with the married women in town. Unfortunately, her father turned a blind eye to Deedra's antics. He proclaimed himself smitten. Again.

Kendall wondered if she would ever know the feeling. Unable to help herself, her eyes flicked to Parks. She flushed when she realized he already stared at her with heat in his eyes.

She needed to pull her father aside and ask him to have Parks reassigned. The man put her off balance. She needed all her concentration right now to deal with the company. Yes, he'd saved her bacon today, because she would have tried to tough the situation out. But that didn't mean he could look at her like he knew her body better than she did.

Her father grabbed his briefcase, then his fleece-lined Burberry trench coat. He turned back long enough to press a kiss to her forehead. "You're doing fine, Kendall. Don't let them rattle you."

She allowed herself to sag against him, just the tiniest bit, before he pulled away. "I know. I just wish all of this were over."

He grinned at her and she was reminded how handsome he still was, years past his prime. Thick gray hair, flashing green eyes so similar to her own. "It will be soon. Your position is all but secured. These old coots may bluff and bluster, but you have a proven, money making track record. You're a shoo-in."

Kendall wished she had the same faith in herself he did, but that would be so far from the truth. Yes, she could act her ass off, but deep inside she floundered. Her father winked at her as he walked out the door.

"Parks, don't let her work too long."

"Yes, sir."

Kendall blinked, unsure she'd heard her father correctly. Did he actually make a joke to the guard about her? She glanced at her security and had to catch her breath.

Grafton Parks was a gorgeous distraction, but when he smiled he became downright deadly to her peace of mind. His variegated hazel blue eyes lightened and his hard lipped mouth softened. Their eyes connected and a shiver shuddered down her spine. She forced herself to turn away, feeling light headed. The man was dangerous to her psyche. She'd already made one mistake because of him. She would not make another.

Kendall gathered her folder and headed to her office. She sat down at the computer and pressed the power key.

"Your father said not to work too long."

She flicked him a glance but continued what she had started. "Yes, and he also said my position is all *but* secured. I'll work, thank you for your concern."

"Ms. Herrington," he drawled, "I think you should reevaluate your decision. You were sick less than an hour ago."

Kendall blinked, but waved a hand, determined not to be swayed. "I'm fine. It must have just been something from lunch that didn't agree with me."

She felt him move closer but refused to look up at him.

"You didn't eat anything for lunch. You know that."

She sighed, exasperated. "Then it must be a bug or something. It's none of your concern."

He moved to the front of her desk and leaned close, forcing her to look at him.

"You're pregnant."

Her hands stuttered on the keys and her heart stopped. No. It couldn't be. Her eyes latched onto his, straight in front of her. He seemed deadly serious. "I'm not pregnant!"

He lifted one black brow, and crossed his arms over his massive chest. Then he stared at her, waiting.

Kendall pulled her organizer across the desk and leafed through, looking for the little marks she used to indicate her period. Then she counted.

And finally swayed in her chair. He could be right.

Parks moved without sound, swinging her chair around and pressing her head down to her knees. "Now, take it easy. You're fine. Breathe. Breathe, Kendall."

His rough voice was a balm to her emotions and his hand on her back so soothing. Too soothing. But she couldn't make herself pull away.

Frantic thoughts ricocheted through her mind. A baby? Seriously? How the hell was she supposed to take care of a baby right now? Her life was devoted to the company. She didn't have time to ski down the mountain, let alone take care of a child.

Wait. Maybe she wasn't pregnant. She lifted her head. "There's a chance I'm not. I mean, it was just the one time and we took care of stuff. It's not possible for me to be pregnant."

She hated the way he lifted that black brow at her, as if she were a damn simpleton burying her head in the sand. But he nodded to her once. "We can get you a test. Then we'll know for sure."

Tears pressed at her eyelids. She forced herself to pull away from his comforting touch to face her desk. Everything had blurred in front of her and she doubted she'd be able to type two words together. Emails needed responded to. The secretary's to-do list needed compiled. She needed to study the prospectus again to be ready for next week.

Kendall shoved away from the desk and paced across to the floor to ceiling windows. Night had fallen in the ultra-exclusive ski resort town. Christmas lights twinkled, though the holiday had passed weeks ago. They'd stay up all year long, just to perpetuate the dream of the holiday. She pressed her hand to the glass, overwhelmed with the need to be outside. Giving Parks a glance, she grabbed her purse from the cubby in her desk and snatched her coat from the tree. Barely taking the time to lock her door, she sailed down the hallway. Rather than be halted at the elevator, she pushed through the adjacent door and carefully clacked down the stairway in her boots.

She didn't even have to look to know that Parks was be-hind her. The only time he slowed her down was just before she passed through the revolving front door and into the cold of the night. He guided her to a secondary, less-used door and exited ahead of her. Kendall allowed herself to reach out and touch his back. Her fist curled into the fabric of his suit jacket and she gasped, desperate for air, until he gave way and let her through. Staggering to the wall of the building, she leaned against it and dragged the bracingly cold night into her lungs. The blind panic began to ease and her head began to clear.

"I can't be pregnant," she gasped.

He squeezed her shoulder. "We'll figure it out."

Kendall floated through the night in a haze. She wanted wine, but didn't know if that would be wise, considering. Parks left without a word and Calvert took over the night shift.

She debated calling her father, but that would be incredibly unfair. He wanted a grandchild, desparately, and something this momentous, that had her emotions so off-kilter, was bound to slip out. Parks had promised to grab a test for her in the morning so that she didn't have to go out and hope not to be recognized. It was bad enough he would be going, because the two of them had been linked for weeks now. Paparazzi still considered her a marketable commodity, just like everyone else in the world. Though she'd been working for her father for the past two years, her previous career had been momentous.

When the former Marine had first started, there'd been pictures of them in every magazine and gossip rag imaginable. They were a striking couple, she had to admit. Calvert didn't receive the same exposure because he preferred night shift, but there'd been a few pictures of him as well. And while the shorter, stockier built blond with the easy smile was good looking in his own way, her eyes were always drawn to Parks, with his springy black hair and knowing eyes. It was ridiculous how in-tune her body seemed to be with his. Men taller than her were few and far between.

Needing to do something, she crossed to the freezer, praying that the maid had restocked.

"Oh, yes."

Snatching a spoon from the silverware drawer, she crossed to the overstuffed chair against the far window. Falling into the softness, she tugged the lid off the carton of classic vanilla bean, sighing in pleasure as the first bite melted in her mouth. Perfect.

CHAPTER TWO

✦

KENDALL HAD MANAGED to curl her body into a ball in the overstuffed chair. The remains of a pint of vanilla bean sat on the carpet, leaking into the fine nap. He frowned at the way her head was angled over the arm. She'd be sore when she woke up.

But stunning.

Every time he walked into a room with her it felt like a punch to the gut. He constantly had to remind himself that he had no business looking at her.

Reaching out, he shook her shoulder gently. "Kendall."

She frowned in her sleep, fine lines puckering her brows. "No," she murmured.

Grif shook her more firmly. "I brought you that item that you needed."

She tried to shift in the seat, but she was too long of leg to be in any position other than what she currently was. With a groan, she pushed herself vertical.

Grif wanted to run his fingers into her pale gold curls to straighten them, but he knew she wouldn't welcome his touch in that way. There were too many other distractions.

She stilled when she spied the bag in his hand and seemed to fold in on herself. She looked up at him, an odd look on her face. "I thought it was a dream," she whispered.

He ached to take her into his arms and hold her, but she didn't need that right now.

"I read the directions on one of the boxes, and it says morning urine has the highest concentration of the pregnancy hormone."

Kendall cringed in distaste, and he cursed silently to himself. He could have led her into it a little more gently. "Sorry."

She sighed and took the plain white pharmacy bag from his hand, unrolling the top. She looked up at him in surprise.

"Three boxes? Really?"

Grif jerked his shoulders in a shrug. "None of them are a hundred percent accurate, but I thought if we tried several of them, we could get a consensus."

She lifted a brow at him, the sleep disappearing from her eyes. "We?"

He could only shrug again and try not to flush.

Kendall flipped each of the boxes over to read the information on the back, then pushed to her feet, one clutched in her hand.

"If you'll excuse me for a moment."

She walked out of the living room and into the bedroom as if she were going to change her clothes, rather than her life. Potentially. He watched her narrow back disappear through the bedroom door, leaving it open barely a crack.

Grif paced across the room, strangely nervous. This was an odd situation to be in. The lines between protector and protect-ee often became blurred, but he'd completely obliterated them this time. He'd done something he'd never done before.

He'd slept with a client.

Unfortunately, he'd do it again if she let him.

The thought that she could be carrying his child right now terrified him more than anything else he'd ever done. More than the three tours in Iraq and Afghanistan, more than the private, covert contract work he'd done after he'd been medically discharged.

The night they'd shared had been short but explosive. Totally unexpected on his part, because Kendall Herrington had done nothing but glare at him ever since he'd taken the job. But half a bottle of wine had loosened her tongue and the desperate hold on her emotions.

That night, that hour, had rocked his world, and hers he thought as well, but all too quickly that wall had slapped back into place. Kendall declared their tryst an aberration and demanded he never say anything about it. For the most part, he'd accepted that. At the time. The depth of his reaction to her had shaken him. He'd never been in a long term relationship before, but she'd been easy to get along with for one night. It made him crave more.

He glanced at his watch. She'd been gone for ten minutes. Crossing to the bedroom door, he knocked lightly. "Kendall?"

There was no response so he eased into the room and across to the bathroom. He knocked on the door.

Sobs came to him through the wood and he twisted the handle. Kendall sat on the floor beside the commode, face pressed to her drawn-up knees. Grif's heart ached at the desolation he heard in her voice. She clutched a white stick in her hand. Even from several feet away he could see the plus sign in the display window.

Kneeling in front of her, he pressed a light kiss to the top of her head.

She jerked away from him and glared at him with fury. "How could you do this to me?"

Frowning, he tried to give her the benefit of the doubt. "What do you mean how could *I* do this to you? If I remember right, you damn near tackled me that night. As I'm sure you are well aware."

Fresh tears filled her luminous eyes, and he felt bad for calling her on her shit. She dropped her head back to her knees. "I know," she moaned.

He reached out and squeezed her shuddering shoulder. "We'll take care of this."

She looked up at him with hope in her eyes and he wanted to lean down to kiss her.

Kendall must have known what he was thinking, because she pulled away and wiped her face with her hands. She took a deep, gasping breath and seemed to pull her control back around her like a cloak.

Grif didn't like the coolness that settled into her expression. But he understood it was how she protected herself.

He grabbed a washcloth and doused it with cold water, then squeezed as much water out as he could against the side of the sink. She took the cloth and held it to her face.

"I'm fine now, hero. You can go."

Fury nipped at him. Maybe it was a good thing she didn't look at him. She'd probably be scared to death if she saw his face.

Without a word, he left the bathroom.

"Do you need me to reassign you?"

Grif gnashed his teeth at Duncan's legitimate question and paused before he barked out a hasty answer. "No, I just need you to be aware I may not be completely objective now. She practically jumped my bones that night, but I was a willing participant. We both need to take responsibility for our actions."

Duncan sighed on the other end of the line. "I wish I could help you out buddy, but you've gotten yourself into a pickle. I'm a little surprised that you allowed such a bad lapse in judgement. I should be pissed."

Grif looked out at the swirling snow, aware he'd seriously fucked up. He'd jeopardized the safety of a client by sleeping with her and now the repercussions were rippling out. They had a kid on the way, her position at the firm was in danger. Hell, her father's health was in danger. Grif genuinely liked the senior Herrington and he didn't want to do anything to threaten the man's life.

"Is anybody free to come out for a few weeks? I'll take a leave while I try to get this worked out."

Duncan huffed on the other end of the line. In his mind Grif could see him swinging around in his big leather chair to survey the whiteboard. "Yeah, I might be able to wrangle somebody out there. Give me a few hours."

The tension in his shoulders eased just a bit. Then he could focus on Kendall.

"I appreciate this, boss man. I'll clean up my mess."

Duncan laughed on the other end of the line. "Yeah, right. Do me a favor and don't fall for this girl. They're dropping like flies around here."

Grif laughed as well. "Has Palmer manned up and asked Shannon to marry him yet?"

"No. But Zeke just found his match a couple weeks ago. They are getting married."

Grif choked back his surprise. Zeke was a good guy, tough, but scarred all to fuck. "She must really be something."

"Oh, she is. I'll get somebody out there for you Grif, but get your life straightened out. You need to be thinking long-term here, not just immediate crises."

"I know," he sighed. "Thanks, Duncan."

"No problem."

Grif dropped his phone into his pocket and took a swig from the water bottle beside him. Duncan was right. He did need to be thinking long-term. The shock of the immediate issue had blurred his head. He had a kid coming.

Grif dropped into the overstuffed chair behind him. What the hell was he going to do with a kid? He certainly had no idea. The thought of being responsible for a tiny little human being like that scared the shit out of him.

His own parents were worthless. His mother was a drunk and his father had been a crook. Get-togethers in the Parks' household consisted of liquor and yelling, with the occasional trip to the emergency room. Hunger had been his constant companion growing up, and when he'd run away from home at the age of sixteen, he hadn't even been missed.

One time in the past ten years he'd gone home. When he walked in the door it was as if he'd entered a twilight zone. His mother sat in the same chair, smoke curling around her head, high-ball glass in her left hand. She'd cracked a cunning smile when he'd walked in and fed him a sob story about his father dying and leaving her broke. Basically, she needed money.

He'd had two hundred bucks in his wallet. He'd dropped it onto the table and walked out, more disgusted with himself this time because he'd still been looking for something that wasn't there.

Did he even have the ability to create a different kind of life for his child? He made good money from LNF, and other than a few toys he'd just let it accumulate. The apartment in Denver would probably not work though. He'd have to get a house with a yard or something, so the kid could play.

Anxiety gnawed at his stomach. He ached for a drink.

First he needed to decide what to do with Kendall.

The woman made his blood run hot. Without a doubt she was the sexiest woman he knew. She'd been in a couple of movies years ago, but her ads for the lingerie company were the ones he remembered. Sultry and too beguiling for her own good. It was a real challenge to correlate that woman with the one in the bedroom now, cold and hard-edged.

It made him wonder which was the real Kendall.

CHAPTER THREE

✦

G RIF STRAIGHTENED THE lapels of his suit jacket and fought to keep from fiddling as the housekeeper walked him through Herrington House. Although that wasn't exactly the right word for the type of dwelling they were in. When he thought of "house", a two bedroom split-level came to mind. Not this overblown cabin. Even "cabin" did not carry the weight that the massive log mansion deserved, though.

The best of Herrington Lumber had been used to build one of the most palatial retreats in Vail. The house was three stories tall, eighteen rooms, with huge soaring windows on all sides to capture as much of the pristine view as possible. The honeyed patina of the logs and the custom stonework, warmed of course, made the house feel rustic and inviting and he genuinely enjoyed working on the premises when Kendall met with her father. The windows were difficult to guard, but the mansion itself hung on an overlook with one meandering driveway up the side of the mountain. Easy to watch. Closed circuit cameras recorded the mountainous surroundings. Several more were strategically placed inside, easing the burden on the four man security team always on site.

Grif tipped his chin to the small bubble camera in the foyer, knowing that Chuck would be watching and reporting.

He had a sneaking suspicion the camera followed him as far as it could. Goodrich, head of security here at the house, didn't appreciate outside talent coming onto his territory and he'd made it clear that the LNF contingent could leave at any time.

Luckily, the choice wasn't up to him. It was up to the man grinning at him from the cushy chair in front of the fireplace in the den.

"Grif. Thank you for coming on such short notice."

The older man made a move to get up, but Grif waved him back down. "Don't get up, sir."

Frank relaxed into the chair and motioned to the one beside him. "Sit down with me."

Grif tried to keep his curiosity in check. He'd gotten a message from one of Frank's many assistants at the company saying that he needed to meet for lunch the next day at the house. Grif had never been there when not watching Kendall, so it seemed a little strange to have the man's attention focused on him.

The housekeeper, a kind, older woman by the name of Emily, brought in a tray with a long neck beer and an iced bottle of water on it. She handed the beer to Frank and him the water. Grif tossed her a wink, knowing it would make her blush.

She held the tray to her side as she addressed Frank. "Is there anything else, Frank?"

He shook his head and smiled at her as she walked through the doorway, pulling it shut behind her. "You know, that woman has been with me for the better part of thirty years. Longer than either of my marriages. She's the best employee I've ever had, and I consider her a friend."

It looked like there was maybe more to the relationship

than that, but he didn't say it out loud.

Frank watched him carefully, grinning at Grif's cool expression. "Not fooling you, am I? Yes, we've been involved for many years. But Emily prefers to keep it quiet. I knew you would spot that."

Grif snorted. "And what does the current Mrs. Herrington think?"

Frank shrugged. "Well, Emily is a good woman and won't be involved with me when I'm with another woman. Deedra knows something is there, but she's not sure what, exactly. She's already demanded I get rid of Emily."

"And are you?"

"Hell, no!" Frank laughed until he fell into a coughing spell. "Emily will be around long after Deedra is gone."

He shook his head at the older man's reasoning. "Why did you marry Deedra then, if you didn't expect her to be around long and she's rocking the boat?"

Frank sighed, staring at the fire flickering in the stone fireplace. "Well, sometimes mortality starts to creep up on you and you look for things that make you feel alive. For a while, Deedra made me feel alive. Now I think she's trying to kill me."

Grif looked sharply at the older man, but he was waved off. "I don't mean literally. Anyway, that's not what I called you here for. What do you think of Kendall's chances with the board?"

He narrowed his eyes at the older man. "Well, it's not my forte, but I don't think she's doing too bad. She has good ideas, it's just convincing the board to implement them."

Frank nodded. "Yes, they're pretty old fashioned when it comes to certain things and Kendall is definitely innovative. I think they would be more open to her suggestions if she were more settled. The modeling thing kind of hurt her."

Grif shook his head. "How can they hold her successful career against her? She worked her ass off to get where she did, then gave it up to work with you. I would think that would speak to her dedication."

"Well, I can see it, but they'll always think I'm pulling for her because she's my daughter, not necessarily because she's the right person for the job."

Frank was right.

God, what would they do when they found out she was pregnant?

Take the company from the Herringtons and give it to that asshat Hunter.

"It would help solidify her position if she were married."

Frank watched the flames dance in the fireplace, but Grif felt like he was under a microscope.

He wasn't normally a sentimental person, but the thought of marrying Kendall didn't send him into a panic mode. It actually gave him kind of a warm feeling in his stomach. There were hidden depths to her he was dying to delve into. Desire wouldn't be a problem. The one time they'd given in and slept together had only fed his need for her.

Did she feel the same? He seriously doubted it. She'd made it perfectly clear he was an employee, no more.

"It would," he agreed slowly. "Although I don't believe she has any prospects."

Frank cocked an eyebrow and regarded him carefully. "No?"

Grif didn't like feeling on the defensive, so he kept his mouth shut.

"Well," Frank continued, "if there were, I think her chances for being voted in to the CEO position would be secure."

Narrowing his eyes, he turned more toward the older man. "Speak your mind, Frank. What are you trying to get at?"

The good old boy attitude fell away and Frank crossed his hands over his stomach. "I think Kendall is going to be heartbroken when the board votes against her, which they're going to do because they don't think she's done her time for this position. I'm willing to do anything for my little girl, even if it means arranging for an option she would never think of to secure her future. You're the first man to come into our lives who I thought would be a good match for her."

Grif sat back in the chair, shocked that he'd actually laid it out on the table like that. "So you want me to marry your daughter in the hopes that a married woman is more appealing than a single woman?"

Kendall's father waved a hand. "Exactly. Hunter is single as well, but you know as well as I do that it's different for men than women."

Granted, but would they be perpetuating the incongruity if they seriously entertained this idea?

Then too, Kendall was a phenomenal woman, but could he actually live with her twenty-four hours a day? Yes, she intrigued him and turned him on physically, but emotionally they didn't seem to have much in common. She was the pampered daughter of a very powerful man, while he was the hard-scrabble kid from the wrong side of the tracks with no father.

Grif didn't know that he would suit anybody emotionally.

"So, have you talked to her about this?"

Frank laughed out loud and ran a hand over his gray hair. "Hell, no, are you kidding? She'd fry me and throw me off the mountain if she knew."

"So, how do you expect me to do this?"

The older man grinned and shrugged again. "You're a resourceful kind of guy. You'll think of something. I would make it worth your while to give up a couple years to stay here in Vail."

Grif didn't like the direction the conversation had taken. He didn't mind working for his money, but that sounded a little shady to him. And disrespectful of Kendall. "If I did decide to marry your daughter, it wouldn't be for you. It would be because we'd decided we'd be stronger together."

Frank raised his brows as Grif wished him a good day and headed for the door.

He left Herrington House more shaken than when he arrived. He climbed into his SUV and made his way back down the mountain to Kendall's condominium, his mind racing. If they got married...fuck, was he really thinking this? He'd gone thirty-four years dodging bullets, but he felt like he was in a kill box with half a dozen scopes trained on him.

He glanced in the rearview mirror and cringed. His control was shot. Sleep had been elusive last night, and he had a feeling it would be even more so tonight.

CHAPTER FOUR

✦

A
S SOON AS the suite door opened, she knew who it was. If she were honest with herself, she'd admit that she'd been listening for him to come in all day. A new guy with an eye patch, Hispanic, had shown up for Parks' shift and she'd been ready to scream with disappointment. Ortiz seemed nice enough, but he wasn't the one she wanted.

Not that she wanted Parks there. She just...hell, she didn't know. Even if she didn't let him into her troubles, she wanted to know he would be nearby in case she did. Spoiled? Maybe.

She'd taken all three pregnancy tests, and all three had told her the same thing. Pregnant. First time in four years she'd had sex, and she got pregnant. Even though Parks had worn a condom.

Just her luck. Trying to land the job of her life and Murphy's Law had to step in to ruin it.

Well, not necessarily ruin her life. Maybe just seriously complicate. She'd always wanted a family. Just not right now.

Dragging the chenille throw higher up her chest, she listened for movement from the other room. Her breath caught when she heard the distinctive sound of logs being settled into the fireplace, then the crackle of sap burning. The fireplace in the living room was the only one that burned actual wood; the rest were gas.

Parks liked the smell of the wood smoke; she knew because he lit the fire every chance he got. She didn't mind as long as he tended it.

There was a swift knock at her sitting room door.

"Yes?"

"Can you come out? We need to talk."

Kendall debated telling him no, but that wouldn't get them anywhere. They needed to discuss what was going on; she just didn't know if she wanted to hear the answers to the questions swirling in her heart.

"Just a minute."

She flung the throw over the back of the settee and crossed to the bathroom. She'd let her hair down for the night and changed into yoga pants and a forest green cable-knit sweater. Not very fashionable, but comfortable. Pulling an elastic from the drawer beneath the sink, she bundled her hair into a ponytail at the base of her neck. Her makeup had disappeared from yesterday and she honestly didn't feel like reapplying it.

He would get her just the way she was.

She flushed as she imagined him taking her any way he could get her. Parks had been very clear that he'd wanted to continue their dalliance, but Kendall couldn't sacrifice her pride to do that. It had been a momentary lapse when she'd given in. She'd been raised better than to be an easy lay and he hadn't hinted at anything more. Being that cold about a relationship just wasn't in her make-up.

Taking a deep breath, she crossed to the sitting room door and twisted the knob.

Parks stood up when she entered the room and Kendall struggled not to bobble. He was one of the best looking men she'd ever seen, which said a lot considering her background.

Grif himself didn't seem to care, though women fawned over him. Kendall thought his eyes drew them in. The shattered, multi-colored look of his irises always caught her off guard. They were so unique.

Walking as purposefully as she could, she crossed to the opposite end of the couch from him and sank down, folding her legs beneath her.

"How are you feeling?" he asked.

Her eyes flicked to his and she was surprised to see genuine concern in them. "I'm good."

"No sickness today?"

She frowned. "Not right now, no."

They didn't say anything for a few minutes and it was a little strange. They obviously needed to talk about things, but it was hard to go from employee slash employer to a man and woman caught in a tangle. Kendall caught herself flicking her thumbnail, a tell that any good businessman would spot and exploit. She'd need to work on her control. This was anything but a controlled situation though.

"I need to talk to you about a few things, and they aren't going to be easy. This is kind of like speed dating, but we've gotten our steps all messed up. We slept together first, now we have to get to know each other. Quickly." He flashed her a crooked smile, which made her insides clench in need.

She tried to respond in kind, but it surely came out as more of a grimace. "Yes."

"I guess the first question I need to ask is: are you going to keep the baby?"

She reared back as if he'd slapped her. "Of course I am. I can't believe you would think otherwise."

He shrugged and made a motion with his hands, palms out. "I didn't know. This certainly doesn't fit in with your career plans. And I honestly don't have much say over what you do with your body, but I wanted to make it clear that I want the baby and I definitely want to be part of his or her life. I want to be there for what you need. If I hadn't let my guard down that night, we wouldn't be in this predicament now."

Guilt tightened her throat with emotion and made her look away. He was taking the blame upon himself, and as much as she wanted to let him do that, it wouldn't be right. "It wasn't just you. I drank too much that night and was feeling...lonely. We both screwed up."

His expression eased and he nodded. "Agreed. We were both at fault. Now we need to rectify the situation."

Nodding, she leaned deeper into the cushions.

"I think we should get married."

Kendall gasped and jerked upright on the couch. "What?"

He stood to pace in front of the fire.

"Well, I've been thinking about this, and I think it solves several major issues. One, it secures your position as a stable, level-headed woman rather than an ex-model who got knocked up by her security guard. The board will appreciate that."

Kendall sank back, floored. She'd thought about the board a couple of times, but she didn't want to believe they would think so harshly of her. That Grif had said it as well made her realize that she had probably underestimated their reaction. She'd thought more of her father, who would support her in anything she did.

"I don't know that getting married is the best option though. I mean, we would be compounding a problem."

Grif shrugged and paused to lean against the fireplace. "Not necessarily. As long as we went into it with our eyes open to what we each wanted out of it, I think we'd be fine."

A cold chill washed over her at his words. "And just what

exactly do you want out of this situation, Mr. Parks?"

He raised a dark brow at her use of his surname. "I think we're a little beyond that now, aren't we Kendall?"

Furious heat rushed to her face and she looked away. Drawing oxygen into her lungs, she tried to concentrate on what he'd said, not what she had thought she heard. It had sounded like he was after money.

"I don't want your money. I know that's hard to believe standing where you are, but I don't. I want my child to have my name to carry on. And I want access to my child any time I want."

She frowned at the implacability in his voice. "I wouldn't try to keep your child from you."

He scanned her face, trying to decide if she were telling the truth or not. Finally, he nodded. "I didn't think you would, but I wanted it out there."

"We can do some kind of pre-nup to get all these details down."

What? Hell, was she actually considering this craziness? The thought of being married to the gorgeous man across from her made her heart race, but it also scared the crap out of her.

Grif smiled and her stomach tightened. A pre-nup was an excellent idea, because she didn't know if she'd be able to keep her head around him.

"I also want to walk into this as if it were a real marriage, not something planned out to serve all parties. I want full marital rights."

Her mouth dropped open. No, surely not.

"What..."

Grif started to walk to her. Her senses went on high-alert. When he dropped to a knee in front of her, she didn't know what to think.

"I know this isn't ideal, but I want you to be willing to give it a try. We will be a married couple for the length of the pregnancy at least. But I want us to actually give the relationship a try. I won't lie to you. I've never seen a good marriage. I'm not into hearts and roses, but I am very strongly drawn to you." His voice dropped as he leaned into her space. "And I know for a fact you are to me. So why don't we make the best of the situation and try to make it work."

Kendall completely stopped breathing, afraid to believe what she'd just heard. After all the weeks of watching him move, talk, feeling his presence everywhere she went, inhaling when he entered the room in the hopes that she'd catch a whiff of his shower soap. Now she would have the freedom to actually touch him, and make love whenever she wanted. She sucked in huge draughts of air, trying to calm her racing heart. The rest of her body had jumped three steps ahead of her mind. Her panties were damp from the mere thought of sleeping with him again.

Though she'd been more than a little drunk that night, she still remembered the feel of his body gliding into hers, and the taste of his mouth as they melded into one.

"You shouldn't look at me that way, Kendall," he rumbled. With a needy groan, he leaned forward enough to press his lips to hers.

Every clamoring emotion inside her stilled as she absorbed the taste and feel of him, unhazed by liquor. She'd kissed men before, a good many in fact, but none had made her forget where and who she was. As his lips moved over hers, Kendall tried to maintain her hold on reality.

Grif pulled back and she moaned at the sudden loss, but he didn't go far. His implacable hand shoved her knees wide enough that he could wedge his hips between her thighs. The tension between them suddenly skyrocketed. Kendall cried out as he cupped her hip in his hand and dragged her closer to the edge of the couch and to the center of his body.

His lips found hers again. He didn't allow her to just ride the wave; he made her participate. When she opened her mouth for the glide of his tongue, he accepted the invitation without hesitation. Damn, he tasted just as good as she remembered. Better in fact. Without the fruity wine aftertaste from the other time, she could taste how decadent and sultry he was.

He rolled his hips and the length of him rubbed against the soaked crotch of her pants. If she didn't say something soon, they would be sleeping together again.

Would that really be so bad…

Grif tore himself away, leaving her panting and sprawled ingloriously on the couch.

"In spite of what I said, I don't think we should do this just yet."

Though she was a little put out, Kendall agreed. Things were moving five hundred miles per hour and she hadn't had a chance to catch her breath yet. "I agree. I think we need to head to bed and think things over."

He cocked a brow at her and she realized how suggestive her words sounded.

"You know what I mean," she huffed, cheeks burning with heat.

Grif grinned and she gave thanks she still sat on the couch, because she surely would have dropped to the ground at the sight of all the masculine charm directed her way. Even that elusive dimple in his left cheek made a brief appearance.

As he pulled away and pushed to his feet, she had a view of how very excited he was behind the placket of his suit slacks.

Her hands lifted, as if to bring him back, before she forced them down.

Her *fiancé* paced away, running his hand through his springy dark hair. At some point he'd taken off the glove on his real hand. It seemed strange to see actual skin beneath his cuff.

Stopping in front of the fireplace, he leaned against the log mantle.

"I'm sorry. I didn't mean to let it get that out of control."

Kendall half wished he *had* meant for it to get that out of control. She wanted to feel him again, completely clear-headed this time.

Last time it had seemed like he'd given in just for her, but this time he seemed invested.

She shifted on the couch, trying to ease the pressure on her body. What the hell, man. She'd controlled every relationship she'd been in, for the most part. Why was her bossy security guard the one who finally made her want to give up all her normal constraints?

GRIF PULLED A notebook from the breast pocket of his jacket and flipped through a couple of pages. "I made some notes. To go over."

Kendall's pale brows disappeared into her hairline at the abrupt change of subject. She tipped her head to hide her face, but he was grasping at straws. With the need still heavy in her expression, it was all he could do to even stand without rushing to her and stripping her down like he wanted to. He had prayed that the first time had been a fluke and that the liquor had rid her of all of her inhibitions. But it wasn't necessarily the liquor; it was passion. Kendall Herrington was a freaking firecracker.

Fuck, he could smell her need from across the room.

His dick screamed for release.

A shudder wracked his body and he knew there would be no way he could talk to her coherently until he did something to get rid of this agonizing pressure. He would not rush her, he vowed. She needed time to get used to the idea of being with him.

"Maybe we can, uh, do this another time. I need to take a breather."

When he looked at her, her clear green gaze had focused below his waist, on his aching erection. He slammed his eyes shut and turned to brace himself against the mantle again. "Fuck, woman, I'm trying to not overwhelm you with everything, but if you keep looking at me like that I won't be responsible for my actions."

He heard a rustle at the couch then he felt her move behind him. A feather light touch landed on his shoulder, pressing him to turn.

She stood in front of him, eyes luminous from the light of the fire behind him. "You don't have to be the only one. I think we're both being responsible for our actions."

Leaning forward, she pressed her delectable lips to his.

Grif groaned, unable to believe she would be willing to go in this direction. None of the details had been hammered out, but obviously her hunger was as sharp as his own. Maybe their mutual need and a shared child would be enough to build a marriage on.

Cupping her head in his good hand, he angled his mouth over hers, unable to get enough of her taste. She moaned into his mouth, pressing the length of her body against his. All coherent thought went out of his head as she angled her hips to align with his.

"Are you sure?" he asked, hating to give her the opening to

shut him down.

She nodded. "I am."

She grabbed his prosthetic hand and tugged him toward her bedroom.

CHAPTER FIVE

✦

K ENDALL GULPED AT her daring, but it felt right. She'd
found that her instincts served her well, in business and
in life. They'd been dancing around each other for weeks,
avoiding eye contact, physical touch. If she hadn't realized she
was pregnant, they'd still be treating each other as if they were
enemies.

Scratch that. If *he* hadn't noticed she was pregnant.

Warmth built in her chest at the thought that he would be
willing to step up to the plate to give their child a stable life.
No, not a declaration of love, but perhaps that would come
later.

Right this minute, she knew no man had ever turned her
on the same way Grafton Parks did. She planned to enjoy every
second of their time together.

Snow fell softly outside her bedroom window, lit from
below by a security light. The only illumination in the bedroom
was from the bathroom, which cast a soft amber glow over
everything. Kendall dropped his hand when she reached the
side of the bed and paused. Grif didn't give her a chance to be
uncomfortable, because he stepped forward to wrap his arms
around her shoulders. Automatically, Kendall tipped her
mouth up to his, willing to be lost in him. His tongue glided

against hers, sending heat straight to her lower body.

One of his broad hands crept beneath the hem of her sweater to cup her hip and warm fingers crept beneath the elastic waistband. His hand slid down, stretching the fabric, to cup her butt.

"I watch your ass all day long, and I can't tell you enough how long I've been waiting to hold it, just like this."

She shuddered at his heartfelt words. "And I can't tell you how long I've been waiting for you to hold it."

He pulled back enough to look into her eyes. "Really?"

She nodded. "Even before I got tipsy on the wine. You're very physically appealing to me."

He shook his head and his lips tipped into a frown. "You haven't seen everything yet."

Kendall heard the warning, but she didn't know how to respond. The night they'd slept together, he'd left his shirt and arm on. The prosthetic itself hadn't seemed to affect anything they did. She wished she had more experience with the disabled, or had asked her father more questions. Something to better prepare her.

"I don't think one part will have much of an impact on the whole."

His eyes narrowed as if to gauge the truth in her words. "Well, let's leave show and tell for another time, okay?"

She nodded because she didn't want any interruptions either. Deep inside, her body ached for his. Pulling away, she tugged her sweater up over her head, tossing it to the far corner. Grif moaned when he caught sight of her breasts in the pale peach satin bra and removed his hand from her ass to run a fingertip over her already hard nipple. Kendall gasped and reached up to cup her breasts in her hands, as if offering them to him. He leaned down and wrapped his lips around one satin cup, licking her through the fabric. It sent a shudder through her, but she knew it could feel better.

Reaching behind her back, she unhooked the bra, tossing it away into the darkness. Grif made a rumbling sound, almost like a lion purring, and it reverberated through her body. His ungloved hand moved to cup her right breast, and it made her want to purr as well. He weighed it in his hand, then drew his fingers in until he pinched her nipple.

Kendall gasped as he rolled it between his fingers and leaned into the pressure. Her own hands grasped his muscular waist, and she realized how overdressed he was. The shirt would stay on tonight, but he didn't say she couldn't explore. Tugging the shirttails from the slacks, she bunched them in her hands until she reached the end of the material. Brushing the backs of her knuckles against his tight abs, she pushed the shirt up his chest.

"Oh, my," she sighed. Black hair furred his muscular chest, heavier over his pectorals, then narrowing into a trail down his stomach. There was just enough light to see a few pale marks on his body. She ran her fingers over one.

"Old scar," he murmured.

Kendall could tell there was baggage there, but she didn't want to deal with it tonight. She moved away from the scar and spanned her fingers over his rib cage.

Man, she'd worked with some hot guys before, but Grif would give them all a run for their money. His body was perfection, all ropey muscle and strength. It made her want to see more.

The button on his slacks wouldn't release, and she thought about ripping the damn thing open, but she probably didn't have the strength to do it. He brushed her away and unfastened it himself one-handed, then let her have access.

Tugging the zipper down slowly, she fought the impatience building inside her. He wore blue briefs and his erection strained the front. Dancing her fingers over his length, she caressed him through the fabric. His hips surged into her hand and his mouth found hers. Kendall moaned, slowly edging beyond coherent thought.

Jerking away, she skimmed her pants down her thighs, then her panties and wool socks. Goose bumps pebbled her skin, both from the chill of the room and from the heat in his gaze. Grif dropped his slacks and stepped out of his underwear, and it took everything she had not to collapse into a quivering puddle at his feet at the sight of his erection framed by the tails of his shirt. Arousal swamped her with heat, and when he pressed her back to the bed, she was more than ready.

As she used her arms to pull into the center of the mattress, he crawled after her. She was a little aggravated that she couldn't see his body, only the hanging white dress shirt. But she didn't say anything.

As he settled over top of her, all her aggravations drifted away. He pressed his hips to hers and Kendall thought she was going to combust. Just the length of him wedging into her slit was enough to make her gasp into his chest. Instinctively, she angled her legs up around his hips.

He grinned at her as he pressed her into the mattress. "Guess we don't need a condom this time, huh?"

She choked on a laugh and buried her face against his neck. "No, I guess not. As long as you're clean."

"I am."

He angled himself to lie on his right elbow, then reached down with his left hand to rub the head of himself into her moisture. Kendall cried out, her nails digging into his bare hips, trying to urge him closer.

"Oh, please," she gasped, tension gripping her. "Inside. Please."

Grif didn't seem to have a great amount of control either, because he surged into her in one long stroke, mouth sealing to hers to catch her cry. Kendall contracted around him, more full than she could ever remember being.

As he pulled back, then slid home again, she knew release was mere seconds away. She'd dreamt and fantasized for weeks, but feeling him plunge into her body was so much better than any fantasy.

He shifted upright, then gripped her knees to angle them up to her chest. Kendall gasped as the head of his dick stroked over her g-spot. "Oh, Grif," she moaned.

He slammed himself into her, over and over again, cranking her arousal higher than ever before. And in a breathless moment her orgasm crashed over her.

Kendall cried out, unable to do otherwise, and contracted around him sharply. Grif groaned and she opened her eyes in time to see pleasure wash over his harsh features as he rocked into her, his body no longer under his strict control. He jerked and his arms contracted around her. Kendall felt the heat from his ejaculation fill her womb and she held on until he collapsed against her.

Even in the cool room, their bodies were slicked with sweat. Kendall's heart thumped, trying to fall into time with his. Grif levered himself up enough to look at her.

"Are you okay?"

She nodded. "Perfect."

He pushed into her two more times, as if relishing the feel, before rolling away to the side.

Kendall blinked up at the ceiling, her body still quivering. "So much better than last time."

Grif laughed aloud. "Well, thank you. I think. For me it was just as good as I remembered."

She rolled her head to look at him, trying to see if he was telling the truth or not. His eyes connected with hers and she could only see sincerity. And that damn adorable dimple.

Looking away, she drew in a deep breath. "Well, I'm going to take a quick shower. You're welcome to join me."

Kendall snapped her mouth shut, angry at having forgotten about his arm. He probably wouldn't be any more receptive now than before.

The silence from the bed behind her echoed as she got up and walked toward the bathroom. As she washed away the evidence from their lovemaking, she waited.

And waited.

But he never came.

When she stepped out of the steamy room a few minutes later, wrapped in a towel, he was no longer in the bedroom. For some reason, it didn't surprise her.

On a purely selfish level, she was a little glad. A lot had happened recently. She didn't want to have to deal with more issues than she had to right now.

The enormity of the decisions she had to make in the next few days weighed on her.

Barely even drying off, she curled up in bed and pulled the sheet and comforter over top of herself.

KENDALL DIDN'T SEE Grif until the next morning, after her so-called breakfast. Now that she knew what the nausea signified, she'd been able to explore on the internet. She was one of the lucky millions of women that had to deal with morning sickness that hit throughout the day. She'd lost weight over the past couple of weeks, but apparently it was very normal in early pregnancies. She didn't have the suggested crackers in her cupboard, so she ate a piece of dry toast. Not the most appealing, but her tummy quieted almost immediately.

Counting back, she realized she was only about two and a half weeks along. It wasn't a difficult date to remember because it had been Christmas night when she'd mauled him. The only excuse she had was that she'd been especially lonely. Her father had gone to a party with Deedra and her mother hadn't answered her calls. She'd found herself alone with a bottle of wine.

And a security guard she'd been having fantasies about for weeks.

When she typed "pregnancy" into the search box, literally millions of results popped up. She clicked on the first one, and lost herself in information.

Grif found her hunched over her laptop keyboard, writing furiously in a notebook. She glanced up when he walked in and was caught by the hesitation in his eyes.

She smiled, trying to appear calm and collected, though her heartbeat picked up as he moved closer to her. When he leaned down to press his lips to hers, she cradled his freshly shaved cheek in her hand. "Good morning."

"Good morning," he rumbled.

He set a familiar green and white paper cup beside her on the desk and she stared at him in surprise. On their way in to work, they always drove through for coffee. She was touched that he had thought to get it for her.

"I thought you might be needing some energy this morning."

His eyes narrowed with humor and Kendall had to laugh. "Oh, you are completely right. Thank you."

She paused to look at him for a moment, struck by how much things had changed in the past few days. He'd been her difficult, unbendable bodyguard less than forty-eight hours ago, but now they were going to have to reevaluate his position. She had a flashback from the encounter last night and embarrassment sent a flush through her cheeks. Maybe job description wound be better phrasing. She rushed to cover.

"The new guard seems nice."

Grif had cocked his head to look at her. She knew he'd seen her embarrassment, but didn't know what had caused it. "Yeah, Ortiz is a good guy. Hyper aware so he'll spot anything out of the ordinary. I've lost my objectivity."

"I'm sorry, Grif. I've put us both in such an awkward position. That night was so out of character for me. I think with the holiday I just got lonely, which made me drink too much. I never get like that."

He shrugged as he pulled a chair from the dining room table, a few feet away. "I think it was inevitable that something would happen. I've been drawn to you since the first time I met you."

She stared at him in surprise. "Really?"

He nodded once. "But I didn't know until that night how hungry you were as well."

Blood rushed into her cheeks in a full-out blush and she buried her face in her hands. "Oh, god."

Chuckling, he tipped her face up with his good hand. "Believe me, I appreciated it. I don't get molested like that very often anymore."

He made a vague motion with his prosthetic.

"Oh, please." She made a face. "You get hit on all the time in the office. And the coffee shops. Hell, everywhere you go you've got women hanging on your every move, waiting for you to flash that dimple."

Kendall snapped her mouth shut, shocked at just how much she'd been bothered by all those women. Not to mention Grif's cool, measured, smiling responses.

The man in question grinned at her, his variegated eyes flashing, until he broke into laughter.

"You're a hard nut to crack, Kendall Herrington. No lie, I thought you were the ice queen from hell for the first week."

She frowned. "I didn't mean to be, but Dad had just told me about hiring you and I wasn't happy. I've had security details before, but never twenty-four hour coverage. With you guys in the separate apartment now, it's hardly an issue. At first it was a pain in the ass."

He crossed his arms, watching her. "Understood. And honestly, with your background, I expected to be babysitting a brat. No offense."

"None taken," she sighed.

It had been the same many times over. Because she'd been a model and had acted in a few things, people expected her to be spoiled and difficult to handle. There were definitely people like that, but she'd prided herself on not being one of them.

She glanced at Grif, shocked at the change in him. But maybe they'd both changed. They realized that at least some of their guardedness had to come down if they were going to make this situation work.

Or not.

"I like you, Grif. But I don't think we should get married."

His expression didn't change, but his eyes cooled.

"Why not?"

Kendall sighed and leaned back in her office chair. "Because we would be compounding a problem. Yes, the pregnancy puts me into an uncomfortable position at the company, but it would still be uncomfortable if I married you on the spur of a moment. It will be embarrassing either way I go."

His jaw hardened and she realized what she'd said. She reached out to rest her hand on his arm. "I'm sorry. I didn't mean that directed at you specifically. Just the situation."

He motioned with the hand she held, disengaging her touch. "What other concerns do you have?"

"Well," she sighed, "I know you're probably a great guy, but we don't know each other. Yes, we're getting along right now, but what about five months down the road when I'm screaming at you because I'm so emotional and we can't stand the sight of each other? That's not a good environment to bring up a child."

Snorting, he stood to cross to the clearest window. "Agreed. What else?"

Kendall shook her head at his stubbornness. "What about your job? I know you're dispatched here for now, but will you technically be my guard if I marry you? Isn't that a conflict of interest?"

"It is. I've already spoken with Duncan. He's willing to let me be on leave for a while until we get some things figured out. Denver is only a couple of hours away. I can just cut back on my long-distance assignments and still work for the agency."

Turning away from the window, he crossed back to his chair. "Are those all of your reasons?"

She nodded, pushing her hair over her shoulder. "For right this minute. I'm sure more will occur to me."

Grif pulled a sheet of hotel stationery from his pocket.

"I had all of those listed as well as a few more. You didn't mention your money. I think we should sign a prenuptial agreement stating that what's yours is yours and what's mine is mine if we do part ways. I don't want or need your support."

Kendall believed him. He didn't seem the frivolous, spendy type. Quite the opposite, actually.

"The pre-nup would also reassure the board. You're fooling yourself if you think they'd let you in, being pregnant, without a man behind you. I strongly suggest you don't even tell them you're pregnant until after you replace your father."

Kendall absorbed what he said and knew in her gut the soundness of his advice. The old men that her father had gone into business with would fight her tooth and nail if she gave them any cause.

"You marrying your security guard is not the craziest thing I've ever heard. It happens. And if you spin it correctly, you can come out looking like a rose."

"As for us not getting along later on," he continued, "well, I don't think that will be an issue. I grew up in a screaming household, and I for damn sure will not subject my child to that. I'll leave first."

She could see the conviction in his eyes, and she wondered what his home life had been like.

Probably as messed up as hers had been.

"I suggest we put a time limit on our contract," he continued. "We'll say two years. This isn't an ideal situation, but I want to go into this with the expectation that the marriage will be a true marriage and we will both put effort into building a relationship that will nurture ourselves and the child."

Kendall blinked, a little hurt by his reasoning. She tried to put her finger on exactly why she was upset, but it wouldn't coalesce in her mind.

Was it because he was doing exactly what she herself should have suggested? Something had shifted inside her and the laid out details, the way she usually appreciated receiving information, wasn't working for her.

For something to do, she reached for the coffee and inhaled. *Oh, yes.* And it didn't make her stomach turn.

"I got decaf. They're not sure caffeine is good for babies."

She looked at him, brows raised. "No way. Seriously?"

He nodded and gave her a commiserating smile, deepening the dimple.

Well, hell. That sucked.

She took a sip of the coffee. Still better than nothing, though she kind of thought it tasted different. But maybe that was a psychological response. If he hadn't said anything would she have noticed a difference? Hmmm.

"I scheduled us an appointment at the Eagle County court house on Monday afternoon to get our marriage license."

Kendall sucked in a breath and sat the coffee on the corner. "So soon?" she pushed away from the desk to cross to the window looking out over the mountains. She felt, more than heard him follow her.

"Well, we don't have to, but the sooner we get it done the less chance there will be that illegitimacy will be an issue with the company."

The Herrington name. Yes, she would have to carry on the name, as would her son or daughter. "Okay."

Tears suddenly burned her eyes and she had to swipe them away with her hands. Taking a deep breath, she tried to force them away, but they seemed to fall all the harder.

When he wrapped an arm across her chest from behind, pulling her into him, Kendall choked out a sob. She turned in his hold and buried her face into his chest. Her difficult, opinionated, handsome, hero security guard held her while she cried.

CHAPTER SIX

✦

K ENDALL LAID DOWN for a nap after her crying jag.

Grif went out and talked to Ortiz for a few minutes, filling him in on the situation and getting the scoop on what had been going on at the agency. It sounded like Palmer was being just as stubborn as ever. But Foster was the surprise. Getting married to a waitress. Grif hoped he knew what he was doing.

Not like he could give him any advice. Every time he talked to Kendall he felt like he floundered. That cool, green-eyed gaze made him lose his concentration. But that no-nonsense businesswoman veneer had faded, to be replaced by a more womanly, softer mentality. They had important decisions to hash out, but it was hard staying on task when she looked at him with fear in her eyes. This wasn't the life she wanted, he knew that, but maybe they could work out a new kind of life.

Duncan had been very accommodating about the leave, but if things changed with the pregnancy he might actually have to leave for good.

The thought of deserting the men that he'd worked with for the past couple of years made him sweat. Because they were all amputees or wounded in some way, there was a lot of preliminary explanation shit that they didn't have to wade through with each other. They said what company or branch they were from and what injury they had, and they moved on. Everybody that worked there had the same global, all-encompassing understanding of what they each went through every day, so they didn't have to explain every little thing.

It was a very liberating, accepting place to be.

At some point he would have to talk to Kendall about his arm, but he had no desire to bare himself to her that way. She'd made no bones about it when they'd first been contract-ed that she thought they were deficient in some way. He wouldn't be rushing to give her any ammunition.

Grif wandered through the condo, looking at Kendall's items with new eyes. They belonged to the woman he would be spending a great deal of time with now. More, even, than when he was her guard. He dropped into the poofy cream colored chair she'd slept in last night and her scent wafted around him, sending a blast of awareness through his body. He's been attracted to her for the past several weeks, and now that he'd had a taste, the need had grown teeth.

Closing his eyes, he let his head rest against the back of the chair.

"Parks!"

Grif bolted awake, disoriented by the expanse of white in front of him. Ah, the window. It was snowing outside.

Kendall stood beside his chair, looking rumpled and beau-tiful with her long blond hair hanging across her shoulders. Her face was a little swollen from sleep and she had a red crease down one cheek as if she'd had folded fabric beneath her head. Her eyes were clear, though, and with her hands on her hips she seemed exasperated.

"I called your name several times and you didn't budge."

He scrubbed his face with his hands, trying to wake up.

"Sorry. I think we're both a little frazzled. I didn't even realize I'd fallen asleep."

She nodded and crossed to sit at a nearby chair. "Well, I'm going to frazzle you a little more. I've thought about this a lot and I apologize ahead of time for the headache. I want a wedding. It doesn't have to be big, just a few close friends, but if I'm going to be married, I'm going to do it the way I want to."

Grif tried not to flinch. He had very little faith in marriage to begin with, and now she wanted to make a production out of it? Fuck.

"Okay," he said slowly. "How big is not very big?"

She shrugged. "Less than twenty or so people. Do you have people you'd like to invite? I mean, if by chance this does work out between us it may be the only marriage we ever have."

He conceded her point with a tip of his head, but inside he cringed. Did he even have ten people he wanted to invite? He thought of his mother, smoke curling around her head in a dirty apartment in Cincinnati. She probably hadn't moved from where he'd left her years ago. Regardless, he didn't want her there. She'd never done anything for him other than use him.

He'd like to invite Duncan, definitely. They'd known each other many years, first in Iraq when he'd worked Ordinance Disposal for Duncan's Marine Company, then later when he'd been hired on as an agent for his civil company. The man had given him purpose several times over.

After working with him for months, Ryan Calvert had become a pretty good buddy as well. He'd like to have him there.

"I do have a couple I'd like to bring. When do you want to do it?"

She blinked at his acceptance. "Well, I need a few days to get some things arranged. I'll have to tell my father. I'd like to get married at the house."

Grif nodded. That would be ideal. The house security could be on watch while they were distracted with the wedding. "Okay. Want to plan on Wednesday?"

She nodded, staring off into space. "I have to get to work," she murmured. But the smile she gave him as she left the room made all the worry worth it.

KENDALL CALLED HER best friend Lilly in New York. They'd basically grown up together on shoots, commiserating when their mothers became too unbearable. For several years they'd been each other's only relief from the stresses of the job. When Kendall had moved out to Vail to be with her father, they'd managed to keep in touch. Lilly was still in the business, managing her own agency now. She promised to be out as soon as she could.

Grif's boss and good friend Duncan arrived on Tuesday night. Wilde was a silver haired devil. Dark brown, deep set, experienced eyes surveyed her up and down when he walked into the room, and Kendall liked his dry humor immediately. Though he needed a cane to walk, he still had the muscular look of a fighter. She had no doubt he could handle anything that came at him.

He shook his head at Grif sadly. "And they continue to fall."

She had to laugh when Grif flushed.

"Shut up, Wilde. Your turn is coming. I'm sure."

The older man made a face. "I think we'll agree to disagree on that point. I'd be a lot for a woman to handle."

Lilly arrived early the next morning, looking very chic and

put together, in spite of the fact she'd just flown through the night to stand up with her at the wedding.

Kendall ran her fingers over her friend's sleek haircut. It was a deep blue black right now, though Kendall had seen it every color of the rainbow. It made Lilly's flawless, pale skin look even more fragile. Her storm gray eyes twinkled with humor, in spite of how tired she must be.

"Why don't you go take a nap for a bit. We've got several hours yet before we need to head to the house."

Lilly waved a hand. "Oh, please. I can't sleep now. We have to catch up!"

So, her best friend in the world turned into the best distraction in the world as Kendall counted down the time to her two o'clock wedding. They finalized plans together and talked about mutual acquaintances.

When Grif arrived with Duncan in tow, introductions were made all around. Lilly seemed taken with the older man, resting her hand on his arm and smiling in a way that Kendall had learned meant she was interested. Duncan was polite but didn't appear as taken with Lilly, although he took care to be solicitous. Kendall hoped her friend proceeded cautiously.

Duncan drove the three of them to Herrington House a couple of hours before the wedding. Grif said he had a couple of errands to run. Frank met them at the door himself and excitement for the day had given his skin a healthy flush. He wrapped her in a hug, pressing a kiss to her temple. "Go on in. Emily has been running since you first called, and everything will be impeccably done, I'm sure. Your dress just arrived and the caterer is setting up in the dining room. Everything is under control."

Kendall felt tension ease from her shoulders. "Thanks, Dad."

She led Lilly through the house, to the guest suite where her father had directed them. There it hung, with her shoes positioned underneath. Lilly teared up when she saw it. "It's perfect for you."

She dropped the accessories bag to the bed and started pulling things out. "Let's work on your hair because that'll take the longest."

Kendall gave herself up to Lilly's expertise, and everything flowed right until a sharp rap sounded on the door. Deedra peeked around the edge then let herself in.

Kendall fought to keep the smile on her mouth. The two of them had never gotten along. Deedra considered Kendall competition for Frank's attention and more than once Emily had overheard the red haired witch badmouthing Kendall. She just had to laugh, though. Deedra's motives for doing anything were so transparent.

The woman walked across the room when she spied Kendall's dress and held it out from the door, as if trying to imagine it on her body, then turned away with a derisive curl to her lips. She caught Kendall's gaze in the mirror and moved toward them.

"Well, aren't you looking just like a bride. Hi, I'm Kendall's stepmother Deedra."

She held her hand out to Lilly, but the other woman gave her a look and nodded her head instead. "Sorry, my hands are full. Nice to meet you."

Kendall gritted her teeth as Deedra fluttered about like the damn flitter-gidget Emily always called her, sticking her fingers into things that didn't need messed with. At one point she wrapped the necklace Kendall planned to wear around her own neck, then dropped it to the vanity. The woman seemed oblivious to Kendall's growing anger. Lilly finally snapped at her to go check on the caterers.

Deedra tossed Lilly a scathing look, then tottered away as quickly as her ridiculously high heels allowed her.

Tension flowed with her out the door. Now that Deedra wasn't twittering in her ear, fretting over things, Kendall could pretend her life wasn't going to change in less than an hour. She looked up at her friend. "Thank you very much."

Lilly grinned. "My pleasure."

The time finally came to put on the dress. Lilly, again, was invaluable. The tiny seed pearl buttons running down the back were no problem for her nimble fingers, and within just a few minutes, Kendall turned to face herself in the mirror.

She'd worn designer dresses before, but nothing like the pale white, strapless confection that now hugged her body from breast to thigh. An intricate design in Swarovski crystals traced from her breasts and down the right side of the dress. The skirt poufed out around her legs, showing glimpses of the matching, completely frivolous, crystal encrusted heels. She'd been incredibly lucky that a designer she used to work for had had them both available at her shop downtown, and had been willing to let the dress out just a bit. Kendall refused to feel guilty for not being the model standard anymore.

Yes, she was getting married in her father's home, but she wanted to look pretty for the few guests that had been able to come on such short notice.

She hadn't seen Grif yet. He'd run down to do errands, but that had been more than an hour ago. Nerves began to chew at her confidence. What if he didn't make it back in time, or got caught in the snowstorm predicted for the area?

She wanted a glass of wine to calm her nerves. She settled for a butter mint Emily had brought her earlier.

Nobody knew about the pregnancy, but Emily had looked

at her with a brow raised, as if she could tell something were different but she didn't know exactly what. Kendall wanted to tell her, but Grif had been right in that the less people that knew about the baby the better. They'd agreed to act as though they were hooked on each other. They probably couldn't pull off looking in love, but they definitely had attracted down.

Lilly had looked at her strangely when Kendall said she liked Grif. But she didn't dig, and she went out to join the rest of the guests.

Kendall had made it a point to invite a few of the stock-holders in the company, some of her father's oldest friends. Hunter and his family would be here as well.

Emily slipped in the room just then and Kendall smiled when she saw her. Mom had refused to fly out to see her get married "in that man's house". She seemed to miss the point that the day was about Kendall, not her years' old relationship with her father. And though Kendall had wished otherwise, she hadn't been surprised.

Emily had been ecstatic to step in and help out, and speechless when Kendall had asked her to stand up for her with Lilly. She'd have done a bigger production than put the little party and dinner together if she'd been allowed, but Kendall had wanted it super small. Just a few close friends. Easy food.

Tears came to the older woman's eyes as she looked Kendall up and down. "You are beautiful, Munchkin. I can't believe you're getting married."

Kendall shrugged. "It seems right, Emily. I never thought Parks would be the one, but he suits me. We click." She shrugged, unwilling to dig a deeper hole for herself.

It really wasn't though. They did get along well, now that they'd thawed with each other a little. She'd only seen him for a few minutes on Sunday because he'd had to run to Denver for the personal paperwork he needed to get the marriage license. Monday afternoon they'd gone to the family lawyer's office to have a quick, complete pre-nuptial done. The older man had paled when they'd told him how quickly they needed it, but he'd come through. Sometimes the Herrington name came in handy.

Nobody asked out-right if she was pregnant, but she could see the question in their eyes. She just refused to answer it. None of their business.

"I have something for you, honey."

Kendall looked at the pale blue square Emily held out.

"This will cover your something borrowed, something blue and something old. My mother gave it to me when I was a young woman, to be used when I walked down the aisle." She shifted uncomfortably and her eyes turned a little glossy. "I never had a chance to use it, but I'm overjoyed that I can give it to you to use."

Letting the gossamer-fine cloth fall open, Kendall gasped as she saw what it was. A very fine women's kerchief, obviously antique, with a stylized 'E' in one corner. Tears started in her own eyes and she reached out to pull Emily into a hug. The woman had been more of a mother to her than her own and Kendall loved her desperately. "Thank you," she whispered.

Emily sniffled and pulled away, then held out a small box. "From your father. Your something new."

Kendall flipped open the lid, revealing glittering diamond studs encircled by tiny emeralds. "Oh, my!"

"If the flitter-gidget had seen them, you'd have never gotten them. That woman's like a damn crow, going for the shinies. I caught her wearing one of my necklaces the other day."

Choking out a laugh, Kendall pulled the velvet card from the box and removed the earrings, inserting them into her ears. Then she peeled down the sweetheart peak of the dress and pinned Emily's cloth inside. When she folded it back, it rested right above her heart.

A few tears slipped down Emily's cheeks. "I couldn't love you any more than if I had actually given birth to you. You've turned into a remarkable woman."

Kendall fought not to break into tears. "Why couldn't you have been my mother, damn it?"

They laughed together and hugged, then Emily helped her repair her makeup and left to check on the details out front.

Kendall paced, too restless to sit down in the expensive dress. Her father came to get her a few minutes later, looking distinguished in his suit. He teared up when he saw her too.

"Beautiful. Just simply beautiful."

Proudly, he offered his arm to escort her through the house and into the wide open great-room. The furniture had been moved away from the massive stone fireplace and turned into an altar where she would exchange her vows. Every chair in the room was filled, and every person rose when she stepped in.

Grif stood at the fireplace, waiting expectantly. He wore a suit every day when he stood guard at her back, and he looked phenomenal, but the Marine Dress Blues put him into a completely different class. She would never have expected to see him in uniform, and it suddenly gave her a greater appreciation for everything he had sacrificed before he came to work for her father. Grif, Duncan and Calvert were all dressed in uniform, medals gleaming from their chests. He hadn't said anything about wearing his uniform to get married, but he must have grabbed it when he went home for his paperwork.

Lilly and Emily stood opposite from the men, looking just as stunning in their own way, waiting for her.

As the wedding march played on the speakers and she walked down the aisle on her father's arm, Kendall did her very best to breathe deeply and not burst into tears. Emotion cinched bands around her chest. When she was a little girl, she'd dreamt of having a normal life where she could go to a normal school, and just be like everyone else. Have a regular family, with a mother and father that loved each other and lived in the same house.

Now, she stood on the edge of her own potential happiness. Terrified, yet exhilarated at the same time.

Grif looked a little pale. He'd shaved recently and his square jaw was clenched. His springy hair had been moussed and combed into shape. His white gloved left hand clasped his gloved right, but the thumb on his left was sweeping back and forth with nervousness. It did her heart good that he appeared just as nervous.

Kendall tried to imprint every single detail into her mind, like the feel of Grif's hand holding hers, and the faint scent of roses from arrangements around the room. His eyes held hers the entire time the officiant spoke and he repeated every word flawlessly. When it came time to exchange rings, she was stunned when Duncan handed him a platinum band with inlaid diamonds and a substantial solitaire in the center. She'd been prepared to wear something more plain, but she fell in love with it upon sight. It glistened in the light as he slipped it onto her quivering finger.

Lilly handed over the band Kendall had chosen for Grif. Platinum as well, but with a darker central band, centered with three understated diamonds. She had a feeling he wouldn't want anything flashier.

As she slipped it on his hand, her eyes lifted to his, and the banked emotion in his expression made her tear up.

"By the power vested in me by the state of Colorado, you may kiss your bride."

Grif covered her mouth with his own and Kendall felt a tear slip down her cheek. He kissed her like she meant something to him. She took that feeling and wrapped it in her heart.

They celebrated for the rest of the night. As they ate the veal chops and grilled asparagus, Emily appeared with an elaborately decorated wedding cake, complete with tiny bride and a uniformed groom on top. Kendall looked up at her in surprise.

The older woman shrugged. "I always wanted to try to make a wedding cake. I think I did a damn fine job."

Kendall's weepy eyes flooded again at the kind gesture and she stood to hug her. "You are an incredible woman."

Hunter wandered over at one point while they were mingling and pressed a kiss to her cheek.

"You look gorgeous, Kendall. I can't believe you pulled all this off without anybody knowing."

Kendall shifted under his sharp gaze.

"Well, we wanted to keep it quiet for a while because we weren't sure where the relationship was going."

"Well, I'm very happy for you."

A hand settled on her waist and she knew without looking that it was Grif. His touch had become very familiar to her.

Hunter offered to shake hands and there was an awkward pause. Grif reached out his prosthetic and shook, then pulled back. Hunter frowned as if he'd been presented with a dilemma. "Is that a…"

Grif turned her away with an, "If you'll excuse us."

"That was very rude," she whispered.

"I don't care. He's been gunning for your spot for a while. Don't give him any ammunition."

Kendall looked at him sharply. "You think I don't know that? He's always tried to be better than me. If his father wasn't my father's best friend, I'd have plowed Hunter under the ground a long time ago."

Grif grinned down at her in appreciation. "Good. I'm glad you realized he was your competition."

She fought not to roll her eyes. "Not really. He can't do anything without his father's approval. He is a true trust fund baby. And I think most everybody knows that."

Her new husband chuckled and squeezed her to his side. "Stay the smart cookie you are."

She returned the squeeze, appreciating the words as much as the action.

"Is Jameson a family name?"

Grif's face darkened with anger and his lips twisted. "You could say that. It's my mother's favorite liquor. She loved it so much she named her son after it."

Kendall cringed. "I'm sorry I asked. I didn't know."

She squeezed him the way he had her just a few seconds before.

"It's okay. There was no way you could have known. No big deal."

She realized it was a big deal, though, because it took him a while to shake it off.

Other than that one aberration, Kendall had a wonderful afternoon. And the guests appeared to as well. The only minor issue, other than the handshaking incident, was the apparent chumminess between Deedra and Hunter. Since he had perfected the art of charm and she the reception, the two of them seemed to get along fabulously.

"I think there's something going on with those two."

She looked at Grif sharply, then glanced back at the two standing off in the corner. The way they moved definitely intimated at some kind of history. "Hm, I kind of think you're right."

But something made Hunter shift away from Deedra, frowning. He shook his head but watched her as she left the room. Kendall glanced around to see if anybody else had seen the little interaction, but she and Grif seemed to have been the only ones. When she looked back at Hunter, he was just disappearing through the doorway Deedra had gone through.

"Looks like a tryst in the works."

Kendall clamped her jaw in anger, tempted to go after the two of them. How dare they do that at her wedding?

"Don't let it ruin your day," Grif murmured into her ear.

Kendall took a deep breath just as Hunter walked back into the room.

"Hm. Nothing happened apparently."

Kendall tried to watch for Deedra to return but she got lost in other things. Grif was right. She had better things to think about than that crazy woman.

The afternoon wore on and guests started to leave. She and Grif weren't going on a honeymoon, so they headed down the mountain to her condo. Lilly and Duncan were going to stay at her father's house to give them privacy for the night.

Kendall felt strangely elated. A week ago she never would have imagined how her life would change.

She looked at Grif. His expression seemed relaxed. He didn't appear to regret anything about the day, which also made her unaccountably happy. She didn't want to be responsible for making his life hard.

Ortiz grinned and folded away a knife when they got off the elevator. "You two look like a cake topper. Congratulations."

"Thank you, Mr. Ortiz. Mr. Calvert is bringing some cake down for you."

Ortiz grinned at her. "I'm sure it will be delicious."

He opened the door for them and they stepped through. Grif closed the door behind them with a frown on his face.

"What?" she asked.

He shrugged and played with the car keys in his pocket.

"I'm sorry I couldn't carry you over the threshold."

Kendall's mouth dropped open. Not what she'd expected to hear.

"It's no big deal. Don't worry about it."

But he shifted on his feet. "Even though it was kind of last minute, I wanted your wedding day to be as complete as possible. Carrying you over the threshold would have been part of that, but I can't bear weight like that on my forearm. I thought about putting you over my shoulder but then I worried about the baby."

The indecision on his face was very out of character, but made her more sure that she'd done the right thing. Grafton Parks was a genuinely good man.

Stepping close, she smoothed her hand down the suit jacket of the uniform, then over the medals on his left chest. "I'm not worried about that part of it. I appreciate the thought, though, truly. And I appreciate this." She held up her left hand. "I never expected it."

His lips spread in a smile. "Good. You weren't supposed to. Lilly gave me suggestions on what you liked."

Kendall leaned up for a kiss. "You did perfectly. I was very touched."

Grif looked at his feet and cleared his throat, nodding slightly. Then he held his own hand up. "I didn't expect this either. I'm not into jewelry, really, but I like this. Very understated."

She smiled, glad she'd been able to pull it off without his input.

"I think we both did really well. The wedding was beautiful. I know it was a bit of a headache, but I truly appreciate you going along with the show."

Shrugging, he ran his finger over the neckline of her dress. "Well, it was for a good cause. And a few hours in my Blues isn't going to kill me."

Kendall was unfamiliar with the term, but she assumed it meant his dress uniform. "Do you miss it? The Marines?"

"Every single day. It's a hard family to leave. Still be there today if it weren't for…" He held up his prosthetic.

The thought of his going back to that environment sent fear flowing through her. "Well, I'm glad you don't have to risk your life like that any more." She glanced toward the bedroom. "This is kind of strange to ask, but are you going to stay here tonight? I would completely understand if you didn't want to," she rushed to add.

Grif seemed to be weighing her words. "I'd like to stay, if you'd have me."

Kendall nodded, almost shyly, and turned for the bedroom.

CHAPTER SEVEN

✦

G RIF REALIZED WHY she'd asked a few seconds later. He started to unbutton his uniform but realized either he would have to leave or she would. He only wore a T-shirt beneath the outer jacket.

Or he could just bare it all and get it over with.

Tiredness beat at him. It had been a stressful day. He didn't know if he was up to an even more stressful night.

"Uh, Grif?"

Shit. She had to be wondering why he'd stood there so long.

"Yeah," he sighed.

"Do you think you can unbutton me?"

He jerked into motion. "Sure. I can try."

She turned her elegant back to him, and when he saw the row of little tiny buttons, he started to sweat. There was no way. The fingers on the prosthetic couldn't even pinch that tiny.

Left handed, fumbling, slower than fuck, he managed to get one button through the tiny satin loop holding it.

"This may take a while. My right hand is useless for stuff like this."

"I'm sorry. I'd have had Lilly help me undress if I had

known it would be an issue."

"It's just impossible for the prosthetic to squeeze this small. And I don't have the dexterity for it even if it could."

"Ah, okay," she murmured. "I didn't really realize that the hand could make movements like that."

It was a subtle probe. Grif found that he didn't mind talking about it as much because her back was to him, waiting patiently for him to move. He started on button number two of fifty. "It can make several movements as long as they're not intricate."

"So," her voice was very soft, "how do you make it move?"

He stopped fiddling with the buttons, realizing that there would be no better time than now to explain it all to her. "If you turn around I'll show you."

Coughing to clear his throat, he took a heavy breath, his heart pounding. Revealing himself to new people was never easy. Hell, he hadn't revealed himself to a woman that wasn't a medical professional ever. Any romantic liaisons he had the shirt stayed on. Period.

Kendall was different. Besides being drawn to her more completely than any other woman, she had now become his wife. She deserved to know what she'd gotten herself into.

The medals on the left breast of the jacket jingled softly as he let it fall from his arms. Without looking at her face, feeling more naked than ever before, he draped the jacket over a nearby chair.

She hadn't said anything. When he looked at her face, he only saw curiosity in her clear green eyes. She reached out to touch him and he raised his arm to her. "Explain to me about this. Does it hurt?"

Her gaze met his and he shook his head. "Not really. Not anymore."

"So, how did you lose your hand in the first place?"

If he'd seen anything in her look hinting at pity or disgust, he'd have clammed up, but she seemed genuine in her need to know.

Sighing, he shook his head in disgust. "I screwed up. I was in an explosive ordinance disposal company in the Marines. EOD. We went in with other Marines and cleared out IEDs and traps. One day a fellow Marine brought in an improvised device that had been disabled. We thought. When he handed it over, there must have been enough charge left in it somewhere that when the wires touched, it detonated. The other Marine was fine, but my hand was obliterated. There was nothing left to save. I had shrapnel in my gut. Lost my sight for a while."

She cringed. "I'm very sorry."

"Not your fault."

Her eyes were soft as he pulled from her grasp to remove the prosthetic, then the soft fitted sock underneath it. As he finally revealed the stump of his forearm to her for the first time, he tried to tell himself it didn't matter what she thought.

Right.

She shocked him when she snorted softly, then reached out to touch it. A shiver coursed through him as she ran her painted fingernails down the sensitive skin, tracing the line of scar at the end. She stepped in close, and wrapped both hands around the end of his arm. "I don't know why, but I thought it would be gross and scary looking, but it's not. I didn't exactly expect it to be bloody, but nasty, malformed. This just looks like your skin was wrapped around the end of the joint. Like a wrapped baseball bat."

The knot in his gut eased. At least she hadn't freaked.

"So, how does the prosthetic work?"

As she seemed to go through life, she wanted to learn

everything there was to know about his amputation. She asked intelligent questions and didn't seem pitying or condescending in any way. Actually, she seemed fascinated that the entire hand could be manipulated by the nerve impulses from his brain. He rolled on the sock, then pressed his stub into the socket, sealing it tight. Then he showed her the reverse process, removing it.

"I have to apologize."

Grif narrowed his eyes at her. "Why?"

Standing there in her wedding dress, looking radiant in spite of the hour and her drooping hair, she lifted her face to his. "Because I wasn't very nice when my father first hired you. I said some things I shouldn't have, within your hearing, and I apologize."

He appreciated her words. "It's over and done with. Don't worry about it. It's not something I haven't heard before. Turn around and we'll see if we can get you out of this dress."

He leered at her and she laughed. Exactly as he wanted.

It took him a long time, but he eventually released enough of the buttons that they could tug the dress up over her head and off. He grabbed a padded hanger from the closet and draped it on, then hung it from the top of the bathroom door. When he looked back, she had unfastened her bra and tossed it across the room, baring her lush, pink-tipped breasts. As he watched she stepped out of her panties to stand before him completely bare.

A bolt of awareness rattled his bones. Kendall Herrington, or was it Parks now, belonged to him, as well as the boy or girl growing in her stomach. Stepping forward, he ran his hand over the smooth expanse of skin, from hipbone to hipbone. "This is going to change."

Her eyes flared with excitement and fear. "I know."

Needing the connection, he wrapped his arms around her shoulders and pulled her into a hug.

"I'm going to shower. Want to join me?"

His cock hardened beneath his pants. "I do."

Seemed to be the night for 'I do's'.

Kendall walked away from him and into the bathroom. Grif watched her perfect ass until she disappeared from sight, then scrambled to shed his own clothes. He took care with his uniform pants, but everything else just got tossed. Seconds after she stepped into the glass enclosure, he stepped in behind her.

There were several jets in this particular shower, projecting in from opposite sides of the stall. She'd turned the heat up high enough to warm their bones, but not so hot to make them overheat.

Grif watched as she lathered and rinsed her hair, then went through the motions of scrubbing her body. Whatever she used smelled phenomenal. A little fruity, yet sexy at the same time.

"May I?" He held his hand out for the spongy thing she was running over her skin. She handed it over and he motioned for her to turn around. When she did, he ran the sponge up and down her back, across her shoulders, down her arms. Kendall leaned against the tile wall, forehead resting on folded forearms. She moaned when he ran it down her sides and gasped when he brushed her nipples.

Grif's cock had only gotten harder as he bathed her. When she gasped, he felt the stirring in his balls. Snugging himself up behind her, he dropped the spongy thing to the floor and ran his soapy hand up her side, then up her breast. Her nipple was rock hard already and he had a feeling she was as aroused as he was.

He leaned down to her ear. "Ever use these benches in here?"

A seat had been fashioned from tile in the very front corner and another along the width of the back. Grif turned a dial and the jets at the back of the stall turned off.

"No, I haven't. I've always wanted to, though."

Sounded like a green light to him.

He spanned his hand across her chest to reach her opposite breast. It puckered as hard as the other one and he fondled the weight in his hand. She moaned as he aligned his dick with the crack of her ass, gliding up and down in the slick water. Tilting her hips back, she sharpened the contact between them. Grif was about to guide his erection down and into her pussy when she turned in his arms and pushed him back. His heels hit the tile and he allowed her to press him down onto the bench.

She followed him down, settling on her knees between his feet. Her long fingered hands glided up his thighs, danced over his hips, then she walked her fingers up his sides. He shifted on the bench, trying not to let her see how ticklish he was, but a grin spread her plump lips.

Kendall set out to torment him. She stoked over his body everywhere except where he wanted her to go-his cock. She massaged his good arm, up his neck, cupped his head in her hands and crushed her mouth against his. Only her luscious breasts touched him where he wanted, and it wasn't enough. When he raised his hand to tweak her nipple, she pulled away and shook her head.

"No. Not this time. You can play next time."

Gnashing his teeth, he tried to be patient, but it was damn hard.

Just when he thought he couldn't wait much longer, she started kissing her way down his body. Biting his nipples gently with her teeth, licking the line down his pectorals, she slowly made her way south. When she finally did wrap those plump lips around the head of his cock, Grif worried that it would all be over before it began. Digging deep, he forced the impending orgasm away. Part of the problem was the view. Looking down at her swaying breasts as she started a delicious movement up and down his cock.

Fuck!

Grif slammed his eyes shut and knocked his head back against the tile to try to distract himself. He wouldn't last if he kept watching her.

Kendall worked him for a few minutes, taking him deep for a few strokes, then lingering high on the furl of the head. That was where she really got him. She stroked her tongue into the slit and over the sensitive, fleshy underside, which made his body quake. Gently, reluctantly, he held her away, desperate to prolong the pleasure. "I want you to ride me."

Kendall nodded. Pushing to her feet, she spread her thighs over top of his erection and lowered herself to his lap. Grif realized almost immediately that he'd made a strategic error. Kendall had become so aroused that he slipped into her body easily. She glided down, moaning as she struggled to accommodate his length. Grif cupped her hip with his hand and even before she started to move, he knew he was a goner.

She started to circle her hips, sealing down as tightly as she could. Grif reached out with his amputation and pulled her hips forward. Kendall gasped as the angle changed and he dragged her forward again. They did this several times before she suddenly lifted straight up, then slammed right back down.

"Oh, damn," she moaned, plunging on top of him again.

Grif felt her grip on his cock start to tighten. Curling forward he took her nipple into his mouth, sucking as she rocked against him, and he felt the split second when her body shattered.

She screamed out, gasping for breath as she slammed herself onto him again and again, riding the wave. Grif finally allowed his own pleasure to swallow him under, straining, reaching to be a tiny bit deeper as he released into her body.

The orgasm rippling through her body prolonged his own, and it was several long moments before she finally collapsed against him.

Grif panted as if he'd run up the mountain, but his satisfaction was complete. As he gathered a quivering Kendall into his arms, he thanked the stars that they'd landed where they had, and that he'd given in that lonely Christmas.

AMAZINGLY, THE WATER was still hot when they separated then stepped under. Kendall lathered her body again and rinsed, then turned to lather his body as well. Grif could have brushed her away, but he kind of enjoyed the attention. She even went so far as to lather his stump.

It was very strange.

For years he'd been responsible for himself, doing everything on his own. Relationships had been few and far between.

"Were you right handed before?"

She stood under the falling water, watching him.

"I was."

Her eyes widened and her mouth dropped open. "So, you had to relearn everything then. Writing, driving, eating."

He nodded and stepped under the water to rinse, closing his eyes, letting her process that bit. She still looked thoughtful as he stepped through the glass door and reached for the towel on the heated bar. Rubbing himself briskly, he tried not to shift under her scrutiny. He secured the towel around his waist and walked out into the apartment.

Calvert had dropped off his overnight bag at some point. Digging through it, he found his briefs and pulled them on, then was faced with a dilemma. He walked back into the bedroom.

Kendall had just walked out of the bathroom and to the dresser on the far side of the room.

"I normally sleep in my underwear. Do you have any issues with that?"

Without turning around, she shook her head, dropping her towel to step into her own panties. Grif forgot what he was doing as he watched the blue fabric slide up her long legs. She tugged them over her butt, then ran her finger down along the elastic leg to make sure it fit her cheek just right. When she finally turned, he had the feeling she'd taken a deep breath before she looked at him.

As they stood on opposite sides of the bedroom, dressed almost exactly the same, a sense of surreality overcame him.

"No. I don't. This is how I usually sleep as well."

Kendall walked into the bathroom and he heard the blowdryer come on.

Crossing to the chair that held his Dress Blue Alphas, he arranged them on a hanger and hung it from the door beside her wedding dress.

Since she was in there, maybe he could slip into bed and get a head start on sleep. But when he crawled under the comforter, his mind began to replay the day.

Kendall had looked stunning. And though he'd seen five hundred different emotions in her face throughout the day, determination had been the strongest.

His face had probably reflected the same. They were both determined to create a life for their child. And to try to make the situation as good as it could be. If he were honest with himself, he hoped deep down that he could make this marriage work for them too.

THEY SETTLED INTO a surprisingly comfortable routine.

Well, other than the morning sickness.

The first morning after they were married, Kendall bolted out of the bed with her hand over her mouth. Grif rolled out of bed to follow, but she slammed the door in his face. As he listened to her retch inside, he wished there was something he could do for her, rather than just stand here and listen.

Crackers!

But there were no crackers in the kitchen.

"Fuck!"

There was ginger ale in the fridge, though. He poured her a glass and sat it beside the bed table. When she came out a few minutes later, she sipped the drink carefully. Once it stayed down, she drank the rest of the can.

From then on, gathering the anti-nausea remedies when it struck was his job. Which he did happily. They now always had about four different kinds of crackers in the cupboards, though she preferred plain, salted saltines.

The nausea itself eased back to morning time only after a couple weeks, then faded altogether in her second month.

During the day he continued to guard her, though Ortiz stayed as well. Grif needed to decide what he planned to do about his job. He couldn't float along on leave forever. Though Duncan had been patient so far, Grif knew something needed to change. Soon.

CHAPTER EIGHT

✦

K ENDALL RAN HER hands down over her body as she
stood in front of the floor length mirror. No, the lump
wasn't very big-she was only about twelve weeks along-but it
was definitely there. She swept up to her breasts, amazed all
over again at how they'd grown.

Grif thought he'd died and gone to heaven. They'd started
to grow, becoming more plump than she'd ever been before.
She had to caution him a couple of times because they were so
sensitive. That sensitivity led to earth shattering orgasms
though, which he very happily coaxed out of her every night.
And some mornings. And some afternoons. She was flattered
in that he never seemed to get tired of her.

And she never tired of him. Though he was around morning, noon and night, they got along well together. They never
fought or even really said a cross word to one another. They'd
settled into married life as if they'd been made for it.

Grif took her on a date one day. He dragged her from the
office and packed her into the truck, refusing to tell her where
they were going. As soon as he turned onto the mountain road,
though, it was obvious he would be taking her up.

As they climbed in elevation, the snow became more pristine. He pulled into one of the many lodges that catered to

tourists and walked her inside. When he spoke to one of the attendants, she was shown to a private dressing area. Grif had brought a bag for her and as she looked inside, she realized he had raided her closet, bringing her woolens to stay warm. The attendant had placed a snow suit inside the door, so she dragged it on after her clothes.

She stepped out of the dressing room, smiling at the thought of coming down the mountain as fast as she dared. In the past few years, she'd become a passable skier.

A young, dark-haired attendant stepped toward her. "Can you follow me please, Mrs. Parks?"

A thrill went through her at the use of the unfamiliar name. She'd been going by Herrington, but if Grif had given her Parks to use, maybe he was trying to tell her something.

She followed the girl through the lobby of the resort, then down a flight of stairs and along a walkway. When they exited a doorway, Kendall found herself on the opposite side of the lodge. Grif stood a few feet away, holding the reins of a very large black horse.

Kendall smiled in wonder, stepping forward to rub the animal on his massive head. "Oh, Grif. He's beautiful. I can't believe you brought me out here."

"Well, we haven't done anything yet, but I thought you might like to go on a sleigh ride with me."

She grinned, realizing the horse's body had hidden the old-style carriage sleigh. Her throat tightened with emotion at the thoughtful gesture and she could only nod. Grif held her hand as she stepped up inside and sat on the bouncy seat, then followed her up. He spread a rustic throw rug over her knees before gathering the reins and clicking to the horse.

"Jack is a very eager boy," Grif told her as they turned toward a trail head.

The horse took off at a heavy, ground-eating trot. Kendall laughed and held onto Grif's elbow as they swished past the evergreens lining the trail. Snow flew from the skids of the sleigh and she laughed with genuine enjoyment. Nobody had ever done anything like this for her before.

They wound their way up the mountain and eventually came to a clearing that had been set up for a picnic. A square patch of snow had been cleared away to make room for a large blanket. Setting on one corner of the blanket was a large wicker basket.

Kendall glanced at Grif. He seemed a little leery of how she'd react, so she let him see the genuine appreciation in her face. "Is this a date? Our first date?"

Grif winced and pulled on the reins, guiding the horse to a nearby tree. "So we've got the order of things jumbled up. Give a guy a break."

Kendall laughed at the look on his face. "Well, I guess I was the one who started everything on the wrong foot."

He raised a brow at her and nodded firmly before hopping from the sleigh to tie the horse. When he returned, Kendall took his hand before stepping down into the snow. The powder was more than six inches deep, but slick underneath. With the temperature rising as they rolled into spring, the ground had begun to warm.

Grif walked her to the blanket, then held both arms as she lowered to the ground. Though she wasn't very big, she appreciated the help. Balance had become tenuous sometimes.

Lunch was a fragrant beef stew with a crusty French bread. They didn't talk about anything important, but managed to find several similarities in what they liked and didn't like. And when the afternoon sun made her drowsy, Grif pulled her into his arms and laid down on the blanket. He tucked her into his side and rested his chin against her hair.

"This was a lovely first date. Thank you," she sighed.

She felt him press a kiss to the top of her head before they both fell asleep.

GRIF SEEMED TO be at loose ends, though. He'd gotten leave from the agency he worked at in Denver, but he needed something permanent to keep busy. She had offered to place him on the payroll at Herrington, but he'd given her a scathing look. She realized now the offer had probably sounded like charity.

The friendliness they'd had after the date had taken a hit that day.

She couldn't worry about it now, though. Herrington had another quarterly board meeting today. She was going to have to come clean about the pregnancy soon because her clothes were getting tight. She wanted to push the announcement off till next month.

Her father called as she was getting ready to go in.

"Hey, Dad. You're up early."

He sighed over the line and she could picture him in her mind as he swung around in his big leather office chair at home. "Well, I've been getting up and heading into the office for forty years. Don't know if I'll be able to turn off my clock when you do take over the reins."

She laughed lightly, but she could hear something in his voice that worried her. "What's wrong?"

"Not sure exactly, but I wanted to give you a heads up. Hunter has been making a few waves, recently, saying you were knocked up and that you had to marry your security man."

Kendall sucked in a breath. She hadn't told her father about the pregnancy yet, but this was the perfect opening. "I didn't have to marry anyone, but what if I was pregnant?"

The subtle squeak from her father's chair stopped abruptly and the silence lengthened. "Kendall Victoria Herrington, are you pregnant?"

"I am, Dad. About twelve weeks."

There was an explosion of sound on the other end of the line that sounded like her father had dropped the phone. There was jostling and banging, then her father came back on. "Are you lying to me because you know how much I want a grandbaby?"

She laughed. "No, Dad. I wouldn't do that. It's completely true. It didn't happen exactly the way I wanted it to, but we're working it out. Grif is a good guy. Marrying him was not a hardship. At all."

She realized then that her handsome husband stood across the room in his standard white T-shirt. He held his prosthetic in his good hand, as if she'd interrupted him putting it on. His eyes were shadowed from her and she wondered if she'd said something wrong. He turned away and disappeared into the bathroom.

She wanted to go to him, to ask what was wrong, but she could only deal with one fire at a time.

"I had planned to wait to tell the board, but perhaps I should beat him to the punch."

Dad hm'ed on the other end of the line, but she could tell he wasn't thinking strategy when he asked her, "Are you going to name it after me if it's a boy?"

Kendall laughed, loving that her once driven father had mellowed enough to want to enjoy grandkids. "Well, we'll see. We've got a long ways to go yet."

She heard whispering through the line, then a woman's voice in the background.

"Emily says she's overjoyed. And that she knew all along."

Kendall laughed again, happy that she had let the two of them in on the secret.

"Well, tell her she's at least going to be official Godmother."

Frank repeated what she said and then huffed into the line. "She just burst into tears and disappeared. I think that means she would love that."

"Well, it was an easy choice."

"Why not Deedra?"

Kendall straightened, aware her father had just thrown her into a minefield. She loved her father, but his choices were sometimes bizarre. Why he'd thought Deedra would be good for him, she had no idea. But it wasn't her place to tear the woman down. Her father would have to see it himself before he accepted anybody else's word.

"Well, I'm sure Deedra is a nice lady, Dad, but…,"

"Bullshit. She's not and we both know it. A little birdie helped me see a few things recently and Deedra's time may be coming to a close. Hell, she didn't even come home last night."

Kendall was torn at the news. The woman had venom running through her veins and her father did not need to be around her. But she held some appeal for her father. "I'm sorry it's not working out, Dad."

"Ah, well, anyway. Back to the baby. I think you should let the board know. But also convey to them how healthy you are and how excited you are to be welcoming another Herrington into the world, to continue the line in our successful business. Most of these men have known you for several years now Kendall. They know what kind of businesswoman you are."

Tears blurred her sight at her father's praise. He didn't give it lightly, she knew. And his support meant the world to her.

"Okay. If you think that's what I should do I will."

"I'm not telling you to do it, but I think you'll have more support than you need. Take your husband with you. He'll back you up if the shit hits the fan."

"I will," she promised.

"In all seriousness honey, he's a good man to have in your corner."

"Oh, I know, believe me."

A knot of tension she hadn't even been aware of carrying for the past couple of months eased. There wasn't a lot she didn't tell her father. Keeping the pregnancy from him and Emily had been difficult.

Walking back into the bedroom, she peered into the bathroom for Grif. He'd just finished shaving and had grabbed a towel to dry his face. She wanted to snug up to him and nuzzle his smooth jaw.

The man seriously turned her on. Yes, she'd always been attracted to him, even when he'd first hired on, but the more time she spent with him the more she loved.

Loved. Yeah, she was getting there.

Grif raised a dark eyebrow and she realized he'd asked a question. "Sorry, what?"

"What did your father say?"

She leaned her butt against the bathroom counter and folded her arms over her chest. "That I need to have faith in the men he's done business with for years. And that Deedra may be out of our lives soon."

He reached for his toothbrush and set it on the counter. The prosthetic moved in to hold it down while his other hand maneuvered the twist cap off the end of the tube. Kendall didn't know if she could do it that way, untwist the little lid with the same hand holding it. He layered the paste on, remounted the lid and started to brush his teeth. "What did Deedra do, did he say?"

She laughed at the froth foaming his mouth. "No, he didn't. Don't care really as long as she's gone from his life."

Grif's eyes met hers in the mirror as he spat in the sink. "Well, he's a smart man. He'll figure it out."

"My dad is a very smart man. He told me to keep you close when the shit hits the fan."

Grif laughed and shook his head. "I like your dad just as much. My father was not a model citizen. Lifetime crook."

"Really?"

"Died several years ago. Before I joined the Marines and lost my hand."

"When did your mom die?"

He gave her a funny look. "She didn't yet, as far as I know. Probably still sitting in the same chair smoking cigarettes and drinking whiskey as she was years ago."

Kendall cringed. "Sounds like the military was an escape for you."

"Oh, definitely. I'd have been career if I hadn't made that one rookie mistake. EOD doesn't have a great record for longevity. We all eventually get blown up."

She cringed at the matter-of-fact way he said it, wondering how many of his buddies he'd lost.

"Now I'm 'combat modified'."

Kendall's heart ached at the term. Though she'd never heard it before, it seemed appropriate.

CHAPTER NINE

✦

T HE BOARD MEETING started off like every other meeting. The men greeted each other and talked about their golf games. Hunter held court at the end of the table, regaling an audience with his most recent exploit. Kendall's father sat at the opposite end of the table, where he'd sat for decades. Although he was a little pale, he seemed to be in good spirits.

Kendall, on the other hand, had butterflies the size of bombers in her stomach. The board would be voting on the CEO replacement today.

As she walked across the room to greet the current CEO, his eyes dropped to her stomach, hidden by the flared jacket of her black suit. She frowned at him as she leaned in for her kiss. "You better stop that," she growled.

The chuckle he gave her sounded a little evil, like he looked forward to fireworks. Kendall hoped nothing was said that would make her have to defend herself.

The meeting started out like it did every other quarter. Her father laid out the big info, earnings and acquisitions. She went over the contracts that had been signed and the leases they were currently going after. They'd had a fire at one of the timber sites and lost some equipment, so she went over the insurance settlement for that. Then her father went into the next year's schedule, which he did at every meeting.

"But as of April tenth, I will no longer be here." He waited till the grumbles from around the room quieted. "My doctor has told me I need to relax. This is not a relaxing business. So, let's move on to the main event. We have two prospects for the position of CEO of Herrington Limited and they each have a little something to say before we vote."

Frank motioned to Hunter, who stood up with a grin and launched into a long-winded, circuitous petition for the job. Kendall had to admit, he had his sales pitch down, but the real estate branch was only a small part of the whole.

When she spoke, it flowed from her heart. The love for her father and the company he had built, as well as her vision for the future of how great the company could be. She ended by resting a hand on her tiny tummy. "I will run this company to it's full potential, so that my son or daughter will have something to look forward to when they come of age."

The men around the table exchanged looks, then stood up and started to clap. Her father stood up from the table as well, taking the well-wishes from the men he'd been in business with for so long.

The only person not happy appeared to be Hunter Groves, sitting at the end of the table with a glower on his face. He pushed away from the table in anger, then circled to the crowd gathering around Frank.

"But she got knocked up by her damn security guard. How white trash is that? It's the only reason they got married."

Frank gave him a warning look, brow raised. The other men shifted uncomfortably.

Hunter plowed through Frank's rebuke. "Well, that and because Frank paid him to marry her."

Kendall stilled, not because she believed what he said, but

because of the guilty look that flashed across her father's face. Grif stood at her back, where she'd always trusted him to be. She refused to turn around and give Hunter's claim teeth, but uncertainty washed through her.

She forced a calm smile to her mouth and shook her head. "I didn't marry anyone because I had to. I had feelings for Grif before we slept together and the baby is a happy accident. Yes, I was pregnant when I got married, but I'm not the type of woman to need a man's support like that. If I hadn't wanted to marry him, I wouldn't have."

"I'd be careful about throwing stones, Hunter."

The younger man looked at her father and smirked.

"Why, Herrington? You know it's the truth. I've got the audio tape to prove it."

The senior Herrington shook his head. "When you play dirty, you have to expect retaliation in kind."

Hunter crossed his arms over his chest. "I haven't done anything to be ashamed of. I would lead this company the way it was meant to be led."

"Nothing to be ashamed of, hm?"

Frank reached a hand out beyond Kendall and she was a little confused when Grif stepped forward with a folder in his hand. He handed it over then turned to her. Pressing a lingering kiss to her lips, in spite of everybody watching them, he stepped back to the edge of the room.

Her father held the folder up. "Are you sure you want to get into morality issues, Hunter? This is your chance to walk away with your reputation intact."

Anger simmered in Hunter's eyes and he shook his head.

Rather than open the folder for all to see, he handed it to Roger, Hunter's father. The older man flicked it open and glowered.

"This is the way you repay the man that put you through school, who's been my friend for forty years?"

Inside the folder, there for all to see, were pictures of Hunter in a wild embrace with Deedra. Neither wore clothes and they appeared to be on Hunter's desk in his office downstairs.

Kendall gasped, her eyes swinging to her father's. He winked at her and grinned. If the pictures had been of her significant other, she'd have been pissed and upset. But there was devilment in her father's eyes. This was why he'd said she wouldn't be an issue much longer.

Turning slightly, she glanced at Grif. A slight smile curled his lips.

The little bird.

Hunter tried to worm his way out of the situation. "She approached me months ago. Said I would win out over Kendall. She came onto me."

Frank nodded. "I'm sure she did. I'm retiring so she's looking for fresh meat. It sounds like one of her hare-brained schemes. And I admire your fortitude in trying not to clear your name. Unfortunately, I do not believe Herrington Limited will be needing your services any longer."

Hunter looked to his father, but Roger would no longer meet his son's eyes. Nobody else would even acknowledge him.

With a huff, Hunter left the boardroom.

Roger reached out to Frank. "I am sorry, Herrington. Not sure what to do with the boy."

Frank shrugged and clasped Roger's hand. "I think the two of them suit each other."

They laughed together as only old friends can, and Kendall knew that their relationship would be fine.

"I move that Kendall Herrington-Parks assume the role of Chief Executive Officer of Herrington Limited, effective immediately."

'Ayes' circled the room.

ONCE THE FUROR had died down over the meeting, she and Grif returned to her office. Grif stood off to the side while Kendall took the guest chair in front of her desk.

"So, was there any truth that you two talked about our marriage beforehand?"

Out of the corner of her eye, she saw Grif shift on his feet. Her question was answered.

"You did." She turned to look at him. "Before you talked to me?"

He blinked, watching her carefully. "We did. We talked about what would be best for your career."

Hurt rolled through her and she rested her hand on her belly. Furious tears filled her eyes, but she refused to let them fall. "And just when were you going to tell me about this little confab?"

Grif stepped forward, head cocked to the side in confusion. "I don't understand your anger. Your father and I talked about you and I getting married. But it was in relation to the job. He didn't know about the baby."

"And how much did he offer you? To marry me? To make me more stable and appealing to the board."

He shook his dark head. "He didn't offer me any dollar amount. When he suggested it, I didn't say anything. The idea had already been floating in my mind as well, but for a completely different reason."

He looked pointedly at her belly.

Kendall didn't know what to believe. Grif seemed to be

telling the truth. Why would he tell her about the meeting if he were trying to hide something?

Maybe her nerves were just frazzled. It had been a hectic day and she had several hours yet to go.

She would definitely say something to her father. Those kinds of actions would only undermine her position in the company.

Moving behind her desk, she clicked the touchpad on her Mac.

"You're not going to say anything else?"

She looked up at Grif. "What do you mean?"

He shifted toward her, looking a little aggravated. "Is that the end of the conversation?"

Giving him a tight nod, she turned back to her computer. "For now it is, until I can think about it rationally. I've got too much in my head right now."

GRIF TURNED BACK to the window, fuming. Kendall never backed down from a fight. He had expected her to lay into him, had prepared for it actually, but now she wasn't going to give him the satisfaction of getting it all out in the open. She would sit at her desk, tight-lipped and cool-eyed, and play it off like everything was fine.

While he was left hanging, prepared to defend himself.

It was only because he felt like shit. No, he technically didn't do anything wrong, but he took part in the situation. Maybe he should have told her what had happened that day, but he didn't want to cause issues between her and her father.

"I didn't do anything behind your back. Frank is my boss. When he called me to the house, what was I supposed to do?" He crossed the room and circled the desk to kneel beside her chair. "But when he offered to make it worth my while to stay in Vail, I knew I didn't need anything to stay, just you. I told him that if I married you it would be because I knew it would make us stronger together."

Kendall lifted her eyes. His gut clenched to see the hurt in her expression. Reaching out, he turned her chair toward him. "I promise you, I would never hurt you intentionally. You've become very important to me, and our life has become very important to me. I've never had this kind of stability in anything. I love waking up in the morning and being boring with you."

She choked out a laugh, even as a tear slipped down her cheek.

Grif reached out and pulled her into his arms. They ended up sitting on the floor with Kendall draped over his lap. As ridiculous as it seemed, it was exactly what they both needed.

"You hurt my feelings," she murmured into his neck, "but I know how my father is. So I can understand the awkward situation he put you in. Hopefully when he retires we'll be able to live our lives without his interference."

Grif pulled back enough to look her in the eyes, brows raised. "Are you talking about the same Frank Herrington I know? The man will be meddling until he's in his grave. Probably even worse now that he won't have the business to run."

Kendall laughed, wrapping her arms around his neck. "You're right. It was a nice dream though."

Rubbing her back with his hand, Grif let himself enjoy her weight, and the tension easing in his chest. As ridiculous as it sounded, he didn't like feeling like he was in trouble with her. He liked Kendall, a lot. He didn't want anything to rock the boat between them.

They stayed that way until his ass was numb and she had

almost fallen asleep. The phone on her desk broke the silence. With a heavy sigh, Kendall pushed herself up and away from him to answer it.

Grif resumed his place at the window, easier with himself now that the air had been cleared. When he'd been in Afghanistan, he'd been responsible for many, many lives over the course of his tours and he'd been known for his coolness under fire. The two-fold responsibility sitting across the room had him sweating bullets, though.

The woman sneezed and he thought it was cute. Puking her guts out because of the baby, *his* baby, inside her body, seemed noble. And when she soaped his back and down his arms, paying careful attention to his amputation, his heart swelled with emotion. The fact that she could take every part of him, without flinching, freaked him out.

A COUPLE WEEKS after Kendall was voted in as CEO, Frank Herrington officially turned over the reins to his daughter.

It made the news. Not just the local stations, but every national station as well. Former-model-turned-CEO was apparently something to talk about. Grif flipped open the paper one morning to find his own face plastered across the front.

Well, hell.

Kendall snickered at the title, *The New Mr. Herrington,* then sobered when he growled at her.

All of the scrutiny made Grif chafe, but his respect for his wife went up exponentially as she handled them all with grace.

"You just have to smile and pretend like you're telling them secrets. They eat it up. As soon as the novelty of it wears off, they'll move on to something juicier."

And they did, for the most part.

It was about a week later when his world shuddered again.

Verna Parks had an interview with one of the national stations. Though it had been years since he'd seen his mother, she hadn't changed much. Wiry gray hair fuzzed around her head and her blue eyes blurred by alcohol, tears tracked down her lined faced when asked about her son. A bottle of liquor, his namesake of course, sat on a shelf beyond her shoulder.

"I haven't seen him for ages, since he lost his arm in the war, but I'm sure he'll come visit now, with his new wife. I'm not doing so good anymore. I'd like to see him before I die."

The fuck she would.

Kendall sat beside him on the couch and he was sure she felt him vibrate with fury. As if she knew what he needed, she turned and wrapped her arms around his waist. He hadn't told her anything about his childhood. Damn humiliating now for one of the worst parts of it to be splashed all over the country. Not to mention his amputation. He didn't know how his mother knew about it, but he didn't care. She'd just broadcast it to the world.

Which brought back the hounds. 'Disabled Veteran Deserts Mother' was one of his favorite articles the next day. The reporter took down every bit of her sob story and printed it, along with his refusal to comment. Grif looked like a damn jackass. He crumpled the paper and threw it against the wall.

"If you want to fight this, we will, but we run the chance of making it a bigger story."

He looked down at his wife and the shared fury in her eyes, and felt what he'd wanted for them to begin with: to be part of a team. Unable to do anything else, he pulled her to him and wrapped his arms around her. The knot of tension in his gut began to unravel. "No. I think we'll just let it go. We have other things to do and plan for."

Kendall's once flat tummy was a little more prominent, now. He loved to cup the child in his palm.

She placed her hand over his and leaned in until she caught his eye. "Hey, we'll get through all this. None of it matters, but this right here does." She tightened her hand on his, pressing a kiss to his mouth.

Emotion tightened his throat and he returned her kiss with everything he had in him. "I know, Kendall, and I appreciate it more than I can ever tell you. Thank you."

It was hard not to tell her he loved her right then, but pride made him snap his jaw shut.

CHAPTER TEN

✦

K ENDALL HAD BENT over to slip on her heel when she felt
something strange in her stomach. She stood and rested a
hand on her belly, waiting to see if it did it again. But nothing
happened. It wasn't until she and Grif were jogging up the
stairs to her office that she felt it again. She paused on the
landing, a bolt of fear going through her. Maybe she shouldn't
jog up the stairs like she did every morning. Maybe it wasn't
good for the baby.

Her tummy quivered again.

"What is it?"

Grif had come back down to her, his face concerned.

"I don't know. I think I may be feeling the baby move."

He raised his brows in surprise. "Wow. Really? What does
it feel like?"

She giggled, relief rushing through her. "It feels very
strange. As if I have a butterfly trapped beneath my skin trying
to flutter out."

The look on his face was a little comical, as if the thought
kind of grossed him out, but he smiled and kissed her.

Kendall was distracted all day, waiting for the little feeling
to return. Then, when it didn't, she fought disappointment.
Her first doctor's appointment was later in the day and she was

dying to know what she was carrying. She'd taken to calling the baby sweet-pea, because it just felt wrong to call him or her an 'it'.

Parks swore up and down he didn't care what it was, but when he murmured to her belly at night, he sounded like he spoke to his son.

When there'd been no response to her pleas, his mother had faded into the gray again. Kendall had debated sending her some money to shut her up, but she had a feeling it would be a never ending cycle. So, she let things lie.

The paparazzi still harassed them occasionally, but even that had faded away. They went to work for the day, then came home. They stayed in, for the most part, because nausea would strike once in a while, just out of the blue. It had started to ease, but occasionally it caught her off guard.

Kendall watched the clock all day, counting down the minutes until they could leave. Grif seemed just as anxious, pacing in front of the window.

"Do you want to know the sex of the baby?"

He stopped when she asked him the question, quiet for a long time. "You know, I don't think so. I think this is one of the few real surprises I'll ever have in my life. I'd like to anticipate it."

Kendall could have cried. She wanted to know, but it wouldn't be fair to Grif if she slipped.

It wasn't until they were actually in the doctor's office and the technician ran the wand over her belly that she decided.

"We don't want to know the sex of the baby."

Grif already held her hand, but his fingers tightened around hers when she said that. "Thank you," he whispered into her ear.

That was a day for tears. She cried when she felt the baby

move, she cried when she followed Grif's wishes, and she broke down and sobbed when she heard the baby's heartbeat for the first time and saw its little face on the untrasound monitor.

"Everything looks perfect. We'll see you in a month."

Kendall left in a daze, feeling adrift in a sea of craziness. Luckily, Ortiz had driven them that day, so Grif could sit in the back and hold her. When they got to the condo, she climbed onto the elevator in a daze.

The little black and white photo from the doctor's office kept drawing her attention. It slowly began to sink in that she was going to be a mom.

"I'm going to be a mom."

Grif unlocked the door and ushered her inside. "Yes, you are. And I'm going to be a dad. Terrifying for both of us."

Kendall nodded and kicked off her shoes. "But I'm not going to be like my mother," she vowed. "You know, she used to not let me play outside because of bruises. They were hard to cover with makeup. And because the sun caused wrinkles."

Grif wrapped his arm around her from behind, nuzzling a kiss to her neck. "You don't have wrinkles."

"Damn, so maybe she was right."

They laughed together and headed to the kitchen for some lunch. As she pulled chicken from the refrigerator, she glanced at Grif. "What do you plan on doing that your parents didn't?"

Blinking, he looked down at the table, and the bread in his hands. "I plan on never letting my child go hungry."

Kendall stared at him, sure she'd heard him wrong. "You were hungry as a child?"

"Every day. Liquor was more important in my house."

Her heart ached at the thought. In this day and age, no child should ever be hungry.

"I was too, but for a completely different reason. My mother used to count out the calories in my food and tell me what I was allowed to have. Usually carrots and cucumbers, broccoli. I can't stand to eat them raw to this day."

Grif shook his dark head. "So, let's plan on doing exactly opposite what our mothers did and maybe our kid will turn out normal."

She nodded, throat tight.

"My…our child will not have to worry about people belittling her little body for any reason."

"Our child will not be called stupid, for any reason, by anyone."

A shudder slid through her body when his eyes connected with hers. They nodded to each other, promising basic courtesies to their child that had been denied them.

Grif set his sandwich down and crossed the kitchen to pull her into his arms, kissing her soundly. "Our child will be important in our lives."

She nodded against his chest. "Paramount. Above everything."

"And our child will know love."

They had a quiet night that night, with she on her computer and Grif watching a ball game on TV. At one point Kendall sat back in her chair just enjoying the companionship. They didn't need to talk all the time; just being together in the same room was nice. When they went to bed that night, they made love with a stronger understanding for each other.

"KENDALL, YOUR FATHER is here."

She's barely looked up at the intercom when her father let himself into the room. "Hey, Dad, this is a nice surprise."

And it was. Her father had retired and the company had

been under her control for two months now. There had been a few minor growing pains, such as finding the new head of the real estate arm of the company, but other than that it had been going smooth. She'd come to realize, however, that the Herrington name did a lot of the paving.

Frank crossed the room and wrapped her in a hug. "It's good to see you, Munchkin." He pulled away and rubbed his hand lightly over the baby bump. "And how is little Munchkin?"

"Little Munchkin is fine. Bouncing off the walls of his cell. The kid is always moving. I'm scared what he's going to be like in a few months."

Dad grinned like the proud grandpapa he would be and nodded his head, as if he expected nothing less than a go-getter.

Kendall realized as she talked to him that he looked better than he had in a long time, at least before his heart attack. His eyes were sharp but relaxed, and his skin was a healthy pink rather than a grayish color. "You look great, I have to say."

He nodded, brushing a hand over his gray hair. "I do, don't I?"

They laughed together and Kendall couldn't remember the last time her father had seemed so lighthearted.

"So, what's up? What brings you down the mountain to see your baby?"

She made a motion to the surrounding offices and he grinned.

"Okay, I admit, maybe I do miss coming in every morning and cracking the whip, seeing people scurry from my wrath."

She laughed, because to some extent that's exactly what he used to do. "You know they've all filed for counseling since you left."

He frowned, until he realized she was only kidding.

"I thought I would see if you have time for lunch today. It's been a while since we had some you and I time. Where's your other half? I thought he would be here."

"Grif had to run to Denver for the day. He still has his apartment and stuff over there because he hasn't decided exactly what to do about his job."

Dad looked confused. "Why not just put him on Security here? Hell, with his experience he could probably head it up."

Kendall sighed, familiar with the argument because she used it all the time. "I know. I keep telling him that. But he doesn't want to feel like he's taking charity."

And she'd realized that the more she argued for it, the more stubborn he became.

"Then hire him as a consultant. If he'd be comfortable leaving you with some of the other guards, he can go site to site and deal with some of the issues that pop up occasionally."

Kendall hadn't thought about him doing that, but it made perfect sense. It wouldn't be all the time, but he could be earning a living.

She understood why he was being so stubborn. He didn't have anything out here. None of his stuff, nothing to mark her apartment as his as well. Guilt chewed at her. She should have thought of that. Maybe they needed to look at a house. But then he'd want to contribute money, which he needed a way to earn. It was a catch-22.

"But back to your original question, yes, I would love to go to lunch with you."

Ortiz had gone down to the security lounge, so she called him and told him they were going to The Chophouse, one of her father's favorite restaurants. Charles, her father's driver, would drive them. Ortiz promised to meet her in the lobby.

They got to the restaurant without incident. June in Vail tended to be busy, though not nearly as bad as in the winter.

Kendall was famished, so the Chophouse, well known for its steaks, suited her perfectly. The baby had taught her to eat more substantial food. Salads and a piece of fruit just weren't keeping her anymore. Protein had moved to the top of her list. The doctor had warned her she would gain weight. Years of cultivated fears kept her off the scale. She didn't want to know how much she had gained, though they told her every time she went to the doctor's office.

Over appetizers, her father finally got around to the reason for his visit.

"My divorce from Deedra is almost complete. My lawyer called me today. I'm going to have to pay her a settlement, but hopefully it will get her out of our lives. She's been at a resort for the past few weeks."

Kendall's brows shot into her hairline. "I didn't know anything about this."

"Yeah, we had a blowup after the last board meeting, and we each retreated to our separate corners for a while. She took a shopping trip to New York—with Hunter, I assume— because he disappeared about the same time, and I stayed home for Emily to take care of me." He grinned at her. "I think Deedra was trying to remind me how much I needed her in my life, but it thoroughly backfired. I enjoyed every minute of her being gone. When she finally did turn up I told her not to unpack her bags, that I was ready to move on."

He paused as the waiter appeared to take away their plates.

"You should have seen her. She was livid. Ripped me up one side and down the other and tried to say her infidelity was my fault."

Kendall choked on her water. "Are you serious?"

Frank's green eyes twinkled as he nodded his head. "She thought I'd been sleeping with Emily the entire time. I have to say, if Emily had consented I probably would have, but she won't take scraps anymore she said. So I asked her to marry me once the Deedra mess is straightened out."

Kendall's mouth dropped open, but for the life of her she couldn't do anything about it. When she could finally catch her breath, she circled the table to give her father a hug. "About damn time! Although I don't know if you should get married again so quickly, even to Emily."

He nodded. "She said pretty much the same thing, so we're just going to take it easy for a while. I might take her on a trip and enjoy some of the money I have laying around."

Kendall nodded as she sat back down. "I think that would be a fabulous idea. Take her on a cruise. It's on her bucket list."

His eyes lit up. "A cruise, huh? Okay. I can definitely do that."

Their entrees arrived then and she dug into her steak. It tasted phenomenal; the fat on the edges burnt crisp just the way she liked it, but pink in the middle. It satisfied the carnivore in her.

They were almost through the meal when the waiter stepped up to their table. "Sir, I am so sorry to interrupt you, but your wife is trying to pay her tab and the card has been declined."

Her father laughed out loud. "Good! I had them cancelled for that very reason."

Kendall laughed, knowing for fact that he'd done it out of spite. But could she blame him?

"Tell my soon-to-be ex-wife that she's going to have to find some other golden goose to pay her bill."

The waiter cringed, but turned away to do as he was told.

"You're making that poor man's day very difficult."

Frank shrugged and grinned, tipping his head to eat the rest of his steak.

Within about thirty seconds they heard a screech from the front of the exclusive restaurant. Deedra barreled back through the room, zeroing in on Frank. "You bastard! How dare you!"

Frank gave Deedra an innocent look. "How dare I what, dear?"

"How dare you cut me off like that. I took care of you for two years, through your heart attack and retirement, and this is how you repay me?"

Kendall couldn't help but snort. She tried to cover it with a cough, but the woman's vicious gaze swung in her direction. "And you, you little pansy ass bitch, how dare you let him do this to me? I was your friend."

Kendall sat back in her chair in surprise. She hadn't known that. "Well, Deedra, I'm sorry you feel I let you down."

The woman's crazed eyes flared even sharper with fury at Kendall's carefully worded response.

"Deedra, you knew this was coming. Your lawyer told you about it last week. I don't understand why you're acting so surprised now."

Her big blue eyes filled with tears and she stepped forward enough to rest her hand on Frank's shoulder. "Because I never thought you'd be so harsh. I was hoping there would be a way we could work all this out, without all the lawyers and legal stuff."

Kendall felt more than saw Ortiz step in from the side.

Frank shook his head and pulled his shoulder out of her grasp. "If you liked the life you had, you never should have jumped into bed with somebody else. You rocked the boat,

Deedra."

She stamped her high-heeled foot in fury. "No, I didn't. You've been sleeping with the housekeeper for years, so it was only fair I slept with Hunter."

Smiling, Frank shook his head. "You know, years ago I probably would have slept with Emily on the side, but I've matured, Deedra. I don't need all the drama anymore. I made a mistake in marrying you. Go back to Hunter in New York."

Deliberately he looked her up and down, then, with a bored look turned away from her and picked up his silverware. "But don't go back to the penthouse. I'm having the locks changed. Your items will be placed into storage unless you take too long to retrieve them; then I'll send them to charity."

People around them snickered.

She gasped in mortified outrage and stepped forward, holding out her hand. "But I don't have anywhere to go," she cried. Tears dripped down her cheeks, but her father just shrugged.

"Not my concern."

With a furious cry, she reached for his steak knife, but her hand never connected. Ortiz was there in a flash, twisting her arm behind her back. Deedra screamed all the way out of the restaurant.

The manager arrived then, apologizing profusely. Frank waved away his apologies. "Don't worry about it. Just know that she is no longer my wife and if she tries to tell you otherwise, kick her out."

Mr. Ortiz returned, straightening his suit jacket as he walked.

Frank held out his hand to the guard. "Good job, Ortiz. Have you eaten?"

He shook his dark head and clasped hands with the older

man. "No, sir."

"Go eat something then. We'll wait for you."

Ortiz nodded and stepped to the side, giving the manager his order. Within just a few minutes his steak was brought out and the guard was putting it away.

Kendall was more than a little shaken. She never imagined that Deedra would go off on her father like that.

When they left the restaurant, the light beaming through the trees blinded her. Kendall held onto her father's elbow as they crossed the brick sidewalk to the black SUV idling at the curb for them. She stepped inside and buckled up as her father slipped in beside her. Ortiz climbed into the front.

"Back to the office, Charles, to drop my daughter off."

The driver nodded and pulled away.

"Grif is going to be upset he missed the excitement. The one day he's gone and the shit hits the fan."

Her father laughed, nodding. "Indeed. Well, we couldn't have known how exciting our lunch was going to be."

He'd no sooner closed his mouth than Ortiz yelled out. Kendall didn't even have a chance to swing her head before the SUV was slammed in the side and her world went spinning. The seatbelt tightened over her tummy as the SUV rolled end over end, landing with a crunch. She thought she might have cried out before her head smacked something hard and her world went dark.

CHAPTER ELEVEN

✦

G RIF FROWNED AT the unfamiliar number on the caller ID. "Parks."

"Is this Grafton Parks, emergency contact for Kendall Herrington?"

The bottom fell out of his stomach. He veered to the berm of the road as the woman on the other end of the line shattered his world. Kendall had been in a rollover crash and he needed to get to Vail as soon as possible. When he asked her about the baby, she either didn't know or didn't want to tell him, because she ignored the question. "We are doing everything we can for her and the baby, but you should be here."

He floored the truck, spitting gravel before it caught on the pavement. The next hour passed in a blur and he honestly didn't know how he escaped the notice of the state patrol, flying the way he did toward the resort town. Duncan called him just outside city limits to tell him that Ortiz, Frank and the driver had been in the vehicle as well and all were being treated at Vail Valley Medical Center.

Pulling into a space, he shoved the truck into park and ran for the door.

The woman at the reception desk smiled at him calmly before requesting the name of the patient. When he told her,

her smile dimmed just a bit as she looked up the information on the computer. "Looks like she's still being seen. Have a seat and I'll see what I can find out."

Grif dropped his ass to the chair, not knowing what else to do. When he looked down, he realized his hand was shaking, and his leg was bouncing a million miles a minute. The clock on the wall across from him read three forty-five.

At four oh seven, he got up to pace. The woman had returned, promising that somebody would be out momentarily to take him back to his wife, but nobody showed.

He stopped at the desk again.

"Can you check on three other names? Frank Herrington, my father-in-law, Diego Ortiz, one of the men I work with and Charles. Not sure about his last name. He works for Mr. Herrington though."

"Because you are a relative, I can tell you that Mr. Herrington has a concussion, a badly broken leg and is being taken to surgery. I cannot release information about the other two men, though, I'm sorry."

Grif gritted his teeth in frustration, but it was more information than he had minutes ago. "And when will he be able to have visitors?"

"Probably as soon as he gets settled into a room after recovery, although it is up to his doctor."

Grif continued to pace the waiting room until a harried looking doctor came through the automatic doors. "Mr. Parks?"

"Yes."

"Follow me, please. I'll take you to your wife."

Grif fell in beside the older man, waiting.

"We get rollover crashes fairly often, but this one is a little different. Apparently your wife's vehicle was T-boned by another vehicle, knocking it over a small embankment. Your wife was on the side of the vehicle not struck, but we still have some issues." He stopped beside a bustling nurses' station and reached for a binder. "She has a pretty serious concussion, and she has yet to regain consciousness. Several scrapes and bruises-"

"And the baby?" he demanded.

The doctor gave him a reassuring smile. "Your son appears to be fine. No signs of bleeding or contractions, and the heartbeat is strong, although it was a little erratic when they first brought them in."

"Son," he said softly. His son. It sounded right to him.

"I'm sorry, you didn't know?"

He shook his head. "As long as he's okay, it doesn't matter."

The doctor held up a cautioning hand. "As of right now he's okay, but your wife concerns me more. The concussion can cause issues if we don't watch her carefully."

Grif nodded, understanding that everything could go to hell in a heartbeat. "Can you tell me about the others in the car with her? Her father?"

The doctor reached for another binder. "Mr. Herrington is going into surgery now to repair his left leg, which took the brunt of the crash. It's broken in three separate places. He has a broken clavicle and a concussion as well, though his is not as serious as your wife's. The Herringtons' driver has already been released with only minor bumps and bruises. But the third man, Mr. Ortiz, is also going into surgery. He did not have his seatbelt on at the time of the crash and was ejected from the vehicle. He has several cracked vertebrae in his neck, broken ribs, ruptured spleen, his left ankle is shattered and too many cuts and bruises to count."

"Fuck."

"Uh, yes. Does he have family? The only name we could find was a contact card for a Duncan Wilde."

"That's our boss. I believe he does have family, although I couldn't give you names or anything. Duncan should be able to though."

The doctor made a note in the folder. Something else occurred to Grif.

"You should know, though, that Ortiz is a disabled veteran and struggles with PTSD."

"Oh, good to know. I'll contact the VA to get his records."

"Can I go see my wife now?"

The doctor nodded, but warned him to be prepared.

Grif shoved the curtain aside, sure that he could take anything he saw, but Kendall lying so pale and lifeless took his breath away. Easing to her side, he reached for her hand, then hesitated because of the IV. Instead, he rested his hand on her arm, stroking lightly.

Somebody had tried to clean her up, but her pale skin still had a few streaks of blood on it. Her long blond hair was mussed around her head and she had an oxygen cannula beneath her nose.

The sheet draped over her stomach and she looked more pregnant than only six months.

They were having a son.

Too many emotions bounced around in his body to separate them, but fear and gratitude were the strongest. Fear that Kendall wouldn't wake up, fear that something would happen to the pregnancy...hell, fear that he wasn't up to raising a son.

And even though the doctor was cautious, he was thankful that the crash hadn't been worse.

GRIF PACED THE small confines of the curtained off area. When a nurse came to ready Kendall to move from the emergency department to a private room, he was glad for the distraction.

As the nurse wheeled her down the hallway, he stayed at her side, watching for any hint that she would wake. But her face stayed calm and quiet.

"I won't tell you not to worry, but I do think she'll be okay. The body knows how to protect itself, and that's what it's doing right now."

He nodded, appreciating the nurse's words, but he wouldn't be satisfied until she opened her pretty green eyes and smiled at him.

The room they walked into would have been good enough for any socialite in the world. And probably had been.

The nurse plugged all the machines in, then a few more, adjusted the fetal monitor around Kendall's belly and tidied the sheets around her.

"Mr. Herrington will be right next door once he's through recovery. If you need anything or if she starts to rouse, call us."

Grif nodded, then dragged a chair close enough to the bed that he could reach over and hold Kendall's hand. Satisfied that he was finally alone with her, he rested his head against their joined hands on the bed. "You need to wake up, woman."

AND SHE DID, just a few hours later.

Her hand tightened on his.

"Is the baby okay?" she whispered. A tear slipped out of the corner of her eye.

"The baby is perfect," he told her, his own throat tight with emotion.

She blinked her eyes open. "Are you sure?"

He nodded, leaning down to press a kiss to her forehead. "I would tell you if he wasn't. I promise."

She sank back into the bed, her eyes falling shut again.

Grif pressed the nurse button. When he told her what had happened, she smiled and promised to let the doctor know.

A WOMAN DOCTOR took over her care, and an OB also checked her over. Both were very encouraged when Kendall opened her eyes and spoke with them. The baby doctor checked the readouts from the monitor.

"Considering what you went through, and the damage to the vehicle, you are a remarkably lucky young woman. And so is that baby."

Kendall seemed more reassured every time she talked to the doctors, until she asked about the men in the vehicle. The doctor, though tiny, had a very strong personality, and she seemed positive that Kendall's dad and Ortiz would be fine.

"Your father has a long road ahead of him, I won't lie. He'll be laid up with that leg for a good while, possibly months, but I expect him to make a full recovery." She smiled. "Not a great way to start a retirement, but you have to roll with the punches."

Her smile lost some of its brightness.

"Mr. Ortiz, on the other hand, is going to be here for a good while, until he's stable enough to transfer to the VA. His injuries are substantial. We're keeping him heavily sedated right now, but his extremity reactions are good, so there doesn't appear to be any long term paralysis."

Relief flowed through her. She'd been so worried when she'd heard about his neck. "He had turned around to look to make sure my seatbelt was on, then when he turned back toward the front, he yelled out. I'm not sure what he saw."

Grif and the doctor shared a look.

"What? Tell me."

Grif sighed. "He probably saw the SUV coming toward him that struck you."

Kendall felt her mouth drop open. "Somebody hit us? And then what? I know we rolled."

He nodded. "They struck the driver's side but toward the rear. I think she was aiming at your father."

"She?"

Kendall knew before he said her name.

"Deedra."

It took a while for it all to sink in.

"And how is she?"

They shared another look, but Grif let the doctor take the lead. "Well, she didn't make it. She died from her injuries."

Shock pushed Kendall back in the bed. "No way. We saw her just a little while before. She confronted Dad in the restaurant."

Grif nodded. "We know about that. The police talked to the manager of the restaurant. They'll probably want to talk to you later, as well."

Nodding, she rested her head on the pillow. Tiredness dragged at her and her body had begun to ache from the beating it had taken. "So, how long will I be stuck in here?"

The doctor's face turned cautious. "Let's take it a day at a time, okay? I at least want to keep you for a couple of days, just to make sure the baby doesn't go into distress."

She was right. The baby needed to come first. "Okay. I'll try to be good."

Grif stood up.

"She will. I'll make sure of it."

The doctor scribbled something in the chart and left the

room.

Kendall felt strangely numb. So much had happened that she didn't know what to think about first. "I can't believe Deedra did that. She tried to kill us."

Grif made a motion with his shoulders. "I think she wanted to kill Frank for humiliating her. You were not her intended target. Although who knows what she was thinking when she rammed you and pushed you off the road."

"I guess I'm glad she did it so close to the restaurant. She would have gotten her wish if she'd hit us on the mountain."

Grif's eyes went cold. "If she had, I would have chased her down to hell and brought her back just so I could kill her again."

Kendall choked on a laugh and reached for his hand. She tugged against him until he leaned down to press a kiss to her lips. "Thank you. I would do the same for you."

CHAPTER TWELVE

✦

D UNCAN ARRIVED LATER that night. Kendall had just fallen
asleep when there was a light tap at the door.

Grif opened the door and stepped out with his buddy,
giving him a shake with his good hand. "Glad you made it."

"Of course. How's your wife and baby?"

"Good, I think." He rubbed his hand over his face, more
tired than he could remember being in a long time. "She had a
concussion and some scrapes, but the baby seems fine. More
than I would have ever thought possible after seeing the truck
they were in."

Duncan smiled and slapped him on the back. "She's a
tough girl. Has to be to put up with your ass."

Grif snorted and nodded. "Agreed."

He made a motion to a couple of rooms down from Kendall's and Duncan fell into step beside him, black cane
swinging. "They put all three on the same floor just to make it
easier. Ortiz hasn't roused since they brought him out of
surgery. Did you get hold of his family?"

Duncan nodded, but didn't seem optimistic. "Diego's
mother isn't doing well, so I doubt she'll be able to come. I
told her I would make sure he was taken care of."

They pushed through the door and Grif caught his breath.

Again. Poor guy was strung up like a side of beef. The soft neck brace had been replaced by a Halo, a wire contraption screwed into his skull and braced against his shoulders to keep his neck immobile. His face was black and blue, giving his Hispanic complexion an odd cast. The eye patch over his right eye was the only part that seemed normal.

Duncan didn't flinch at all, but then Grif hadn't expected him to. The man had seen more in his forty-odd years than any man should. That experience made him as solid as a rock.

When he crossed to Ortiz's side and rested a hand on his shoulder, Grif's throat tightened with emotion. They'd all been in and out of hospitals over and over again. It was just wrong that Ortiz would be here for possibly months because he had turned around to check on Kendall's safety.

Grif would be ready if his fellow Marine needed anything.

As soon as she was allowed to get to her feet, she wanted to see her father. The doctors and nurses had told her he was okay, even Grif and Emily, but she needed to see for herself. So, hand clutching the silk robe Grif had brought her from home, she headed down the hallway to see him.

Grif glared at her the entire trip and held his hands out as if to catch her if she fell.

"I'm fine, damn it. Just let me walk."

Her father's face crumpled into relief when he saw her and they both battled tears as she leaned over to hug him, carefully. She shook her head at him when she pulled away, because his entire left side was a mass of bruises and casts. His leg was suspended to a frame over the bed and the cast reached all the way up his thigh. There was also an incision over his clavicle.

Frank followed her gaze. "They put a pin in here, to help it heal."

"You'll be setting off airport scanners wherever you go."

Her father grinned at her, though he seemed a bit weak.

Grif brought a chair over for her to sit in and she sank down. She gave him a smile, feeling bad that she'd snapped at him earlier. He'd only been looking out for her.

"Grif tell you what's been going on?"

Frank nodded, frowning. "I never would have suspected she'd do something so crazy. I can't tell you how sorry I am for bringing her into our lives."

"No need, Dad. It's done."

They visited for a while before they both began to tire. Emily came in just as he fell asleep.

She didn't seem surprised when she saw Kendall at her father's bedside. "He asks about you all the time. I'm glad you were able to come over."

Dropping her bag to the chair, she turned to give Kendall a careful hug.

The housekeeper's arms were so comforting, she let herself sag into them for a moment. Emily seemed to need the connection just as much, because it was a long minute before she released her and stepped back.

Before she went back to her room, she wanted to see Ortiz. Grif told her reluctantly where his room was, so she headed down there. He followed close on her heels. Then held her as she cried for the wounded Marine.

THEY RELEASED HER the next day.

Kendall had never been so glad to see the outside of a building. June in Vail was truly spectacular and she'd missed being able to get out.

Though she was cautioned to take it easy for at least a week and to come in for anything at all, they didn't think there was any risk for the baby. She was to follow up with her regular OB next week.

She thought for sure they'd have to wade through reporters, but there didn't seem to be any around.

"They think you're at Herrington House."

She didn't know how he'd managed that, but it made her happy.

Grif drove her home as slowly as the law allowed. Kendall thought she'd be a little freaked getting into a big SUV, so similar to the one she'd crashed in, but it didn't bother her. Pulling the seatbelt across her lap bothered her more, because she had bruises from the crash.

She smiled as Grif looked across at her again. "I'm fine. Just drive. You're watching me more than the road and it's freaking me out."

Tightening his jaw, his head swung forward and he kept it there for the most part.

She watched the evergreen scenery flash by and wished she had sunglasses. There was still a bit of an ache on the right side of her head, but she'd been assured it would go away within the week.

The baby dragged something across the inside of her right belly and she rested her hand there. One of the ultrasound techs had told her it was a foot, but it felt bigger than that. She rubbed it a bit and was rewarded with a bump. *Okay, maybe it is a foot.*

When Grif walked her off the elevator on her floor, Brian Calvert, the blond bodyguard, already stood outside her condo door.

He smiled when they reached him.

"Mrs. Parks, can I just say how very glad I am that you and the baby are okay."

She smiled as he brought out a small bouquet. Kendall was unaccountably touched. She didn't know Mr. Calvert very well at all, but he seemed to be a really nice guy. "Thank you very much. I appreciate that."

Though she'd only been gone a few days, the apartment smelled musty, like it hadn't been opened at all, which she knew wasn't true. Grif had returned several times for items she needed.

Dropping her clothes to the floor as she walked in, she headed straight for the shower. "I need help in the shower, Grif."

His rich blue eyes flared with heat. Kendall adjusted the faucets while he took off his clothes, the prosthetic and the neoprene-like liner from his arm. The skin on his stump seemed irritated. She cradled it in her hands to look closer.

"Why is it red like this?"

He pulled away from her touch and stepped under the water.

"You haven't been taking care of it like you're supposed to, have you? You've been busy taking care of us."

Kendall carefully walked into the stall. The water flowed over her shoulders, breasts, then belly and it felt so good. The disinfectant stink from the hospital had pervaded her pores, souring other scents. Reaching out, she rested her hands against Grif's chest. Knowing he wouldn't let her fall, she rolled her head forward to let the water loosen the knots in her neck.

She indulged herself for a couple of minutes before turning her attention to Grif. He'd been by her side, or Ortiz's, or her father's the entire time they'd been in the hospital. She doubted he'd taken care of his amputation the way he was supposed to in that time. He'd told her he was supposed to wash the sleeve out every night. There wouldn't have been a place to do that. Knowing Grif, he wouldn't have deliberately hindered himself by taking off the prosthesis in the hospital room. He would have been on guard for her the entire time.

Lathering the bath poof with his soap, she urged him to face away and began to lather him down. He groaned, sagging against the wall of the shower. His amputation hung on her side, so she carefully lathered it as well. The skin looked red and aggravated in patches, as if he had poison ivy. She turned him into the water and held his arm up toward the faucet to make sure all the soap was rinsed. Then, with a quick shampoo and a final rinse of her own, she urged him out of the stall.

She wrapped one towel around herself, knotting it at her breast, then began to pat him down with another. "Do we need to put anything on these spots?"

He shook his head. "They'll heal up pretty quick if I leave them to air dry. It's just where moisture had built up inside the sleeve."

She turned to the sink, where he'd left the sleeve. She had watched him wash it out before, so she started to run water inside it.

"Don't do that, Kendall. I can take care of my own shit."

Continuing to slosh water inside the device, she crooked a brow at him. "I know you can, but you haven't been because you've been taking care of other people. You are just as important."

"No, I'm not. Don't. That thing stinks. I'll do it later." He tried to pull her away from the sink, but she resisted.

"You might as well let me finish. Do you need to put soap in it?"

"No," he sighed. "Just water."

Water sloshed inside as she closed the end with her fist and shook it back and forth, then dumped it again. She repeated the process half a dozen more times before he told her it was enough.

"Let it drip for a minute then put it on the rod to dry."

The appliance to dry the sleeve looked like a paper towel holder with a rounded top. Positioning it carefully, she left it, not convinced she'd done it correctly.

"It's fine, Kendall. Leave it. You didn't have to do that."

"Yes, I did. And I'll do it many more times in my lifetime, I'm sure."

His look sharpened on her face, but she turned away.

"I'm ready to just relax. I'll dive into business stuff later."

Unwrapping her towel, she ran it down her legs, then squeezed her hair to get out the excess moisture. Padding across the bedroom, she crawled into the bed naked. It had gotten to the point that any sleeping position other than her side was out of the question, so she laid down on her left side to watch Grif dry off.

They were both needy. She smiled when she realized he had already begun to harden. It had been almost a week since they'd made love, the longest they'd gone without since they'd married. A tingle of arousal swirled down through her body.

Grif tossed the towel aside and crawled into bed facing her. He ran his fingertip over the pouting tip of her breast and she gasped. They had become so sensitive.

He shifted up onto his right elbow and ran his left hand over every part of her body he could reach, swirling around her belly, then lower to her ready heat. Pressing his mouth to hers, slipping his tongue inside her mouth, he mimicked every action his finger made in her slickness. As he circled her clit, hovering on the high side like she liked, he whispered into her neck and ear how much he'd missed loving her.

Kendall ran her fingers over his chest, then up his neck. Stubble had begun to darken his jaw and it rasped under her nails as she pulled him close, panting into his neck as he sent her into a white haze of rippling pleasure. When she'd caught her breath, she ran her hands down his body, pulling him to her. Lifting her right thigh over his hips, she angled for him to enter her.

When they made love this way it was slow and easy, but this time there was an urgency that hadn't been there before. As if they were conscious of exactly how close she and the baby had come to dying. Even as he surged into her body, he clutched her to him, mouth never leaving her own.

They both began to move faster, searching for that perfect resonance that would carry them to that peak, and they both found it at the same time. For a breathless moment, they hovered on that brink, before tumbling into climax. Kendall cried out, arching against Grif as he spasmed and released into her body. Heat spread through her womb as his hips continued to surge, no longer under any kind of control.

It took several long minutes for their heart rates to return to normal and their bodies to stop quivering, but they held each other the entire time.

"Well," he sighed, "I don't know about you but I'm ready for a shower."

Kendall giggled, knowing he spoke the truth but not wanting to move. Lethargy had moved in with a vengeance and it was all she could do to keep her eyes open. "Just let me close my eyes for a minute."

He snorted but pulled her closer anyway. "Okay."

GRIF WATCHED KENDALL sleep and felt a contentment he'd never known before. She'd drifted away as soon as she'd closed her eyes, but he didn't blame her. This week had been the most harrowing of his life, even more so than when he'd lost his hand, and it had been just as trying for her. Constantly wondering if the baby would be okay had put shadows under her eyes. Her father's health had also kept her on edge because of his cardiac history. She'd whispered to Grif one night that she worried his heart would give out from all the crises going on at once.

But Frank now seemed stronger than before, as if the lack of Deedra's malevolent energy in his life had finally begun to let him heal. It didn't hurt that Emily now catered to his every whim.

As if she hadn't before.

Movement in his peripheral caught his attention and it took him a moment to realize the baby had moved. Grif stared, waiting for another bump, but he had quieted. Just when he was about to turn away, the baby moved again. Conscious of not waking Kendall, Grif rested his hand against her belly.

The baby kicked, as if to say hello. Tears came to Grif's eyes at the thought of looking into his child's determined little face for the first time. The boy would be hardy, just like his mom and dad. Grif had been desperately afraid he would never get the chance to do that this week. Happiness didn't normally stop into his life, certainly not to stay, so the past few months had been like a dream. He'd been waiting for the other shoe to drop.

Kendall's hand moved from her hip to cover his on her belly as the baby continued to kick. When he looked up, tears had seeped from her eyes to the pillow beneath her. "He loves you as much as I do."

The whispered words didn't register at first. "What?"

Her smiled faltered and another silver tear spilled to the

pillow. "We love you. I love you. When they were telling me everything we'd gone through, all I could think about was that I hadn't had enough time with you yet. And that I hadn't told you that. And then I didn't know if I should tell you in case something happened with the baby. I didn't want you to feel obligated to stay with me."

He cringed at her assumption that he was only with her because of the baby. Then he realized he hadn't given her any reason to think otherwise. "Even if there wasn't, I would still be here for you. I have no idea if anything I do will be right, but I love you too. Have for a long time, I think. The baby was just a fortuitous excuse to get you to marry me." She choked out a laugh and burrowed into his chest.

"Are you sure? It was my mess up and I don't want you to feel like you've had to sacrifice your life for my mistake."

"Honey, do you seriously think I couldn't have pushed you away that night? It was a mutual mistake, but I've come to realize that we were meant to hook up, if not then it would have been soon."

Some of the tension left her body and she snuggled into him, her belly pressed to his.

Grif cradled his wife and child to him and wondered, truly, what he'd done to be given this gift.

Three and a half months later...

KENDALL SMILED DOWN at him, sleepy and rumpled. "Good morning, sleepy head. I'm sorry to wake you, but I need your help."

Grif lurched into a sitting position. "Sure babe, what do you need? Glass of water?"

He scrubbed his face, blinking against the light from the bathroom.

"I need you to run me to the hospital so I can have our baby."

Grif lurched to his feet, tiredness being replaced by fear. "What? Are you sure? Are you in pain? They're not the Braxton things you've been feeling?"

Kendall's head nodded and shook as each question was asked, and it would have been ridiculous had it been any other type of situation.

"My water broke, Grif."

He blinked at her.

"Get your ass moving, Marine!"

Grif bolted for the bathroom and his arm. He rolled on the sock and slammed the prosthesis on as quickly as he could, then lurched for the bedroom and clothes. He realized in passing that Kendall was already dressed in a flowy dress and sandals, and her bag sat at her feet. "How long have you been up?"

"About half an hour." She held up a notepad. "I've been timing my contractions and they're getting closer."

"How close?"

His gut quivered in fear as he paused for the answer.

"I'm not going to tell you because it'll freak you out. I need my calm-headed hero to get us to the hospital."

Fuck!

Grif ripped on clothes as fast as he could, stumbling into the wall as he bounced on one foot trying to get his shoes on. Kendall giggled and sailed out of the room ahead of him. "I texted Calvert to let him know we're leaving. Here are the keys."

He caught them one handed then bolted for the door. Then realized what a dumbass he was and went back to grab the hospital bag from her hand and guide her to the door.

"Grif, chill. Calm headed, remember?"

Grif did not chill until three hours later, when he looked down at his screaming son in the clear bassinet. He reached out his hand to brush against the tiny little fingers and the boy's entire fist suddenly opened to grip his finger.

"Wow, you are a hoss, little man."

Grif knew he looked stupid in his shorts and long-sleeved button-down shirt, but he didn't care as he looked down at his red-faced boy.

"It's a good thing you got here when you did," the nurse told him. "Any later and you'd have been delivering him yourself."

Grif actually felt himself pale. Damn. That had been too close for comfort.

The nurse swaddled his son in a striped baby blanket, wrapping him up like a little burrito. Then she lifted him and held him out to Grif.

He and Kendall had practiced this, because it had been a fear that he wouldn't be able to handle him with the prosthetic. They'd 'rented' a life-size baby from the hospital, same weight, same everything. And it had been a breeze.

As he took his son now, though, all that practicing went out the window. He nestled into the crook of Grif's elbow, with the prosthetic hand beneath his butt. Grif's real hand was then free to do what he needed it to. The nurse smiled at him in encouragement and he turned to Kendall.

Though she'd been in labor for hours and her hair was mussed, her face flushed, tears tracks down her face, she somehow still managed to look glorious. She smiled when she saw him holding their son and held a hand out.

"You look very natural doing that."

Grif grinned. "You know, I feel natural. It's my son, so

how could I not?"

She nodded against the pillow. "I have a suggestion for a name."

He raised his brows. "Did you settle on one?"

They'd tossed hundreds back and forth for months, but nothing had sounded exactly right.

"I do, but you may not like it."

Grif narrowed his eyes at her. "Why?"

"Jameson Herrington Parks."

Emotion tightened his throat and he tried to clear it, but it didn't work. Tears made his vision blurry as he blinked down at his son.

"We need to make your legacy a good one, and I don't want you to have pain because of that name anymore."

She reached out to them both, cradling them against her as he fought with his past and future. For years he'd been resentful of the name, but he realized now that Kendall had eased him past that. When he pulled away and nodded, pressing a kiss to her lips, she began to cry.

"I think it's perfect," he admitted.

EPILOGUE

Six months later...

T HE BRIDE WAS truly radiant. As she walked down the aisle on his arm, Grif couldn't help but beam as Emily took calm, measured steps toward her future husband. When they reached the altar Grif pressed a kiss to her hand and gave it to Frank, who stood tall and strong in front of the minister.

Grif took his place just behind Frank's shoulder and glanced across the aisle to his wife, who had tears in her eyes. He smiled at her and she sent him a subtle nod, then turned back to listen to the proceedings.

Considering this was Frank's third wedding, he should have been an old hat at it by now, but Grif knew the truth. His fingers quivered when he took Emily's ring, and he would have dropped it if Grif hadn't grabbed it. Emily, on the other hand, looked sedate and satisfied. She'd been waiting for this for a long time, and he prayed Frank kept his shit together.

Jamie squealed "ma" in the back of the room. When that didn't get her attention, he started to chant it, making some in the audience giggle. Kendall glanced at him long enough to give him a little wave, which seemed to appease him.

As the ceremony drew to a close and the husband kissed

his bride, the audience cheered. They walked down the aisle arm in arm.

Grif held his hand out to his wife. She snugged up against him as they walked down the aisle behind her father. Friends lined the walkway, and he wanted to be done with the requirements so he could talk to them and mingle. He was very curious about the woman Duncan had brought. His boss couldn't seem to take his eyes off of her.

Ortiz stood just outside the door in the vestibule, as close as he could get considering the group of people. Grif shook the guard's hand, glad to have his man back in action. The Halo had come off weeks ago and the scars on his forehead had finally begun to fade away.

Lilly brought Jameson out. The little boy lunged into Kendall's arms, patting her cheeks. "Ma."

Kendall giggled and tried to straighten his little suit, but it was kind of a lost cause. "I see you, little Munchkin."

The wiggly boy crawled across Kendall to latch onto his arm. Grif turned and caught him, pressing a kiss to his dark hair. He smelled of Cheerios and sweetness, but cuddled into his arms as if he'd been waiting for him for hours rather than minutes.

Jameson rested his head against his shoulder and Grif used his other arm to pull Kendall in closer, stunned yet again that this gorgeous woman had consented to join her life with his. He'd been a little freaked at first, but he was so glad they'd done it the way they had.

Everything had started to fall into place.

The cabin they were building was almost complete. The three of them would be able to move in within the next few months.

Frank had run his own investigation, with Grif's help, to find out who on the security team had been spying into his personal affairs and recording conversations. It certainly hadn't been done with Frank's authorization. They'd traced the leak back to Goodrich, the head of security, who had been sleeping with Deedra ever since she'd come into the house. He was the first to be fired. Two other guards were also terminated for knowing about the crime but not saying anything about it. Frank found himself with a one man security team and desperately in need of more.

He'd been the first contract signed with the Vail branch of Lost And Found Investigative Service. News of Ortiz's heroism had gained them a lot of attention before they'd even opened. They were now flooded with contracts.

Kendall leaned into his shoulder. She looked as radiant as she had on their own wedding day, months ago. Considering everything they'd gone through, it seemed like he'd been with her for a lifetime. "I want to amend our pre-nup."

She looked at him, brows raised. "Really? What part?"

Grif pressed a kiss to her forehead. "I want to take the two-year trial out of the wording. I'm in it for the long haul. I love you, Kendall. I can't imagine being with anyone else."

Her face softened with love and she leaned around Jameson to press a kiss to his lips. "Well, that's a good thing. We were going to have to scrap it anyway with the other baby coming."

Grif leaned back to look down into her face to see if she were telling the truth. The devilish glint in her eyes confirmed that she was. Exhilaration raced through him. "Another baby?"

"Another baby."

Jameson patted him on the cheek and he thanked the stars that they'd landed where they had. And that he'd given in that lonely Christmas.

The End...

SEAL'S LOST DREAM

J.M. Madden

Dedication

Hear our humble prayer, O God, for our friends
the animals,
especially for animals who are suffering;
for animals that are overworked, underfed and
cruelly treated;
for all wistful creatures in captivity that beat their
wings against bars;
for any that are hunted or lost or deserted or
frightened or hungry;
for all that must be put death.
We entreat for them all Thy mercy and pity,
and for those who deal with them we ask a heart
of compassion
and gentle hands and kindly words.
Make us, ourselves, to be true friends to animals,
and so to share the blessings of the merciful.

Albert Schweitzer

Author Note

This story is not for readers under 18.

The Military War Dogs that have taken part in the war in Iraq and Afghanistan are the unsung heroes of the wars. Numbering at about 2500 working animals, it is believed that they have saved more than 10,000 lives.

There isn't a lot of publicity about these dogs, so I have had to take some liberties with the story, but I tried to stay as true to what I know as I could. I hope you enjoy it!

CHAPTER ONE

✦

"**Y**OUR BEARDED MYSTERY man just pulled in."

Dr. Willow James looked up at her assistant Nicky leaning in the doorway. "Uh oh. What'd he bring me this time?"

Nicky shook her dark head. "Not sure. Sue is helping him now."

Willow tied off the last stitch of the spaying she was doing on Donna Sharp's new little cat Skittles. "Put him in room one and I'll be there in just a minute. Whatever he brought, I'm sure it's critical."

Her vet tech nodded and disappeared.

Wiping the little tabby's belly, she picked her up and carried her to the holding cages in back. Laying Skittles in the basket, she tucked a piece of fleece over her to keep her warm as she came out of the anesthesia. In a few minutes she'd send Nicky back to check on the cat.

Willow walked toward room one with dread in her stomach. 'Flynn', as he called himself, had been coming to her vet practice for about the past year, hauling in animal after animal for her to treat and try to find homes for. Or dispose of respectfully. Dogs for the most part. Usually strays. A couple had been micro-chipped and eventually returned to their grateful owners. She'd asked him once where he found them all. Hard, shadowed gray eyes had flashed to her for a moment. "They find me," he told her quietly.

And she believed him.

The man was imposing. Six-three anyway, thick dark brown hair and beard, tight t-shirts that showed off more muscles than should be allowed on any man. He wore jeans that cupped his ass but hung low on his hips. A knife was tucked into the corner of the pocket. Pretty damn delicious. His personality, though, left a lot to be desired. For the most part, he snapped or grumbled at everyone. After seven years in practice on her own, he made her feel ridiculously inadequate at her own job. She wasn't sure why he kept coming in. There were a hundred other vets in the Denver area he could patronize. If she hadn't seen the way the animals themselves reacted to him, she'd have probably asked him to go to another vet.

But the animals loved him. Dogs with no more will to live gave him a final grateful lick before they faded away. Feral cats calmed under his broad hands as if they'd been waiting for him forever. She didn't know what he did in real life, but he should have been a veterinarian. Or a K9 officer. Maybe Search and Rescue. Something where he could use the skill he had.

With the stealthy way he walked into a room, she thought perhaps he had military experience. She'd learned early on that making him wait in the waiting room put other customers on edge because he glared at them. The staff tried to get him into a room as quickly as possible.

It was a shame he was so abrasive. The man was positively gorgeous. Dark haired and light eyed. Scrumptious.

Stupid vanity made her tighten her gut and lift her boobs as she walked into the room, ready for anything.

FLYNN DIDN'T ALLOW the relief he felt at the sight of the sexy vet show on his face, but the knot of tension in his gut began to ease. With barely a glance at the table, she crossed to the sink to wash her hands, tossing her long black braid over her shoulder.

"Tell me what you have, Flynn."

"It's a dog."

She frowned at him as she dried her hands. "Are you sure?"

He understood what she meant. The scrap of bones on the table barely classified as anything. It weighed less than thirty pounds, according to the scale out front. The frame of the animal was built for much more.

Dr. James leaned over the dog, ran her hand over its head and tilted its face up to look in the eyes. Unhooking the stethoscope from her slender neck, she held the end to the dog's chest, listening for a moment before moving it to the belly.

Flynn hated this part of the ordeal. The waiting. The scales teetering. When the animals were this bad, he knew chances usually ran at about eighty-twenty on the negative side whether or not they could be saved. The dog was skin and bones, and hadn't moved from the painful curl he had found her in an hour ago.

The dog's brown eyes had latched onto his, and he'd known he couldn't leave her behind that fence. A cable hung from her neck, but he couldn't find the clasp end. It had embedded into the flesh and grown over.

There seemed to be something else going on with her, though.

The doctor leaned over the table toward him, ruffling the buttery-golden hair on the dog's neck area. Even over the odor of the dog, her fresh laundry scent tickled along his skin, tugging at him to lean closer. Flynn braced his hands on the edge of the aluminum table and stayed where he was. He didn't come here to see the shapely doctor with the broad smile.

Right.

She reached for a strange, paddle shaped device hanging on a wall hook, waving it over the dog's shoulders. He knew the distinctive sound the machine made when it detected a microchip, but it didn't happen this time.

"No microchip. And this cable has rusted apart. Whoever owned this dog didn't care that it grew into her skin, but she worked to get free, it looks like."

Fury made the hairs of his arms bristle. "You think they knew it had grown in?"

Dr. James nodded, her soft, whiskey colored eyes meeting his. "This isn't something that happens over night. It takes weeks, if not months for it to get this bad." She fondled the fur for a moment, then peeled back the hair to show him.

Flynn clenched his jaw to keep from turning the air blue. The fuckers needed to rot.

"We'll trim her up and see how bad the neck wound is. Body score; she's between a one or a two. More toward a one. This pretty girl hasn't been fed for a while. No gut sounds at all."

The knot in his stomach began to ease at her words. After a year of bringing animals to this soft hearted woman, he knew when she started to personalize the animal she was going to do her best to save it.

The doctor flexed the dog's legs, then began to palpate her stomach.

"Oh, no."

"What?" he demanded.

The doctor blinked up at him, frowning. "She's pregnant."

Flynn looked down at the emaciated thing on the steel table, unable to believe she had anything to give a litter of puppies. "Are you sure?" he snapped.

The doctor looked up at him with that look she had. "Yes, I'm sure. Not very many, but there are at least a couple in there." She ruffled the dog's head. "Okay, Mama, we're going to fix you up."

This was normally the point where Flynn bowed out of the scene and left the doctor to work her magic, but the dog turned her head to look at him as if she knew what he was thinking. Unable to help himself, he reached out to rub along her jaw. Her fluffy tail thumped against the table.

"Where did you find this one?"

"Industrial district."

Dr. James frowned. "Hm. She looks like she could be a decent dog if they'd just taken care of her. But they left her to strangle. I'm glad she got away. Bastards."

Flynn seconded her exclamation. If a person didn't plan to take care of a dog, why would they have it in the first place? The animal looked at least part Shepherd, with her dark face and lighter body, but he couldn't be sure.

Nicky, the vet tech, stuck her blond head in. "You've got an emergency coming. Hit by car. They're about ten minutes out."

The doctor nodded her head, examining the cable around the dog's neck. "Okay. Thanks, Nicky. Why don't you carry Mama here back to the cages? We'll work on her after the emergency."

"Mama? She's pregnant?" She stepped more fully into the room. "No way. You poor thing."

Nicky reached to pick the dog up, but Flynn waved her

away.

"I'll move her."

The women stood back as he lifted the dog carefully into his heavy arms. Nicky pointed down the hallway. Flynn knew the way; he'd done this before. Kneeling in front of the biggest cage on the bottom, ignoring the twinge in his hip, he leaned in and placed the dog carefully on the padded mat. The doctor held a blanket over his shoulder and he used it to tuck around the dog. Her dark-chocolate eyes watched every move he made but she didn't seem fearful. He paused before he closed the door to run his hand over her head one more time. Then he forced himself to his feet and walked out of the practice.

WILLOW WATCHED FLYNN'S broad back disappear down the hallway. The man was such a chatterbox. She snorted to herself in derision. His nice ass kind of made up for his lack of conversation skills, though.

She took care of the dog hit by the car. It was a big old yellow lab, with more happiness than sense. He wiggled his whole body for her when she walked into the room and snuck in stealthy licks wherever he could. There was a long scrape on his rear leg and some weakness, but no breaks. She x-rayed the dog, but didn't see any reason to be concerned. Cleaning his would, she wrapped his leg in bandage, talking to the distraught owner the entire time. But her thoughts were on the mama dog and her future. She would have to be careful with the anesthesia; she didn't want the puppies to go too far under. Mama was already stressed.

Nicky had everything set up by the time the Lab was released and they worked quickly to shave the mama dog's neck while they waited for the drugs to knock her out. Once asleep, with her neck shaved, Willow truly got mad. Usually she could disengage herself enough to care for the animals, but some-times their circumstances worked their way through her hard shell. This dog had suffered for a long time. The cable had been around her neck long enough that the skin had complete-ly grown over it. The only break they got was the infection that had set in. When Willow pulled on the exposed end of the cable, it slid through the slimy pus and out. She irrigated it as much as she could, then stitched in a couple of drainage plugs so the infection could leave the area. Nicky smeared the entire band with antibacterial ointment just as the anesthetic began to wear off.

Willow stroked the dog. "Hi, Mama. You did good today. Good girl."

The dog's tail thumped weakly but she didn't raise her head. Willow didn't blame her; she'd been through a lot. And she still had a long way to go.

FLYNN WAITED FOR a solid week, seven days exactly, before he allowed himself to stop at the vet's office to check on the dog.

The plump, gray-haired receptionist smiled at him when he walked in the door.

"Where's the vet?"

Sue, he thought her name was, blinked behind her owlish glasses, looking beyond his shoulder. "Not another already?"

Flynn shook his head once. "No."

Pushing to her feet, she went through the door at the back of the office, behind her desk. She spoke to someone on the other side, then returned to her chair. "She'll be in in a minute."

Flynn paced the almost-empty waiting room, tempted to walk out through that door. Now that he'd committed to seeing the dog, he wanted to *see* the dog.

Assuming she was still alive. He didn't want to think about what he would do if she weren't. Her eyes had haunted him all week.

Dr. James stepped in from the back door then and grinned when she saw him, her white teeth flashing. She looked a little excited to see him.

"Come on back, Flynn."

He walked around the end of the counter, behind the receptionist and through the door at the back. Outside there was a concrete patio with a large kennel at one end. It was roofed and had been sectioned into several smaller kennels. In a fenced-in area off to the right, the dog he had brought in wandered the edge of the fence. Her blondish-brown colored coat was shaved down to the skin on her neck, but even from a distance he could tell she had already gained weight. Hell, she was on her feet. That was an incredible change from last week.

The dog spotted him when he walked out and stopped in an alert pose, ears pricked, then started toward him. Her face was darker than the rest of her body, but her eyes were bright. The way she walked highlighted the roundness of her belly. As she drew near, she whined, then sat patiently in the grass.

Flynn wanted to lean down and ruffle her fur, but he forced himself to stay away from her, his feet rooted to the patio.

"You can pet her."

He glanced at the vet. Her arms were crossed over her plump breasts, and she was smiling at him a little oddly. The bright summer sun shone down on her glossy hair and pinkened her round cheeks. His behavior probably seemed strange, but it was as much as he could do right now.

"No, I just wanted to check on her."

The doctor's too-knowing eyes watched him for a moment,

then she smiled slightly. "She'll recover fine. The cable came out of her neck easier than I expected and amazingly she hasn't gotten any more infection in it. I'll take the drains out next week and she should be good to go. Once she bulks up a little bit, she'll be a good-looking dog. She looks like she has Belgian Malinois in her, so I may be able to adopt her out to a local PD or something. I think whoever had her before realized she would be a handful. Even pregnant, she loves playing ball. We've named her Maya for now, till someone takes her."

Flynn clenched his jaw as an automatic argument filled his throat, but he did not give it voice. His chest tightened to the point that he couldn't breathe, and whispers of smoke burned his eyes.

No. It's not real. It's a dream. It's not real.

For the first time, the flashback let him go without dazing him. Maybe it was the sun shining down, or the fact that he knew he had an audience. Either way, awareness returned quickly.

Two pairs of eyes, whiskey gold and chocolate-dark, stared at him hard. Dr. James had moved just a couple of feet in front of him, and her hand was held out above his arm as if she'd been about to touch him. Turning sharply away from her concerned face, he walked to the back door of the office.

"She looks good. Thanks, Doc."

He stopped at Sue's desk long enough to drop a few hundred dollar bills on the surface, then walked out the front door.

WILLOW HAD TO keep her feet planted so that she wouldn't chase the enigmatic man down.

What the hell had that been?

One minute he'd been looking at the dog, and the next his face had tightened as if he expected pain. She'd stepped forward but had hesitated to touch him. Something about the way he'd clenched, as if he were prepared to fight, set her senses on edge. But his eyes had cleared seconds later.

If she didn't know better, she'd think it was some kind of attack.

He'd made a reference that had sounded military before, but that had been months ago. They talked when he came in, but it tended to be short and to the point with him.

She looked at the dog on the inside of the fence. Maya stared at the door as if waiting for him to come back, a slight whine coming from her throat.

"I know, Maya. He's intriguing, isn't he?"

The dog looked at her as if she understood Willow's words, and plopped her bottom into the grass.

WILLOW HAD HAD the dog for two weeks when she went into labor late one night. Every evening she did a final walk-through to make sure all of the animals were good before she headed home. She was especially glad she had that night, because the first oversized puppy would not have survived if she hadn't been there to help.

Maya quivered and strained but couldn't deliver. Running out of options, Willow had to sedate her and do an emergency C-section on the poor thing. She'd called Nicky back at the first sign of distress and the assistant arrived just in time to clean the three good-sized puppies. While Nicky dealt with them, Willow spayed the dog and sutured her closed. As soon as the anesthetic wore off the determined mama dog cleaned her puppies and made them her own. Willow grinned at the dog's single-minded determination, so glad that her maltreatment didn't seem to have affected the whelps at all.

Walking home that night through the exercise yard, Willow

debated calling Flynn. He'd paged her answering service once to get in touch with her, so she had his number. Actually, it wasn't the first time she'd thought about calling him. But her reasons weren't necessarily professional. They were more along the lines of hurry-up-and-ask-him-out-so-you-can-get-shot-down-and-get-on-with-your-life reasons.

Hell, he probably had a skinny little wife at home. Not all men wore jewelry if they were married. And as good looking as he was, if he didn't have a girlfriend or wife, he was either a player or gay. Neither of which she needed.

In the end, she erred on the side of safety and decided not to call him. If he wanted to know about the dogs, he could call or stop in like everyone else did.

Besides. If he couldn't commit to a dog, she doubted he would be good dating material.

CHAPTER TWO

✦

I T WAS ANOTHER three weeks before Willow saw Flynn again. She happened to be standing at the reception desk talking to the final patient of the evening when his big black truck pulled into the parking lot. He jogged around the back of the truck, and she knew whatever he'd brought her was in bad shape. She hurried outside to meet him.

More grim faced than normal, mouth clenched, he glanced at her as she neared but didn't wait for her help. Hoisting a blanket-wrapped form into his arms, he turned from the truck.

"Get the doors," he snapped.

Willow slammed his truck door shut then dodged around him to get the office door. "Room one."

She followed his broad back into the room, not bothering to wash her hands. She had a feeling it wouldn't matter with this patient.

Flynn placed the bundle on the stainless table, then began to unwrap it from the blanket. "I found her laying on the edge of a country road. I think she'd been there for a while."

Willow forced back a cry as she saw the dog for the first time. Obviously, she'd been hit by a car. The long line of her broken jawbone was exposed and Willow could see through to her raw tongue. Ticks were on every spare inch of her body, some so engorged with blood they'd fallen off onto the blanket. The dog's chest lifted in a slow breath and Willow couldn't believe the poor thing was still alive. Her dull eyes blinked slowly, glazed with pain.

"I think her back is broken."

Willow reached for the dog's spine. Not only was it broken, it was shattered. There were no complete vertebra from her diaphragm on. She reached for the dog's rear foot and pinched her toes. They were cold to the touch and didn't respond to the pressure.

Sadness made her throat tight as she looked up at Flynn. His gray eyes were hard, but she could see the desolation he tried to hide. He knew as well as she did there was no hope for the dog. It was why he'd brought her here.

Throat tight, Willow readied the shots to put the unfortunate dog to sleep. There was no flinch as the needle slipped into her skin, only a shallow sigh as she went quietly to sleep. The pain in the line of her body eased.

As Willow administered the second shot, she reaffirmed to herself why she'd become a vet. To help those that she could, and to ease the suffering of those she couldn't.

Fitting the stethoscope to her ears, she pressed the paddle to the dog's chest and listened to her heartbeats slow, then stop altogether. She listened for a few more seconds, then drew away, re-covering the dog with the blanket.

Flynn stared at the bundle, shaking his head slightly. "Why am I always the one to find them?"

Willow was surprised at the personal question and responded to the pain she heard in his heart. She circled the table and dared to reach for the man's broad hand. He stiffened but didn't pull away. When he looked up at her, she smiled at him. "Because they know that you will care for them like no one else ever has, in the most vulnerable time of their lives. I'm happy she found you, because nobody else brought her in. You did. And I was able to end her suffering. She'd been laying beside that road for a couple days at least, in incredible pain. Now there's no more pain. As traumatic as this is, I look at it as a wonderful thing. We've eased her suffering."

Willow let go of his hand, surprised he'd let her hold onto it as long as he had. She moved to the sink and scrubbed.

"Wash up, I need to show you something."

Flynn blinked at her but moved to do as she instructed. Once he was done, Willow led him through the office, out the back door and down the paver path behind the dog run. She glanced at him once to make sure he followed.

When she'd been looking for space to open her office, she'd come across this piece. The office on the corner used to be to a human doctor's office, and the adjoining house on the opposite street had been where he'd lived. It had suited her needs perfectly, and she'd paid a little more than she'd wanted to in order to have it.

Her stomach quivered a little as she opened the door to her screened in porch, on the other side of the exercise yard from the office. Bringing strange men into her home was not normal, but he needed to understand the good that he did.

Maya looked up when Willow entered and wagged her tail. But when Flynn stepped in behind her, the Belgian Malinois stood up from her nest, dislodging three wiggling bundles. The dog lunged at Flynn, crying, wagging her tail as fast as it would go and stood on her back legs to get closer to his face.

"Down," he growled, but it seemed instinctual, and he followed the command with a ruffling of her shoulders when she obeyed. He knelt to the floor and was almost knocked over as she paced happy circles around him.

Willow moved to the floundering puppies, picking up the fattest. He curled into her chest, snuffling, and she walked him across to Flynn.

He took the pup from her hands with no argument, holding him up in front of his face to look at the little brown dog. "How many did she have?"

"Three. Two boys and a girl. All fat and healthy, thanks to you finding Maya here when you did."

Flynn frowned, narrowing his eyes and started to shake his head.

"Don't you dare deny it," she broke in. "She had problems delivering. I had to do a C-section. If you hadn't found her when you did and brought her to me, they all four would have died. And it would not have been quick."

Maya licked at the pup in his hands and Willow could see the reluctant acceptance settle onto his face. Cradling the pup to his chest, he reached out to pet her.

She basked in his attention, pushing as close to him as she could.

The tension that Willow normally saw in Flynn's face eased and she wondered if he had a pet at home. She hoped not, because it looked like Maya planned to adopt him. The dog leaned against him as he played with her three babies, looking up at him as if he hung the moon.

All too soon though, the shutter came down over his face. Though he didn't say anything outright, she could feel him withdrawing and it made her heart ache for him.

He pushed to his feet. "They look good. You're doing a good job with them."

Willow drew her eyes away from his molded chest to focus on his face. "I didn't bring you over here to tell me what a good job I'm doing. I brought you over to show you what you are doing. By helping these dogs."

His mouth worked beneath his beard, as if he heard her words but didn't want to say anything. With a final stroke, he handed over the puppy in his hands and gave Maya a final rub. Then he was gone.

Willow sat back on the floor, wondering if she'd ever see him again.

FLYNN WORKED AS much as Duncan would let him. When he'd rolled out of the SEALs, it hadn't taken him long to figure out that sitting in his damn lonely apartment was a terrible way to live. Hell, even going to therapy was better than stewing in his own juices. The job at Lost and Found Investigative Service, working for and with other disabled vets, had come at a critical time for him. He'd found the camaraderie there he needed to work on his issues. No, his weren't as obviously physical as the other guys that worked there, but they were just as crippling.

The therapists continued to tell him that his PTSD would ease. Someday. Three years after he'd left the Navy, he was still waiting for someday.

Mace was everywhere. When Flynn worked out, he saw him out of the corner of his eye, just sitting quietly and watching. When he slept in bed, he could feel the weight of the dog's body curled against his feet, same as always. He found himself tossing treats over his shoulder that were never eaten.

The psych doctors told him it was all illusion, brought on by the guilt of the dog's passing. They dosed him with stronger and stronger pills, but the dreams persisted. Until he finally called a halt to all the drugs. Being slightly delusional was better than being delusional and drugged out of his mind. He needed to stay alert.

The dreams had started to change a little in the last few months, though. Yes, he still saw the dog, but now the voluptuous vet was there as well. Sometimes she'd be working on Mace and she'd look up at him with that bright, beautiful smile she had, her golden eyes shining with pleasure. Other times she'd look up at him with tears rolling down her soft cheeks and he knew he'd lost him all over again. Those were the nights he woke with tears on his own cheeks.

Flynn wanted to go see the vet again, because he felt a little less crazy when he was with her. She was a woman who obviously loved and appreciated animals. He didn't feel like he needed to hide that part of his personality with her. While he moved through life looking for stability, she seemed to walk through life creating stability. Frantic owners arrived at her doorstep every day, but she had the disposition to ease them into a better headspace. That was very appealing to him.

Maya tugged on his heart too. Flynn was kind of afraid to talk to the vet again, because he didn't want her to tell him she'd found the dog a home. It was heading into fall now. The puppies were seven weeks old, surely old enough that she'd started to look for homes for them as well. If his life were different, he'd think about taking her in, but he didn't feel like he'd be a good owner to her.

Every time he passed the vet's office on his way to work, he debated pulling in. But he forced himself to keep the steering wheel straight and steady, avoiding temptation.

Duncan swore up and down he needed another dog. Had even promised to adopt him a retired Military War Dog if he could find a way to use the dog. Flynn had turned him down, though. Several times. The disappointment in his boss's face— the man who believed in him not to lose his shit on a daily basis—made Flynn feel like an even bigger loser.

Stepping out of the shower, he grabbed the towel from the bar and started to dry off. His hands slowed at his lower abdomen, fingers running over the puckered scar of the gunshot wound that had changed his life. He remembered the mind-numbing pain as if it were yesterday.

Forcing himself into motion, he tried to shake off the melancholy.

When he drove by Dr. James' office just a little while later, the woman herself stood in the parking lot talking to an older gentleman. She wore dark blue scrubs and a lighter colored top. Her long black hair had been pulled up into a high ponytail and for a fraction of a second her eyes flashed up to his truck before he passed. Her hand raised in a wave before he lost sight of her, and a curl of warmth spread in his belly.

Willow looked up at the sound of the familiar truck, fear clutching her stomach at the thought of Flynn bringing another patient. But when she spotted the truck, it was driving past her office. Before she could stop herself, she waved.

There was no reaction from the man behind the wheel, and that was probably best. She didn't want to break his heart if he stopped in to see Maya.

The man in front of her shifted, bringing her attention back to him. "Sorry, thought I had another patient coming in."

Bill smiled at her, a little too friendly, and patted his dog on the head. The French Bulldog cringed under the attention and Willow cringed with her. "You know, Violet would probably appreciate being stroked on the head rather than pounded."

Bill's expression hardened at the subtle correction. "She appreciates any attention she gets, believe me."

Willow didn't like the way the man looked at her, but it wasn't offensive enough to actually say anything about. "Hm," she said doubtfully. "Well, she's fine for another six months.

Just watch how many treats you give her. She's starting to gain a little weight."

She knew by the glint in his eye that she wasn't going to like what was going to come out of his mouth.

"I like my girls a little fuller figured."

It was all she could do to keep in a disgusted moan. It was too early in the morning for his gross come-ons.

She put on her glossy doctor smile and turned away. Bill watched her ass the entire walk into the office, she could tell. Her ick factor was at an all-time high as she slammed the door behind her.

Sue laughed at her disgusted face when she walked in. "I told you he was in rare form today. He called yesterday and just had to get his precious Violet in. Sorry, Willow."

She moved to lean against the counter. LoveBug, one of the cats who lived in the office, rubbed against her arm. Willow scratched her on the head. "You're not a very good guard-cat. Why didn't you swat him when he shoved you off the counter?"

The little cat purred her answer, arching under Willow's hand.

"It's okay, Sue. It'll be a crazy day when I can say no to a pair of eyes like that. Violet, I mean. She's such a cutie."

Her receptionist nodded. "She's too good for her owner, I know that."

Wasn't that the truth...

Willow waded through the rest of her clients for the day, but she found herself looking hopefully out the window way too often. Had Flynn driven by for a reason? Had he thought about stopping when he'd seen her in the lot?

She'd been thinking about the man a lot recently. Fantasizing. When Maya had left, she'd debated calling him to let him know, but she didn't want to be responsible for hurting him. The man had been through a lot. She could see the ghosts in his eyes without him saying a word.

As much as he appealed to her physically, she didn't know if she wanted to deal with his emotional hang-ups. She had enough of her own.

Maybe she could just screw him and get him out of her brain.

She snorted. Right. Like that would ever happen.

FLYNN TRUDGED UP the dark path to his apartment building that night in a daze. He'd worked his regular shift, then gone for a five-mile run before sliding into his truck for the drive home. His hips ached like a son of a bitch and he knew he would be hurting even more tonight.

When he saw the shape of the dog out of the corner of his eye, he thought it was Mace. His old buddy was always there to commiserate with his pain, jogging along at his side. But when the light caught on the brighter colored fur, he had to pause to look closer.

For a moment, he thought he'd been hallucinating even that much, until Maya suddenly lunged at him from the depths of the bushes beside the building.

Flynn sank down to his knees to greet the dog and looked around for Dr. James. She was nowhere to be seen. He'd never given her anything with his name on it, let alone his address, so how the hell would she know where his apartment was?

"How did you get here dog?"

Granted, he only lived a few blocks away from the vet's practice. She could have run here. But how did she know where here was?

Maya wagged her way around him, sneaking in stealthy

licks when she could.

"Sit," he growled.

Maya dropped to her haunches but her butt continued to wag and she whined at him for attention.

Flynn shook his head, laughing. How on earth had she found him?

Pulling his phone from his pocket, he paged through the contacts until he found the number for Dr. James' answering service. He left a message that the doctor needed to call him, then waited. Within a half minute, his phone rang.

"This is Dr. James."

Her throaty voice wrapped around his tired soul and he took just a moment to enjoy it.

"Hello?"

"Flynn," he snapped. "Do you know where Maya is right now?"

There was a sigh on the other end of the line. "No, I don't. She ran off two days ago and I haven't seen her since. Why?"

"How the hell could you lose her?"

"I didn't lose her. She escaped. Jumped over the fence like it wasn't even there. Took off like a bat out of hell, too. Wait. How did you know to call me? Did you find her?"

Flynn paused and looked down at the dog. "No. I think she found me."

"No way. She tracked you down? Damn, she's smart. Give me your address."

Flynn reeled it off without hesitation, then cursed his lack of discretion, but the doctor was already gone.

"Well, I guess you can come in for a minute, dog. Come on."

He turned back up the sidewalk, waving the dog to follow him, but she bounded ahead and disappeared into the open stairwell of his building. When Flynn arrived at his door on the second floor, she waited for him.

"Okay, dog, you're freaking me out."

Unlocking the door, he swung it wide for her to enter. She did a circuit, sniffing here and there, before returning to sit in front of him, whining. Shaking his head at the manipulative female, Flynn moved to get her a bowl of water. He kept tins of dog food in his pantry for strays, so he grabbed one and dumped it into a second bowl.

Maya had eaten two tins of soft food and curled up in front of the couch on the carpet by the time there was a knock at the door. Flynn crossed the room to open it. Dr. James stood on the other side, round hip cocked and an inquisitive smile on her face.

Dressed in tight blue jeans and a black t-shirt that cupped her boobs to perfection, she was a vision. For the first time her long black hair was loose, hanging over one shoulder. She had a scrubbed look, pink-cheeked and fresh, like she'd just gotten out of the shower. His gaze drifted back to her breasts.

Maya lunged across the room to greet her, but gave her the 'I've been bad' look that dogs had. Laughing, Dr. James leaned down to pet her.

"You bad dog. You made me worry!"

Flynn didn't know what to do. Guests never came to his apartment and he realized as he looked around that he wasn't really set up for entertaining. He had one couch and a well-worn recliner. And more electronic equipment than any one man needed. Well, she wouldn't be staying long.

"Did you bring a leash?"

The doctor looked at him with an odd expression on her face. "No, I didn't actually. I just came over to check on her, make sure she hadn't hurt herself when she'd been on the streets. I'm not taking her back. She's made her decision on where she wants to be."

A shiver of white-hot fear rolled down his arms. "She can't stay here."

"Why not?"

He shook his head, unable to give voice to the five million reasons why it would be so wrong to put this dog with him. "What about her puppies? She can't leave them and I certainly can't take them."

The doctor grinned, her white teeth flashing. "She weaned them herself last week. They'd been eating soft food since they were a month old anyway. It was easy to find adoptive homes for them."

Panic poured through him, sending a wave of heat over his body. The puppies had been the biggest reason why he couldn't take the dog. Fuck.

"I'm not set up to have a dog."

She lifted a sleek brow in question.

"I'm not, damn it. I have a job. What's she going to do when I'm at work?"

"You can bring her to my office for a while. Until you get into a routine."

He blinked at the easy answer, then looked at the dog lying on the carpet. Her head lifted when he made eye contact. She was extremely sensitive to the people and the environment around her. Flynn got the distinct impression she *knew* they were talking about her.

He shook his head, scrubbing at his beard. "Dr. James…"

"Willow," she interrupted. "I think we can get rid of the doctor part. You've been bringing animals to me for a year now."

"Willow." Flynn didn't like how easy it was on his tongue.

He cleared his throat. "I can't have a dog. Seriously."

She smiled at him softly. "Then you better tell her."

Flynn turned away from the two of them, scraping his hand through his hair. Emotion boiled through his gut and, if he was honest with himself, excitement as well.

The dog had curled up on the floor but continued to watch him.

"I don't think you're going to pry her away from you."

He glanced at the woman standing in his doorway. He probably should have invited her in, but he didn't know if he wanted her in his space. She already invaded his dreams too much.

Willow apparently took his silence as agreement because she turned to leave. "If you bring her by the office in the morning we'll watch her for you. I've missed her the past couple of days anyway. Maybe we can share custody."

Flynn found himself nodding as she pulled the door closed behind herself and left. He caught a glimpse of her amazing ass before she was gone.

Man, what incredible game you have, Flynn. Only woman that had been in his apartment in years and he made her stand in the doorway.

Limping to the recliner, he eased down into it. Maya continued to watch him. She seemed to understand that her presence there was tenuous at best.

"What the heck am I going to do with you?"

WILLOW LAUGHED SOFTLY as she jogged down the steps. The look on Flynn's face had been priceless. It was obvious he'd just gotten back from the gym, or something, because he was dressed in jogging shorts and a fitted blue t-shirt. The slight tang of his sweat drifted in the air, taunting her to inhale more deeply, and his dark hair was damp at his temples. What was it about a sweaty man that was so damn sexy?

Maya, on the other hand, had looked extremely satisfied with herself.

It was amazing that the dog had found Flynn. Yes, he only lived a few blocks away apparently, but still. The dog needed to be trained for search and rescue work. Talent like that should not be wasted.

When Flynn pulled into the lot the next morning a few minutes after eight, Willow had just let herself into the building. She watched as Maya jumped out of the truck and kept pace with Flynn as he walked toward the door.

Flynn seemed to be limping, though.

"Are you okay?"

He looked up as soon as they came through the door and seemed surprised to see her there. "I'm fine," he snapped. "Are you sure you can watch her today?"

Willow nodded, leaning over to pet the happy dog. "I can. We'll keep her in the office or I'll put her in one of the kennels. She won't slip away again. How did she do last night?"

Flynn scowled at her. "Fine. Why do you let her sleep in bed with you?"

Willow jerked back in surprise. "Her? I don't even let my own dog sleep in bed with me. Maya stayed on the porch the entire time I had her." She narrowed her eyes at him. "Why? Did she get into bed with you?"

Just uttering the words sent a tingle through her body. Damn. Could she be jealous of a dog?

Flynn's scowl became even more fierce before he turned away. "I should be here by five. Don't lose her."

Laughing at the non-answer, she watched Flynn walk out the door, cross the lot and climb into his truck. Maya whined.

"Don't worry, sweet girl. He'll be back."

And he was, right on time. They settled into an odd schedule over the next couple of days. After the first day of pacing, Maya soon realized that he would return for her, so she settled in as one of the 'locals' as Sue like to call them; the animals that nobody wanted that ended up staying long-term at the office. LoveBug the office cat, Tom the mouser that liked to stay out back around the kennels, and now Maya. Occasionally Willow brought her own dog Guinness over to socialize when her appointments ran long.

On Thursday night she locked up the office and walked the dogs out to the exercise lot. It was after seven and Flynn hadn't arrived to pick Maya up yet, so Willow thought she'd run her through some exercises to see how she did. Leaving Guinness at the fence with a firm order to stay, she led Maya to the center of the lot. Willow knew the dog was strongly food motivated, so she wore a little belted pocket around her waist, full of soft treats.

Maya seemed to understand she needed to pay attention, because she sat patiently and did everything Willow requested of her. The basic sit, down, stay were no-brainers. The dog did them quickly, and Willow realized she was responding to hand movements as much as to her voice. Somebody had put in some training time with her.

Willow pulled a tennis ball from her pocket and threw it across the yard. This was a game that Maya loved. Literally, she would chase the ball for hours on end.

Once again, Willow wondered if Flynn would consider using her for Search and Rescue work. Though she was a little old, she had the natural prey drive that was needed for the tough work.

Willow paused to think, wondering how she could get her

into the program. That was when she realized she was being watched. Flynn stood at the back corner of the office braced against the wall, long legs crossed, sunglasses over his eyes. The evening sun glimmered on his hair, and his arms were crossed over his bulky chest. The immediate twist of arousal in her belly made her turn away. The man was too good looking for his own good.

Maya spotted him then and took off, leaping the four-foot fence to run to him.

Willow shook her head and waved her hand. "Did you see that? That's how she took off to find you!"

Flynn shook his head at the dog, grinning, and rubbed her.

"Did you see what else she was doing?"

He nodded without looking up. "I did."

"She has incredible drive. You ought to think about training her. She needs a job desperately."

His grin faded. Even beneath the beard, she could see his jaw tighten. "Then somebody else will have to give it to her. I'm not."

Willow frowned, planting her hands on her hips. "Well, maybe I'll train her then."

His chest jerked, as if she'd wounded him with her words. "I think that would be best."

Well, hell. She'd only said that to make him realize *he* should train her.

"She's not my dog. You should do it."

Flynn shook his head, finally meeting her eyes. "I can't."

There was something in his voice that made her pause, mouth open, before she laid into him. It wouldn't do any good to fight with him about it, not if he wasn't open to the job. She had a feeling Flynn whatever-his-name-was had more knowledge about training than he was letting on.

But the pain she heard in his growl made her back off. She walked closer to the fence, calling her Lab mix to her side. "This is my dog, Guinness. I've had him for about six years now, and he's a state certified Search and Rescue dog."

Flynn pushed away from the wall to step toward the fence, but his right leg suddenly collapsed beneath him. He caught himself, but the grimace on his face told her he had to be in pain.

Willow clenched her mouth shut, unwilling to be snapped at if she asked if he was okay. Her body thrummed with the need to leap to his aid. Wrapping her palms over the chain link fence pipe, she waited for him to look at her. "Can I get you some ibuprofen? Whiskey?"

One side of his mouth tipped up. "I might take some ibuprofen if you have them laying around."

Willow turned for her house, hoping that he would follow. Guinness jogged at her side as she slipped through the gate and turned right on the path, toward her house. She couldn't hear his footsteps behind her, so she wasn't sure if he would actually come in or not.

She retrieved four pills from the bottle she kept in the kitchen cupboard, along with two bottles of water from the fridge. Flynn had let himself into the porch and was trying to lower himself into the patio chair. He kind of plopped down at the end, as if his legs gave out, and he bared his teeth in pain. Willow held the items out to him, hoping he would take them and be fine. She was surprised he let her see him like this at all. He was normally all bad ass. Turning, she sat in the chair opposite from his.

Curiosity badgered at her. "Did you get hurt today?"

Maya's head rested on his thigh and he stroked her. "A bit. It was my own doing though. I just came back from a jog."

Willow frowned. "If it hurts that much, why do you do it?"

"To make sure I still can."

She shook her head at his reasoning. "Just because you can do it doesn't mean you should."

One side of his mouth lifted in a smile. "Agreed. But I have to."

The hidden smile slipped away as his eyes flicked to the left, then back. Okay. That was a bit strange.

"How did you get into the search and rescue work?"

Willow blinked at the question he threw at her. Was he actually trying to engage in conversation? Or throw her off the track?

"Well," she sighed, "I was hiking the Devil's Head Fire Lookout several years ago and got involved in a search. That was before Guinness; before I even thought about doing SAR work. But there was a team there that just impressed the hell out of me. Waded into that dark forest and brought that hiker out within a couple hours. Most impressive thing I've ever seen. I was bitten. I adopted Guinness from a local shelter and we've been going ever since. Twenty-two searches later and we're a solid team. We get called every couple of months. Found a few people. One little girl who stops into the office every once in a while to bring me a homemade card. It's very satisfying."

Flynn seemed surprised. He'd crossed his arms over his pecs and looked at Guinness lying on the floor. "He was a rescue, huh?"

Nodding, Willow reached over to scratch the dog's broad head. "Once he came home, he settled in as if he'd always been here. And the work was easy for him. He needed a job." She glanced pointedly at Maya. "Like she does."

For a minute, Flynn looked incredibly sad when he nodded, and Willow noticed that he seemed depressed. She had a feeling he was gearing up to let her down. Maya seemed to sense it as well, because she lifted a paw to his thigh.

"Before you say anything, just think about it for a while. She's not suffering right now. If you don't mind me working with her a bit, we'll see how she does. And maybe the next time I get a call-out you both can go with me. We always need more eyes at a search. She may not want to work when she gets into an environment like that."

Willow knew that would not be the case, though. Maya had such intelligence wiggling through her body.

Flynn nodded, but didn't seem convinced.

"So," she crossed her legs. "Can I ask why you were jogging yourself into an early grave?"

He blinked at her, then down at the dog. "Trying to outrun ghosts."

Her heart ached at the pain she heard in his soft voice, and she blinked at the echo of her own observation. "And did you? Outrun them, I mean."

"Some," he sighed. "Others are still here."

Flynn sounded so matter-of-fact that she had to believe him.

"I'm sorry, Flynn. Is there anything I can do?"

He looked up at her as if he was surprised by the question, but he shrugged away her concern. "Nah. No biggie."

Bracing his hands on the arms of the chair, he tensed to stand up, but his legs didn't seem to want to cooperate. Willow started to get out of her own chair to help him, but he waved her away and forced himself that much harder. He made it to his feet, but wavered. Maya stepped in to lean against him, as if she understood that it would kill him to crash in front of her. Willow watched the pair, ready to leap out of her own chair to help if it seemed necessary. But they steadied. And she realized she was a little disappointed. Flynn was about to leave. Again. And she didn't want him to.

"Thanks for the pills," he told her. "And for taking care of Maya. I do appreciate it."

Willow nodded once. "She's no problem. Really." She took a breath, gearing up to be hurt. "Hey. Would you like to stay for dinner?"

Flynn looked shocked that she'd asked. His mouth fell open a little and his dark brows furrowed over his eyes. "Uh, sure. I guess we can."

Willow fought not to giggle hysterically. First man she'd ever asked to dinner and she got an 'I guess'. Awesome.

"I didn't plan anything special. Maybe I can whip up some fajitas or something."

His gray eyes lightened. "I can put away some Mexican."

She grinned at the enthusiasm in his voice. "Well, okay then."

Willow led him into the house and parked him in front of the TV. When she glanced at the couch a few minutes later, Flynn had passed out. His mouth hung open as he breathed deeply. Maya had parked herself on the couch beside him, head across his lap. Even in his sleep, Flynn rested one hand on top of her head. Willow smiled at the peaceful look on his face. It was the first she'd seen. The frown that had furrowed his brows so deeply had disappeared.

Willow cooked the chicken fajitas but didn't wake Flynn when they were done. As exhausted as he appeared, she didn't have the heart to interrupt the sleep he was getting. So she ate her dinner with Guinness as she did every night.

CHAPTER THREE

✦

F LYNN WOKE, IMMEDIATELY aware he wasn't in his bed. The room was dim, but he knew without being able to see much that he wasn't alone. Soft light filtered in from an adjoining room, and as his bleary eyes cleared he remembered where he was. Willow's place. Even as he thought it, he realized the woman herself was curled up on the end of the couch opposite him.

His heartbeat steadied as the details in his environment settled into place. The last thing he remembered was the doc showing him how to elevate his legs on the recliner end of the super-comfortable couch before she disappeared into the kitchen. Wonderful smells had drifted through the house, but the exhaustion he fought against every day had dragged him under.

Maya hadn't moved, though. Her head still rested on his hips, and was the perfect, natural resting spot for his hand. Her eyes rolled up to him when he moved, but she didn't do any more than that. He laughed at her softly.

Willow roused at the sound, stretching her arms to the air. Flynn found himself staring at her breasts, then the pale glimpse of skin at her belly as her shirt rode up. Arousal coursed through him at the sight of her softly rounded shape and he was glad Maya hadn't moved yet. His dick had suddenly taken notice.

Clenching his jaw, he looked at the luminous numbers on his watch. Two-thirty. Fuck. He couldn't believe he'd…wait, slept for six hours. Straight through.

He looked at his watch again, unable to believe he'd gone six straight hours without moving. Normally he catnapped. Two hours at a time. Never more than three. It seemed like he'd just fallen asleep.

Willow sat up beside him on the couch, just a few feet and the warm body of a dog separating them. She smiled at him, her long black hair rumpled around her face.

"Dude, you crashed hard. As soon as Maya laid down beside you, you were out like a light."

Flynn shook his head and leaned forward, forcing down the leg part of the recliner. His hips ached, but he could tell he'd be able to walk out of here with no problem. Maya slid away from him to pad to the door with Guinness, waiting to go outside. Willow stood to let them out, then returned to sit on the edge of the couch. Soft golden eyes surveyed him, waiting.

"I can't believe I slept like that. I'm sorry."

She shrugged, grinning at him. "Believe it or not, I've had worse dates."

Well, fuck. She'd considered this a date. Now he felt even worse.

Then his stomach growled.

Willow laughed out loud, pushing to her feet. "Want some fajitas? Go let the dogs back in while I warm it up."

Flynn found himself eating Mexican food at two-forty-five in the morning, feeling more relaxed than he had in a long time. Willow teased that he snored, but he scowled. "It was Maya."

The dog cocked her head when she heard her name and came to his hand. He fed her the end of a tortilla and she tried to climb into his lap for more.

"You're starting a bad habit," Willow warned. "She's very food motivated."

Maya certainly didn't mind, and neither did Guinness when he slipped him a piece of chicken beneath the table.

"So who is Mace?"

Flynn froze, the food turning to wool in his mouth. He choked the bite down his throat and looked at his plate as he tried to formulate an answer.

"You mumbled his name when you were sleeping. It sounded like you were very close," she murmured.

"We were," he breathed.

Did he dare tell her about him? The counselors were always urging him to open up, but did he know her well enough to do that?

"He was my Military War Dog in Afghanistan."

He heard her softly indrawn breath.

"Wow. I wondered if you'd been in the military. Army?"

Flynn looked up at her. "Navy SEALs."

Watching the shock on her face was a little gratifying. And disheartening.

"The beard makes sense now."

Frowning, he ran his hand over the thick bristles, realizing they were getting a little long. He normally kept it trimmed up and presentable. Recently, though, he'd been run a little ragged.

"So, you said 'was'."

His stomach twisted, shocking him, and he smelled smoke. Clenching his hand on his thigh, he tried to force the vision away. He'd thought he'd gotten over Mace's loss. "Yeah, he died over there."

Visibility began to fade away and he felt the stifling heat of the dessert. Maya whined and planted her two front paws on his legs. Flynn was a little startled, but he reached up to pat her on the side. "It's okay, girl."

He glanced at Willow. She had tears swimming in her golden eyes.

"I'm so very sorry," she whispered, reaching across the table to hold his hand.

Flynn's throat tightened with grief and he knew if he didn't get out of here there was a very real possibility he would break down. Shifting away from the table, he pushed up from the chair. Maya landed beside him, looking up at him. Though it hurt to do so, he pulled away from Willow's comforting hand.

"Thank you for dinner," he told her. "Or whatever this was. I guess it's a little late for dinner, or even a midnight snack. But it was really good."

He snapped his mouth shut and turned for the door, but she caught his arm. Before he could pull away, she'd wrapped her arms around his waist and squeezed. The feeling of receiving lush comfort like this was so alien it shocked him to stillness. His family tried to commiserate, but they treated him as if he were being a child, moping after a 'damn dog'.

Mace had been everything to him. The MWD had saved his life, and that of his team more times than he could count, identifying insurgents before the men had even had a hint. He'd spotted landmines, snipers, suicide bombers. When Flynn blundered into situations with more balls than caution, Mace had taken up the slack, scanning the environment for anything that might damage his handler. They'd slept together, shared many MRE's together, and now shared blood.

As Willow held him, with her head resting on his chest, some internal guard built into his psyche snapped. He told her about the best friend he'd ever had. The best friend he'd lost. He wrapped his arms around her head and leaned his cheek against her soft hair, allowing himself to remember the details he'd tried so hard to push away.

Willow held him tight, until his back started to ache from standing in one spot for so long. When he shifted to ease the discomfort, she pulled back enough to look up at his face. The condemnation and recriminations he expected to see in her eyes weren't there, only vast amounts of understanding.

Flynn felt physically and emotionally drained. His body seemed to weigh twice what it normally did. Everything was fuzzy, like he was on the anti-psycho drugs again. When he glanced at the wall clock, the hands wavered and he realized it was just after four in the morning. They'd been standing there for more than half an hour. He started to pull away, but Willow tightened her hand on his, tugging him into motion. She led him into a bedroom and sat him on the edge of her bed. Tugging his tennis shoes from his feet, she nudged him to raise his legs and lay down. Flynn didn't have it in him to fight her. Closing his eyes, he let her cover him with the comforter.

When her weight eased in beside him, he turned on his side to pull her close. Maya jumped onto the bed behind him and curled into his back.

Flynn let himself drift away, more secure than he'd felt in a long time.

WILLOW HELD FLYNN'S hard body to her, trying to stem her tears. They dripped down the bridge of her nose, one after another, wetting the sheets. The loss in his voice had undone her. Made her ache for him. It didn't seem like he'd talked about it much before, so though she'd gotten tired, she'd waited right there with him as he remembered his dog.

She'd waited for the story of his passing with fear in her heart, because she probably would have broken down sobbing. But that part of his story he kept to himself.

He'd seemed wrung out when she'd pulled back to look at him, dazed, too brittle to try to drive home. So she'd tucked him into her bed. And curled in after him.

Though she was sorry for his loss, maybe it had helped him to talk about it.

Willow woke up at seven, thanks to Guinness's cold black nose nudging her awake. Time for breakfast. She slipped out of bed, leaving Flynn to sleep, and dressed as quietly as she could.

Crossing the paver path to the office, she fed the animals there and checked on her cases. Sue came in a bit later and Willow headed home to take a quick shower. Flynn had already disappeared. Maya was on the back porch and a note had been propped on one of the small tables.

'Thank you.'

Disappointed that he was gone, she went through the house, dropping clothes. The hot shower felt good after the chilly Colorado morning. They were moving into fall now and she had a feeling the search and rescue calls would start coming faster. She'd only had three over the summer. Once the colorful fall leaves started to hit the ground, people seemed to lose a lot of their sense. They took off on trips into the mountains unprepared for anything Mother Nature threw at them.

Willow's day was busy, to say the least. A dog came in that had eaten two pounds of chopped sirloin, Styrofoam tray and all. It was obvious by the pain he was in that it wasn't moving, so off to surgery they went. She'd no sooner gotten out of surgery than a cat came in with a thread and needle in her throat. So off they went again. An African Gray arrived squawking with a mangled wing; broken after the owner had tried to clip his toenails himself and squeezed the bird under his arm too tightly.

The calls came one after another, so when she heard Flynn's truck pull into the parking lot, she sighed. It figured. She hadn't had a second to herself, other than the single time she'd stopped to go pee a couple hours ago. Her braid was unraveling and she was fairly certain she didn't smell so good right now thanks to an overzealous puppy. Last night had been shoved to the far corner of her mind because she didn't know exactly what to do with it. If Flynn came in all surly and angry, she could probably infer he was defensive about what had happened. But he shouldn't be. It was obvious he'd needed the release. And the rest.

They were in a bit of an odd relationship, though. They weren't actually friends, but they were certainly more friendly than they were a year ago. There was attraction on both their parts, she knew that; she'd felt his eyes on her breasts a lot, but they hadn't acted on it.

Maybe they never would.

That thought truly made her sad and she had to close her eyes for the briefest second to absorb the impact. She'd been thinking about him for so long that him not being there shocked her.

Willow walked down the hallway, more anxious than she wanted to allow herself to be. Flynn stood at the counter, smiling slightly, which was shocking in itself. His big hands were curled beneath something small and furry, but it didn't seem to be an emergency. In spite of herself, she rushed forward to see what he had.

FLYNN TIGHTENED HIS spine as Willow walked down the

hallway toward him. But as she looked up at him with bright curiosity in her burnished golden eyes and her cheeks lifted with her broad smile, he felt something clutch in his gut. Willow had a wispy, soft beauty. Her hair was a mess again, but it was who she was. She didn't try to make herself into something she wasn't.

The jeans she wore outlined her voluptuous shape, even under the ridiculously nondescript black t-shirt she wore. Her nails were blunt and a little ragged, but he knew for a fact she had the softest touch imaginable.

Emotion tightened his throat as he thought about last night and the way she'd completely taken him over. It had been...a revelation. That he could be that open with somebody and not feel like a freak.

Her plump pink lips were moving and he slammed back into his head to respond to her query. "I, uh, found him hiding under my truck tire when I left work."

Willow took the fluffy, dirty kitten from his hands and propped it against her breasts, cooing to it. "This is exactly what I needed at the end of a long, tough day. Thank you."

She smiled up at him and he was struck with the urge to lean down and kiss her to tell her she was welcome. He'd never felt the urge so strongly before and he wasn't sure what to do with it, so he stayed where he was, just gazing down at her.

The little cat rumbled in happiness at the attention it was receiving.

Willow held him up high enough to look at him. "He seems fairly healthy. Weight is good." She lifted the kitten's lip to press at his gums. "Good color response, so he's not fighting anything obvious. I wonder if he just didn't wander away from someone's house?"

Flynn shrugged, unable to come up with words to respond.

He felt dumb just standing there, but he wanted to watch her. He didn't care if she gave the kitten a rectal exam, he'd watch her.

Actually, he wanted her attention on him again. Last night had been surreal. Blocks of time were gone. But he felt lighter in his skin than he had in a long time.

"Do you want to go grab a pizza or something?"

Willow looked up at him in surprise, but almost immediately smiled. Her eyes flicked to the side, then back to him. "I would love to, Flynn. Can you give me some time to clean up?"

He nodded, remembering too late that they weren't the only ones in the office. Sue had a mile-wide grin on her face and the vet tech stepped forward to take the kitten. She had a sly smile on her face as well, and he felt a little embarrassed at inviting their boss out so abruptly.

Not so smooth anymore, Flynn.

"Why don't you move your truck over to the house and I'll meet you there. Maya will be glad to see you."

He nodded and escaped the stares of the three grinning women, his skin prickling.

The drive took all of fifteen seconds, but he sat there in her driveway, hands clenched around the wheel as he tried to decide what kind of nut he had turned into. He hadn't been on a date in years, but the evening suddenly stretched in front of him. What were they going to talk about? Do? Should he take her out or stay inside? The thought of crowds made him shudder. Crowds watching him make a fool of himself on a date made him feel sick.

This was an incredibly bad idea. His hand reached for the key in the ignition, then stopped. No, he couldn't leave. He was man enough to go on a freaking date, no matter where they went. He'd been a SEAL, for fuck's sake. *Man up.*

Flynn slid from the truck and circled the house to the backyard gate. Letting himself through, he smiled when Maya bounded out to meet him. Willow had just let herself through the gate from the exercise yard.

"Give me a few minutes to get cleaned up and we can go."

He almost told her not to bother, they could just order in, but he didn't want to voice his insecurities. Or disappoint her. So he let her disappear into the house.

Maya leaned into him, tail wagging. Guinness came over to investigate the visitor, gave him a lick on the hand, then wandered away to chew on a red rubber Kong.

Willow came out the back door just a few minutes later and Flynn almost swallowed his tongue. The black t-shirt had been replaced with a pretty, delicate, blue shirt and skirt outfit. Her long black hair had been curled toward the ends, and drawn back into a wide clip to sway across her back. Subtle eye makeup made her eyes positively shine. Her pink lips were even pinker than normal, and glossy. Flynn felt his mouth water at the thought of tasting those lips, to see if they were as sweet as they looked.

A hard slam of need hit him in the gut, and it was all he could do to stay where he was. He did stand and offer her a slight smile. "You look very nice, Willow."

She beamed at him, her cheeks flushing. "Thank you very much. I don't get a chance to be pretty very often."

"You're always pretty."

She stared at him for a long few seconds, then glanced away to clear her throat. "Thank you, Flynn. I think that's the sweetest thing I've ever been told."

Shit. He'd made her cry. He didn't mean to do that.

The next time she met his eyes, though, she'd blinked away her tears. "We can go anytime."

Flynn nodded and turned for the gate, not saying anything. He held it open for her to cross through, then jogged ahead of her to open the truck door.

Trepidation swamped him as he slid behind the wheel. The thought of being around a lot of people had him walking the edge of panic. "I, uh, don't go out very often, so I don't know what kind of pizza places are around here."

Willow looked at him out of the corner of her eye. "Can I make a suggestion?"

"Please."

She gave him directions to a narrow brick building on the west side of town in Arvada. Flynn wasn't wild about the area they drove to. Too many hiding places. And some of the locals seemed too interested in what they were doing.

Or maybe that was just his own paranoia reading more into the situation than was actually there.

"Please tell me you don't come here alone," he grumbled.

Willow smiled up at him as he walked her to the front door. "Okay, I won't."

Flynn glanced at her, unable to believe she would tease him. But she stepped into the restaurant before he could tell if she were lying or not.

Willow knew the woman at the hostess stand by name. They chatted like old friends as the younger woman led them to the back of the restaurant. Flynn was surprised when she led them to the very last corner booth. Willow sat on the door side, leaving him with the wall at his back. Flynn looked at her. Did she realize what he needed or were things just falling as he needed them to?

The waiter came to the table, and again Willow knew the young man by name. "Water please, Aaron."

The kid's eyes flicked to him, and Flynn felt like he was

being judged. "Same."

Aaron disappeared. Flynn leaned over the table.

"Do you know everyone here, or is it my imagination?"

She shrugged and grinned. "I used to work here. On the weekends when I was working my way through medical school. They paid well, I got to take home leftovers, and they knew my family before they moved to Florida."

Flynn sat back in his seat as Aaron brought their water. He glanced at the menu, but took Willow's suggestion on a pizza they could share. One of the waitresses dropped off a plate of cheesy garlic bread, redolent of fresh spices.

Willow reached for one before the woman had even left. "You'll love the bread. It's a house specialty."

The bread was truly incredible. Eating it gave him an excuse not to talk. Willow didn't push, though. She sat eating her own bread and sipping her water. Occasionally she brought up topics for discussion and he participated as much as he could, but he could tell she was a little disappointed. She went into a discussion about her family in Florida, but he only half listened. Flynn hated feeling like he was letting her down. He had a million questions, but articulating them as he sat in such an open environment proved difficult. The wall at his back, which he thought would be a good idea, turned not so great as servers kept popping through the doorway beside their booth. Flynn turned so that his back was angled to the corner of the booth.

Willow chewed thoughtfully, but didn't say anything as his anxiety ratcheted up.

"There's a window in the top of the door. Would it help if I let you know when someone was coming through the door?"

It would, but he refused to admit that to her.

She seemed to understand that though, too. Her eyes flicked up and a second later a waitress sailed past their table.

Willow kept her head high, and when she saw somebody coming through the door, her eyes flicked in that direction.

Some of the rigid tension in his spine eased. Whether she realized it or not, Willow had just become a part of his team.

Mace wagged his tail beneath the table of the booth across from them.

Willow's golden eyes tracked a person coming toward their table, and Aaron appeared carrying their pizza. He set a little stand beneath the pie and gave them each a plate, then disappeared.

Flynn didn't know if he could eat or not. Willow pulled a piece from the pie to her plate, then put one on his plate. "It would be a shame to waste this pizza. At least try it."

She sat with her eyes on the door, giving him time to take a bite. Flynn had to agree it was one of the best pizzas he'd ever had.

They made it through dinner, packed up the few leftovers and left. Flynn felt like a schmutz, ruining their date the way he had.

"I'm sorry," he told her, holding the truck door open for her.

She glanced at him and frowned. "I'm not. I had a lovely dinner with you."

Flynn leaned between the door and the frame, needing to explain more.

"Crowds mean danger to me." He flicked his gaze back to the restaurant. "There were twenty-three people in there, probably too many for me to take on alone." He couldn't help but grin. "But I would have done my best."

Willow laughed at his bravado and reached out to hold his cheek. Flynn forced himself to stand, unmoving, as she caressed the bristly beard down to his chin, and he felt obligated to be blunt. "I'm not a regular guy, Willow. I can't take you out dancing or to a fair without planning exit strategies and collateral damage. I've been stateside for three years now, but I still live as if I'm in a war zone. To some extent I probably always will. I don't know that anything will ever change that. And I don't know that that would be a good environment for you."

She raised a brow at that.

"Do you see me pulling away? Cringing at what you do?"

She waited for him to shake his head.

"Did I not give you the backup you needed for that situation?"

He stared at her, shaken that she could understand the fear he did not want to give name to.

"Dancing is overrated, although we may have to work on the county fair. That's one thing I simply cannot miss. I love animals more than people, so as long as you make an effort every once in a while to get out, I think we'll be fine."

Leaning in, she pressed a soft kiss to his lips.

Flynn felt like he was drowning; in her scent, her taste and the emotion she stirred in him.

He opened his mouth to taste her, and a visceral need erupted. It had been so long since he'd been with a woman, but he didn't even think that was it. It couldn't be just any woman. Willow was the one who had been taunting him in his dreams for so long.

Willow saving him from himself.

She tasted of Italian herbs and lemon. Angling his head, Flynn forced her mouth wider, needing to taste everything she had. She met him move for move. Fingernails dug into his ribs, then burrowed beneath his shirt to his skin. Flynn shuddered at the first intimate touch he'd felt in years.

He stepped closer, unable not to. One of her hands drifted down to his ass cheek and squeezed, and he hardened to the point of pain. Oh, hell...

The hairs on his neck rose, and he realized how exposed he was, kissing her out here on the street. With a final, lingering nibble, he pulled away. He scanned the surroundings, but didn't see any immediate threat. It was probably just his own unease. Circling the truck hood, he slid into the vehicle.

Willow had dragged the seatbelt across her midsection, but still looked a little dazed. Flynn grinned at her hazy expression. "Are you okay? You look a little flushed."

She gave him a smack on the arm. "Can I help it if I'm recovering from one of the hottest kisses ever?"

Flynn swallowed and looked at her, trying to decide if she was bullshitting him or not. She looked totally sincere. And aroused. The erection he'd been trying to tame renewed, making him shift uncomfortably.

Willow leaned toward him with a satisfied look on her face. "Yeah, I'm not the only one, am I?"

Grinning with her, he started the truck and shoved it into gear.

WILLOW RUBBED HER fingers against her thumb on her right hand, remembering the feel of his hot skin. And he'd been muscular. It was obvious he worked out because the man didn't believe in loose fitting t-shirts. Seems like everything he had fit him like a glove. But she wanted to *see*. She wanted to be like any other woman and drool over a hot body.

Hell, if he showed the inclination she would maybe do more than that. In spite of how she felt about her own body.

It wasn't like they didn't know each other. He'd been coming into the office for the better part of a year, once, sometimes twice a month even.

Something occurred to her suddenly, and she sat back against the bucket seat. "I don't even know your whole name. Or what you do."

Flynn glanced at her, his face lit by the lights of the dash. His teeth flashed for the barest second before he turned back to the road. "My name is Flynn. You know that."

She narrowed her eyes at him. "You had your tongue down my throat. I think I can know your name."

She lifted a brow at him, waiting.

He seemed to be mulling something over, but he tipped his head slightly. "Joe. Joe Flynn."

Hm.

"But if you call me Joe, I probably won't respond to it. I've only ever been called Flynn."

She tucked that little tidbit of information away, happy that he'd given her another piece of himself.

"And I work for an investigative service on the north side called Lost And Found. Background checks, surveillance, that kind of thing."

Willow turned her whole body to him in surprise. She hadn't expected that. "How interesting! You get the dirt on everybody."

He shrugged his broad shoulders. "Sometimes. Other times it's sitting in a car for eight to ten hours a day doing nothing, day after day."

"So where are you from Flynn? Seems like I still don't know very much about you."

Turning onto the 265 on-ramp, he glanced at his mirrors, then her.

"My family is in a little town outside Atlanta. Mom, a couple sisters. My dad died years ago."

She frowned in sympathy. "What made you join the Navy?"

Merging into traffic, he shrugged his broad shoulders. "My dad had been Navy, so I always kind of had the idea I would have to join before I did anything else. Where I come from, there's not much of anything to do but join the military."

"And fight the Walkers, right?"

Cranking his head around, he laughed out loud.

Willow grinned, tickled that he'd gotten the pop culture reference to *The Walking Dead*. Joe Flynn just got a little cooler, in her eyes.

They chatted about five million things on the way back to her place, and even when they pulled into her driveway they sat there and continued to talk in the darkness.

Flynn had restrictions about what he could talk about in relation to his service. Most of it was covert ops. Willow wasn't concerned about that, as long as it didn't affect the now. She had a feeling Mace had played a huge part of his life over there, but when she asked, he shook his head.

Willow's natural curiosity chafed at being stifled like that, but she guessed she understood. Lives depended upon secrets. Especially in places like Afghanistan. And if he didn't want to talk about his lost partner, it was his prerogative.

Flynn left her at her door with a knee-melting kiss. It was on the tip of her tongue to invite him in, but she didn't think either one of them were quite ready for that. So as he walked out the door with Maya at his heels, she allowed herself to watch his fine ass disappear from view and dream about when the time would be right.

CHAPTER FOUR

✦

I T SEEMED LIKE Willow had just gotten to sleep when her
phone rang. Two hikers had gone missing on the Chicago
Lakes Hike near Mt. Evans. They were supposed to have
returned the previous afternoon but had failed to check in with
family. Heart racing, she promised to be there within an hour
and a half.

Guinness was already on his feet, tail wagging. When the
phone rang during the night like that, he knew it was a good
possibility they would go to work. Willow used the bathroom
and dressed, debating whether or not to take Flynn and Maya.

What the hell.

She dialed his number and he answered on the second ring,
totally clear voiced. "Hey, I was just thinking about you."

Willow grinned, glad that he'd been as restless as she had.
"Well, as much as I appreciate that, I just got called in on a
search. Did you want to come with me?"

Silence stretched on the other end of the line and she wondered if she were moving too fast for him. When she'd
mentioned going on a search, he'd seemed agreeable, but
maybe she'd read him wrong.

"Sure," he told her quietly. "How much time do I have?"

"I'll be by to pick you up in twenty minutes. Will your boss be okay with this? You'll need to be off at least a day."

"I'll call him to check. I should be fine. I'll be ready when you get here."

Willow hung up, then called the office line to leave a message for Sue to reschedule patients or to ship them on. Willow had worked out a partnership with another local vet to take her overflow when she had searches come up, so she called that vet's line as well and left another message.

Then she started packing her trail bag. Essentials were already inside; she just added a couple liter bottles of water and a couple of apples. There were enough provisions in her pack to last several days if she needed to.

They were out the door within fifteen minutes of the initial call. And in front of Flynn's apartment building ten minutes after that.

Maya bounded out like she was going on a great adventure, making Willow laugh as she opened the back door of her full-sized SUV. The dog leapt in as if she'd been waiting forever, greeting Guinness like old friends.

Flynn tossed his backpack in the back, then climbed into the passenger seat. There was a pinched look around his eyes, and she wondered if she'd made the right choice in bringing him.

"Are you okay? I can do this alone. You don't have to come with me."

He met her eyes in the gloom of the cab. "I'm fine. Seriously."

Shoving the truck into drive, she didn't question him any more than that.

It was a quiet drive for the most part. Flynn asked for details about the operation. He had hiked the Bierstadt trail before, but not the Chicago Lakes trail. He requested details on the op.

Willow grinned at the way he made it sound military.

The missing hikers were supposedly experienced, so she was curious why they'd gone missing. Injury landed at the top of her list. The trail was treacherous; one of the most dangerous in the Colorado range. Hopefully only one was injured, but the other was smart enough to stay planted, caring for the other.

They wouldn't know until they got there.

When they arrived at the trailhead, several ranger trucks as well as private vehicles crowded the parking area alongside the road. Willow parked where she could and pulled her pack on. Guinness whined with excitement as she slipped his neon orange reflective harness on. She tossed a similar harness to Flynn for Maya.

"This particular mountain is a little deceptive because it goes down before it goes up. Put that on her, but once we get there, hang back from me at least twenty feet. Do you have your pack?"

Flynn nodded. That worried, pinched look still tightened the skin around his eyes, but they glinted with excitement. The darkness would perhaps help him feel more secure as they walked toward the large group ahead of them.

Ranger Roger Thompson, her contact for the operation, met her in the middle of the road that lined the lot. He held out a hand and shook hers briskly.

"I appreciate you coming out, Ms. James. I tried to get one of the teams out of Vail, but they were tied up."

"No problem, Mr. Thompson. Tell me what's going on."

His flashlight flashed as he moved it toward a green Suzuki wagon. "The car's been here since yesterday. A couple, Mike and Katie Gerhardt, left yesterday to summit, but they haven't been heard from since about 2 p.m. yesterday. They called her mother when they reached the peak, then started down the slope. But they never got here. Her mother is the one who called us this afternoon."

"Nobody else saw them? This is a fairly popular hike."

He shrugged in the dimness. "Nobody's stepped forward."

No, that would be too easy.

"Okay, if I can get something from the car, we'll head out."

She pulled her jacket around her. It wasn't winter, but chilly. If you were caught out here without the proper protection, hypothermia was a definite possibility. Flynn had put on a long-sleeved Henley and sweatshirt, and he had a nice pair of hikers on his feet.

It was only a little after three a.m., so she wouldn't have light for hours yet, which would make the trek that much more treacherous.

One of the local deputies had Slim-Jimmed the driver's side door. Willow found a discarded flannel in the backseat and held it out to Guinness. The dog buried his nose in the fabric, tail wagging. "Seek, Guinness. Seek."

She turned to Maya and encouraged the dog to smell. Maya sniffed at the shirt, but didn't inhale the same way her dog had. Willow placed the shirt in a large Ziploc and stuffed it in the top of her pack.

Guinness was already at the end of his twenty-foot lead, pacing back and forth across the dusty, leaf-strewn ground.

"Are all your people out, Thompson?"

"Yes. As soon as we realized we were calling you in, we pulled everyone out." He handed her a radio. "It's on the channel you need. Let us know when we can start up the trail. There's an access road for the Idaho Springs reservoir after you hit the creek. We'll meet you there and wait for your go ahead to follow."

Willow nodded, familiar with the area. She'd hiked this trail a couple times before, although it had been a while.

Certainly never in the dark.

With a final wave at the gathered rangers, she gave Guinness his head. The dog found the trailhead easily, then started fanning back and forth. So many people had already cluttered the air with their scent it would probably take him a while to find that of the missing hikers. There was also a campground not far away. She could smell the wood fires.

Willow turned on her headlamp and handed her spare back to Flynn. "These are good for conserving the batteries in your flashlight. If you have problems, let me know. With the way he's acting, I think Guinness may have picked up a hint of something. Try to get Maya to watch."

"Roger."

Willow dug into the climb. Just as she was getting warmed up though, the trail headed downhill. She knew the trail had to sweep down to the creek, then back up to the first lake. Then, further up, was the second of the Chicago Lakes.

Guinness paced back and forth, steady and strong. His tail wagged constantly. Willow had never seen another dog love his job so much, and she was thankful he had chosen her at the animal shelter. He'd come to the wire door and stared at her until she'd had to take him out. It had been love at first lick, on both their parts.

They'd worked together seamlessly. She patted the right hand pocket of her cargo pants, making sure she'd brought his favorite tennis ball.

She glanced back at Flynn and Maya. The dog was sniffing along, but she didn't have the same interest as Guinness. The dog didn't seem to mind the activity, though. She paced along like she'd been hiking before.

They crossed the small wooden bridge that crossed the creek, then started to climb. They were given a bit of a reprieve from the climb when they hit the flat access road. Thompson and three of the other trucks had pulled up and parked, and they were gearing up to hike.

"I sent a team on to Summit Trailhead just to be sure they weren't up there."

Willow waved a hand in acknowledgement of Thompson's words, then hiked on.

She glanced back at Flynn, who seemed to be walking easily. "We'll be on this road for a little while, then the serious climbing begins."

He gave her a thumbs-up and a grin, which made her happy. Maybe he was actually enjoying this.

Worry about the hikers kept her pace up. When they came to the trailhead leading up to the first lake, she didn't hesitate. Guinness still ranged back and forth, but he seemed to be keeping more to the trail now. With so many different odors to wade through, she was constantly surprised when he was able to single just one out.

The trail in this section climbed, then leveled out, then climbed again. She knew they had to be getting close to the first lake, but they wouldn't be able to see it in the meager light from the quarter moon. After another mile, she paused to take a drink from her water bottle. Legs burning, she paused long enough to offer Guinness a drink as well, but he wasn't interested. His breath fogged the early morning air as he panted.

Flynn knelt beside her. Even he seemed to be a little winded, but the expression on his face appeared exhilarated. Willow kept her headlamp pointed at the ground. If you looked somebody full in the face, it totally ruined their night vision.

"Are you doing okay?" she asked.

"Definitely. Although I have to admit, I can't wait for dawn. The lamps don't pick out all the rocks."

Willow laughed and nodded. "Isn't that the truth... Seems like a lot of my hikes are at night, though, so I've learned to wear taller hikers. Better ankle support."

She held her boot out for him to look at and he nodded.

Willow offered Maya a drink, but she wasn't interested. Pulling the plastic bag from her pack, she gave both dogs another whiff of the shirt.

"Seek, Guinness. Seek."

The lab took off like a shot, tugging at the lead. Willow hurried after him. He had the scent now.

Almost two miles later, Guinness plunged into the trees on the downside of the trail. Willow stopped him long enough to mark on her GPS where they veered off the trail, then followed along behind, careful of the hidden dangers Guinness seemed to be plowing through. For several hundred yards, he went over and under trees, circled boulders and dragged them through untamed brush, single-minded in his determination to find the source of the scent. In the lee of a towering pine, he stopped to sniff at an area that seemed to have been beaten down. Willow could see signs that somebody had been here recently.

She was puffing from the exertion, but excitement gave her adrenalin. She glanced at Flynn once but he seemed to be keeping up, so she continued on. They entered a dense stand of pine, and Guinness literally began to jerk on the lead. They were getting close.

"Mike," she called out, rousing a nesting bird. "Katie!"

There was no response, but she continued to call out, then

strain her ears for an answer. They continued to hike for another half hour before they finally heard a call back. The lay of the trees and boulders distorted the sound, so she continued to follow Guinness. In another hundred yards, they finally found them. She gave a whoop and threw the dog his tennis ball, so proud of him.

Mike Gearhardt lay on the ground, nestled against a boulder and Katie stood over him protectively. The woman burst into tears at the sight of the dog, then when she saw Willow she dropped to her knees. "You found us, you found us."

Mike was rough-faced and haggard, but he forced himself to sit up.

Willow knelt down beside him. "Are you injured?"

He motioned to his right ankle. "We got off track and I climbed this boulder to try to get a lay of the land. But I landed a little off, and it snapped. We've been here since yesterday. Do you have any water?"

She pulled a liter out of her pack and handed it off, cautioning them to drink it slowly. Then she radioed for help, marking it on her GPS receiver. She was dismayed to see how close they actually were to the trail. The Gerhardt's had gotten disoriented and wandered for too long, tromping circles in the bush.

Willow leaned over to look at his ankle. It had been wrapped in a spare t-shirt or something and had turned purple. Then it had swollen hugely. The foot would have to be splinted. If they tried to move him without stabilizing it, there was a chance it could be injured further. She dug in her pack and pulled out the first aid kit. It had bandages in it, and luckily, one set of splints.

Flynn knelt on the other side, ready to help.

"Katie."

The other woman didn't respond to Willow, just continued to weep.

"Katie!" Willow shook the other woman's shoulder, worried that she'd gone into shock. "You need to sit with Mike. We have to splint his foot, okay?"

The bedraggled woman nodded, her eyes clearing. Mike smiled at her reassuringly. "We're going to be okay, honey. They'll get us out of here."

"We have rangers tailing us and I gave them our location. They should be here in just a few minutes."

Mike and Katie nodded.

"Mike, I'm sorry, but I have to splint your foot and it's going to hurt like a sonofabitch."

She caught his nod in the darkness.

Flynn held the splints to the elevated foot while she wrapped it, and she appreciated his help. Yes, she could have done it herself, but it was nice to have backup.

The rangers arrived as she was finishing up the wrap. The bouncing lights were welcome in the darkness, but when she looked up, Flynn had gone still.

IN SPITE OF the ache in his hips, Flynn was loving life. The search had gotten his blood pumping, excitement coursing through his body. Maya seemed to be having fun on the hike, but she didn't seem motivated like Willow's dog. Guinness was in his element. The happy dude had plowed up the mountain, through streams, over brush, completely in the dark. He'd flushed out a couple of quail and crossed paths with an opossum, but his single-minded push to find the target didn't let him get distracted. Finding the targets had finally released him from the drive.

Guinness hadn't been the only one, though. Willow had

impressed the fuck out of him. Following her, watching her work, had been an eye-opening experience. Flynn knew he was in good physical shape, but she had kept him puffing. Granted, they were climbing in elevation as they searched, but he'd lived in Colorado long enough that he should have adapted to the thinner air of the mountains. Willow had showed him serious gaps in his training.

The dark night enclosing them on the search had reminded him sharply of working ops with his team in Afghanistan. More than once, he'd looked down at Maya's back and imagined it being Mace's darker, sleeker coat. Willow's bobbing light ahead of him could have been that of his buddy Reed, who he'd always backed doing entries into buildings.

When the injured man needed splinted, she'd jumped to it as quick as any doc on the battlefield.

At some point though, the mountainside beneath him faded away, and the lights coming toward him were those of the insurgents they'd been hunting. Smoke drifted into his eyes, making him cough. He drew back, searching for his weapon in the litter on the floor. It wasn't there. A light shined into his eyes and he lurched to his feet, ready to bolt.

Mace whined, confused at his actions. Flynn looked down at him, fearing he'd been hurt, but something wasn't right. Mace's hugely expensive vest, with its mounted camera and canvas handles, had been replaced by a reflective orange vest.

But it wasn't Mace.

"Flynn!"

He looked at the woman in front of him but didn't recognize her. Even with her dark hair, she didn't appear native Afghani. Her hands were held out in front of her and she was saying something.

Wiping the smoke from his tearing eyes, he focused on her

pink-lipped mouth. *Pink-lipped* mouth.

"Willow?"

Smiling, she stepped forward, nodding her head. The dog that wasn't Mace stood on her rear legs, with her front legs against his waist. "Hey, Maya."

Flynn ruffled the dog's coat and she started to lick the crap out of him. As the fogginess lifted from his brain, he realized he wasn't in Afghanistan. Nowhere close, even.

The early morning sky was beginning to lighten, and he wondered how long he'd been out of his head. Willow stood in front of him with her hand on his shoulder, but she didn't seem alarmed. Actually, she was grinning. "Are you back?"

He nodded, glancing around. They were the only ones in the immediate vicinity. "Where did the rangers go? And the people we found?"

She made a motion with her head. "Back to the trail. They're going to try to carry Mike down the mountain. Let's sit for a minute."

Dropping the nylon pack to the ground, she sat cross-legged on the leaf-littered slope. Flynn lowered himself a little more cautiously, his hips aching. "Did I do anything?"

A sleek black brow lifted over one eye as she glanced at him. "You mean during your flashback? Nah. Nothing major. I think you were spooked by the rangers' headlamps, but you kind of just backed away into the darkness, all military-like. At one point it looked like you lifted a rifle and you were whispering to somebody. But you didn't strike out or anything."

The sick knot in his stomach unraveled. Good. He'd never hurt anybody in any of his flashbacks, but he'd been taught to kill with his bare hands for many years. It was one of his greatest fears that he would break during a flashback and seriously hurt or maim someone. Rubbing a hand over his face, he pinched the bridge of his nose.

The thought of hurting Willow made his heart stutter.

"Here."

She shoved a protein bar under his nose. As unappealing as it sounded right at that moment, he knew he needed it before they headed down the mountain. Ripping the package open, he took a big bite.

Maya had planted herself on his lap and he sank his hand into her coat.

"You called her Mace."

Willow took a bite of her bar, watching him digest her words.

Shrugging, he took a bite of his own bar. It tasted like sawdust, but he forced it down. He was surprised when she ran a hand over his back.

"If you ever want to talk about him, I would love to hear."

He nodded, unable to say a word because his throat was so tight.

As the dawn began to lighten, they finished their protein bars and washed them down with water. Willow tossed the dogs a couple of treats and played for a few minutes off leash, then they packed up to go.

When she led them to the trail and explained how the Gerhardts had wandered, he was stunned at how close they had been. It was obvious they had been lost for hours. If they had only picked this direction and walked a couple hundred yards…

Flynn realized that going down the trail was as difficult as climbing it. Willow was a well-built woman, and now that he'd seen her work he knew why. It was from ascending and descending mountains. This wasn't a Fourteener, what the locals called a fourteen thousand foot mountain, but it had to be close.

Maya stayed right beside him on the trail. She seemed to sense that the remnants of the flashback were still bothering him. More than once she shoved her nose into his hand, making him ruffle her fur. Flynn appreciated her single-minded attention.

Within about twenty minutes, they had caught up to the ranger party. Flynn could hear Mike moaning the closer they got. He felt for the guy. The injuries weren't life-threatening, so trying to justify a helicopter rescue was out of the question, Willow told him.

The rangers each gave him a considering look, but didn't mention anything about his behavior.

One of the more heavily built rangers had given up his pack and gear to piggy-back Mike down the mountain. The narrowness of the trail required that they travel single-file on this section. Flynn watched the sure-footed ranger descend, in spite of his load, glad that the morning was lightening.

When the trail widened, two other rangers arranged to carry Mike between their locked hands. Still awkward, but it gave the larger ranger relief for a while.

That was how they made their way down the mountain, transferring Mike back and forth between the group to carry. Flynn offered to carry at one point, handing his leash off to Willow to hold. He clasped hands with another ranger and the big one, Chambers, lowered Mike to their support. It was more awkward to carry a man that way than he expected. Mike didn't weigh that much to begin with, maybe a hundred and sixty pounds, but every step made him feel heavier in their arms. Almost immediately, Flynn felt the ache in his hips, but he clenched his jaw and powered through several hundred yards. The trail began to narrow and they were getting ready to transfer Mike back to Chambers when the man opposite Flynn slipped in the leaves. Suddenly Flynn was bearing all of Mike's weight. He did his best to maintain his hold, but he was severely overbalanced, and he felt them slipping off the edge of the trail and down the slope. Rather than let Mike go down first, Flynn used all of the training and strength he had in his body to twist and get himself underneath. As they hit the ground, Chambers was close enough to stabilize Mike before he hit, but he couldn't keep all his weight from landing on him. Flynn gasped and accepted the blow, trying to breathe through the pain as they all three slid in the leaf litter. Mike cried out, throwing his arms out to try to break his fall.

It was several long seconds before they stopped moving and the dust had cleared. Flynn was still on the bottom, but Chambers was sitting right beside him, and had taken most of Mike's weight. The poor guy was almost crying with pain from being jostled.

"We're almost down, buddy, we're almost down," Chambers told him over and over again.

Katie, up on the trail was crying, but she calmed when Chambers carried Mike back up to her. Flynn shook his head at how easily Chambers clambered up the bank. The man must be part goat.

Maya licked his face in concern and he buried his hand in her ruff, appreciating the connection. Willow leaned down beside him and offered him a hand up. Flynn had a feeling he may have hurt himself on that slide, so in spite of his pride, he took her hand.

Pain ran down through his right side as he let her pull him up. She seemed to sense that he wasn't at his best, so she was careful with her movements. When he stood vertical, he took a minute to evaluate what hurt.

The right hip, his old nemesis, throbbed. For a minute, it felt like it had been out of joint, but with a little grinding it settled in. As he turned to head up to the trail, though, the pain made him grit his teeth. Willow followed behind and he hated feeling like she was the stronger one, but this was definitely her area of expertise. All through the climb and descent, she'd powered on like a workhorse, never letting up.

It's why her ass was so well-shaped and luscious. Snorting, he dared to glance back at her.

She had turned her head to watch the rangers escort the Gerhardts down the mountain. The foggy morning had softened her features, making her seem more ethereal than normal. When she met his gaze, she lifted a brow in question. "What?"

His smile widened. "I just realized why your ass is so luscious."

As her cheeks turned pink, he laughed. She smacked him on the shoulder. "You're bad." She paused. "Why?"

He motioned with his hand. "Because you hike up and down these mountains like they're nothing. I haven't seen you hesitate or stumble at all. Hell, you've barely paused to breathe in spite of the crazy elevation change we've done. As someone who has gone through BUDs training, swam more miles than I can count, served three tours in Afghanistan, I truly admire your mettle." He paused. "And your ass. Especially in those cargo pants. They look like BDUs."

Flynn forced his legs to power him up the bank before she could swat him again, but he paused to catch his breath once back on the trail. That was why he didn't mind accepting her help. In the squads, if a man went down the rest of the team took up the slack, carrying that man out if need be. It was just what they did. A long-ago, flashing, pain-filled night scrolled through his mind. They'd carried them both out that night.

Gritting his teeth, he glanced at Willow. There was a sad, thoughtful look on her face. "What's wrong?"

Golden eyes flashed up to his, then away. "It's just funny, because I'm a good-sized girl. Most men don't..." she shook her head. "I get hit on, but mostly by guys who think I'm desperate for attention. I'm not."

Flynn stepped closer to her, ignoring the pain radiating down his side. He didn't like the insecurity he heard in her voice. With the slope of the trail, she stood on the uphill, eye level with him now. He turned her chin until she looked him in the face. "I'm going to tell you a couple things, and I want you to remember this. Number one, I'm a Navy SEAL. You can't even compare me to most men, so don't lump me in with them." He waited for her laughter to subside. "Number two, I don't care what you've been told or by whom. Your body fucking rocks. Men don't want to make love to twigs. Way more than will admit it want a lush, cushioning body to welcome them home."

Reaching out, he cupped her hips in his hands, tugging her into him. "I would not change anything about you. Not one single thing."

With her face so close and her eyes so misty, he had to kiss her. She wrapped her arms around his neck and returned the kiss with enthusiasm, brushing her hand down his cheek.

They pulled away slowly, content to let the others go on without them. Willow stared at him as if trying to decide whether or not to believe him. The relationship developing between them was new and fragile, but even if it didn't survive, he hoped she would accept his words at face value.

After a few seconds, she smiled. "I appreciate you saying that. I really do." She leaned forward and gave him another, quicker kiss. "We should probably go. I don't know about you but I'd like to go to bed sometime today."

Flynn grinned at her. "I'm good with that."

When she realized what she'd said, she shook her head and dodged around him with a muttered 'you know what I meant'. He chuckled, forgetting for a moment the pain about to hit him. Gritting his teeth, he let the pull of the mountain guide his feet down the trail.

When they reached the *flat* access road, he almost moaned out loud in relief. The throbbing in his hip had jumped up to almost-excruciating. Willow paused to dig something out of her pack. She held out four ibuprofen to him along with a bottle of water. He downed them gratefully, then started limping along. When he realized Chambers had waited to give them a ride back to the parking area, saving them a solid hour of hiking, he could have kissed the big guy. By the look on her face, Willow thought the same thing.

When they got back to the parking area, Willow had to dictate a short statement to be added to Thompson's incident report. Flynn sat in the truck with the dogs waiting for her. The lack of motion and strain against his body was such a great relief he started to doze off.

Willow climbed into the truck just a few minutes after he did and pulled away. She went through a drive-thru for coffee once they got back on the highway, then she headed for home.

Flynn forced himself to stay awake. Willow had to be as tired as he was, but they couldn't afford to fall asleep. He asked her about Guinness's training. That was the best subject he could have brought up, because she was very passionate about the dog and his abilities. Curiously, she hadn't said anything about Maya. He finally approached her about it.

"So, do you think Maya would be able to be trained for

search and rescue?"

Willow looked at him briefly, before turning back to the road. Eventually, she shook her head back and forth. "I think she could be trained for anything, but I think I know what she needs to do."

"What?" Flynn demanded.

Willow avoided the question, promising she'd tell him after she'd thought about it a while.

Flynn reached back and stroked the dog's head where she was curled up on the seat. Though he didn't want to admit he wanted to keep her, he did.

"My boss has been after me to adopt another War Dog," he told her, surprising himself. He hadn't planned to tell her about that. "To use at the company."

She glanced at him, her face lit by the dash. "And what do you think about that?"

He couldn't say anything for a long time, because a lot of emotion was running through him. Mace had been an incredible dog, well worth the astronomical amount the military had spent on his training. Just the vest he wore when working had cost almost thirty grand. But it had been outfitted with armor, a GPS tracking device, an infrared camera. More times than he could count, Mace had been the first 'man' on the line, rushing into buildings, over walls, under vehicles. And he'd saved many lives.

Did he even want another dog? He stroked Maya's head, realizing that he didn't really have a choice. The attachment now ran both ways.

"I wouldn't mind having another working dog, but I don't think I want to be on the front lines in the same way. This was interesting." He waved a hand at the mountain. "But I'm not the man I used to be, at least physically."

"What would the dog be doing at work, though? Tracking suspects, locating items? It's not like you'd be under gunfire every day."

"True."

Flynn sat back against the seat, mulling over her words, and replaying Duncan's in his head. His boss hadn't been out of line by suggesting they use Flynn's experience for the company, but Flynn had shut down completely at the thought of bringing another dog into his life. Maya had kind of forced her way in though, and his work outlook had begun to change.

"I think you could train Maya to go to work with you and do those things. You were a Navy SEAL K9 Handler. I would think teaching her how to track down an item or protect a person would be a breeze for you to do."

Flynn appreciated her confidence, but... "The dogs are trained for the most part by the time we get them. We maintain their training and tweak it for our individual situations, but the basics are already set."

She frowned at him in the dim light. "I think you're downplaying your abilities."

Maybe.

Flynn glanced back at Maya, wondering what she would be capable of if he spent time with her.

CHAPTER FIVE

✦

I T WAS ALMOST nine a.m. by the time they got back to town. Since he wasn't going in to work, Flynn took Maya with him for the day. Before he left, he leaned in through the driver's side window and pressed a kiss to her lips. Willow wanted to melt into the seat right there, but she kept her wits. She brushed her hand down his cheek. The arousal faded as she watched him limp up the sidewalk to his apartment. Though he hadn't said a word, she knew he was in serious pain. That skid down the slope had hurt him.

Willow went into the office long enough to check her post-ops and sign releases for a few. Sue had arranged everything else, so Willow headed home. As soon as she walked in her door, she crashed. Hard. Guinness nosed her around five p.m. to go outside. Willow ate a banana as she stood at the counter, staring into space, as she waited for him to finish his business.

She wondered if Flynn had gotten up yet. Actually, she wondered if Flynn *could* get up.

Unpacking the perishables from her trail bag, she restocked it and set it in the closet, ready for the next call. Then she puttered around the house. Did a load of laundry. All the things she normally did after a trip. But worry pestered at her. Flynn had been seriously limping this morning when she'd dropped him off. She wanted to call to check on him.

Screw it.

She grabbed her phone to call and realized she'd missed a text.

Maya misses you.

Willow grinned. Flynn wouldn't say it, but apparently Maya could.

She tapped out, *I miss her too.*

Maybe you should come over to see her?

Grinning, Willow headed to the bathroom to shower, suddenly energized and humming with arousal.

SHE ARRIVED AT Flynn's forty minutes later, Guinness in tow. The door opened as soon as she knocked, surprising her. Flynn stood, hand on the doorknob, and waved her in. He'd just taken a shower too and she inhaled as she stepped close enough to press a quick kiss to the edge of his lips. Growling when she tried to leave, he tugged her back, his mouth sinking into hers. Awareness tingled down through her body. The tips of her breasts rubbed against his chest and she moaned, aware of a languid heaviness in her lower abdomen.

Willow had hoped that he would welcome her this way, but she hadn't expected how readily her body would respond. Faster than with any other man she'd been with. At the same time, she also became aware that Flynn enjoyed what they were doing as much as she. Unable to help herself, she gave a subtle rub against his erection with her hips.

Flynn gasped and stilled. "If you had any idea," he whispered, "how long it's been for me and what a narrow edge I'm walking, you wouldn't do that."

As soon as he uttered the words, she wanted to bump him over that edge. Just to see what he would do. She had a feeling the experience would be momentous.

Resting her hands on his sides, she rubbed her thumbs back and forth beneath the edge of his gray t-shirt. Her heart thudded in her chest, shaking her whole body. Through the shirt, she could feel the delineation of his muscled body. Turning her head, she pressed a kiss against his neck, then his jaw and cheek. Before she lost all willpower, she pulled away.

Willow settled into a chair catty-corner to the couch. Maya came over and buried her head in Willow's lap as if she had actually missed her today. Rubbing her ruff, Willow allowed her fingers to run over the scar around the dog's neck. The hair was growing in nicely. Within a couple months the wound wouldn't even be noticeable.

Flynn moved behind her to the well-worn brown recliner and she was shocked at how painfully he was moving. "Are you injured?"

Flynn gave her a grim smile as he lowered himself to the seat of the chair. "No, just banged up from the slide yesterday. Or this morning. Whenever the hell it was. A little muscle sore."

Willow frowned at his answer. He'd fallen into a skid but she didn't think it had been that bad. "I didn't realize you'd hurt yourself that much."

He shook his head and ran his hand through his dark hair. "It aggravated a previous injury."

Like when he tried to outrun his ghosts.

"Is there anything I can do?" She wiggled her fingers. "I've got great massage hands."

For a minute, he looked intrigued before he shook his head. "Nah, that's okay. I didn't bring you over for that. I thought I'd see if you wanted to stay for lunch? Or dinner..." he smiled at her sheepishly. "It'll have to be takeout, but there's a pretty good Chinese place that delivers."

"Sounds good to me."

She watched as he pulled a well-worn takeout menu from beneath the table beside his chair and handed it to her. Willow looked it over and decided quickly, handing it back to Flynn to order. Her doctor's brain had moved on to other things, namely the injuries he kept alluding to that seemed to still cause him so much pain.

"If I had known it was going to hurt you this much, I wouldn't have taken you along."

Irritation flashed across his features. "I don't need to be coddled like a child."

She raised a brow at his words. "It's not coddling. It's being careful of an old injury that obviously still causes you issues. Climbing that mountain wasn't easy, and if you had fallen and hurt yourself more, I would have felt like shit. Then we would have had to carry your ass home."

Flynn snapped his mouth shut, eyes narrowed as he took in her words. Eventually he nodded. "You're right. It wouldn't have done either one of us any good if I had injured myself. But I had to do it."

He shrugged his broad shoulders, giving her a little grin. She shook her head at him, knowing in her heart that if they stayed together, she would have her hands full.

"We'll talk next time. Chicago Lakes is a difficult trail, but not the most difficult around. You did really well until right there at the end when you tried to do too much."

Eyes darkening, he frowned, looking down at his hands. "You're right. I tried to step up and be part of the team and I bit off too much. I'll try to leave it to the younger shooters next time." He winked at her, grinning fully, but the shadows stayed in his eyes.

Willow knew it had to be hard taking a step back from the action. Flynn had limitations, but he'd been trained as a SEAL to meet those limitations then exceed them, in spite of his pain and everything else that might get in the way of his objective. She'd watched documentaries about SEALs before and it wasn't an easy life.

Maya snugged her head into his lap, interrupting his resigned introspection. Willow wondered if he even realized how many times a day she did that for him. His face immediately lightened, and a smiled tipped up his lips beneath the beard.

"I heard from Ranger Thompson," she told him. "The Gerhardts are fine. Mike's ankle had to have surgery and he had some hypothermia and dehydration, but they expect to release him from the hospital in a couple of days. Katie was dehydrated as well, but she's already been released."

Flynn shook his head. "I knew they'd be fine. The hypothermia was probably his worst issue."

Willow nodded. "Definitely. He had compromised blood flow to the broken foot. A couple of his toes might be numb here and there, but I think it's a small price to pay for their lives."

There was a knock at the door. Willow stood up automatically, reaching for her cash, but Flynn waved her away. "I've got it."

She followed him to the door anyway to take the bag of food they'd ordered. Adjusting a few things on the coffee table, she spread the boxes across the surface. Flynn limped back to the chair and she tried not to watch how painfully he moved.

The Chinese was delicious as he'd said, and conversation slowed as they each enjoyed the food. Flynn shifted back and forth in the recliner, though, as if he couldn't find a comfortable position. Maya sat at his hand next to the chair arm, licking his hand every chance she got. Maya knew he was in pain.

Willow tried to eat her own food, but worry made her tense. If she asked what had happened to him, would he tell her? Maybe she had to come from a different direction. She was debating how to open the can of worms when he cracked the lid for her.

"So, were you serious about that rub?"

Flynn regarded her steadily as she pondered the question. He knew as well as she did that the next few moments could potentially change the course of their relationship, because they had reached a point where things were becoming physical.

Willow's heart thudded in her chest as she thought about her answer. With a quick blink and a single nod, she took their relationship to the next level.

Willow stood up and closed the lids on the food boxes, trying not to show him how affected she was. "If you want to get comfortable, either on the couch or the floor, I'll put these in the fridge if that's okay?"

"Sure. I'd appreciate it."

She stacked the boxes in the bag and walked the bundle to the refrigerator. She wasn't surprised at the sparseness of the food inside, but she was surprised that there was no beer or even soda for that matter; only bottle after bottle of water and fruit juice.

When she came back from the kitchen, Flynn had just appeared from a hallway, wearing a pair of thigh-length running shorts and the same t-shirt from before. He glanced at her before retrieving a pillow from the couch, then moving to an open expanse of space at the end of the couch. With a grimace, he lowered himself first to his knees, then to his belly on the floor.

It was all Willow could do not to tackle the man from

behind. His tight t-shirt gathered and bunched along with his expanding and contracting muscles. And his ass... she shook her head to clear it.

You need to get a hold of yourself.

Dragging oxygen into her starving lungs, she knelt on the floor to the right of his hips. Her hands reached out and smoothed up his spine. They glided fine on the cotton of the t-shirt, but she wished they didn't. Then she'd have an excuse to ask him to take his shirt off.

At the top of his spine, she started by carefully massaging the muscles of his neck, up to the base of his skull. Her fingers brushed against the short dark hair of his scalp, and she smoothed it down. Squeezing with her thumb and fingers, she worked her right hand down his neck. Bringing her other hand up, she started to pinch the muscles between his neck and shoulders. Then, spreading her fingers, she began to knead her way around his shoulders and across his back.

Flynn groaned into the pillow beneath his head and Willow knew she must be hitting good spots. She made sure not to press too hard though. Using the thumb of her right hand, she ground it into the muscle aligning his spine. Starting at mid-back, she worked her way down to his hips, then switched to the other side to go up to where she'd started.

Tension seeped from his body and she felt him almost sink into the floor. Touching him was unlike anything she'd ever felt. Even through his clothing, he was hot to the touch, and there was so little spare flesh on his body. No love handles, no paunch. She wanted to run her hands down over his ass just to see if it was as firm as it looked. A man's eyes turned her on, but a nice ass came in a close second.

Shifting to his feet, she lifted his right into her hand to start manipulating. As she moved up his calves, he moaned again, and mumbled something into the pillow.

"What?"

She leaned over him to try to hear what he said. Flynn lifted his head long enough to catch her gaze. "That feels phenomenal."

Willow grinned and lifted his other foot, giving it the same attention before moving up his calf again. Then, shifting a little bit, she started to rub his hamstrings, first his right, then his left. Flynn groaned loud and long and pretended to cry.

"You're killing me woman, but it feels so good."

Willow couldn't get a good grip on his thigh because of the nylon fabric of his shorts. "Don't freak."

Before he could say anything, she'd slipped her hands beneath the leg of the shorts, gripping the large muscles. She massaged up and down, then shifted over to the other leg, doing the same thing. He didn't say anything about her touching him so intimately. Willow wondered if he would stay quiet when she massaged his butt.

Climbing and descending mountains put a lot of stress on the heavy muscles of the lower body, especially the thighs and the buttocks. As sore as his thighs seemed to be, his gluteus muscles had to be just as sore. Swallowing heavily, she allowed her hands to rest on the cheeks of his perfect ass before she dug her fingers in.

Flynn gasped in painful pleasure. God, Willow hadn't been kidding when she said she had massaging hands. As she dug her fingers carefully into the muscles of his ass, he feared she would hurt him more than he already was, but she applied the perfect amount of pressure. He'd fallen on his right side and she made sure not to rub that side as hard as the other. Not that she could see the bruises, but they were there.

He felt her shift to his other side and she started at his

calves again. Flynn fought with a ton of guilt, because there was no way he could pay her back for what she was doing to his body. Yeah, he was strong, but that mountain had seriously kicked his ass. Running five miles on a flat paved surface had left a huge gap in his training, he realized now.

She started to work his left hamstring and he wanted to pull away, but he stayed still, breathing through the pain. She found every knot, then slowly worked it away. As she moved up his left ass cheek, he realized it was more sore than the other side. Well, he'd been babying his injured side, so it made sense that the opposite side had worked harder. His eyes watered and he clenched his fists, but when she started to move up his back, he realized that his legs and ass felt better after her attention.

He was also getting hard. As if it weren't enough that she was touching almost every square inch of his body, she'd also been rocking his body. His cock had appreciated the attention whether she realized it or not.

She worked up his back again, paying attention to a million hurts he didn't even realize he had.

"Do you want to turn over?"

Flynn choked out a laugh. "I don't know if you want me to," he mumbled.

Her hands paused and he felt her heat as she leaned over his back. Her long hair drifted over his shoulder, smelling of lavender. "Why?"

"Because I'm harder than a rock," he growled.

Willow's hands pulled completely away and she leaned back. "That's okay. If you want the front of your legs rubbed, turn over."

Flynn debated whether it would be prudent to take her up on her offer, or if he should tell her thank you for her time and send her on her way. Hell, maybe he was reading more into the situation than she intended. Maybe she would actually rub his legs and leave it at that. She may not even want what he had.

Disgusted with his own indecision, he followed what his gut told him to do, and flipped over.

Flynn felt the brush of Willow's gaze along the length of his cock before she deliberately looked at his legs. Reaching out, she started to knead the heavy muscle at the front of his right thigh. Once again, he lost himself in the feel of her magic hands moving up and down the length of his upper leg. She paused at the upper part of his thigh and he felt the tips of her fingers trace the puckered line on the outside of his right hip. "Jeez, Flynn, that's a hell of a scar."

He sighed and rested his arm over his eyes, unwilling to see her face just then. "I had to have a hip replacement."

Even without looking, he knew he'd shocked her. He waited for her response and was surprised when he felt her rest a hand on his chest. Moving his arm, he glanced up at her.

Concern had dimmed the light in her eyes. "I'm sorry you had to go through that."

He didn't know if she meant the surgery or the war or what, but it didn't really matter. The sincerity in her face really touched him, but he forced a shrug. "It was part of the mission. Not how I wanted it to end, but it happens to the best of us."

Forcing a grin, he tugged on the end of her braid.

Willow leaned forward, resting her lips on his for a timeless moment. Wrapping his hand around the back of her head, Flynn refused to let her go, tugging her down against him. With a gasp, Willow's lush body rested against his, exciting him all over again.

Instinctively, her thigh slid over his, sliding against his

erection.

Flynn rolled them over, till he cradled her head and hip beneath him. God, she felt good. She'd already sent gallons of endorphins cruising through his body because of the rub, but this pleased a completely different part of his body. His dick nestled into the V of her pelvis.

Willow gasped, surging against him, spreading her legs to pull him closer to her. Flynn stopped moving for the barest second. "If you don't want this, Willow, you need to tell me now."

Rather than respond, she ran both hands beneath the elastic band of his shorts, squeezing. "You have a beautiful ass," she whispered.

Flynn chuckled, grinding against her. "If you say so."

Willow wore a plaid button-down shirt in shades of green. Very pretty, but the damn buttons wouldn't release for his blunt fingers. The need to see her plump breasts was almost overwhelming. He'd been fantasizing about them for so long.

Willow seemed to sense how needy he was, because she started to undo the buttons herself. When the sides of her shirt draped open, Flynn groaned. Even wrapped in satin, her breasts were truly gorgeous. She did a little shimmy beneath him, reaching her hands behind her, and the satin fell away.

Taut, brown, pebbled nipples begged for attention. Resting on his elbow, Flynn weighed the left one in his hand, strumming his fingers over the tip. Willow panted and cupped both breasts for him to pay attention to. Leaning down to taste one nipple, he continued to fondle the other with his hand until she cried out, shuddering.

He skimmed his hand down the pale skin of her belly, fascinated at the downy-soft feel. At the waistband of her jeans, he ran his fingers across the fabric, then unfastened the button.

When he peeled back the sides, the zipper went down, revealing a pair of dark-blue satin underwear.

Flynn clenched his jaw, burying his hand inside her jeans and against her belly, rubbing as far as he could reach. He couldn't get enough of the feel of the fabric on her soft skin, and he rocked his hand back and forth. Lunging to his knees, he gripped the sides of her jeans, tugging. Willow lifted her hips and let him drag them down her legs. They landed in a pile at the end of the couch. He nestled himself back between her thighs, grinding his hard length against the fabric he'd revealed.

"Fuck, I could come just like this. You feel so damn good."

Willow grinned at him, rocking her hips up into his cock. For the briefest second, Flynn's vision actually dimmed as the need began to blind him to everything else. Slipping a finger beneath the soaked gusset of her panties, he ripped them away from her body. He pulled back to look at the soft dark fuzz he'd revealed, trimmed to a narrow band just above her slit. The tingle in his balls threatened orgasm.

Ignoring the muscle pain, he shoved to his feet, reaching for her hand. Willow grinned as he jerked her to her feet and led her into the bedroom. He guided her to lay on the bed and she did, in her own way. Backing onto the mattress, she stretched sinuously, stretching one arm high to lift her breasts. Then she glided both hands down her body, and one finger slipped into her glistening cleft. Her golden eyes drifted shut with pleasure.

Flynn ripped his own clothes away, uncaring what she thought about his battle-worn body. Willow watched him through slitted eyes and opened her arms to him.

Flynn crawled up the bed and between her legs. Without giving her a chance to protest, he moved her hand away and pressed an open-mouthed kiss to her slit, then arrowed his tongue to burrow in. She tasted of wild honey. Willow cried out as he circled her clit and shifted beneath him. Her hands fell to the bed and she fisted the sheets, rocking her hips up into his movements.

When he slipped a finger into her wetness, he flinched at her heat, imagining what it would feel like enveloping his dick. Plunging his finger deeper in time with the movement of his tongue, he tried to curb his own excitement even as he built hers.

Willow was a sensual woman. She had no problem telling him exactly what she wanted. Within seconds her first orgasm rippled through her body. Flynn opened his eyes to watch the pleasure wash over her. God, she was beautiful. She shuddered and quivered, and her moan was the sexiest thing he'd ever heard. Even as the aftershocks rippled through her body, she opened her arms and guided him into her heat.

Flynn seated himself in her body and stilled. Willow's body still shivered with aftershocks and she cried out as her body accommodated his. As he started to move within her, slowly at first, then faster and faster as his control frayed, those subtle shivers turned into quakes as her body tightened with another orgasm. Her pleasure and excitement fed his own, and Flynn let himself go. It had been too long to hope to put it off. Three hard, deep plunges sent his body supernova, blinding him to everything but that hard point of release. Willow cradled him to her as his body played out its movements, her face nestled into his neck.

It took several long minutes for his pleasure to finally ebb. Willow still cradled him to her, her legs wound around his. Flynn pulled back enough to press a kiss to her jaw, then tugged her back into the curve of his body. It just wasn't in him to move in the near future. The house could be burning around him and he would die happy, part of her.

They fell asleep still joined.

CHAPTER SIX

✦

WILLOW WAS PRODDED awake by a heavy erection gliding into her from behind. A hard hand cupped her breast, and his other hand glided down her belly. As she gasped at the invasion, Flynn buried his mouth into her neck. The bristles of his beard sent shivers dancing along her skin, but it cranked her arousal to catch up with him.

Flynn loved her like a starving man. Willow had a feeling he hadn't been with anyone since he'd returned stateside, so it made her acceptance into his life all the more precious.

And it wasn't as if she were unaffected. Flynn appealed to her on a level no other man had and she already felt like her life was woven with his. As he surged into her, pushing her over the edge of pleasure, she knew for a fact that love was a breath away. It was on the tip of her tongue to whisper the words as he groaned in her ear, losing himself in his own pleasure, but she held them back.

It was simply too soon.

With a final series of surges, he reluctantly pulled out of her body.

Willow shuddered with aftershocks. Flynn rolled to the side, boneless, and grinned at her in the dark bedroom. She saw the flash of his bright teeth in the meager light from the bathroom. "Sorry to wake you up."

She lifted her brows at the false apology. "Yeah, right. I could tell how apologetic you were as you yelled out you were coming."

Flynn chuckled and pulled her tighter against his body. "What can I say? You're damn good sex."

She frowned at the off-hand way he said that. She hoped she was becoming more than that. Leaning up, she pressed a kiss to his jaw. "Do you mind if I use your shower?"

"Nope. Go right ahead."

She waited for him to join her, but he never appeared. When she left the bathroom, the bedroom had begun to lighten with dawn, and Flynn snored lightly. She smiled at his relaxed, leg-sprawled pose, until her gaze drifted down over his lower abdomen. On his right hand side, same side as the long scar on his thigh, there was a fist-sized area of pale silver skin. A couple of silver lines crossed through the middle. If she didn't know better, she would think it had been a huge gunshot wound.

Hell, she would bet on it. The man had been a SEAL, some of the most elite of the military. She watched the national news every night. Had he been one of the many injuries or attacks she'd seen listed over there?

She glanced around the room. Most of her clothes were out in the living room. Her gaze landed on a small picture frame on the wall and she stepped forward to look more closely. Flynn was young but recognizable, though his beard seemed fuller now. There was a daring, devilish smile on his face as he stood next to another man, both dressed in desert camo. Both held leashes to dogs sitting in front of them.

Willow leaned in further. That must be Mace. The dark-faced, lean Belgian Malinois looked ready to go, ears pricked to attention. He almost seemed to quiver with excitement. As she looked between Flynn and the dog, she realized they were both ready for anything, both just waiting for any excuse to leap into action.

It made her sad that Mace was no longer with them. She wondered about the other team, and if Flynn ever talked to them anymore. They seemed close in the picture.

With a final glance at his naked shape, she walked out of the room to get dressed. Unable to find anything else, she jotted a note on the Chinese menu and left it on his chair where she knew he'd find it. Maya and Guinness whined to go out, so she walked them down the steps to the yard. They did their business and she urged them toward the SUV. Maya was reluctant to leave but eventually complied.

Willow didn't see Flynn till later on that night. He knocked on her back patio door, then let himself in. Maya went into a wild jumping fit, she was so glad to see her human. Willow laughed at her antics, even as nervousness churned her tummy. The day after sex always seemed awkward to her, because neither side wanted to be rejected, yet both expected it. Flynn eased that worry as soon as he saw her, though. He crossed the floor, took her in his arms and laid one of the hottest, open-mouthed kisses on her she'd ever had.

When he lifted his head, he grinned down at her dazed expression. "I hope I didn't scare you."

She shook her head, pushing her hair behind her ears. "No, of course not, just took me by surprise a little bit." She grinned at him. "Looks like you're feeling better."

Flynn laughed and Willow had to stare. For the first time she could see the devil-may-care attitude she'd seen in the picture from years ago. The setting sun was bright enough to require sunglasses, and the wraparound shades he wore sat rakishly on top of his head.

She grinned at his light-heartedness and wondered if she dared broach the subject she'd been researching all day. Eh. She took the coward's way out and avoided it for now. "Your butt must not be hurting you anymore."

"Not like it was yesterday. Thank you for that massage. I really do think you shortened my recovery time."

It was Willow's turn to shrug. "I felt bad for truckin' you up and down that mountain. It was the least I could do. Can you stay for dinner?"

His eyes darkened with intent and he stepped toward her. "Any chance we can have dessert first?"

Surprise made her mouth fall open and she took an instinctive step back, then another. Flynn followed, staying just within reach of her. Willow giggled at the silly play and dodged around a chair, keeping it between them. Eventually, he gripped the arm of the chair and jerked it away, stealing her cover. Willow tried to dodge through the door into the house, but he caught her from behind. Laughing until she could hardly breathe, Willow turned in his arms, wrapping them around his neck. He took her mouth in a crushing kiss and she could feel the grin against her mouth.

This lighthearted Flynn fascinated her. When he came into the office, it was usually to escort a critically ill animal. She'd only ever seen him as somber, snappish. This lighter version thrilled her. And excited her. As he walked her backwards through the house, tugging clothes away from her body as they went, arousal beat a steady tattoo through her body.

When they reached the door of her bedroom, he was significantly overdressed. Willow dragged his t-shirt up over his head. Hard-wrought muscles flexed and bunched as he stripped for her. A light covering of hair covered his nipples and pecs, then streamlined down his abdomen. Her glance skipped over the scars on his right side and straight to the extraordinary erection he fisted and stroked.

Willow dragged her panties down her thighs and ripped her socks off, the last of her clothing. Then, stepping toward him, she moved his hand from his cock so that she could wrap her hand around it.

Flynn groaned and pressed his lips to hers, skimming his tongue into her mouth. Willow groaned, pressing her breasts into the wall of his chest. As she started to stroke his erection, one of his hands swooped down her belly to her wet core. She'd been wet and aroused all day, remembering the loving he had given her the night before.

Brushing her nipples back and forth against the wall of his chest, she opened her mouth wide beneath his questing tongue, drowning in the flavor of need.

Flynn wedged his cock between their bodies, rocking his hips to rub against her soft belly. "Get on the bed."

Willow quickly moved to do as he instructed, but he shook his head.

"No, I want you up on your knees. Right here on the edge."

A shiver of arousal shuddered through her, and her clit tingled. She shifted to her knees and presented herself to him, arching her back.

Flynn groaned and swept a finger into her wetness, circling her aroused clit. Willow's hips shifted with his movements, trying to guide his finger. When he started to rub her with two, she completely melted down. Rocking her hips faster, she reached for the pleasure he offered her, crying out sharply as she tumbled over the edge.

He waited just a few seconds for the peak of her climax to

pass before he guided his length inside her. His timing was impeccable because as he rocked into her, harder and deeper than she'd ever been fucked before, her second orgasm rippled through her. Flynn's rhythm faltered at the feel of her body gripping his, then increased frantically as his own orgasm rushed at him. As Willow melted into the bed, she felt his body release into her own.

As they tried to catch their breath, Flynn rolled away from her but kept his arm just barely touching her own. Willow appreciated that. Yes, they were sweaty and sticky and had just had some of the raunchiest sex of her life, but she loved the closeness, and he seemed to enjoy it as well. She didn't know what his dating habits had been like previously, but he seemed to really enjoy being close. It had been a little difficult getting into his tough shell, but now that she had, she truly enjoyed the man he was showing her.

She leaned up on her elbow to look down at him, shoving her hair over her shoulder. "You don't act like you're hurting."

Flynn grinned. "It's not like I could feel anything else. As soon as I saw you I had to have you. Single-minded determination."

Willow laughed and reached out to run her hand down his tight abs, coming to rest near the scar. "This looks like a devastating injury. It's amazing you can move as well as you do."

He rocked his head toward her. In the dim light, his eyes were already shadowed, but the laughter had faded from his expression. She hated to put a damper on the evening, but she wanted to talk to him about some things.

"It is amazing," he admitted. "The bullet destroyed a couple sections of bowel, shattered my hip. I was in the hospital for months."

Unable to think of anything else to do, she leaned forward and rested her lips against the silver flesh. "I wish you didn't have to go through that."

He shrugged, resting his hand on her back. "At least I came back. A lot didn't."

She continued to rub, debating how to proceed. "Were you injured at the same time as Mace?"

He blinked at her once before rolling to sit up on the edge of the bed.

Willow thought she'd pushed too hard. She waited for several minutes and was about to head to the shower when he sighed.

"Yes, we were injured at the same time. Hell, same bullet even."

She crawled to where she could see his shadowed face. "The same bullet? Are you serious?"

Flynn nodded. "One of those crazy freak things that happen. As SEALS, a lot of times we had bounties on our heads. The dogs, too. As soon as we went outside the fence, we had targets on our backs."

Willow stroked her hand over his back, wishing she could ease the pain she heard in his voice. "Can I ask what happened?"

Broad shoulders rippled with a shrug. "We were heading out on an op. In this quiet little village at night looking for a target. We were easing up when Mace spotted the ambush a few yards away from our position. He'd just started to jump over a pile of trash to engage when the first insurgent fired. The bullet went through the leghole of his vest, shredded his heart, through his belly and hit me."

Flynn fell silent for several long moments, his face buried in his hands. Willow crept closer to him and wrapped her arm around his shoulders.

"I knew as soon as he fell he was gone. It took me a few seconds to realize I'd been hit as well. Then I went down like a ton of bricks. My team carried both of us out of there, fighting the insurgents the entire way."

Willow rested her head on his shoulder, tears dripping down her cheeks. "He protected you."

Flynn nodded. "If the bullet hadn't lost some of its momentum before hitting me, my pelvis would have been shattered. I would have bled out before the Medevac could get there. As it was, it hit the ball of my femur, totally obliterating it. They flew me to Landstuhl then to the States, where I had the hip replacement."

"How long had the two of you worked together?"

"Four years," he sighed. "Three combat tours. Too many individual ops to count."

Willow continued to rub his back. What a horrendous event. She could only imagine what would happen if something that traumatic happened to Guinness. Leaning forward, she gave him a smile, trying to lighten the mood. "So, you have a part of him in you. Any urges to sniff crotches or chase balls?"

He stared at her incredulously for a few seconds before belting out a laugh. Catching his breath, he looked at her again and continued to laugh till tears glistened in his eyes.

Willow grinned as he wrapped his arms around her. She wanted to hear about his lost partner, but she didn't want him to dwell on issues that he couldn't change. Over the past year Flynn had, for the most part, been a pretty dire human being. She would have liked to think she'd begun to thaw him out a little.

Flynn pressed a kiss to the top of her head. Willow lifted her face and he captured her lips for a long, heartfelt kiss.

Maya whined outside the door. The emotion inside the room had reached pretty epic proportions, so she probably wanted to be part of it. Willow pulled back enough to look into Flynn's eyes.

"I want you to observe something, Flynn."

She crossed the room to the door and let Maya in. The dog immediately went to Flynn for reassurance, not for herself, but for Flynn. The dog's concern was almost palpable.

"What am I supposed to be observing?" He looked up at her as he stroked Maya's head.

"Her reaction to your emotional state. I talked to a buddy yesterday and I think you should consider training Maya to be a state-certified PTSD dog."

The movement of his hand on her head stopped and he looked down at the dog, then back up at her in consternation. "What?"

Willow took a breath. "That dog reacts to your emotional and sometimes physical state. You've had a couple of flashbacks since you've had her and what has she done?"

Flynn frowned and shook his head.

Willow waved her hand at the dog's current position. "She parks her head within reach of your hand. Even when you sleep and you have dreams, she's right there with you. It took me a while to figure out that she was reacting to your emotions, not her insecurities."

"When we were on the trail," she continued, "and the rangers came with their lights, you had a flashback. She stayed right there with you, even when you lost the sense of who she was. You called her Mace, but as soon as you touched her, you started to calm."

Flynn looked down at the dog beside him, thinking about what Willow had said. Could it be that the dog was reacting to his emotions like that? He tried to remember the flashback on the mountain, but it was a little too foggy. Mace had been there, of course, but he had seemed solid. Had it been because another dog had taken his place?

He glanced around the room, but Mace was nowhere to be seen. Now that he thought about it, he hadn't seen him in a couple days.

Maya looked up at him with her concerned brown eyes. It was a little disconcerting to think that *his* insecurity had been the motivating factor to her attention, not her own.

"Are you sure? I haven't been with her long enough to have developed that kind of bond with her, or she with me. It took Mace weeks to get used to me and for us to build a solid working relationship."

Willow shrugged. "They're different dogs. I've watched her, though. She's consistent. Nothing shakes her up. Until you get upset. When you get quiet in your mind and something's going on, she's right there to be with you."

Dragging in a breath, he looked down at the mutt. She stared up at him, unflinching. For the first time in three years, he wanted to have a flashback to see how she reacted. The bad part was, he would not necessarily remember having it. He had been stressed a few times, though, and Maya *had* come to him without coaxing on his part.

As if she were reacting to his stress level...

Flynn sat back, deep in thought. For years he'd been unable to cope with certain situations. Crowds, especially. Crowds at night, even more so. If there were a chance Maya could be trained to help them out there, his life would change. It would be like having Mace back.

His throat tightened at the thought of his lost companion. Nobody could take his place.

"Did any of your counselors ever talk to you about getting another dog?"

Flynn blinked up at Willow, standing a few feet away. "They did, but I was pretty closed off to the idea. I think a couple even talked to me about the PTSD dogs, but I wasn't interested."

Willow gave him an ironic look. "I think she's kind of decided for you. If she's that attuned to your personality, you would be a fool not to train her to help you out as much as she can."

He frowned, agreeing that it would make sense.

Did he want to be that dependent on another dog though, that would leave him long before he was ready?

Willow seemed to understand he felt overwhelmed with the subject, because she smiled and crossed to the bed to drop down beside him. "There's no pressure and you certainly don't have to decide anything right this minute. This is just an option that is available to you. I'll support whatever you want to do."

Flynn dropped a kiss to her mouth, appreciating the care he could see in her face. It was more than he'd ever gotten from his family or anybody else. "I'll think about it. Promise. We need to get ready for work, though."

Willow sighed. "I know. Let's go."

FLYNN MOVED THROUGH the day waiting to see Mace. The apparition of the dog usually appeared to him at least once a day, but it had been less frequently recently. Duncan could tell he was battling some issues, so he let him off again. Heading home, Flynn tried to let his mind wander. Mace usually appeared out of nowhere.

As he thought about it, though, he realized that was wrong. Mace had only ever appeared when he felt some kind of stress, either physical or emotional. Jogging, pushing himself in situations, crowds.

Flynn turned the truck toward Arvada and the pizza restaurant Willow had taken him to. It was almost noon, so the lunch crowd should be growing.

Luckily he didn't recognize any of the wait staff. He requested the very back booth and sat against the same wall as before. The waitress came and took his order and disappeared through the door that had caused him so many issues last time. This time, Willow wasn't here to spot for him. Every time a body plowed through that door, he tensed, ready to fight. None of the staff paid him any attention.

Flynn glanced beneath the table across from him. No Mace.

The waitress brought his meal and drink, but he couldn't touch either one. His eyes scanned the room for threats and he craved the feel of a gun in his hand.

Movement out of the corner of his eye caught his attention. When he looked over, Mace sat beneath the table across from him. His dark head was cocked as if he were trying to understand what Flynn was doing. Even as he watched, the dog pushed to his feet and jogged out of the restaurant. Flynn dropped cash on the table and followed him out, but once on the bright street, no longer saw the MWD.

Frustration burned through him. Feeling like a pansy ass in the middle of a restaurant was not how he'd ever envisioned himself.

Decorated former Navy SEAL found hiding under a table in local restaurant...that news and more at eleven.

The thought of snapping in the middle of a group of people like that chilled him to the bone. He had no doubt he would kill somebody if it ever happened. The thought of breaking in a group of people like that with Willow present made nausea surge. No way would he allow himself to do that.

Discouraged, disgusted with himself, he turned for his truck.

CHAPTER SEVEN

✦

W ILLOW WADED THROUGH a backlog of patients. When the Search and Rescue call had come in, she'd rescheduled as many of the routine appointments as she could. Now it was time to play catch up.

Not that she minded the work. She was just worried about Flynn. He'd seemed a little shell-shocked when she told him about Maya. And honestly, if she'd been in the same situation, she probably would be too.

A dog like Maya came along only once in a great while, and there was still the chance that if they did send her to be trained, she would not pass the tests for certification. That worry was so minor, though. She was already doing exactly what Flynn needed. Getting Flynn to accept her as a therapy dog would be the big thing.

Five o'clock rolled around and her excitement began to build. Would Flynn be over tonight?

She checked on the animals one last time and was about to leave the office when an emergency call came through. A Chihuahua had had an altercation with a door. She had no choice but to wait for the owner to bring the little dog in. Nicky waited along with her, and she was glad for the assistant's help when they had to put pins in the tiny little leg to hold the break together.

It was past seven o'clock by the time Willow headed down the paver path to her house. The dogs were so happy to see her. As she let them through the gate into the exercise yard, she grabbed up a couple of tennis balls. They would play for a while, in spite of her tiredness.

When Flynn didn't show by eight, she went ahead and ate dinner by herself. Maya watched the door and paced, just as anxious as she was. Willow debated sending him a text message, but tossed the phone away. If he wanted to talk to her, he would.

Half an hour later she picked up the phone again, unable to keep her worry in check.

Maya misses you, she typed out.

She plugged the phone back into the charger then cleaned up her dinner mess. When it buzzed on her counter a few minutes later, she forced herself to walk calmly across the floor.

I miss her too.

She grinned at the response, the same one she'd given him days ago.

But I miss you too, he continued. *Can I come over?*

Willow frowned at the question. *Of course you can!*

Why hadn't he just come over? Weren't they beyond the tentative beginning stage?

The fact that he felt the need to ask her was worrisome. Maybe she just felt like she was further along in the relationship.

While she waited for him to come over, she started a load of laundry. And puttered around the house. Brushed her teeth.

Maya gave an excited yelp when she heard the back door open. Willow got there just a few seconds later, but stopped at the jamb until she could see what kind of mood Flynn was in.

Dressed in running shoes, t-shirt and shorts, she had an idea where he'd been. As he looked up, eyes dull with tiredness, she had to shake her head. "Why do you keep doing this?"

His grin flashed for a moment before he stepped forward and wrapped his arms around her. Willow buried her nose against his neck, pressing a kiss there, but pulled away to frown up at him. "You don't smell very good. Hot shower time?"

He nodded gratefully. "Join me."

Willow smiled. "I'd be happy to."

They left a trail of clothes all the way to the bathroom, then had to stand on the cold tile and wait while the water warmed. Flynn used the time to run his hands over her ass and around to her belly. "I love your shape. You're so soft and welcoming."

That was one of the sweetest things anybody had ever said to her.

It was so strange. She appreciated his hard, cut-muscled shape, but he appreciated her softness. They were a pair.

Willow was taken aback at how thoroughly Flynn paid attention to her that night. He washed her hair and body, dried her completely, then tucked her into bed. Disappointment filled her when she realized he planned to go to sleep, but concern for him outweighed it by a mile. He'd been running from ghosts again and was worn out.

Maybe someday he would tell her about his ghosts.

When they woke in the morning, his somber mood was gone. They made love like she'd wanted to last night, and it was as wonderful as all the other times they'd done it. But he seemed to have something weighing on his mind.

Willow took another shower and started to dress for work. Flynn met her on the patio with scrambled eggs and toast.

"Wow. Thank you! I was just going to grab a banana but this is much better."

They sat at the patio talking about what they had planned for the day, but Flynn avoided the topic of training Maya.

"And you need to know," Willow told him, "that you are welcome here at any time. I can give you a key, too."

Flynn frowned at her, his gray eyes narrowed. Willow felt like she'd blundered somehow. "You don't have to come over, but I want you to know that you can. That's all I'm saying."

Some of the strain left his face. "I appreciate that, Willow. I better get going."

They gathered up their dirty dishes and put them in the dishwasher. Willow turned her face up for a kiss and Flynn pulled her into his arms, squeezing her between the counter and his hips. Though they'd made love less than an hour ago, she could tell he was ready again. When she lifted her brows he grinned at her. "What can I say? You bent over to drop your plate in and all thought disappeared."

She wiggled against him. "I guess so. If I had more time I would take you up on this."

"I have a lot of making up to do, so you'd better be ready later."

Heat swamped her body and hardened her nipples. Flynn's need was the most potent aphrodisiac she'd ever encountered. Made even more thrilling because he'd opened up only to her.

"I'll be ready." She gave him a lingering kiss, knowing that his need would only get worse.

She pulled away before he could make her any later. "I…'ll see you later."

Damn. She'd almost said she loved him.

Willow left the house and headed to work, unbalanced and insecure all over again.

FLYNN FELT RESTLESS and unsettled. When he'd returned stateside, he'd been seriously damaged. Counseling had helped take the edge off, but not enough to make him polite for public consumption. Working with the guys at Lost and Found had actually helped more than anything. They accepted all his quirks and allowed him to build an environment he could function in and become productive. Duncan, his boss, had truly created a haven for all of the veterans he had hired, and Flynn could never express to him the gratitude he felt.

When Duncan came into the rec room at lunchtime, requesting a talk, Flynn had no problem with that. Though they hadn't served together, hadn't even been in the same service branch, Flynn could tell that Duncan had been an awesome leader. Every one of the men in the company respected him. There was an undercurrent of reserved command in Duncan, but they were truly all friends.

They moved to the group of couches and chairs in the back corner of the room, away from the few other guys present in the office. Flynn frowned in sympathy when Duncan lowered himself to the cushion, using his cane as an anchor. He took the chair to the right from Duncan.

"I just wanted to check on you," his buddy told him. "I hadn't seen you for a while."

Because he'd been hiding out.

"I know. Working on some things outside of work." He cleared his throat, suddenly nervous. "I've kind of been seeing somebody."

Duncan's dark brows slid up his forehead and he grinned, leaning forward enough to grip Flynn's shoulder. "Congratulations, Flynn. That's really something. Can you tell me about her?"

Flynn felt a little embarrassed. "Well, she's a great lady. A veterinarian, actually."

Duncan frowned. "A veterinarian. Really? How did you meet her?"

Flynn gave him the truncated version of the past year and the animals he'd found. Before he could stop himself, he told him about Maya, too.

"And does she know about your service and Mace?"

He shrugged. "She knows parts of it, but not all."

"And Mace," Duncan asked softly. "Does she know about him?"

With a heavy frown, Flynn shook his head. "She knows how we were taken down, but I haven't told her about the delusions."

He stood to pace the area in front of the flat screen TV mounted to the wall.

"But the thing is I haven't been seeing him like I was before. Ever since Maya latched onto me, I haven't seen Mace as much. I actually tried to make him appear yesterday, did all of the things that normally bring the apparitions on—went out to lunch in a restaurant with a bunch of people, went running on the trail—I saw him for a few seconds at the restaurant and he ran out, leaving me behind."

"So, is that good or bad?"

Flynn stopped and frowned at his buddy. "I'm not sure. It kind of feels like I'm losing him again, but the fact that the delusions are disappearing is good. Right?"

Spreading his heavy arms across the back of the couch, Duncan grinned at him. "I can understand your need to hang onto Mace. I think he's been a coping mechanism for you for a long time. But if you've become stable enough to let him go, I think it's a wonderful thing."

"Willow thinks I should train Maya to be a PTSD dog."

"I think Willow sounds like a brilliant woman," Duncan told him firmly, grinning. "I'd like to meet her. I've tried to tell you before you needed to get another dog."

"I thought you wanted it for the company, though?"

Duncan shook his head. "Nah, only if you wanted one. I think a companion dog would be perfect for you."

Flynn dropped back down into the chair, things realigning in his head.

"Sounds like this woman has really been good for you."

Flynn had a flash of Willow, dark hair flying around her face as she grinned at him in the sunlight. "She's been incredibly good for me. I don't know if I'm good for her, though. She's had to adapt to a few things already."

Duncan shrugged. "If she loves you it doesn't matter. Look at John and Shannon."

Snorting, Flynn thought of the abrasive partner and his petite woman. They had definitely overcome a lot to be together.

John hadn't had the same problems he did, though.

"I worry that she's putting more into this relationship, into me, than what I'm returning. She's a beautiful woman, runs her own business, does phenomenal volunteer work..."

"And you feel like more of a liability than part of the relationship."

Flynn looked at Duncan, stunned at the man's insightful words. "Yes, exactly."

"You need to get out of that self-destructive loop because it doesn't do either one of you any good. Enjoy being with her. Don't worry about all the exterior crap. If she's happy having you in her life, relish it. Do you love her?"

Scenes slammed through his mind, one after another of Willow looking at him with that calm smile in her eyes. "I think

I do."

A sad look flickered over Duncan's face. "Then enjoy it. For as long as you can."

Using the cane to help himself to his feet, Duncan motioned to Flynn. He lurched to his feet, clasping Duncan's hand in a heavy shake. "Thanks, boss man. You're not bad for an old leatherneck."

Duncan laughed at the familiar dig.

"And you're not so bad for a frogman, Flynn. Let me know how it goes."

"I will."

As he walked out of the office later on that day the receptionist, Shannon, caught his eye and he walked over to her desk. There was a huge bouquet of blue and white flowers on the corner of her desk.

She looked up at him expectantly, smiling. "Can I help you, Flynn?"

Every thought went out of his head and he had no idea what to say. The only reason he'd walked over was because of the flowers. "Those are beautiful. What kind are they?"

"Oh, these are carnations." She leaned down to smell them. "John knows they're my favorite."

Flynn leaned forward to smell them, and he was struck with the ridiculousness of the situation. He'd never given a damn about flowers before, but he hooked up with a woman and suddenly everything changed. He pulled out the one thing he did know about flowers. "I thought roses were good?"

"Oh, they are," she smiled. "But carnations usually live a lot longer. I love them. So he got them for me for Sweetest Day."

Flynn frowned. "Sweetest Day? Really? There is such a thing?"

Shannon nodded. "Yep. October nineteenth. My family is from out east. It's kind of a regional holiday but John remembered."

Flynn made some kind of response and left. Valentine's Day was the only holiday he knew for lovers, but Shannon and John apparently knew more than he did. Should he get Willow something? Would she even care?

Deciding to err on the side of caution, he stopped at a florist on the way home. There was only one woman inside the shop and she was more than happy to sell him a big bunch of carnations. Flynn was ashamed to admit he didn't know what Willow's favorite color was, so he got a mixture of what the woman had.

Walking to the truck with the big bouquet in his arms, he felt ridiculous. Unwieldy, exposed. Drawing too much attention to himself.

All of that aggravation faded away as he walked in the back door of her house and through to the kitchen. Willow stood at the stove stirring something, and when she turned around and saw him holding the bundle, curiosity filled her expression, then pooling emotion. Holding the bouquet out, he stepped toward her.

Swiping her fingers beneath her eyes, she took if from him, burying her nose in the blooms. "How did you know carnations were my favorite?"

Grinning, promising Shannon another thank you, he shook his head. "I didn't."

"What are these for?"

Flynn frowned. "The receptionist at work says it's Sweetest Day. Some holiday candy makers created out east." He handed her the bar of dark chocolate.

Willow laughed but took it. "Thank you so much, Flynn. I

never expected this. I've never gotten such a beautiful bunch of flowers."

He found that hard to believe. "Well, you can pay me back for them later."

She laughed, punching him lightly in the arm. "I think I can do that."

Pulling her close, Flynn pressed a kiss to her lips, surprised all over again at the spark of need that hit him immediately. If his response was anything to go by, he would not soon be getting tired of Willow.

CHAPTER EIGHT

✦

W ILLOW'S GAZE WAS drawn to the flowers over and over again. She'd never heard of Sweetest Day, but she certainly appreciated Flynn's gesture. It had been totally unexpected.

As she dipped out a bowl of creamy tomato soup, she watched him playing with Maya. The dog had been ecstatic to see him, of course, but Flynn seemed to be treating her differently somehow. She couldn't put her finger on it.

She flipped a grilled cheese onto a plate, placing it on the table, then went back for her own. The fruit salad was already there, so once she dipped the soup she called Flynn to eat.

When he asked about her day, she filled him in on the animals that had come in. Only one minor emergency. All the rest had been routine check-ups and vaccinations. A pretty boring day, overall.

Willow asked him about his day and a strange expression crossed his face. "I was good. Talked to my boss about a few things. I think I may do what you suggested. I'll at least talk to the trainer."

Happiness filled her. "Wonderful. I would never have suggested it if I didn't think it would benefit you."

"Well," he said slowly, "I think she may have helped me

already. I, uh…"

Flynn pushed to his feet, running his hands through his hair. It was obvious he had something important to tell her, but didn't know how to do it.

"You don't have to explain anything, Flynn, really."

He shook his head in frustration. "It's important. I just don't want you to think I'm crazy." He tossed her a self-deprecating grin.

Willow smiled back, leaning deeper into the chair, wishing she could help him through this. "I don't think you're crazy at all."

After a long pause, he dropped back to the chair, elbows resting on his knees.

"Mace was a great dog. Picked things up like he'd been training for years. Had an instinct unlike anything I'd ever seen before. When I went into the SEALs, I was all balls. I'd just graduated BUDs training at the top of my class and I thought I knew everything. Well, more than once that dog corrected me."

Grinning, he shook his head at her. "A couple of times, he would refuse to go into a building. Just flat out refuse. If I tried to make him enter the shit went downhill fast. I learned to trust that damn dog like you would not believe."

She leaned forward, at the edge of her chair.

"I was out of it for a solid week after I got injured and shipped stateside, but when I woke up, Mace was right there, guarding over me."

Willow frowned in confusion. "I thought…"

"…he was killed." The gray of his eyes darkened with pain. "He was. But it took me a while to realize that because he was everywhere. When the doctors came into my room, he was there curled up on the end of my bed. When I had a bad day in therapy, he would walk me back to my room. It took me a while, like a week, to realize that he wasn't actually there and that I was the only one seeing him. The doctors and nurses went along with everything I said at the time because they didn't want to threaten my progress."

Emotion tightened her throat at the obvious pain he still felt. "I'm so sorry, Flynn."

Shrugging, he buried his hand in Maya's fur. She'd materialized from somewhere, sensing that he needed her.

"After a couple weeks they brought in the psych doctors. There was nothing wrong with me other than occasional flashbacks and I saw my partner everywhere, so they let my recovery continue the way it had been. It wasn't until they released me from the hospital that they started to be concerned with my visions. They dosed me up with drugs and sent me to counseling, but nothing got rid of the apparitions. I've had them since I was injured. It wasn't until I started coming to see you that they started to ease. Since Maya has crashed into my life, I've seen Mace less and less."

Willow didn't know what to say or think. The fact that he'd been beleaguered by visions made her sad, but certainly not fearful. If anything, she felt bad that he wasn't seeing his friend as much anymore. "So, how often do you see him now?"

Flynn's jaw firmed and his expression looked a little defensive. "Not very often."

Willow didn't like the way he phrased that, as if she wouldn't be with him if they were still here. Pushing away from the table, she moved to the chair closest to his and mirrored his position, elbows on her knees.

"I think it's fascinating that Mace has been watching over you all this time. It shows his diligence and loyalty to you, his partner. It doesn't bother me that you have these visions. As long as they don't harm you or anyone else."

He shook his head. "They never have. He shows up when I'm under strain, for the most part."

Reaching out to rest a hand on his knee, she smiled up at him. "One of your jogging buddies?"

The tension in his face eased. "Sometimes. At first I tried to outrun him, but he was there when I finished."

"Was he at the restaurant the other day?"

He gave her a sharp look. "Yes. He was."

"So," she said slowly, choosing her words with care. "He comes when you're stressed."

Flynn tipped his head once.

"Well," she continued, "that completely makes sense to me. He was your partner for many years in a total hell-hole. He knew where the danger was. I think this is your mind's way of compensating. You have issues being in crowds and unfamiliar situations, like the first time you came here."

His eyes narrowed and a smile tipped up his lips. "I wondered if you'd caught that, the first day."

"I did," she confirmed, "but your stress level has changed recently. I would like to think you're comfortable with me, and with Maya when she's around. Mace is fading away because she's taking that burden."

Though his expression seemed a little sad, he nodded to everything she said. "I think you're completely right."

He stroked his hand over Maya's head.

"I actually tried to make a vision of him appear yesterday, and he did just for a minute, but he didn't stay."

She shrugged, unconcerned. "If you see him, it doesn't bother me. Whatever you need to deal with a situation. I think training Maya to react when you have anxiety or a flashback is a more proactive approach, but I'm not going to make you feel like you have to bury that part of your personality."

Flynn leaned forward enough to press his lips to her own, a weight slipping from his shoulders. Willow reached up and tugged on his beard, making him grin. "Don't stress about this. After what you've been through, you're allowed to have a few blemishes in your armor."

She pushed away from the table and moved to the sink.

Flynn sat back, stunned. When he'd gone through the scenario of telling her he saw apparitions, he'd imagined tears, screaming, being kicked out of her house, a plastic smile. The total, easy acceptance had thrown him for a loop.

Willow acted as if it were no big deal. He didn't know whether he should be offended or appreciative. Or if he should feel anger that she didn't seem concerned. Maybe she just didn't care. Somehow, the anger surged. Did he mean so little to her that she didn't need to know any more details?

"As a doctor, at least, I thought you would be concerned with my prognosis, but I guess I was wrong."

Willow turned back to him with a frown, planting her wet hands on her hips. "Of course I'm concerned, and as more than a doctor, I might add, but I know that you are able to police your own medical issues. You're a grown man, former SEAL, so I have faith that you know what you're doing. I think if it's something I need to be worried about, you would tell me. Or am I mistaken?"

Flynn blinked at her, his anger fading away as he shook his head.

He watched as she started to clean up the dinner mess, unconcerned.

Now he felt ridiculous for his aggravation. Was he looking for something to rock the boat? The sense of rightness he felt as he watched her putter and clean up was a little offsetting. He felt as if he had found where he was supposed to be.

And more importantly, he had found who he was supposed to be with.

But was it too easy?

Crossing the kitchen, he wrapped his arms around her from behind, tucking his nose into her wispy hair. Desire shuddered through him when she rubbed her butt against his hips. "You'll never get the dishes done if you keep doing that."

She bent over a little further, daring him. "I think they need to soak."

Flynn gripped her hips in his hands and rubbed himself against her. The relief and acceptance he read in her body language was exhilarating. More than he'd ever hoped for when he'd planned out the evening.

Grabbing her hand, he tugged her through the house and into her bedroom. Once there, he started to strip her out of her clothes. "You can't say I didn't warn you."

She giggled and turned in his arms. "You didn't need the warning at all. I'm up for anything you throw at me, Flynn." She pressed her mouth to his, nibbling at his lips before plunging her tongue inside.

Flynn groaned, his need ratcheting through the roof as she pressed her bare breasts to his chest. Leaning away far enough to rip his t-shirt over his head while her fingers worked at his zipper, Flynn tried to remember the last time he'd been so consumed by anything.

Not since he'd worked Mace through Afghanistan with the rest of the team.

He buried his nose in her hair, pressing kisses along the length of her neck. Using his teeth, he gently nipped her earlobe. She shuddered in his arms and curled into his chest.

Flynn felt the way he used to years ago, before Afghanistan, strong and healthy, confident. He wanted to fight

Willow's dragons. And get back to living life.

Willow suddenly dropped to her knees in front of his erection, and he didn't remember anything for a very long time. As her mouth enveloped him with heat, he tried to imagine what he'd done to deserve her.

WILLOW RAN HER hand over Flynn's broad back as he laid facedown on the mattress, exploring the striations of the muscles. The man had made her drool from the first time she'd seen him. Now that she'd enjoyed his body and knew what it was capable of, she couldn't turn off her need. But it was so much more than physical.

His lean face turned sideways on the pillow to look at her.

She thought about pulling a t-shirt on or something, but the appreciation in his eyes made her grin. Where other men had seen chunky, he saw voluptuous and curvy. He'd told her that over and over again just in the way he ran his hands over her, as if he couldn't get enough.

Willow felt more secure in her body than she ever had before, because he appreciated her. She was afraid to hope that this could be a long-term relationship. As gorgeous as he was, he could choose any woman out there.

But he was here with her now.

She leaned over to kiss him on the cheek and his gaze followed the sway of her breasts. Laughing, she pecked him on the cheek again and sat back.

"I think you're a hound dog."

The half of his face not planted in the pillow winked at her. "I don't think I'm the only one."

Willow carefully straddled his lower thighs and ran her hands down the divots of his spine. "How can I not be a hound dog with this luscious ass within my reach?"

His body shook with laughter beneath her as she squeezed his ass cheeks. Twisting beneath her, he managed to turn himself face-up without dislodging her. Willow was happy enough to plant herself on his flaccid cock, knowing that just a little bit of grinding would get him ready for her again.

But when her eyes connected with his, he'd gone serious.

"I've heard it's against post-coital protocol to talk emotions after sex, but I have to tell you how much I, I…enjoy being with you. I can't believe how lucky I was when I spotted your office sign."

Her heart clutched in her chest at the hesitation. Was it possible he was as insecure as she was?

Then she realized what he'd said. She raised a brow at him, laughing. "You stopped because of my sign?"

Grinning, he shrugged beneath her. "I was looking for something close to the apartment when I moved in last year and I remembered your sign from the drive to work. The dog is cute."

Shaking her head at him ruefully, she leaned down enough to press a kiss to his lips.

Cupping her breasts, he lifted his knees, pressing her higher against him. When she would have shifted away, he pulled her deeper. Willow moaned, knowing that she could go again.

Instead, he pushed her vertical again.

Willow sat up on his semi-erection, tempted to grind enough for him to slip inside.

Strong hands tightened on her hips as he stared up at her. "I want you to know that I appreciate everything you've done for me."

She shook her head. "I didn't do anything."

He frowned at her. "Just listen for a minute. You have.

Over the past year you've been nothing but nice, even though I was pretty abrasive when I started coming in here. I apologize for that." He ran his hands down her arms to her hands. "I feel like I'm not up to being in this relationship."

Cold fear shot down through her and she rocked back, all thought of sex gone. "What?"

"I haven't been in a serious relationship for the past few years. I had a girlfriend when I went over, but it wasn't serious enough to keep together over deployment. I have no idea what I'm doing."

Willow started to lever herself off. "If you need time…"

He grabbed her thighs to keep her where she was and sat up in the bed, hardly straining as he adjusted her weight. "You don't understand. I don't need time. I need guidance." Another hand swiped through his hair. "I'm going to fuck something up and this is too important for me to do that."

Relief flowed through her. He wasn't trying to break up.

"Don't worry about fucking something up. As long as you talk to me when you're not sure, we'll be fine. I'm not perfect. I can count on one hand the number of relationships I've been in and most of them were with animals."

Flynn snorted. "You know, I can see that."

Willow tweaked his right nipple, making him grin.

"I do know that we're different enough from everybody else that we're going to have to create our own reality. But that's part of the fun."

He nodded at her words. "I'm good with that. I just want you to know that I will give my all to this. And to us."

"Then that's all I can ask," she whispered, leaning forward to press her lips to his. Drawing in a deep breath, she reached for a star. "I love you, Flynn."

His gray eyes darkened with intensity. "And I love you, Willow. You've completely changed my life."

Tears clouded her vision, but she was secure because he wrapped his arms around her.

"And you've changed mine," she whispered.

EPILOGUE

✦

WILLOW WATCHED HER man walk toward her, struck all over again by how handsome he was. Women turned to watch his tall, muscled frame in the too-tight t-shirt as he skirted the crowd to her table. The wraparound shades hid his eyes, but she knew they would be scanning back and forth, searching for threats.

She never thought she'd get him to come here.

When he drew close enough, she smiled up at him as she took the big glass of lemonade from his hands. "Hey, Gorgeous. Thank you!"

With a final broad look behind, he settled onto the bench across from her. As Willow took a heavy swallow of the sweet drink, she glanced over his shoulder to make sure no one had gotten too near. "You're doing perfect. I don't think I need to tell you that."

He grinned at her and nodded. "Nobody said anything about Maya and they kept a wide berth once they noticed her vest."

He and Maya had grown tremendously together through the months of training and she wore her red service dog vest proudly. But this was a huge step for both of them.

It was the middle of the day, so the serious noise hadn't

started on the midway yet of the Denver County Fair, but it was still busy. People wandered through the animal barns and ate fried food, enjoying the bright August day. The games were just starting to open up, but the rides wouldn't start for a couple hours. They'd be gone by that time, but this would still have been an awesome trial.

A little boy of about three wandered over from one of the nearby tables. He only had eyes for Maya though. The dog wagged her tail as he walked closer but glanced behind to Flynn, as if seeking permission. Flynn nodded and only then did she lick the little boy across the cheek, sending him into giggles. The little one patted her on the head, laughing when she nuzzled his cheek.

Flynn barely tensed when a woman rushed over to snatch up the boy. Willow saw her glance at the vest and cringe. "I'm so sorry he bothered you. He's just so fast."

Flynn waved a hand and even smiled at the woman. "No big deal. The dog appreciates the attention."

The boy's mother relaxed and even smiled at Flynn, a little dazed, before turning back to her own table. Once seated she glanced behind her for one more peek.

Willow watched the exchange with interest. "I think that's one of the most laid-back reactions I've ever seen you have."

He turned his head to her and she wished he would take off his glasses so she could see his clear gray eyes. "Maya knows when something's not right. Like that guy last week. I've learned to follow her lead."

Willow nodded. The two of them had been on an embezzling investigation last week and when Maya and Flynn had sat in on an interview, one of the suspects had put Maya on edge. She'd paced and whined and stared until the man had been intimidated enough to confess. Not what she'd been trained for, but it had worked out that day.

Man and dog had learned to rely on each other more and more. Maya had learned to anticipate trouble areas, sometimes sooner than Flynn did himself, and she guided him out of them faithfully. If he called her Mace here and there, she didn't seem to mind.

"Still, though, it's been an amazing year."

"It has," Flynn agreed softly. He leaned toward her across the table, pushing his shades up onto his head. Willow met him part way to press a kiss to his lips, tickled that he'd shown her his eyes. When she would have pulled away, he cupped her head in his hands. "I can't tell you enough how much I appreciate you. If you hadn't seen what you did and suggested training Maya for companion work, I wouldn't even be here." He turned his head enough to glance around, before focusing back on her.

Tears filled her eyes but she wiped them away. "I love you, Flynn. I think you would have found a way to live again eventually, but I can't say I'm not happy to be the one to bring you out of it. I think Mace sent you to find Maya and you were meant to walk through my door with her in your arms. Because I know in my heart I was meant to love you."

He nodded and swallowed heavily, pressing another kiss to her lips before pulling away. There was a sheen to his eyes now, too, which choked her up all the more.

Willow was shocked at how quickly the year had flown by. As a couple, they did everything together, but it was never enough. At night, as they rocked each other to oblivion, then held each other afterward, they both agreed that if they could become one with the other person, they would do it. Their connection had strengthened to the point that just a look could convey an entire conversation.

Sometimes, when he seemed sad, it was because he hadn't seen Mace in a long time. At those times, though, he would always reassure her, telling her 'I've lost one dream but gained another'.

There was no limit to the amount of love she felt for her SEAL.

As he left his bench to circle around the table and settle behind her, she interlaced her fingers with his and rested them on her tummy, softly rounded with another of their dreams.

The End...

UNBREAKABLE SEAL

By

J.M. Madden

Dedication

As always, I have to thank my husband. If he hadn't allowed me to give the characters in my head the chance to run amok, I wouldn't be here now. I truly love you. You are my very own happy ever after.

To my semi-tolerant kids. Thank you. For staying outside when I needed you to, watching cartoons on a super low volume and bringing me icy diet-Cokes. I love you guys.

Acknowledgements

Bruce, you rock! I appreciate your time and effort in ensuring this book is as concise as possible.

Donna and Robyn, awesome crit partners, I'm so lucky to have you. Thank you for taking time out of your crazy schedules to make sure Max and Lacey were as yummy as possible. Love you guys.

Robinetta and Rebecca, this book would not have happened without your nursing input!!! Thank you so much!!!

And to my other beta-readers, Mayas, Sandie, Karla, Susie, you guys rock! Thank you so much for the support.

Mary, you kick my Comma-Queen ass, woman! But I appreciate it. Thank you!

To our men and women in the military, thank you from the bottom of my heart. I wish I could take you all out to dinner and give you a great big hug, because you all deserve it. Thank you for serving this beautiful country!

Readers, I hope you love Lacey and Max as much as the other characters in the Lost and Found series. Yes, DUNCAN's book is coming!

In a while…

CHAPTER ONE

MAX SWEPT HIS hand down his arm, but the spiders kept coming. They'd grabbed onto him when he'd opened the door of the Starbucks. At first there had been only one, easily dismissed. Then they had begun to multiply, tracking little points of blood across his skin as their feet dug in. Clenching his jaw, he scraped his hand down his arm again, praying nobody had seen, but the blood remained. The spiders began to come faster.

When they started to bite him it was aggravating more than anything, but as they started to dig deeper into his skin they became harder to ignore. His breaths began to speed up and he closed his eyes, counting in his head.

The training he'd worked for all his life began to unravel. Glancing around from beneath his brows, he wondered if anyone could see what he did. There were only a few people in the shop, one of which stood behind him.

As he stepped up to the counter it took everything he had to open his mouth to place his order, then count out money. The pain was excruciating. Even now he could feel the poison moving through his blood, sapping his energy. His traitorous body began to quake in an effort to combat the venom and his knees quivered, but he gulped in oxygen and straightened his spine.

He gave the grinning teenager his name and moved aside for the person behind him to order. Allowing himself to rest a hand on the counter, he counted off the seconds as he waited for his coffee. As his name was called, he swiped his hand down his arm one more time but the spiders just shifted out of the way, then back. He grabbed the cup and all but raced out of the shop.

As the cool ocean breeze brushed across his skin, the spiders began to multiply, then they began to crawl up his neck near his left ear. Goosebumps pebbled his skin and raised the hair on his nape. Lurching around the corner of the coffee shop, Max quivered with the restraint he was using to keep from freaking out. The cup dropped from his fingers and he turned to face the brick wall, planting his hands against the rough surface. The feel of the brick beneath his palms helped to center him, but the spiders continued their march, spreading poison as they did.

Max knew he had to wait the hallucination out, but when a particularly vicious one sank its fangs into the tender skin behind his ear, he could hold out no longer. Smacking his hands all over his head and arms, he pounded the spiders away. They only moved. They didn't leave. Panic gripped his throat in a vise and he could hardly breathe as he frantically tried to rid his skin of the infestation.

One of the biggest spiders crawled down his back, sharp feet stabbing as it went along his backbone. Max thought it was leaving but instead it settled mid-back. The pain that came from the pinchers digging into his spine was excruciating and he fell to his knees in agony.

LACEY KNEW THAT her crazy instincts were going to be the

death of her one of these days, but she followed her gut and the tall military man. The guy had drawn her attention as soon as she'd seen him. Actually, his ass had. Tight, luscious buns encased in khaki shorts always drew her eye. His muscular bearing screamed military, but the unkempt dark hair and stubbled jaw kind of threw her off. Former military, maybe? SEAL?

The guy seemed familiar to her. Maybe she'd seen him at the clinic.

Then her senses sharpened and she'd begun to watch all of him. When he swept his square hand down his muscular forearm the first time, she'd thought nothing of it. The second time had drawn her eyes. The third had made her frown. She realized that there was a subtle shaking moving through the man's body. As he'd placed his order and moved to lean on the counter, she waited to see what he would do.

As soon as the barista handed over the cup, he shoved through the door of the coffee shop. Her nurse senses jangling, she followed him out of the building, catching sight of his perfect ass turning the corner of the building. Without hesitation she followed him.

The poor guy had dropped the cup of coffee and was braced facing the wall. His fingers flexed against the brick and his arms strained. When he arched and cried out, then began swiping his palms down his arms, she moved forward. Lacey didn't see anything, but he was acting as if he'd walked into a swarm of bees. Her eyes scanned for anything that would make him act like that, but she couldn't see anything.

Knowing from experience that if she reached out to touch him she risked her life, she stopped a few feet away. "Sir, I need you to look at me. Whatever it is you think is attacking you isn't there. I promise you. Can you look at me?"

It only took a moment for him to look at her, but it seemed ever so much longer as she watched him strike himself over and over again. Obviously he felt it was the only way to rid himself of whatever he thought was after him. She continued to speak to him in the calm voice she'd used on many frantic patients until his movements began to slow.

"Hey, buddy, I know you can fight it off. Can you look at me?"

His dark head lifted and fierce, brilliant, yellow-gold eyes latched onto hers. Lacey felt like she'd just landed on a lunch order. She smiled at him as reassuringly as she could, then dared to step forward. She reached out a hand but he jerked away.

"No," he snapped, deep voice taut with strain. "They'll get you."

Lacey pressed forward, hand outstretched. "There's nothing there, I promise you."

She rested her hand on his quivering arm and ran it down his skin to clasp his broad wrist. His frantic gaze followed her movement, then he turned to her and looked her arm up and down. Blinking, he shook his head, then held his own arms out in front of himself. When he lifted his eyes to her, she knew the hallucination was gone.

She tried to put all the reassurance she could into the smile she directed at his dazed expression.

"What did you see?" she asked.

"Spiders," he gritted out. "Stabbing at my skin as they crawled up my body."

Holding his arms out again, he skimmed his palms down their length, as if brushing away the experience.

Lacey realized as she stood there that his eyes still seemed a little dazed. Was that normal?

She held out her hand. "Lacey Adams."

The man straightened and clasped her hand. "Maxwell Tate. Thank you."

Lacey gasped as he tugged her into his hard arms, then allowed herself to be bear hugged. She expected to be released quickly, but instead he held on, as if he needed the contact. The man smelled incredibly good, as if he'd just rolled in laundry softener. Relaxing, she allowed him to take what comfort he needed from her. She'd actually been hugged many times like this, as if she were the last lifeline in the world. She looped her arms around his waist and rubbed his back. He would let her go when he was able.

When she felt his nose nuzzle into her loose hair, sudden shivers danced down her spine and the tenor of the hold changed. She became aware of how solid his arms felt around her. Muscular pecs rested just above her breasts and he was curled over her to accommodate his size. Heavy thighs pressed directly against hers.

When he eased back, she thought he was releasing her, but instead he shifted his strong hands to cup her jaw. Before she could breathe out a question or protest, his head lowered and his mouth settled against hers.

Lacey's normally level-headed brain short circuited as his soft, full lips began to move over hers. The stubbly hair around his mouth tickled, but arousal surged through her body and she opened her mouth when his tongue glided over the seal of her lips. Damn. It had been an embarrassingly long time since she'd been kissed like this. Against her better judgment, she leaned into him, tilting her head.

The man groaned at her compliance and one of his arms wrapped around her arched back, clutching her tight. He shifted forward until their hips were more tightly aligned and she could feel exactly how much he was enjoying their kiss.

Then he jerked away.

Lacey blinked, shocked at the sudden loss. Her heart was thudding with anticipation, then suddenly bereft. She looked up and the guy was looking at her as if he didn't know who she was. Well, he didn't actually, but he'd instigated the kiss. Why was he looking at her as if she'd been the one to grab him?

He frowned down at her for several long seconds before his eyes cleared. "I'm sorry, do I know you?"

Surprise had her mouth falling open inelegantly. She cleared her throat. "Uh, no, not really." But as she looked at him, that sense of familiarity nagged at her again. "I'm an RN with Dr. Petrovic's office. Maybe I've seen you there?"

The man squinted. "Can't remember right this second."

Lacey eased back, straightening her purple t-shirt. "I thought you might need some help."

His eyes hardened and a shift settled over his body. Though he didn't move, tension saturated the air. "I'm fine now." His cold gaze drifted over her lips, then skimmed down her body. "Thank you for the *help*."

Lacey Adams seldom was at a loss for words, but as she watched the scrumptious man walk away, it was all she could do not to breathe fire. Of all the rude insinuations she'd ever been slammed with, that had to top the list as the most reprehensible. And she had a huge list. Hell, she'd worked at Walter Reed for years, caring for some of the most wounded warriors to come home. Some of the things she'd seen and heard would peel the paint off a car. She'd had one guy whose answer to everything was 'fuck you', but she'd even gotten along with him eventually. Still talked to him occasionally. And she'd done it because she'd genuinely loved doing her job. In spite of the hurtful things the men said, for the most part they *needed* the help and care.

And that's what she needed to remember. He didn't seem to know what he was doing. If he were in his right mind, he never would have said something so hurtful. She hoped so, anyway.

Lacey turned back toward the front of the store. She passed his drooling coffee cup and in a fit of aggravation kicked it across the alley, spattering coffee on her white tennis shoes. The little outburst felt good but guilt overwhelmed her as she stepped onto the sidewalk. Cursing her inner goody-two-shoes, she stomped back, picked up the cup, and dropped it into the trash before she went inside the store for her coffee.

Now she really needed it.

ONCE SHE HAD a few minutes to think about things and get over her outraged hurt, Lacey realized the guy needed help. It was obvious to her he'd been dealing with a serious hallucination when she found him. What would he have done if she hadn't intervened?

Concerned, she called Anna, the receptionist from the office. Though it was a Saturday, she knew Anna would remember a guy like him. The younger woman was always on the look out for bangin' hot guys, as she liked to call them.

She picked up on the first ring, sounding out of breath. "Hey, Lacey. What's up?"

Her voice sounded rushed and Lacey wondered if she'd interrupted something important. "Sorry to bother you at home, Anna, but do you remember a patient by the name of Maxwell Tate?"

Anna was humming on the other end of the line, as if someone else was drawing her attention. "Uh, I can't think of one right now. If I do I'll let you know. Okay?"

And she hung up.

Lacey grinned, knowing that Anna would have a juicy tale when she came into work on Monday.

As she walked down the street toward her apartment, basking in the glorious Virginia spring, she wondered if she would ever see the man again.

CHAPTER TWO

✦

M AX THOUGHT HE was having another damn hallucination. Two in the same day was not a stretch.

And what were the chances that she lived in his apartment
complex? The girl woman that had kissed him stood at the
bank of mailboxes at the end of the line of apartments. Her
thick dark brown hair was drawn back into a tight ponytail,
blowing over her shoulder as she dug in one of the boxes. His
bleary eyes traced down her back, settled on her heart-shaped
ass, then drifted down her lean legs. His body stirred for the
second time that day. Damn. She'd caused the first spark of
interest, too.

When he'd opened his eyes and found her in his arms,
confusion and embarrassment had swamped him because he
didn't remember how he'd gotten there. He'd lashed out. Yes,
he realized *he'd* kissed *her*, but it was easier to shift the blame.

Guilt nagged at him. She hadn't deserved that. He'd been
the one in the wrong. Before he could talk himself out of it, he
walked forward, catching her attention.

Her bright blue eyes widened under her thick bangs and
her mouth fell open a little. Slamming the door of her mailbox
shut, she turned to face him, arms crossed beneath her
substantial breasts. Max was momentarily sidetracked as he

caught the size of her…attributes. How the fuck had he forgotten the feel of those pressed against him?

When he looked up, she was glaring daggers at him. *Hell, not so slick anymore, Tate.* He'd just been caught. Royally. "Sorry about earlier," he forced out. "It wasn't your fault." He tried to give her a smile, but his mouth only twisted. Trying to salvage some of his pride he turned to walk away, but she followed.

"Hey, wait a minute! Mr. Tate!"

He turned back to her, waiting.

"Do you live here or are you stalking me?"

It was his turn to be confused. "I live here. On the fourth floor. Why?"

She shook her head. "You just looked familiar to me is all." Her eyes had softened. "I appreciate the apology. But I think you need to see someone…"

Laughing sharply, he turned away again. "Thanks for the advice," he tossed over his shoulder before he took off at a jog. He refused to think he was running away from an issue.

She hollered something behind him, but he couldn't quite make out the words as he pounded down the line of cars and up the stairs to his door. When he pushed it open, he realized he was a little out of breath. Seriously? He'd jogged maybe a quarter mile and he was out of breath? He'd never hear the end of that shit…Then he remembered. Nobody would be giving him shit again for not performing up to par.

The woman thought he needed to see someone. That was just hilarious. Who had he not seen in the past five months? Doctor after doctor, scrip after scrip. They'd rather shove pills at him than try to fix what was broken. But he was okay with that, really. He looked at the time. It was early, but he could take a couple now.

Crossing to the fridge, he looked at the calendar on the

door. It took him longer than it should have to realize he was looking at the wrong month and he rubbed his temples in aggravation. How the hell had he lost so much time?

Forcing his eyes to focus on the calendar again, his eyes drifted to the line of previous months along the bottom. Unerringly, his eyes found February 22nd. The night his world fell apart on a beach in Yemen.

Jerking his eyes away, he flung open the door and reached for a beer. It was the only thing inside his fridge. And he had enough to get wasted tonight.

LACEY FOUND HERSELF watching for Max everywhere. She even went to the Starbucks for the next three days hoping to see him again, but she didn't.

As she drove home from work that day her gaze scanned the area, looking for his broad back and dark hair. She pulled into her spot and her gaze drifted to the assigned parking spot for 4C. The motorcycle. Of course. She should have known. The damn thing had caught her eyes several times zipping through the lot and down the street. And now that she'd met him, she realized he had been riding it. The sleek black bike had to be the most dangerous thing in the lot. Because every man suffering from hallucinations needed a contraption to hurtle over a hundred miles per hour.

She shook her head as she walked past it and headed for the stairs. As she made herself jog up to the second floor, she wondered what else she could have done. She maybe could have called the cops, but what would they have done? *Hey officers, yeah, this guy dropped his coffee and kissed me, and says he has spiders on him.* They would have loved that. Probably would have hauled her ass off.

When she got to her door, her neighbor from directly

above her leaned against her doorjamb, waiting.

Lacey grinned at the young woman. Hannah Campbell was a livewire, but she made Lacey laugh. Petite and tan, she was her opposite in almost every way, but they clicked like sisters.

"What are you doing here?"

Hannah pushed away from the doorjamb and moved to take a couple of grocery bags from Lacey's hands so she could unlock the door.

"Just waiting to see if you want to go out tonight. It's the weekend and I know for a fact you haven't been getting out much."

Lacey cringed and pushed the door open. "I don't really want to go out, though. I appreciate the invitation, but wading through bars looking for the one guy who might give me the time of day is not my cup of tea. I'm a little old to be doing that kind of thing."

Furrowing her brows, Hannah shook her head. "Oh, please. You're thirty-two, yes, but you're not dead. You've been here for two years but you've only gone out with me three times. You're freaking gorgeous. Men fall all over themselves when you go out with me. Tell her Frank."

The tabby blinked at her sleepily when he heard his name but didn't leave the sunny windowsill he lounged upon.

Laughing at the over-thirty crack, Lacey set her bags on the kitchen counter and started to unload. Hannah took the fruits and veggies, leaning into the fridge to put them in the crisper drawer.

"Men don't fall all over me," she scoffed. "I know I'm boring, but I kind of like my boring life right now. It's a relief to not have the same stresses as I had before at Walter Reed. I'm enjoying the ease of it."

Hannah folded the bags in her hand and turned to face her,

giving her a scathing look the kind only a true friend could. "I think you're full of shit. You could have any man you gave the slightest encouragement to. And I think you miss those cases you had. I've seen your eyes get all excited when you talked about working there. You don't do that when you talk about Peter-dick's."

Lacey cringed at the name Hannah had given her current boss, but wondered if she were right. Yes, her private practice job gave her a manageable schedule, good pay. No sudden revamps in authority like at the military hospital.

And she didn't have to see the cases that broke her heart anymore. The soldiers that came in so wounded that it was a miracle they had survived as long as they had. The guys that were so courageous and stalwart in the face of what the staff had to do to help them.

After years of taking care of those guys, the constant strife and worry had worn her out. Before she left, Lacey had joked with one of the younger nurses that maybe her PTSD would dissipate if she were off the floor. And it was the truth. The constant anxiety had slowly whittled away at her soul. She'd gone for counseling for a few months after she'd left just to be able to sleep at night.

The private practice work gave her a chance to breathe. Yes, there were still military personnel that came in, but it wasn't the pressure cooker Walter Reed had been. Actually, it was damn boring at times.

She thought about the guy a couple floors above. "Have you met the guy above you? Max? Tall, dark-haired, has eyes the color of gold."

Hannah sighed and rolled her blue eyes dramatically. "Oh...my...god! He's so freakin' hot! Have you seen him on that motorcycle he rides? I've tried to get him to go out with me, but he seems oblivious. Barely even recognizes the perfection standing in front of him." She popped a hand onto her curvy hip, posing.

Lacey grinned at the younger girl's enthusiasm, but was secretly a little relieved. She took the reusable shopping bags from Hannah, stacked them together and put them in the cupboard where they belonged.

She didn't have any business wondering about the man upstairs. But she did. It was one of her downfalls when she worked at Walter Reed. Every single one of her patients had left an impact on her and she wondered about them long after they were gone. There were a few she still talked to occasionally, but not many.

Hannah eventually got bored and took off. Lacey crossed to the window to stroke Frank. The cat purred and rolled over so she could stroke his fat belly. She glanced down at the parking lot but didn't see anyone moving around. She looked down the street, hoping for a glimpse of a motorcycle, then shook her head at her foolishness.

CHAPTER THREE

✦

H ANNAH CALLED HER several days later, panic lacing her voice. "Lacey, you need to go check the guy upstairs. I think he wrecked his bike!"

"What?" She rubbed the sleepiness from her eyes. The credits to *Grey's Anatomy* were rolling on the flat screen across the room.

"I just passed him on the stairs. He's got road rash all over him and didn't even seem to notice he was bleeding. I asked him if he was okay, but he told me to fuck off. Seriously? I was being nice and he told me to fuck off. Who does that?"

Lacey sighed and pushed up from the couch. "Okay, I'll go check on him. He's probably in pain. Don't worry about it."

She hung up on Hannah before she had to listen to any more. Then, grabbing her bulging first-aid kit from the bathroom, she headed for the door. She glanced down at her sleep shorts and t-shirt, but decided she was decent enough to go out. Jogging up the steps, she waved at Hannah, head poked through her own door on the third floor, then continued up to the fourth floor. 4C was directly to the left and the door was cracked open. There was a smear of blood on the door.

Lacey leaned her head toward the crack, listening, but didn't hear anything. "Mr. Tate?"

She rapped her knuckles on the panel, but there was no response. Pushing the door open, she looked inside.

The apartment was almost completely bare. A recliner sat in front of a dark TV. But there was nobody around. She stepped into the room. "Mr. Tate?" she called.

Again, no response. Daring to walk further into the dim apartment, she flipped lights on as she went. This apartment was set up exactly the same as hers, so she headed toward the back. The bedroom door stood wide open and she paused on the threshold. In the light from the hallway, she could see Maxwell Tate lying on a messy bed on his stomach, staring at her. Lacey cringed when she saw the blood dripping from his dangling right hand onto the carpet. A sizeable puddle had already formed.

"Mr. Tate. Can you hear me? I wanted to check and make sure you were okay."

He blinked but didn't move. Lacey hit the light switch but nothing happened, so she moved forward cautiously. "I need you to say something so that I know you're with me."

His pale eyes angled up and focused in on her. "I'm here."

"Good." She smiled. "Can I check you over? I'm a nurse."

Frowning, he nodded against the mattress.

Lacey slipped on a pair of gloves and moved closer to the bed. She grabbed a discarded towel to drop beneath his slowly dripping hand then leaned around, looking for the source of the blood. "Mr. Tate Max may I touch you?"

"Please," he sighed, eyes latched on her.

Lacey grasped his wrist in her left hand and lifted. The entire underside of his long arm was scraped up, as if he'd slid for a good ways on pavement. She cringed and pulled a penlight from her bag, skimming it over the abrasion. It looked like a fairly clean scrape, but he definitely needed to have it cleaned. She let his arm dangle again and flashed the light over his back. She couldn't contain a gasp as she caught sight of his scraped skin through the ripped black t-shirt.

"Max, I need to do a quick exam, okay? Can I listen to your back?"

He didn't tell her no so she drew out her stethoscope and listened to his breath sounds. Sounded clear, although a little inhibited. Maybe just because of the way he was lying. She wrapped the blood pressure cuff around his opposite arm. Surprisingly good. He flinched when she ripped open the Velcro and gave her a dirty look, then fell back to his belly. Lacey checked what she could reach and what he would allow her to.

"Were you wearing a helmet, Max?"

"No," he sighed.

"I'm going to check your head, okay?"

He didn't answer, so she reached down and ran her fingers over his scalp. There was a goose egg on the back of his head about the size of a golf ball, but no obvious blood. Kneeling in front of him again, she reached forward to rest her hand on his brow. His eyes had fallen shut and he flinched when she touched him, but allowed her to flash the penlight into his eyes. They responded exactly as they were supposed to. He slammed his lids shut and turned his head in the opposite direction, away from her.

Back on her feet, Lacey flashed the light down his long legs. She could see blood on the sheets where he'd shifted them, but couldn't find the source of the blood.

"I think you need to go to the ER."

Those golden eyes snapped open in the dim light. "No."

Lacey sighed, shaking her head at how obstinate men could be. Military especially.

She prodded at him. "Max, you need to hop in the shower to wash off this blood and dirt if you're not going to go to the emergency room."

He mumbled something but didn't respond.

Crossing to the bathroom, she flicked on the light, happy when it actually worked. Her eyes were drawn to the counter and the black gun resting there. "Hell," she muttered. Picking the Sig Sauer up she cleared the chamber, a little chilled when she realized it was loaded, with one in the barrel. She put the gun under the cupboard and the clip in the mirrored medicine cabinet, then turned the shower on.

Max hadn't moved an inch during her time in the bathroom.

"Max, you need to get up. I have the shower running."

He mumbled something then pushed up on the mattress, muscles bulging. He sat at the side of the bed, staring into the hallway.

"Max."

He looked up at her, his shadowed golden eyes desolate.

Lacey felt her heart lurch in her chest. She'd seen sadness many times over in her career, but the absolute anguish in his expression made her eyes burn. Unable to turn from him, she sat down on the mattress beside him. "What's wrong?"

He blinked and shook his head. "They're gone."

Lacey had a feeling she knew what was wrong, but she asked anyway. "Who?"

Max sighed and looked away, then ripped his t-shirt over his head, not even acknowledging the pain he had to be in. Lacey ran her eyes down his chest, telling herself she was doing it for medical reasons, but she couldn't help but remember how that cobbled stomach felt against her breasts.

He stood up and started limping for the shower, shoving

his running shorts down his hips as he went. Once again, she was torn between checking the scrapes on his back and admiring his rounded, tight butt. Something caught her attention and her gaze drifted up. There was a deep scar on the right side of his body, almost an inch deep and about the size of a fist, just below his shoulder blade. Before she could drag her eyes away, he disappeared into the steam. What the hell had done that?

Lacey shook herself, wondering why she'd lost her focus. Yeah, the guy was good looking, but damn. She'd never become so distracted by a man's body that she couldn't function. Hell, ninety-nine percent of her patients were male, but this one was truly affecting her.

Removing the gloves, she folded them into themselves. After the shower she would be able to disinfect the scrapes. Then she could get out of here.

As she waited for him to get out of the shower, she glanced around. There were no decorations on the walls. The bed had sheets on it and a light blanket, but that was it. Dirty clothes were scattered everywhere. The drawers of the single bureau were out and a little twisted. As if he'd tried to push them home but a corner had caught.

Unable to help herself, she kicked his dirty clothes into a pile in the corner. She planned to strip the bed but couldn't find spare sheets in the hall closet. Only a tall gun locker. Really?

She did what she could with what she found, but ended up running down to her apartment and grabbing a spare fitted sheet. She threw his in her washer and jogged back upstairs to make his bed. Frowning, she looked at the open bathroom door. He should have been out by now.

"Max?" She knocked on the panel loud enough that he

should have heard her, but there was no response.

Creeping forward she peered inside, but didn't see his form behind the shower curtain. Concerned she crossed and ripped the plastic back.

Max sat on the floor of the shower, head bent. Even from a distance she could tell the water was ice cold. "What the hell are you doing?"

His dark head stayed bent but he flinched as if he awoke. She shut the water off and knelt on the floor, then rested her hand on his nearest arm. "Max."

Finally, he blinked up at her. "Oh, hey Angel."

She tried not to be affected by the endearment, because it was probably just a symptom of his psychosis, but it had been a long time since she'd heard anything like it. Giving him a look, she tried to urge him to his feet. Tendrils of blood were starting to curl away down the drain and she saw the raw scrape down his right thigh. Did she even have bandages that big?

She stood and held her hand out to him. "Come on. You need patched up."

He looked up at her hand, then her face, and seemed to come to a decision. Using a hand on the floor, he pushed to his feet. Lacey reached for a towel from the rod but he stepped out onto the rug before she could even hold it up.

Max's hand drew her gaze though when he reached past her to set a lethal looking eight-inch black knife next to the sink before taking the towel. Where the hell had that come from? She'd scanned the bathroom after she'd found the gun, but hadn't seen anything else.

Lacey looked up into his face, searching for the explanation on why he would have had a knife like that in the shower with him. Did he think she was a threat? No. She wasn't naïve.

She'd had patients commit suicide on her floor before.

Was Max one of those that were looking for that release?

Tears burned against her eyelids, but she refused to let them fall.

He took the towel from her and wrapped it around his hips. Lacey motioned to the toilet seat lid. "Have a seat, Speed Racer."

He dropped to his ass, lean muscles of his abdomen tightening, towel edge slipping down between his strong thighs. For the first time she noticed a wide, stylized tattoo on the back of his shoulder, opposite from the deep scar. From this angle she could see feathers but not what it was exactly.

The extra-large first aid kit sat on the counter. Lacey pawed through it, looking for the broad pads and the antibacterial salve.

Max didn't move when she lifted his arm to blot the fresh blood away. He shifted his gaze to her, scanning her face. Lacey gave him a smile as she ran her fingers over his cold skin. "Aren't you chilly?"

Shaking his head, he let his eyes fall to the floor. "Didn't even feel it," he murmured.

"Well," she told him, "you can take my word on how cold it is." She shivered dramatically.

The corner of his very full mouth tipped up in a slight grin, then his eyes fogged over again. He moved his arm when she guided him to, but he didn't talk to her anymore, no matter how many times she tried to start the conversation.

As she tugged the towel away from his thigh there was no hint of modesty. She tried to drape it to cover his distracting nakedness, but ended up just drawing more attention and embarrassing herself. She spread antibacterial from the point of his hip down almost to his knee, then she started bandaging.

Lacey prided herself on having a complete, sufficient first-aid kit, but by the time she was done with Max her bag was feeling empty. The big, silent man had also started to shudder with cold.

Her heart ached for him. Against her better judgment, she was truly concerned.

"Max, do you have meds you need to take at bedtime? Max?"

He blinked his golden eyes at her. Then, without even looking at what he was doing, he reached for a pillbox on the counter. It was separated into days of the week. Narrowing his eyes, he looked at the box, finally selecting a full section of pills. It wasn't even Thursday, Lacey noticed, just the next full one. He tipped a pile of pills into his hand and threw them into his mouth dry. Cringing, Lacey quickly ran a glass of water from the faucet and handed it to him.

She looked at the pills in the next slot and observed several psychiatric and psychotropic medications. As she recognized what they were, she shook her head, confused. There were several here that did the same thing, and several more that treated completely opposite things. In total, he took eleven pills at night. Some of them very addictive.

Surely he wasn't prescribed all of these at once.

"Where are your bottles, Max?"

Without looking, he tugged open one of the drawers in the vanity. All of the bottles were there and as she started reading, she realized they were indeed prescribed at the same time and for opposite things. There were also five different doctors' names listed on the amber bottles. Petrovic, her own doctor, was one of them. So she *had* probably seen him at work.

Cupping his rough chin in her hand, she made him focus on her. "Max, how long have you been taking all these pills?"

Shrugging, he frowned. "Not sure. A while. They help with the dreams."

And created new ones. One of the most powerful pills in the box had a well-documented history of inducing hallucinations.

The spiders.

Knot in her throat, she urged him up off the toilet. The towel fell at his feet, but they didn't pay it any attention. Lacey walked the big man to the bed and knew that she was going to have to get involved. She snorted to herself. Like she wasn't already.

Max sighed as he flopped into the bed, burrowing his head into the pillow. Lacey tugged the light blanket over his lax form, taking the barest moment to brush her hand over his granite hard shoulder. Feeling bold, she pulled the corner away again to look at the tattoo. A stylized eagle screamed down his back, talons out, clutching a three-pronged trident. Navy SEAL. She should have known.

Lacey pulled the blanket back over his shoulder.

CHAPTER FOUR

✦

M AX WOKE WARM and content, as well as surprisingly at ease. What was up with that? The first time he shifted in the bed though, he had to groan. *What the fuck did I do this time?*

Flipping the blanket away, he sat up enough to look down his legs. Bright white bandages covered the outside of his right thigh and the inside of his right arm. As he held it up to look, he caught sight of the sheet beneath his bare ass. Confusion swamped him. When did he get blue sheets?

Swinging his legs to the side, he planted his big feet and looked around. The window was dark beyond the blinds, but he had no sense of 'when'. Must be evening. Pushing to his feet aching in places he didn't remember hurting he padded to the bathroom. It was as he was taking a leak when he realized something was off. Looking around, his gaze fell to the counter.

What had he done with his piece?

He finished his business and went into the bedroom, searching the bedside table. Not there. Bureau top. Empty, as always. More than concerned now, he headed for the living room.

And stopped dead.

A woman was curled up in his brown leather recliner,

sound asleep.

If she hadn't been in *his* brown leather recliner, he'd have been worried he'd walked into the wrong apartment again.

He eased around a few feet to get a better look at her face. Recognition teased at his brain, but he couldn't say exactly where he had seen her before. There were a lot of people that lived in the apartment complex; maybe she was one of them.

But as he continued to survey her delicate features, the fine dark brows arched prettily over her even features, he felt like he knew the taste of her very kissable dark pink lips. Which was ridiculous, right?

As his eyes traced down her curvy shape, it was obvious she had no bra on beneath that thin t-shirt. He wondered what she would do if she woke up with a naked man standing over her. As he looked down at himself, he smirked. Make that an aroused, naked man.

As if she'd heard his thoughts, her bright-blue eyes fluttered open.

Then widened with shock.

Max tried to hide himself, but it was difficult when he was erect.

A hectic flush of color darkened her cheeks and for a moment he felt bad for embarrassing her. Then he remembered this was his apartment.

"Mind if I ask what you're doing here?"

She blinked at him sleepily and straightened in the recliner. "No, sorry, I fell asleep. You were having some problems earlier, so I helped you out."

Max scowled. "What kind of problems?"

Brows raised in surprise, she motioned to the bandages on his leg. "I believe you wrecked your motorcycle. Not sure how else you would have gotten that much road rash."

Max cataloged his injuries. That sounded feasible with the long scrapes decorating his body. His arm felt like it'd been filleted. He had a flash of skidding on pavement, then everything going dark. *Fuck.* His bike.

Turning from the room and her, he went to the bedroom long enough to pull on a pair of athletic shorts and shoes. He snatched a t-shirt from the dirty-clothes pile, scowling again when he realized she must have straightened up. Walking back into the room, ignoring the grating pain down his right side, he frowned at her. "Where's my Sig?"

Lucky for her, she didn't pretend ignorance. "The gun is under the cupboard. The clip in the medicine cabinet."

Without a word, he retrieved his weapon, slipping it into a holster inside the band of his shorts. Her eyes focused on the lump at his waist when he walked into the living room, but she didn't say a word.

Gritting his teeth against the scalding rawness of his injuries, he jogged down the four flights of stairs to the parking area. The woman followed along behind silently.

Oh, hell. No... His mint condition Buell Firebolt XB12R was in shambles. He hadn't even parked the damn thing, just dropped it on its side. At least he was in the right parking spot. Max started to kneel down but the ripping pain in his side stopped him. Instead, he planted his hands on his hips and glowered.

When he looked up, the woman was gone.

Another kick in the balls.

Scrubbing his hands over his hair, he gritted his teeth to keep in the howl of rage. After all the shit that he'd gone through, why the fuck couldn't he get a break?

Max rubbed his eyes, trying to remember what had happened with the motorcycle, but the last day was a blank. Maybe he'd cracked his head.

Retrieving the key from the ignition, which he'd forgotten earlier, he turned for the stairs. Every step he climbed hurt more than the last. All he could think about were the pills at the top of the stairs. They would remove the pain.

By chance, he glanced up at 2C when he circled the landing. The door with its cheery flower wreath stood open and he saw the woman that had been in his apartment pass the open doorway. She turned to him when he paused and he was shocked at her tear-stained cheeks.

"Have you seen Frank?"

Max started to shake his head, not knowing who the hell Frank was.

"My cat," she explained. "I came down from your apartment and my door was cracked open. He must have slipped out."

Fresh tears trailed down her cheeks and Max felt something shift inside him, thawing. He felt bad she'd lost her cat. The hopeful expression on her face implied she would like him to find the damn thing. It had been a long time since anybody had depended upon him.

Was he worth depending upon? Damn, he needed the numbness back. But as he looked at her heartbroken face, and felt the bandages she'd put on his arm and leg, he couldn't just walk away. It just wasn't in him to be so cruel.

He sighed, fighting away the biting need for oblivion. "What does he look like?"

"Tiger striped with a white diamond on his chest. He has a blue collar on."

Max turned to look around, but there was nowhere a cat could hide on the landing. Without a word, he limped back down the steps to the ground level. He'd never had a cat in his life, so he had no idea how to even call one or find one. If he were a cat, he would be looking for pussy, he smirked, or food. At the base of the steps he looked around.

He had no idea what time it was, only that it was deep into the night. Nobody moved. No vehicles on the street. As he peered under bushes and around cars, he prayed nobody called the cops on him.

Using the flashlight on his phone, Max found the cat across the small patch of yard between complexes. It was curled up under a bush, eyes wide and dark with fear. When he reached under the bush for the animal, it spat and took off. With a mighty lunge, Max grabbed the damn thing by the tail and reeled it back, then grabbed it by the scruff of the neck with his other hand. It continued to spit and hiss as he carried it back to his building, then up the stairs to her apartment.

The woman cried out when she saw them and rushed forward to take the monster from his hands. It immediately curled into her arms, purring to beat the band but turned its head enough to glare at him. Max shook his head. "He was across the way, at the next apartment building."

She cringed and he assumed that was a long way for the cat to go.

"Frank's not allowed outside. Thank you so much for finding him."

As he looked down into her blue eyes, with their dark rings around the iris, his chest swelled a little that he'd actually done something good. As ridiculous as it sounded, it had been a long time since he'd felt like he'd contributed to anything. She would have a little less heartbreak in her life.

As he turned to go, she reached out to touch his elbow. "Wait, Max."

She carried the cat inside the apartment and he heard a

door close deeper inside. When she returned, she was cat-less. Pushing her door open wider, she motioned him inside.

"You've ripped open your bandages."

She motioned to his thigh.

He'd felt something pop when he'd lunged for the cat, but the pain had been a constant burn. The blood that coated the nylon of his shorts and ran down his leg meant he'd ripped it pretty good. Of course. No good deed goes unpunished.

Max shrugged away her concern. "No big deal. It'll stop eventually."

She raised a brow at him and rested her hands on her hips.

Max wanted to believe the concern was for him, but he thought it was just her nurse bossiness.

How the hell did he know she was a nurse? Was that another detail he'd lost, like the fact that he'd wrecked his motorcycle at some point and totally didn't remember it?

"Are you a nurse?" he asked, curious if he was right.

She nodded her head. "I told you that last night. My name is Lacey."

Lacey. He had known that. And as he looked at her face, he realized he remembered her, too. *Angel.*

She tilted her head at him. "We've met several times, actually. You were at a Starbucks last week and had an issue and you ended up kissing me. Do you remember that?"

His jaw fell open and she could have knocked him over with a feather. "I kissed you?"

She nodded, eyes flashing.

But now that she mentioned it, he did remember kissing her. Explained why he thought he'd known her taste.

Max nodded his head, dazed. "I think I do remember."

Actually, he was horrified. The Starbucks trip sounded vaguely familiar and kissing her, but nothing else. "What issue?

What did I do?"

Dark brows furrowed over her eyes. "You were hallucinating that you had spiders on you."

Oh, yeah. Shuddering, he looked down at his arms. The spiders weren't there, but he remembered the feel of their feet stabbing into his skin. Unable to help himself, he swiped his hands down his skin.

Lacey stepped forward and took his hands into her own. "I'm going to tell you something and I want you to listen to me. This is the most coherent I've ever seen you and I want you to hear what I'm saying. You're not going to like this, but you need help. You are on too many medications."

Max snatched his hands away.

"They are cancelling each other out," she continued, "and causing you more problems. I don't know what your original injury or illness is, but the pills that you're on are making it worse."

Confusion swirled in his mind but what she said had the ring of truth. There were too many inconsistencies in his life and he'd been flirting with a reckless death for too long. But why bother to stay around? It wasn't as if anybody needed him. The government was releasing him from his service because he wasn't any good to them any more. Since Yemen he had the lung capacity of a newborn. His family didn't care. In his heart, he knew he'd been taking too many pills, but they had him in their grip now, and he didn't have to worry about all that other crap when he took them.

She seemed to sense what he was thinking, because she stepped forward into his space, a finger pointing at his face. "And let me tell you something, Bub, you better not be thinking about offing yourself. No Navy SEAL I know would dare even think that."

He choked out a laugh, somehow not shocked she'd guessed his branch. "You'd probably be surprised."

Dreams of suicide haunted him nightly. And daily. He'd even kind of tried a couple times. Hell, once he'd written a note to his parents and everything, then sat in the tub with the muzzle of his beloved Sig in his mouth. It was one of the greatest personal humiliations of his life that he hadn't gone through with it. That had been a few months ago.

Lacey caught his neck in her soft hands and pulled his face down to hers. "You are so worth fighting for Max Tate. I don't know what has happened to you in your life, but I refuse to let you be one of the twenty-seven men that kills themselves every day."

The number sank into his mind and he wavered. But what the hell did she know about what he'd gone through?

"You have no idea what you're asking," he growled.

Tears filled her eyes. "I do."

For several long seconds he held her liquid look, but he finally had to turn his head away. It was too close to a promise, holding that determined gaze.

Regretting he had to do it, he pulled from her grip on his neck. The hope in her expression dimmed and he felt like he'd just stomped on a kitten's tail, but she let him go. Her soft, comforting hands fell to her sides.

Max felt bereft, as if he'd lost his team all over again, but he straightened his spine. This woman was nothing to him. And she was seeing what she wanted to see. All women looked at men like they needed to be saved.

Forcing himself to back away, he gave her a mock salute. "Have a nice night, Angel."

He was almost to the door when she called his name. Unable to deny one last glance of her he turned...and caught her in his arms as she pressed up against his body. Strong arms wrapped around his neck, then her lips found his. Shock held him immobile for several long seconds, then he let himself sink into the heat of her mouth. She tasted of hope and sex, two things his life had been completely bereft of for too long. Unable to do otherwise, he took everything she had to give. Cupping her jaw, he tilted his head for a better angle.

Max lost all sense of time and space as he cradled her to him, basking in the warmth she poured into his soul. It burned away the fogginess he walked through every day and sharpened the need he'd felt, but tried not to acknowledge. He hardened against her lush belly. Flexing into her softness, he let his hands drift south to cup her hips.

Lacey cried out against his mouth and rocked her pelvis into his erection. Max could have easily dropped to the floor and satisfied them both, but some niggling sense of chivalry made him hesitate. What right did he have to take advantage of her kindness that way?

Max shuddered as he slowed his movements and prayed he had the strength to actually let her go. Lacey tugged herself out of his arms though, leaving him feeling more bereft than before. Her bright eyes were languid with desire and her cheeks were flushed with arousal. The lips he'd feasted at were puffy from his attention.

Max had never seen anything more beautiful.

Lacey rubbed her face with her hands and folded her arms beneath her sharp-nippled breasts. "I didn't mean for it to go that far. I'm sorry I attacked you that way."

Chuckling, he stroked a finger down her cheek. "It was definitely unexpected." He paused, knowing he had to create some distance. "I don't know if we should do it again, though. You're a nice lady, Lacey, but I'm not a good bet."

Her eyes narrowed on his and he could almost feel the ire building. "You damn well could be, if you gave yourself a chance. You need help, Max, to see what I see."

Turning away, she crossed to a small desk and grabbed a pen and paper. His eyes traced down her narrow back as she scribbled something down, then added another line of script. For some reason his throat was tight, as if he'd just missed his boat.

Lacey returned and held the paper out to him. Max took it reluctantly, reading the neat lettering on the page. *Eric O'Hanrahan*. There was a string of letters after his name Max assumed meant he had a lot of schooling.

"I don't need this."

He tried to hand the paper back but she held her hands up defensively. "You need it. Your doctors are trying to medicate the problem away and you're not dealing with the underlying issue. I've seen it before when I worked at Walter Reed. And it's not something you can kick on your own."

Max's eyes narrowed on her and her assertions suddenly took on weight. If she'd worked at Walter Reed, maybe she *was* seeing something he didn't. Without saying anything more, he took the paper from her hand and folded it away, then walked out the door.

CHAPTER FIVE

✦

LACEY FORCED THE tears back as she watched his strong back disappear through her door. Dragging in gulps of oxygen, she tried to make sense of what she'd just done.

Hopefully enough to get him to seek help.

Technically he wasn't a patient, but her professional demeanor had completely gone out the window with Maxwell Tate. What the hell had she been thinking, kissing him like that?

Pushing the door shut, she leaned her back against it, praying that he would use the information she'd given him. He was seriously overmedicated and those medications were making him suicidal. Was that the complete answer? Probably not. But the pills concerned her the most.

No matter what he'd done he deserved to be treated with the utmost care by the medical community he depended upon, and it wasn't happening. She had a feeling they were all trying to medicate the problem away.

She'd seen it before.

MAX PUT THE paper on the fridge door, though he doubted he would use it. He'd already been to so many doctors and counselors it wasn't even funny. They couldn't make him feel better about getting his team killed. Only the pills dulled the pain enough to make him forget. Yes, he knew he probably took too many, but he didn't know any other way to deal.

Over the next few days, every time he went to the fridge for a beer, the swirly, feminine writing on the butterfly paper caught his gaze, silently demanding attention. At the bottom she'd written her name and her phone number. He'd long ago memorized it. In frustration one night he crumpled the paper and tossed it in the trashcan. When he reached inside the fridge for a beer, he realized he'd already emptied it.

Cursing roundly, he went to the bedroom for his pants and wallet. His bike was still in the shop, so at the base of the stairs he turned for the street. The closest gas station was only a couple blocks away. He could walk to it.

He trudged toward the lit corner, falling into a mindless rhythm. When the attack came from behind, he didn't even have the chance to defend himself. Fists pummeled him from every direction, stealing his air and sight almost immediately. When he hit the ground, kicks started flying his way. He felt something snap and assumed he'd just lost a couple of ribs. When a boot sailed toward his head, he was too slow to protect himself. His world went dark.

LACEY ROLLED OVER in bed, reaching blindly for her phone. Carrie Underwood's *Blown Away* blared. As she fumbled it to her ear, she had a flashback of receiving calls from Walter Reed.

It wasn't Walter Reed on the other end of the line. It was the local hospital. The woman on the other end described a man they had in their ER that sounded like Max.

"Yes," she confirmed, "that sounds like my upstairs neighbor."

She listened to the nurse on the other end of the line for several long seconds, then told her that she would be there in a few minutes.

As she pressed the screen to end the call, she wondered what on earth had happened to her mundane life.

The ER was fairly quiet when she walked in. An aide led her to a curtained off area, and when she pulled back the curtain, she found Max sprawled on a gurney, apparently asleep. The nurse escorting her smiled gently. "We gave him a sedative because he was agitated, but as soon as we told him you were coming he calmed. The police haven't found who mugged him."

Lacey gave her a weak smile and stepped to the side of the bed. Max had a new bandage on his forehead, the corner of his mouth was swollen and there were other scattered bruises and scrapes down his body. His right eye was purple. All of the bandages she'd put on him hours before had been replaced.

"He has three cracked ribs and a bump on his head, but no concussion. Looks like he was recently in a crash or something."

Nodding, she took the pill pack of pain pills the nurse handed her but dropped them in her purse. "Wrecked his bike last night."

The woman nodded with a knowing shake of her head.

"Everything else looked okay. Keep him quiet and make him take deep breaths occasionally, even though it hurts."

Lacey nodded, familiar with the routine. Reaching out, she ran her hand through his thick, dark hair. Lion gold eyes popped open and stared straight at her, as if he'd known where she would be standing.

Lacey forced a smile. "Hey, big man. You wanna blow this

pop-sicle stand?"

Without a word Max sat up with a surge, but he couldn't contain the wince and gasp. He leaned on an arm, favoring his injured left side. Lacey held a hand out, but he ignored it and slid off the gurney. When the release nurse pushed a wheel-chair forward, he dropped into it, again without a word.

Max situated himself down into her car carefully, one broad hand clutching the doorframe. Once inside he rested his head on the headrest, eyes closed. When she parked the car, he climbed out to limp beside her. It wasn't until Lacey let them into her apartment that he spoke.

"I'm sorry they had to call you," he told her. "Your number was the only one I could think of. They took my wallet and my bike's still in the shop. The cops didn't find my keys."

Lacey tried not to wince. In other words, if he'd had any-body else in the world to call, he would have. At the last minute, she'd written her number below Eric's on that paper she'd handed him days ago. Apparently he'd memorized it. She wondered if he'd called the other number.

"You're fine, Max. I'm glad they called me. We'll get in touch with maintenance tomorrow to get you new keys for your apartment."

He nodded and looked a little lost, standing in her living room.

"Please, make yourself at home. Can I get you anything to eat or drink?"

Shaking his head from side to side, he sank down onto the edge of the couch. Lacey turned on the TV and handed him the remote control, then walked down the hallway to put fresh sheets on her bed. She'd changed them just the other day, but Max sleeping in the same sheets she had seemed way too intimate. If he took the bed, she could sleep on the couch. Like she did every night before the infomercials woke her up.

When she returned to the living room the screen had gone dark. Max was propped in the corner of the couch, body tilted at a strange angle to accommodate his sore side. He looked up when she stepped into the room.

"Come on. I've made you a bed."

He pushed to his feet without a word and followed her down the hallway, hand across his midsection. When she led him into the master bedroom, he paused. "I don't want to take your bed. I've already inconvenienced you enough."

Lacey shook her head. "You're not inconveniencing me. I sleep on the couch a lot anyway."

Without arguing further he sat, then lay down, moving slowly to not jar himself.

"If you lay on your hurt side it usually feels better," she murmured, dragging the sheet over top of him.

Max rolled onto his left side and sighed. "You're right," he whispered.

Then, between one breath and the next, he was asleep, snuffling softly. Lacey stared down at him, once again wondering what the hell she was supposed to do with him. He was a borderline suicidal prescription drug addict who refused to get help. And he tied her heart in knots. After years of nursing experience, she had no way to distance herself from him.

She went back out to the living room and lay down on the couch, pulling a quilt over top of herself.

But, seemingly minutes later, something roused her. She padded to the bedroom door and peered in.

Max had pushed the covers away and lay on his back, brow furrowed in pain. His fists were raised as if he planned to fight phantoms. Lacey called his name and he startled, but his head rocked toward her. For several seconds he blinked, obviously trying to right his reality. His fists released and he raised one hand to his head. "I can't make sense of anything right now," he whispered.

And with those few words, her heart ached for him even more. She crossed to the bed and sank to the edge, her hip resting against his. "I know, Max. Just know that you're in a safe place right now, okay? I can stay right here with you if you'd like."

Without a word he curled onto his left side again, but this time he wrapped his arms around her and buried his face into her thigh. Lacey wrapped her arm around his shoulders and tried to fight back tears. All her life she'd helped people, but she'd never been so affected by a tortured soul. What was it about this man, right now, that wouldn't let her let go?

She sat on the side of the bed like that for a long time, dozing off a few times. At some point, Max shifted back and she lay down beside him, pulling the sheet over them both. He wrapped his heavy arms around her and spooned her from behind. Lacey was a little worried when he wrapped his arms around her so tightly, but her body seemed to know everything was cool. Within seconds they were both asleep.

MAX OPENED HIS eyes then slammed them shut again. The damn window shades were open. He moved to roll over and realized his left arm was trapped. Panic gripped him until he realized that he wasn't exactly being held down—there was just something on his arm. Slitting his eyes against the brightness, he opened them.

An angel lay facing him, dark curly hair fluffed around her face, her full lips parted to breathe. Lacey. He remembered calling her to the hospital after he got mugged, but not much after that.

Humiliation choked the air in his throat. He was a god-damned Navy SEAL, and he'd been mugged like a common citizen. He'd been so out of his head for a beer that he'd walked into an area muddle-headed from pills. Disgust coated his tongue and made his stomach twist. Thirty-two fucking years old and he was being mugged by kids and relying on women to come to his rescue.

He was sick of this. Waking up wondering what the hell he'd done the night before. Losing time. Existing in limbo. Not being the man he remembered striving to be.

Lacey raised her head, allowing him to pull his arm out from beneath her. He moved to sit up and was suddenly reminded he had broken ribs. And a knock on his skull. Along with five million other aches and pains. His skin burned form the road rash as the bandages chafed against it. Oh, yeah. "Fuck," he breathed.

Lacey sat up beside him and rested a hand on his back. "Can I get you some ibuprofen?"

He nodded, holding his body as still as he could. He'd had a broken rib before, but not three. When Lacey returned with four small brown pills in her hand, he took them quickly. Then didn't know what to do. Glancing at the clock on the bedside table, he saw it was too early to call the apartment management for keys. Easing back down against the mattress, he took a careful breath.

"Dude, you've got the biggest black rain cloud following you right now," Lacey told him. "Is your life always like this? One calamity after another?"

He rolled his head to look at her and sighed. Damn, she was something. Mussed and her eyes a little swollen from sleep, but still incredibly beautiful.

"No," he answered finally. "At least not up until a few months ago. Then things truly went to hell. I will admit that the past two days have been spectacular."

She laughed a little, then laid back down beside him, her eyes drifting to a slit. "If you want to talk about it, I'm willing to listen."

Did he want to talk about it? He never had, other than detailed debriefs after the mission. Max blinked and looked up at the ceiling. He'd never had anybody interested enough to ask. "I lost men and my career when I took a bullet to the back. I have no air to do anything. I get winded running up the stairs."

"Wow," she whispered. "I'm so sorry."

Emotion suddenly tightened the grip on his throat and he had to blink repeatedly. She didn't say anything, just lay with him as he remembered his men and tried to control his emotions.

"I wondered about the scar on your back," she whispered. "I've seen enough gunshot wounds to recognize them when I see them."

He rolled his head to look at her. "I bet you've seen bad stuff at Walter Reed."

"Mm," she agreed. Her eyes drifted shut and he realized she was suddenly the one fighting not to lose it in front of the other.

"I'm sorry. I shouldn't have asked."

Lacey's eyes opened and she gave him a weary smile. "That's okay, Max. I think we've both seen more than we should have in our lives. But I've seen truly miraculous things as well." Reaching over, she gave him a half hug but pulled away entirely too soon. She gave his undamaged arm a pat and stood up from the bed. "If you don't mind, I'm going to take a quick shower. Then I'll make us some breakfast."

He nodded, watching as she dug clothes from a bureau. There was a flash of red panties before she buried them in the pile. As she disappeared into the bathroom, his senses sharpened and he listened to her movements inside. The shower came on, then there was rustling as things dropped to the floor. During a quiet pause, he imagined her standing naked in front of the shower, waiting for the stream to warm. Then came the sound of splashing water as she stepped inside.

Arousal flowed through his body, in spite of the innumerable aches and pains he was dealing with and he took a minute to wrap his hand around his dick. It had been a long time since he'd been interested in anything, so he allowed himself to enjoy the feeling for a moment. In another life he'd have joined her in that shower without hesitation.

He must have dozed off listening to the water fall and his hand on his dick, because when he next opened his eyes, Lacey stood at the side of the bed. Her damp, dark hair was pulled to the side of her neck and her face was clear of makeup. She smiled at him and held out a steaming cup. "Thought you might like a cup of tea. Sorry it's not coffee."

Max pushed himself upright in the bed as carefully as he could and leaned back against the headboard, taking the mug in his hands. He had to smirk when he read, *Yes, I'm your nurse. What stupid fucking thing did you do?* on the side of the cup, but decided it was very appropriate. What stupid thing *hadn't* he done recently?

Lacey disappeared down the hallway, returning a few seconds later with a plate of food. Max stared at it for several moments before taking it from her hands. It was more food than he'd eaten in the last week. Definitely healthier than the microwave shit he usually subsisted on. He set the tea on the bedside table and dug into the scrambled eggs and potatoes.

His stomach didn't know what to do at first; it went into shock. Once it realized real food was being supplied, it began to growl. And it didn't stop until his plate was clean.

Lacey smiled when she took it. "Looks like you were hungry," she commented.

Max choked out a short laugh, holding his ribs. "You have no idea."

Now that the food was gone though, his eyes began to get heavy.

"You should take a nap," Lacey told him.

That was the last thing he remembered for several hours.

When he next woke, the sun had moved up the sky beyond the window frame. There was a sandwich under plastic on a plate next to the bed, with a note tucked underneath. 'Had to go out for a while. Be back soon. L.'

Max pushed up from the bed, feeling fairly rested. He padded into the bathroom to take a leak and decided to hop in the shower, get some grime off of him. He was disgusted with himself when he realized he still had crap on him from rolling in the street while he got his ass kicked, and he'd taken it to her bed.

It took him a while to get all the bandages off his appendages. When he was done, he decided he'd been less scary with them on. Snorting, he stepped into the shower, the hot water scalding as it ran down his battered body, but there was an edge of pain that actually felt good. He'd been floating through a fog for so long, just drifting along waiting for fate to realize she'd forgotten to snatch him on the way out. Lacey's concerned, tearful look when she'd sat with him last night gave him hope that somebody in this life would regret his leaving it. His parents were oblivious, living separate lives, shaking their heads at their wild child. They'd long ago washed their hands of him and the constant worry.

His team…well, his team was gone. And there was nobody to blame for that but himself.

Max lowered his head under the water, letting it sheet down his face.

Lacey was a nice lady. And as tempting as she was, he didn't think it was fair to get involved with her. Already he wanted to just open up and talk about everything that had ever happened to him. He wasn't normally so open, but he wanted to bask in her calm-headed, easy personality.

Using her fruity shower soap, he scrubbed himself as clean as he could around all his scrapes and stepped out, grabbing a towel from the rod. It was only when he was fairly dry that he realized he didn't have any clean clothes to put on. Damn. He needed to get into his apartment.

Anxiety began to creep in as he sat on the bed and took a bite of the sandwich. He'd missed his morning meds. His skin began to crawl as he looked at the clock on the table. Twelve hours without anything.

The sandwich turned to dust in his mouth as he imagined the flashbacks that were going to invade. The pills controlled most of that. Sweat began to bead his brow.

As gross as it was, he put his dirty clothes back on to call maintenance. Frustration ate at him though when he realized they weren't on site. It was Sunday, the only day the office wasn't staffed. He listened to the answering machine message and wrote down the emergency number. This was definitely an emergency.

Three hours. No sooner. When he finally got through to the head of maintenance, the man was on the beach down the coast. It would take him a few hours to get back.

Max began to pace.

CHAPTER SIX

✦

WHEN LACEY GOT back an hour later, Max was at a boiling point. It was obvious he'd worked himself into a lather worrying. About her or what was going on with his life, she wasn't sure.

"Max, what's going on?"

His fierce eyes targeted her. "I need to get out of here. I have no fucking clothes, no pills, I don't even have a key to get out of your place without being locked out. You left me stranded."

Lacey blinked at the aggressiveness of the outburst. "Actually," she murmured, "I didn't."

She crossed to the bedroom and returned with the note she'd left beneath the sandwich. Taped to the bottom was a gold house key. Not that he'd have known that, because he hadn't eaten the sandwich or even moved the plate.

Max let out a harsh yell of frustration and for the first time, Lacey actually feared what he would do. He gripped his head in his hands and headed for the door. Lacey reached out to grab his arm, but he flung her away. She had just enough time to see him disappear through the doorway before she tripped on the startled cat. She crashed to the floor, her head cracking on the tile.

FEET POUNDING THE black asphalt, Max ran in five-minute bursts until he started to see spots in front of his eyes. He couldn't breathe and the pain in his ribs was excruciating, but it kept him grounded enough that he wasn't breaking into random houses looking for meds like his own to ease his anxiety. He wasn't a great judge of time, but when he thought an hour had passed, he started back to his building. The maintenance supervisor would be there soon and he needed to apologize to Lacey for his outburst. She'd only been kind to him. In return he'd been shitty and difficult.

Maybe he could beg some more of those ibuprofen from her.

When he trudged up the concrete steps to the second floor her door was open. Lacey sat at her dining room table, a bloody dish cloth held to the back of her head. Another woman, a tiny blonde who looked vaguely familiar, stood over her fussing. The blonde looked up, her eyes furious, and stomped toward him.

"Who the hell do you think you are taking advantage of Lacey this way? All she's been is nice to you and this is how you repay her. Leaving her bleeding in her own living room."

Though he'd caught his breath from running, those spots danced closer in his vision and he focused in on Lacey. He'd left her bleeding?

Dodging the blonde, he walked forward and dropped down in front of Lacey. "What did I do?"

She shook her head, wincing. "It wasn't you, really. I tripped over Frank and went down. Don't worry about it, Max."

His fists clenched in frustration because he knew she was lying to protect him. Leaning up, he peeled back the cloth. Blood welled from a small cut on the back of her head and he felt like the lowest scum. Another mark on his sterling record.

"Does this need stitches?"

She nodded. "I'm going in to the office to do it. Dr. Petrovic can do it in there. I just wanted to wait long enough to let you know what I was doing. You don't read notes very well."

She gave him a crooked, chiding smile. Max's throat tightened with emotion and he had to look away. She leaned forward to press a kiss to the top of his head and he all but lost it. Wrapping his arms around her, he held her tight for a long minute, gathering his scattered control. Arms quivering, he kissed her back on the chest, just above her heart and pulled away. "I wouldn't hurt you for anything," he whispered.

She nodded against him. "I know."

Swiping his hands over his eyes, he made sure there was no evidence of his loss of control when he turned back to the neighbor.

"Be careful driving her in."

The woman nodded, eyes watching him carefully as he lifted Lacey to her feet. In spite of his aching chest he walked her down to the car and watched as they pulled away. He trudged back up the steps but turned to sit on the top one, deflated. His emotions over the past week had bounced from one extreme to the other and he craved the fog he'd lived in for the past few months.

The fog dulled the pain and let him hide from his ghosts.

He could admit to himself though, that his life was going to hell. Lacey, as little as he knew her, had become the brightest shining spot in his life. She was vibrant and actually made him feel better about himself.

Which was incredibly sad. A woman he barely knew had become what he was going to live for.

The maintenance supervisor arrived and let him into his apartment, handing him a spare set of keys he'd had made on the way. Max accepted them gratefully, feeling less like a total leech now that he could get out of Lacey's apartment.

He walked into the bathroom and tugged open the medication drawer. For the first time in a long time, he actually took inventory of all of the pills he took every day. There were a lot of fucking pills. He read the label of each one and realized that there were several that did the same thing. The symptoms were what caught his attention though. He took pills to get rid of the violent flashbacks, but others he took for his anxiety caused flashbacks.

No wonder he was so fucked up.

The thought of trying to get an emergency appointment at the VA made his head hurt. And his regular check-up was months down the road. He walked to the kitchen and dug in the trashcan. The paper with Lacey's pretty writing was at the bottom of the can. Looking at the numbers for several long seconds, he made himself pick up his phone.

WHEN LACEY ARRIVED home with three fresh stitches in her head, she was concerned that Max wasn't in the apartment. The maintenance man had probably arrived and let him in his place. That didn't necessarily ease her worry though.

Hannah puttered around, trying to make sure Lacey was as comfortable as she could be. She even offered to run upstairs and check on Max, but Lacey shook her head. "No, if he needs something he knows where I am."

In her heart, she wanted him to come down and check on her because he was concerned, not because he felt guilty.

But she didn't hear from him all that night.

Hannah stayed with her overnight, even though Peter-dick

didn't believe she had a concussion. Lacey frowned at the nickname she'd begun to adopt. It was going to get her in trouble one of these days. He had released her from work on Monday, though.

As soon as Hannah headed up the stairs to her own apartment the next morning, Lacey gave in to her curiosity and headed up to Max's. There was no response when she knocked on his door.

For a long moment, fear held her immobile. What if he'd finally done it? She knew he'd thought about suicide. It was in his eyes. The desolation and despair. The need for some kind of release.

The day wore on and there was still no word from him. When she went down to get her mail from the bank of boxes, she found the butterfly stationery she'd written Eric's number on for Max. A note had been scrawled on the back and shoved into the slot.

Lacey,

I appreciate the help you've given me this past week. You've seen me at my worst but still been able to smile for me. You have no idea how precious that is.

I have to go away for a while, but I will contact you as soon as I'm able. I know, after what I did to you yesterday, I have no right to ask, but I'm going to anyway. Think about me when I'm gone.

Max

Lacey's throat closed up and it was all she could do not to burst into tears as she read his words. Of course she would think about him.

And she did.

Lacey settled into a routine, going to work, coming home,

meeting with friends and in general keeping herself busy. She took drives down the coast to explore and went to the beach. But it wasn't enough. She was lonely for Max. When she got home from work every day, her eyes drifted to 4C in the parking lot, though it stayed empty. She didn't know if Max had gotten his bike back from the repair shop or not.

Though he didn't contact her directly, he let her know that he was thinking of her. One day she came home and there was a box on her doorstep. Inside were six of the plumpest, juiciest chocolate covered strawberries she'd ever seen. Using extreme willpower, she allowed herself to eat just one of the divine treats, then put the rest away. All week she nibbled on those strawberries.

Then a couple weeks later she arrived home to another box, this one long and narrow. Inside were twelve pale yellow roses. They made her cry because her father had been the only other man to give her roses, on her graduation from nursing years ago. He'd died not long after that. The roses had been the last things he'd ever given her and the last time she'd seen him.

Lacey sat and stared at the flowers for a long time. When she went to bed that night, she dreamt of her father, urging her to walk on the stormy beach. Max sat on the sand with his back to her, but he looked up at her and smiled when she stopped beside him. And while the storm raged around them, they were safe and cocooned in a little bubble of love. Lacey woke up smiling at the hoaky dream, wiping tears from her cheeks.

If only he'd left her his cell phone number…

She took the time to hand write a note, then sent it to Eric at the center. It would take a few days to get there, but her mind would be eased that she'd told him thank-you and that she missed him.

When she came home one day in summer, two and a half months after he'd left, there was a sporty red Fiat parked in Max's spot. Throwing her crap inside the door of her apartment, Lacey rushed up the stairs to the fourth floor and pounded on Max's door. A woman answered, looking surprised at the commotion.

"Oh," Lacey sputtered. "Sorry. I thought Max was home."

The pretty red-haired woman shook her head. "Nope. Sorry. Is he the guy that lived here before?"

Lacey nodded and forced her hand out. "Welcome to the building. I'm a couple floors directly below you."

Ashlynn Crane seemed like a nice enough lady, but she wasn't Max.

As Lacey trudged down the stairs to her apartment, choking disappointment overwhelmed her. There had been no word from Max for ten weeks now, other than the gifts, and she was worried. She debated calling Eric to check on him, but she doubted her friend could even tell her anything with the HIPAA laws in effect.

He couldn't have been redeployed. Even if Eric had worked miracles, Max wouldn't have been ready physically or emotionally. Whatever had happened to him months ago had been bad, so bad that he'd medicated himself to the point that he didn't care. And the doctors had helped him do it. That couldn't be fixed quickly.

Lacey tried to be outgoing and engaging, but it was hard. Twice she'd made the four-hour drive to her old stomping grounds, hanging out with her girlfriends from Walter Reed. But even that didn't satisfy her. There was a general feeling of discontent in her life that was very irritating. Ideally, she had everything she needed. Friends, a good paying job, a nice place.

The only thing she didn't have? Max.

CHAPTER SEVEN

✦

M AX LOOKED AT himself in the full-length mirror, tugging at the tight collar of the button-down shirt. He looked like a damn banker.

"Quit messing," Eric grumbled. "You look fine."

"It's just going to look fucked up when I get off the bike anyway."

"No, it won't. I don't think she'll actually care what you're wearing anyway."

Max looked at the guy who had become one of his greatest supporters. Eric O'Hanrahan, with too many letters after his name to remember all the certifications, had been as great as Lacey had said. When Max had called him that day weeks ago, Eric had balked until Max had mentioned Lacey's name. Then he'd arranged for a taxi to pick him up and deliver him to the drug and alcohol treatment center in Silver Spring, Maryland. When Max had realized where he'd been delivered he'd almost turned around. Silver Spring Rehabilitation Center. But as he'd looked over the grounds and the people moving around, it had seemed like a decent place to be. Eric met him at the car and as soon as he'd met the man in person, Max had felt at ease. As they walked around the grounds of the facility, he hadn't had the skeevy reaction he'd expected.

Eric admitted that they were fully booked at the time, but that special arrangements had been made to make room for him. And there was a clerk assigned to making sure the government covered his treatment.

"Lacey must have been a pretty good friend," Max commented, unable to keep the curiosity from his voice.

Eric had glanced at him and his lean face cracked into an easy smile. "Lacey Adams is a gem. She's not a counselor, but she has the instincts of one. She was there for me at a time when I truly needed it."

Eric leaned down and lifted his right pant leg. A metallic prosthetic shone in the light.

Max lifted his brows in surprise. He hadn't even noticed a hitch in the man's gait.

"She cared for you at Walter Reed?"

The other man nodded. "Lost it in Fallujah eight years ago. Then I had shrapnel in several other places they had to dig out. I was in the hospital for about five months. Lacey was my nurse from beginning to end. And when I had issues letting go of the props, like you are it sounds like, she guided me to get treatment. Even years ago she was aware of the dangers we faced when we came home."

Max frowned. He must have been so obvious to her. But she'd still taken a chance.

Eric started him off with a bang, so to speak. A full detox from everything he was on. Max occupied one of the few locked areas in the treatment facility for a solid week, and dealing with the detox quakes and tremors while he had three broken ribs was one of the most painful physical things he'd ever done. They gave him more drugs to counteract the tremors and nausea, but they didn't work as well as promised.

Once he'd made it through the worst of the detox, the

actual counseling kicked in. Max realized that most of the patients here were former military, all branches. Many of the counselors themselves were former military. Eric was a former Marine. There was an understanding that the situations could be talked about, just not the specific details of the ops themselves. Even knowing he had the option of doing that didn't make him any more comfortable about talking through the most traumatic event in his life.

Max left the lock-down facility feeling more clear-headed than he had in six months. Most of the drugs were out of his system and he was on a drug that supposedly helped with addictions. It seemed backwards taking more pills to get off the ones he was on, but the process seemed to be working. Since he'd only been on the overload of pills for a few months, the addiction hadn't set its claws as deeply as a long-time user.

The only hiccup came when he realized there was no bed for him in the main facility. It had been overbooked for years, literally, dealing with all of the returning service members that Walter Reed couldn't get to.

Eric offered him the spare bedroom in his own home. "Dude, you don't have to do that," Max protested.

Shrugging, Eric had given him that easy smile. "I owe Lacey. She's sent me people before, but I can tell you're different."

Max looked away, praying what the other man said was true.

He had the option of writing Lacey, but he had no idea what he would say. He refused to beg for her to wait for him any longer than she already had. That seemed too lame. She knew he was safe. Maybe when he was further along in his treatment, when he knew it would stick, he'd send her a letter.

Eric grew to be a true friend. Once Max started to open up

about that botched op in Yemen that night, it became easier to talk about. Would the guilt ever be appeased? No. But he was learning that just because he was guiding the boat that night, and boat team leader, he wasn't required to accept all the blame. Max had followed SOP and had landed the craft exactly where they'd planned. The only wrench in the machine was that they had been outmaneuvered. Out of all the hundreds of miles of empty shoreline, they'd managed to find one of the busiest smuggling routes in the country, loaded with traps for the unwary. They'd been ambushed as soon as they'd hit the beach. Four SEALs had died in the abduction the two in his own team while protecting the boat and two from the boarding team they were transporting. The terrorists had overwhelmed them with men and guns. Being in charge of the boat, with all comm destroyed, he'd been forced to barter for the lives of the survivors.

As Max's hands were secured behind his back and his face partially buried in the sand, he'd watched the light leave Terry Sharpe's eyes. His best friend in the world had died right in front of him. Taye Williams, his other buddy, had died in the original volley on the beach.

Also as boat team leader, he'd been treated to the deluxe bungalow eight feet down in the rocky ground. Unfortunately he'd had to share the accommodation with some of the indigenous residents, a couple of spiders he'd found out later were similar to black widows from the States. When they crawled over him, he'd been unable to get away from their pinchers.

Three nights later another SEAL team had come to their rescue. The only hiccup had been the spray of bullets the terrorists had sent in Max's direction as they were running away. One went through his back just below his shoulder blade. His right lung had been penetrated and it had never recovered completely. It was why he was out on medical. If a SEAL couldn't breathe, he wasn't a very good SEAL. Plus he had a muscle deficit in the back of his shoulder.

But the worst part of the entire thing was losing the two best friends he'd ever had in the world.

Talking about the fun they'd all had together had helped ease some of the pain. But then, it had also made the loss that much sharper. The three of them had been almost inseparable on the boat and off, because they'd trained constantly. Trained exactly for the situation which went to hell.

At the twelve-week mark, he wrote Lacey a note.

Lacey,

I know it's been too long. You can yell at me when you see me.

Eric is as great as you said and more. I'm off all the pills except for three, and I feel stronger now than I have in a very long time. Guess this rehab thing is working.

I think about you every day. Every minute.

Maybe we can go out when I get back?

Max

God. How lame that had been. He'd been gone for weeks and all he could do was write her an eight-line note. She'd written him a full-page thank you for the roses, telling him about her dad. It had made him feel closer to her than ever. The note was dog-eared from his constant handling.

Eric leaned into his line of sight, sandy brow raised. "You okay there, buddy?"

Max blinked and nodded, remembering where he was suddenly. "Yeah, I'm fine. I think this'll do."

Stepping back into the changing room, he changed out of the outfit they'd chosen for him to go home in. More dressed up than what he usually went for, but maybe Lacey would appreciate it.

LACEY GRINNED AT the note and folded it closed. It sounded like he was doing so well. Shutting her mailbox door, she dropped the rest of the mail into her shoulder bag and turned for the stairs. A chilly ocean wind whipped her hair around her face. The sky was dark with thunderclouds, but she couldn't be upset at the weather.

Frank greeted her at the door, meowing plaintively. Lacey stooped to pick him up when her cell phone rang.

Digging it from her purse, she pushed the door shut behind her, dropping Frank to the couch.

"Hello?"

A voice cleared on the other end of the line. "Hey."

Lacey dropped to the couch. "Max?"

"Yeah, it's me. I'm not bothering you, am I?"

"No, of course not! I just got in from work and found your note in my mailbox. Max, I can't tell you how proud I am of you."

There was silence from the other end before he cleared his throat again. "Thank you for telling me that. I really do appreciate hearing it."

"Well, it's true. I know it hasn't been easy for you."

He sighed on the other end. "No, but Eric has really been something. There are other counselors I work with too, but he and I have really clicked. And I don't think it's just because he worships the ground you walk on."

Lacey laughed. "Is he still going on about that? I was a friend to him when he needed one."

Max got quiet for a minute. "Sounds like you still could be if you gave him the chance."

Lacey laughed, a little uncomfortable. "No, he knows it will never go anywhere. He's a great guy, but not really my type."

The silence lengthened again.

"So what is your type?"

Somehow she'd known the question was coming. "Well, he has to be confident in himself and kind. Intelligent. Willing to be a partner. I don't know what else. It depends upon the situation."

"Hmm…Okay. Well, I realized when I sent that note that it wasn't very… personal. So, I wanted to ask you if you would go out with me sometime?"

Emotion made her blink rapidly and she was glad he wasn't here to see her get weepy just from a question. "Yes, I will, Max. But I had already decided I would just from the note."

He chuckled. "I'm just covering all my bases."

She laughed with him, more light-hearted than she'd felt in a long time.

"When are you coming back?"

"Well, when Eric says. But I don't think it'll be very long. We're working on some career counseling right now. I have to decide what the hell I'm going to do for the rest of my life."

"What do you like to do?"

Max hesitated and she felt bad for putting him on the spot. "Never mind. I was just curious. It's none of my business, actually."

"No, it is. I love it that you're interested. Be patient with me on this relationship stuff. Eric has been working with me but I'm still getting used to it." He sighed, sounding frustrated. "I'm just not sure. I mean, I'm not old enough to have been thinking about retirement already, so I hadn't given it much thought. I guess if I could go back I would train the kids coming through BUDs. Or get into some kind of tech specialty. I've always been good with wiring things."

Lacey folded her legs to the side and relaxed into the cushions of the couch. She loved the sound of his rumbly voice in her ear. Frank curled up against her, purring.

"Well, consider this an adventure then, Max. You're older and wiser. What would you do if you could choose anything in the world?"

She heard him inhale and hold it for several long seconds. "I never wanted to be anything but a SEAL. Guess I'll know when I see it. What about you?"

"Me?" she asked, genuinely surprised.

"Yeah. Do you like your job?"

Lacey frowned. Did she like her job? "I like being a nurse. I like helping people. Do I think I'll work at Peter-dick's the rest of my life? No."

Max burst out laughing on the other end of the line and Lacey realized what she'd said. "Petrovic! Sorry."

He was still laughing and she could tell he pulled the phone away from his face for a minute. "Peter-dick? Really? Did you come up with that?"

"No," she admitted. "Hannah calls him that. I'm going to get in trouble and say it out loud someday at work. He's a really nice man."

"Yeah, okay," Max laughed. "If you say so. Sounds like you might have some discontent too."

Lacey sighed. "I do. Not sure exactly what I need though. I enjoyed working at the military hospital, but I was getting burned out. Giving so much all the time. I loved the soldiers, though. That's why I thought Virginia Beach would be a good place to be with the heavy Navy population, but I'm still not happy. We're both in kind of the same boat right now, huh?"

"Yeah. The thought of coming back there and not being

part of the population is disturbing to me."

"I'm sorry, Max."

"It's not your fault, Angel. I think things just change and you have to be willing to change with them or move on to something better."

She smiled at the endearment he'd slipped in there. "I think you're right, Max. So we'll leave our options open, right?"

"Right. Hey, I'm gonna have to go. I have to meet Eric in about twenty minutes."

Lacey sighed. "Okay. It was very nice talking to you, Max, and I'm so happy you're doing well. I'm anxious to see you."

"I'm anxious to see you too. And kiss you. Not long now, I don't think. Bye, Angel."

"Bye, Max."

Lacey tapped the hang-up button on her phone and flopped against the couch, happier than she'd been in a long time. Months, even. Just from a damn phone call.

Frank looked at her curiously, making Lacey laugh.

Damn, she was almost giddy just from a five-minute conversation with him. What would she do when he came back and she was with him even more?

Fall more in love.

The thought sobered her. While she'd always hoped for love, she'd never expected to actually find it. Dad had loved Mom, but she didn't think Mom had appreciated him when he'd been alive. George Adams had died from a massive heart attack. After everything he'd been through being deployed in Asia with the Army, Lacey had thought he was invincible. But her mother had shredded his heart many times over. Lacey had his medals in a box in the closet because Mom hadn't wanted to keep them. Made the other men uncomfortable, she admitted.

Charelle Adams, or Cherry as she liked to be called, lived a free and easy life, moving from one boyfriend to another. Occasionally she settled down for a while and actually got married, but they didn't usually last long.

Lacey had learned to take care of herself and be responsible at an early age. It had made her leery of her heart. She'd thought she'd been in love before, but what she'd felt years ago didn't even compare to the excitement and arousal she felt while talking to Max.

She was in serious trouble.

CHAPTER EIGHT

✦

F IVE DAYS LATER on a beautiful Friday afternoon, he stood
at her door, clean-shaven, dark hair trimmed and more
handsome than she ever could have imagined. His face had
filled out and his lion-gold eyes were crystal clear and targeted
on her. When he grinned, his bright, even teeth gleamed. A
deep blue, button-up dress shirt hugged his shoulders and his
long legs were encased in pleated khakis.

Holy hell he was too good-looking!

Lacey stepped forward to wrap her arms around him, nestl-
ing her face into his neck. Some spicy cologne tickled her nose
and sent a swirl of need through her.

Max wrapped his arms around her neck, cradling her head.
Lips pressed against the top of her hair. He moved back far
enough to get one of his hands to her face, tipping her mouth
up to his. Lacey caught her breath as his lips settled on hers
and began to move. Oh, she'd forgotten how good he tasted.

He cradled her head in both of his hands, angling his
mouth tighter against hers. Lacey parted her mouth, inviting
him inside and he took her over, sweeping deep with his
talented tongue. Lacey moaned, shocked at how quickly he was
consuming her.

When he did finally pull back, his cheeks were flushed but

he was smiling. "Hello."

"Hello," she giggled. He hadn't even made it into the apartment! They stood in her open doorway where anybody could see them.

Shaking her head at her impatience, she tugged him into the apartment. The tiredness from her day at work had disappeared. "Why didn't you call?"

Max grinned, his eyes crinkling at the corners. "I wanted to see the look on your face you just gave me. The unrestrained, unplanned emotion." He shrugged his heavy shoulders. "I wanted to catch your natural response."

Lacey smiled up at him all the wider. She could understand his insecurity. "Well, I'm thrilled to see you. You've made a dull day one of the best I can remember."

"Let's go make it better." He winked at her playfully. "Get changed. We're going on a date."

Blinking, she glanced down at her scrubs. Hell, yes! "Give me a few minutes."

Lacey stood in front of her closet for a solid two minutes, wondering what on earth she was going to wear. Wait...She scraped hangers back and forth on the rod until she found what she was looking for. Not normally a dress kind of girl, she'd bought it on the spur of the moment a few weeks ago. Pale cream with little pink and green flowers over it, the summer dress had capped sleeves and a sweetheart neckline that looked great on her boobs. And the angled hemline showed off her decent legs. Slipping on a pair of low sandals she unearthed from the closet, she moved to the bathroom. Normally she wore clips at work to keep her hair away from her face. Pressing the power button on her curling iron, she brushed out her hair, realizing how long it was getting. She needed a trim, but that was a worry for another day.

Anxiety skittered through her stomach. She hadn't been out on a date for a couple of years, sadly. And the last date certainly hadn't created this excitement in her belly. Her hands shook as she curled a few pieces of hair around her face and crown. Pretty but not overdone. Turning the power off she reached for her makeup bag. Again, just a touch to highlight her eyes and lips. If she was lucky, he would kiss it off anyway.

Surveying herself in the full-length mirror on the back of the door, she paused, actually surprised at how good she looked. Running her hands down her hips, she walked toward the living room.

Max swallowed as Lacey walked into the room, wondering what the hell he'd done in his life to get her to take notice of him. Was the black cloud finally drifting away?

Without even realizing he'd done it, he walked forward to cup her face in his hands, pressing a kiss to her dark pink lips.

In deference to her dress, they took her car. They spent the evening on the beach, hitting all the heavy tourist spots. They paused in front of the huge statue of King Neptune and his three-pronged trident. Max's gut clenched at the familiar symbol of the SEALs and wondered if he would ever get over the way he left. The ocean pounded away against the sand and he could almost imagine it squishing between his toes as he trained.

"You're still a SEAL," Lacey told him, drawing his attention. "Just because you're not running with the teams anymore getting shot it doesn't mean your accomplishments are diminished. What happened to you is part of the job. I'm sure there are many other SEALs out there not on active duty. I know at least some of you actually retire."

She grinned up at him and he couldn't help but grin back.

"I know what you're saying," he admitted. "It's just a hard

transition right now because I don't know where my life is going."

She nodded, tucking her flying hair behind her ears. The ocean wind just grabbed it again, vexing her. Turning her face into the wind she let her hair blow back, capturing it in a fist. With her other hand she dug in her little purse for a black elastic. With a couple of twists, she had secured the heavy weight of it.

The movements were incredibly feminine and he could tell she'd done it many times before. He smiled as a couple of stray tendrils escaped their confinement.

When she realized he had watched her the entire time, she shrugged and smiled, then gasped as a gust ripped at her skirt. Skimming her hands down her thighs, she held the fabric close, laughing. "I can't win. I should have worn shorts!"

Max laughed with her, loving her obvious joy.

They headed down the boardwalk, rubbing elbows and bumping into each other, just enjoying the casual contact. When he guided her toward Rockfish, a popular seaside eatery, she sighed happily. "I've wanted to go here for a while."

Max had worried about going out and feeling like he needed a beer, but he didn't. If it had been with a group of guys it may have been different. Lacey was a water drinker, which suited him as well. They shared a platter of the restaurant's famous crab cakes and laughed at stupid things, becoming more comfortable with each other. As the night wore on though, the glances lingered. He caught her staring at his lips at one point when he tried to explain something and the bolt of heat that rolled through his body was truly epic.

It was too soon to sleep with her. Max realized he was worried that he would move too fast, fouling any chances of a relationship. But when she looked at him like he would taste like a scrumptious chocolate treat, his control weakened.

Lacey declined dessert, but when she caught sight of his gooey brownie sundae, she agreed to take a bite. As her lids fluttered down and her mouth swept the cream from the spoon, she moaned. Max hardened at the sound, wishing they were somewhere else completely.

Lacey seemed to think the same thing, because she drew in a heavy breath. His gaze dropped to her full breasts. Through the thin cotton of the dress and her bra he could see the shape of her nipples. When he lifted his eyes, she was staring at him, hard. She dropped her napkin beside her plate and gathered her belongings. Max waved the waitress down to give her the check and they left. As they stepped outside to the boardwalk, he grabbed Lacey's hand and pulled her to a stop. When she turned with an inquisitive smile, he captured her mouth with his own. She tasted of brownie and ice cream, like he probably did, but it was way sexy on her. As she moaned into his mouth, he debated finding a dark corner and taking her hard up against a wall.

She wouldn't go for that, not in public anyway. The thought of doing it in her apartment sent dangerous images through his mind.

They walked down the boardwalk hand in hand. Max didn't normally go in for the whole PDA thing. He'd had girlfriends before who clung to him, which drove him nuts. He needed to have his hands free and be able to do what he needed to do without a woman hanging on him. It was a defensive issue. Lacey was different though. He needed to hold her hand as they walked because he didn't want to not be touching her.

"Is this okay?" he asked.

She grinned up at him, nodding.

So they walked back to her car hand in hand. She handed

him the keys to the little Toyota sedan and as he drove them back home she kept her hand under his on his thigh.

Max didn't remember the drive, only the feel of her hand through the fabric of his pants, inches from his aching dick. He parked the car and went around to open her door but she'd already gotten out. He followed the sway of her ass up the flight of stairs to her door and nibbled kisses against her neck as she unlocked it.

"If you don't want this," he murmured, "you need to tell me before I come in."

She glanced over her shoulder at him, her blue eyes dark with arousal. "I know."

Pushing the door open, she tugged him inside by the hand.

Excitement surged through him, and a little fear. Lacey was a wonderful woman. She deserved better than he could give her, but he followed her into the bedroom anyway. Maybe if he took care of her better than any other man ever had, she'd keep him around.

Lacey stopped at the side of the bed and reached for the buttons down the front of her dress, but Max stilled her hands. "I want to do this."

First he captured her lips, trying to convey to her how beautiful she was. He hadn't even undressed her but he knew she was going to rock his world. Settling his hands against her rib cage, he teased the underside of her breasts with his thumbs. "You know, you have incredible breasts."

She grinned and nodded, but the smile drifted away as he cupped her weight in his hands. His thumbs brushed over her hard nipples and she cried out.

Urgency pressed at him, making his fingers fumble as he unfastened her dress. Again, she did a purely feminine shimmy and stepped out of the fabric, revealing a pale peach bra and panty set. She reached behind her and released the bra. Max could not contain a groan. Simply beautiful. As she lay down on the bed in front of him, dark hair spread beneath her, Max had a genuine worry he wouldn't last long enough to enjoy the feast before him. But they had all night.

Shucking his clothes, he stood before her, proud and erect. Lacey smiled and sat up to reach for him. "No more road rash and bruises. And you've been working out."

Max had and his battered ego loved that she'd recognized that. He took a moment to reach into his pocket for his wallet with the condom inside and rolled it on. Then, stepping forward, he eased down on top of her. Lacey's legs fell open in welcome and he wedged himself against her panties. Lacey gasped, hands tightening on his sides. Covering her mouth with his own, Max shifted against her, loving the feel of her breasts cushioning his chest. Slipping his tongue into her mouth, he rocked against her. He could feel her arousal climbing as he kissed her.

Leaving her mouth, he moved lower to her chest. Dragging one dark pink nipple into his mouth, he drew it tight against the roof of his mouth. Lacey cried out, cupping his head in her hands. She didn't move him away though. As his mouth played with her breasts, he reached for the gusset of her panties. They were soaked with her excitement. Max had to stop and breathe for a moment to tamp down his own impending orgasm.

When he thought he could continue, he shifted enough to draw her panties down her long legs. Moisture glistened against the dark curls. With a single finger, he eased between the plump folds of skin. She was drenched with excitement and shifted beneath his touch, angling her hips into his fingers. Max circled her clitoris once and she cried out.

"More," she gasped.

He made the same movement twice more and she quivered. Letting her catch her breath, he focused on her breasts again, blowing cool air against the moist tip closest to him. Shuddering, she clutched the sheet beside her hips, panting faster. Max kept her on that edge for several long minutes, taking her almost to the peak, then drawing back to cool her off. When she was crying out his name, demanding he come to her, Max almost slipped inside, but he had a feeling she could come several times. Doing steady, hard circles around her clit with his fingers, he gently bit her nipple.

Lacey cried out and convulsed in his arms, her orgasm ever so more beautiful because he had caused it. Her smooth tummy clenched and her legs shifted as the driving tension eased. Max gave her a couple of minutes to catch her breath, then eased over top of her. As her hazy, languorous gaze caught his, she gave him an exquisite smile.

Emotion made Max pause at her entrance, feeling as though he was on the edge of something momentous. He inched forward, wanting to etch every moment on his memory. In spite of what he wanted, as her tight, slippery heat pulled him in, he lost all sense of himself. Rocking forward, he basked in the sensations coursing up through his body. Euphoria like he'd never felt before overwhelmed him, making him surge harder. Within just a few heavy plunges, he was at the edge of orgasm.

Max stilled, panting into her hair, trying to maintain some sanity. Lacey moved beneath him, peppering kisses up his neck to his jawline. Max tilted his head just a little to meet her hungry mouth and the enthusiasm she showed him cranked his own need. Without even moving, his orgasm loomed closer.

Then she raised her legs higher on his hips, rocking into him, and every thought of restraint left his head. Surging deep and sure, he took what she offered.

The orgasm struck him hard. He'd denied himself for so long. As the pleasure consumed him, he arched his back and cried out, unable to curb it. Then came the spasms, involuntary as he emptied himself into her, but delicious. Lacey echoed his cry as another orgasm consumed her as well.

Lacey's arms were clamped around his body and she was pressing kisses to his jaw when he finally caught his breath enough to look up at her. She arched her brows at him. "You okay?"

Max nodded, too overwhelmed for words. She gave and gave with her mind and body and soul, and she was asking him if he was okay. "I'm beyond anything I can express. I truly think that was the most perfect thing I've ever experienced."

The words were true. He'd had sex many times before, but something about Lacey and him together felt totally different. No one else had pulled the emotion and need from him that Lacey had. And the appreciation.

The appreciation was a little confusing. Was he so wrapped up in her because she was the only one who had seen through the drugged-out mess to the man beneath? The thoughts were too deep to think right now.

Lacey stroked his back, just at the edges of the scar. He was conscious of where her hand was, but no longer anxiety-ridden about what she thought of it.

Though he regretted pulling away, he had to dispose of the condom. As soon as that was done though, he pulled her back into his arms.

LACEY WOKE TO kisses being planted down her spine and a heavy shape looming over top of her. She glanced over her shoulder, brow raised.

Max looked up at her and grinned.

She giggled. "Again? Really?"

Though she teased him, her body began to respond. Just the thought of his sex made her center go liquid. They'd loved all through the night but she was ready to go again.

Max laid her flat but propped her hips up a little. Lacey arched, knowing he was coming in from behind. As she planted her hands against the mattress, the head of his dick breached her opening.

"I don't think I was the only one ready for another round this morning."

She chuckled as he glided deep in her moisture, then moaned. They fit together like they'd been built for each other. As he began to rock his hips into her, Lacey began to pant.

"Fuck, you feel so good this way," he gasped. "I'm not going to last."

Neither was she. As he seated himself deeper and deeper with every surge, rubbing over that bundle of nerves at the front of her pubic bone, the tension in her lower belly wound tighter and tighter until it couldn't tighten any more. She shattered. As the orgasm rocked through her, prolonged with every plunge of his body, she wondered if she could stand it. Max responded to the clutching of her body, heaving deeper as his own orgasm caught him in its grip. He slammed into her, spasming over her back, crying out. Lacey arched harder, extending his pleasure, until he finally collapsed on top of her. He forced his heavy shoulders to the side so that he wasn't crushing her and panted into her ear. "I don't know where the hell you learned to do that, but you need to do it again."

Lacey laughed, swiping her sweaty bangs away. "I wasn't taught to do it but it felt right."

"You're not kidding," he murmured.

She could tell he was falling asleep. His arms tightened around her and they ended up spooning. Lacey's own eyes drifted closed.

When they woke a little later, they were both famished. They stumbled to the kitchen, intent on filling their bellies. Lacey wanted an omelet loaded with as much crap as she could get in it, so that's what she started. Max wanted the same but with toast. When everything was ready, they sat at her little dining room table across from each other.

"I haven't been this hungry in forever," Lacey murmured around a mouthful of ham and egg.

Max leered at her. "I've been starving for a long time."

Lacey chuckled, knowing he was referring to sex. "How long has it been?"

His eyes sobered. "Well, I got injured in February, but we'd been in and out for months before that. I haven't been involved with anyone for more than a year and a half." His dark brows furrowed into a frown. "Damn, that sounds bad."

Lacey grinned, shaking her head. "It's been longer than that for me. More like a couple years."

Max scowled. "I can't believe nobody's snatched you up. You're sexy and incredibly smart. Sane."

She gave him a narrow-eyed look. "Well, normally I avoid military men. When you live just a few miles from the largest Naval station in the world though, that becomes a little difficult."

"I can see that. Why do you stay here?"

Lacey looked at her plate for a long minute. "Well, not sure exactly. I guess because it's what I'm used to. I love the feel of a military area."

"But you don't want to be connected to the military?"

Frowning, she shook her head again. "I was burnt out

dealing with all the trauma that came through Walter Reed. I loved it there, but I had to have counseling when I left because I would wake up crying, dreaming of the next trauma rolling in. I still don't sleep right all the time. When I saw you, I knew exactly what you were going through. And the help that you needed."

Max set his fork down. "I'm sorry I took so long to convince. When I walked into your apartment that night and saw that bloody towel against your head, I almost threw up. I knew I had to change if I had any kind of chance with you."

Lacey's eyes teared up. "I knew you didn't mean to hurt me, but I'm kind of glad it happened if it got your butt moving in the right direction." She brushed her eyes with her hands.

Max stood and circled the table to kneel at her side. He took her hands in his. "You mean a lot to me, Lacey Adams. I have a feeling I'd do just about anything for you."

Those damn tears blurred her vision again and all she could do was wrap her arms around him, loving the feel of him wrapping himself around her.

"Do you have family?" he asked.

She shook her head. "Not close. My mom lives in Florida but I don't talk to her much anymore. She's always been a little more involved in being her than taking care of her kids. I have a brother in design at New York University. A few cousins here and there. Nobody very close."

"I'm kind of the same. Parents were in London last I heard, but that was a few years ago. My lifestyle was too reckless for them, they said. No other close relatives. Grandparents on my mother's side died years ago, but my grandfather on my father's side is in a nursing home in Florida."

"Do you get to see him very often?"

Max shrugged. "Every once in a while. It's been a couple

years though. He's got dementia and doesn't remember who I am."

"Hm. That's hard."

They talked all through the night, comparing childhoods and schools. All of the miscellaneous things couples talk about early in their relationships that they had missed out on while Max was gone. It was the best night of Lacey's life.

THEY SETTLED INTO an easy relationship. Too easy, Lacey thought sometimes. Max moved back into his apartment. The woman had been the relative of one of the guys from his old team. She'd been in town for business for a week and had needed a place to crash.

Lacey was glad the woman was gone. She'd had some crazy thoughts about her being Max's ex or something, moving in to rekindle a relationship.

The only reason she'd been thinking that way was because she was insecure.

Max greeted her as soon as she got home, sometimes even jogging down to give her a kiss in the parking lot and carry her things. He continued to go to counseling, to a guy Eric had suggested in town. Again, they avoided the VA and got more immediate treatment, which was better for all involved. Yes, he still struggled with flashbacks and anxiety attacks, but for the most part he stayed on an even keel.

Lacey was amazed at the change and humbled that he credited her with setting him on the right track. She didn't like wondering what would have happened if they hadn't hit that wall that night. Or the floor, as it were.

The only thing that wasn't working for them were their careers.

Max's medical disability paperwork came through and he

was in a funk for days. Being a Navy SEAL was truly a calling, and when he couldn't do what he'd loved most in the world, it hurt. His old team had moved on to other missions, calling only when they were back in town. And even then they couldn't share what they'd done or where they'd been.

"I don't know what to do with myself," he murmured, lying in bed with her that night. "I watch the clock waiting for you to get home. I've looked at school and I guess I can do something I just have no idea what."

Lacey propped herself on his chest, hands stacked beneath her chin. She'd been thinking about something for the past couple weeks, but didn't know how he would react. "What do you think about moving?"

Max cranked his head around to look her in the eye. "Where?"

Lacey shrugged a little. "Away from the military that we can't be a part of anymore. Away from all the reminders. I know we haven't talked much about where we are going," she wiggled a finger between them, "as a couple, but it may be an idea."

Max looked at her as if he were debating a problem in his head. "My life is a mess right now. As crazy as I am about you I don't know if it's fair to tie my life to you when I'm floundering."

Lacey looked away, swallowing hard. "I understand."

She rested her head on his chest and listened to his pounding heartbeat, but tension had crept between them. They'd lived together for the better part of two weeks now, so the thought of him not being around made her chest ache.

Max shifted, sitting up in the bed cross-legged. Lacey sat up as well, adjusting her sleep shirt. Max ran a hand through his dark hair. "This feels like something big we should talk about.

If there's one thing I've learned from the hundreds of hours of counseling I've done in the past couple of months it's that you open your mouth and speak up to get things settled. Talk to me."

Lacey knew he was right, but she didn't want to pressure him to do anything he wasn't ready for. She looked into his golden eyes, wondering if she was about to send her SEAL running. "I think in order to keep my sanity I need to change some things. And I have an idea for you, but I need to make a phone call. It may not pan out, but it's been niggling at me for a couple of weeks."

Max pressed a hard kiss to her forehead, then craned down to reach her lips. "I trust you implicitly. How can I not? I love you. You've never led me wrong on anything."

Lacey reeled back. "Wait, you love me? Where did that come from?"

Grinning, Max shrugged his muscular shoulders. "It just seemed like the right time to tell you. I'm kind of surprised you didn't know."

She shook her head, dazed, but elation began to fill her. Lunging forward, she tackled him to the bed, giggling. "I love you too, damn it. I can't believe you told me like that. I thought you were breaking up with me!"

"Why the fuck would I break up with you?"

"You just said you didn't think it was fair to tie your life to mine."

"I know," he admitted softly. "But I don't think I can ever give you up."

She giggled as he nibbled kisses down her sensitive neck.

"That's good," she gasped. "Because I don't think you could force me away now. I've been freaking out over telling you I love you for weeks."

His eyes sobered. "Weeks? Really?"

She nodded, dropping a kiss to his chin. "At least. I fell in love with you when you sent me the yellow roses."

Max wrapped his arms around her, holding her tight. "Thank you," he told her softly, leaning up for a kiss. "I never imagined I could be this happy after the past year I've had. You really are the best part of me."

"I think we bring out the best in each other," she whispered.

Relaxing into his hold, she set out to show him again why they were so great together.

EPILOGUE

✦

M AX LOOKED AT the piece of paper Lacey handed him three days later. "What's this?"

"Your interview time and address."

Duncan Wilde, Lost and Found Investigative Service.

She handed him a narrow folder. "And your plane ticket."

Max shot her a narrow-eyed look, peering in at the ticket. "Colorado? Really?"

She nodded, hands clutched together in front of her.

"This is the phone call you had to make?"

She nodded again. "Duncan was a patient of mine years ago. Actually, I know all three partners of LNF. When they were in the hospital they got the idea to create the company."

As cool as the guy sounded, there was one big issue. "I'm not an investigator."

Lacey smiled that chiding, encouraging smile she had. "No, but you could be."

He mulled the idea over, more interested than he would have expected. "And what would you do?"

Lacey grinned. "There's a great VA out there. I asked around and they're always looking for experienced nurses. I could be helping vets but not be drowning in the emergencies and critical care that I did at Walter Reed."

Max narrowed his eyes on her excited face, surprised at the animation he saw there. Hell, if a job in Colorado could do this much for her spirit he'd haul trash or clean sewers. "Why don't we both go out?"

Her blue eyes widened with surprise. "Well, I could maybe."

"Why don't you call out there and try to set something up? If we're going to do this we may as well jump in with both feet."

Max laughed as she disappeared into the living room, task in front of her. The two-hour time difference worked in her favor. She caught one of the nursing supervisors before she went off shift and set up an interview for four days from then, on a Friday. When she hung up the phone, she did an excited little dance and jumped into his arms.

Laughing, he held her against him. Lacey was a level-headed woman, but this had definitely motivated her.

On the plane two days later, she vibrated with excitement. "Oh, it's so pretty," she sighed as they caught sight of the snow-capped mountains below them. Max had to admit they were gorgeous. And as they drove through town in their rental car they found more and more things that they enjoyed. There were exercise trails everywhere, which appealed to him. No, he didn't have his air lung capacity like he used to, but the more he worked out the better it got.

They drove by the well-kept VA in the center of the city and found the entrance she was supposed to use for her appointment. Then they headed toward the north side of the city and drove past LNF. Looking up at the glass building, Max got a good feeling about being there.

They ate at a popular chain restaurant, lingering over dessert afterwards.

"So, what can you tell me about Wilde?"

Lacey set her fork down. "He came in with terrible injuries but the man is strong. Not just physically. He has one of the strongest spirits I've ever seen. You'll see what I mean tomorrow."

They decided they would go together to the appointment. Lacey hadn't seen Duncan for years and she desperately wanted to.

When they walked into the reception area of Lost and Found Investigative Services, they didn't expect to find a man in a wheelchair holding a woman in his arms and spinning circles with her. The petite, curly haired woman was giggling and clutching his neck. "John, you have to stop," she gasped. "There are people coming."

The man laughed but looked up and slowed when Max and Lacey stepped into the room. The woman's eyes got saucer-wide with embarrassment and she scrambled from his lap.

Lacey recognized John Palmer immediately, but he got a funny look on his face, like he'd seen something that befuddled him. She stepped forward and raised a brow at him. "I'm not wearing scrubs but I don't look that different, do I? Come on, Gunny."

The confusion cleared and John pushed forward with a whoop. "Lacey!"

She leaned down to loop her arms around his neck. "Still as sexy as ever, I see," she whispered in his ear.

The big man laughed out loud, shaking a finger at her as she pulled away. "I remember what you told me that day."

Lacey giggled. "I told you fuck you. And then I told you that there was some one out there that would love you, warts and all." She glanced at Max. His brows lifted over his eyes because she didn't normally speak like that.

John lifted his hand to the woman he had been spinning. "Lacey, I'd like you to meet my girlfriend Shannon Murphy. Incredibly, she doesn't mind my warts. Shannon, this is the best damn nurse at Walter Reed. She took my abuse and gave it back to me the same way."

Shannon reached for Lacey's hand, pumping enthusiastically. "You must be quite a woman to put up with this guy back then."

Lacey laughed. "You too. I doubt he's changed that much over the years."

They all laughed like old friends until Lacey held out a hand to Max. "Gunny, this is Maxwell Tate, Navy SEAL. He has an interview with Duncan in a bit."

Duncan himself stepped out then, probably drawn by all the noise they were making. And he looked good. Lacey had always had a soft spot in her heart for salt and pepper haired men and she wondered if it had started with Duncan years ago. More gray on the sides now, but his face was lean and healthy, and his dark brown eyes as sharp as ever. "Lacey Adams. I didn't know you were coming with Mr. Tate. You're not trying to sway my opinion, are you?"

Lacey grinned and stepped forward to wrap her arms around the tall man, conscious of the slim black cane at his side. "No, I don't think I need to, Duncan. How the heck are you?"

"I'm good," he assured her. "Running ragged trying to put fires out right now, but managing. Come on in."

He led them into his office, a comfortable space with a huge whiteboard on one side of the room. Lacey chose a leather couch against the wall, folding one leg beneath her when she sat. Max dropped down beside her with his elbows on his knees, hands held between them. She squeezed his arm in encouragement as Duncan took the chair to her left, and John stopped just beyond the coffee table.

"So, Lacey, how have you been? I haven't heard from you in a while."

"Well, I left Walter Reed a couple years ago, before all the bad publicity, luckily. I'm working at a private practice right now. Is Roger still here?"

Duncan gave her a single nod. "He is. Graveyard shift. One of the best men I've ever hired."

Lacey smiled happily. "I'm so glad. I knew he would be perfect here."

Duncan looked to Max. "Lacey here was my one-man pitch team at Walter Reed for a while. She'd send me guys she thought would fit in well with what we do here. I only hire disabled vets and they need to have a certain skill set. She said you were a SEAL?"

"Yes, sir, Special Boat Operator 2nd Class onboard the *USS Carl Vinson*, lead coxswain on a RIB crew. For the most part. But I've been everywhere and done everything. Can I ask what you do here?"

"Personal surveillance, divorce cases, embezzling, cyber investigations," John listed, running a hand over his short dark hair. "Hell, even doing deed searches through court records. Whatever we need to do to get a job done. And we have jobs for every vet's skill level."

Lacey thought it sounded fascinating, and by the look on Max's face he did too. "I didn't know there were companies out there that only hired vets."

"There aren't very many," Duncan admitted, "and we were one of the first. And while we don't normally hire Navy," he looked Max up and down, "occasionally we make exceptions."

Lacey laughed, shaking her head. "You all fight for the

same country. I don't understand the rivalry."

Max sighed and the other two gave her dirty looks.

Duncan leaned back in his chair, stretching out his legs. "So, explain to me what's going on here. You guys are together, right? Lacey, are you going to move out here if he gets a job?"

Lacey took a breath and nodded. "Yes. I've already spoken with the VA downtown. I have an interview there tomorrow. While I don't want the Walter Reed craziness, I want something more than I've had for the past couple years."

"The VA is a good place to be then," John told her. "A lot of our guys go out there for counseling and PT."

Lacey was glad that they knew of the hospital and that it seemed to be a good facility.

Duncan held his hand out for the folder Max carried and he handed it over.

"When can you start?"

Without even checking the contents, Duncan had slid the folder beside his thigh. Max lifted a brow. "You're not even going to look at it?"

Duncan shook his head and motioned to Lacey. "Nah. Your resume is sitting right there. She's sent me some of the best men I've ever hired. You won't be any different. When can you start?"

Emotion choked her throat. He was seriously going to give him the job just on her word? Max seemed just as surprised. He stood from the couch and shook Duncan's hand, then John's. "I'll do everything I can to prove you right."

Smiling, Duncan pushed to his feet, cane at his side. "I know you will," he murmured. "Now, the question was serious. When can you start?"

Max looked down at Lacey and she shrugged. "I won't

know if I have the job or not till after tomorrow."

Duncan and John shared a look. "Okay. As soon as you hear, let me know. I have a man out right now with injuries and our third partner, Chad Lowell, is in Texas with him. The ship's running a little light right now."

Max nodded. "As soon as we hear we'll call. Tomorrow we'll start checking out apartments too."

Lacey reached out to hug Duncan again, then John. "It's so good to see you guys again and you're both doing so well. How long have you been dating Shannon, John?"

"Almost a year now," he admitted.

Lacey frowned at him. "Almost a year? Are you engaged?"

He frowned, rocking the wheels of his chair in agitation. "No."

She shook her head at him. "If she's been with you this long she'll stay with you, but you'd better make it official."

Glowering, John pushed away, grumbling, "I know".

They made their goodbyes to Shannon and took the elevator down. On the sidewalk below, they paused, then flung their arms around each other. Max lifted her off the ground, squeezing her tight and making her laugh in joy. When he pulled back enough to press his lips to hers she sighed with contentment.

"I can't believe how easy it went," he admitted, setting her to her feet. "All because you said the word."

Lacey shrugged, a little self-conscious. "I don't think it would have gone as easy if I hadn't sent him those other men and they hadn't proven as good as I claimed. Believe me, you'll have to show him how good you are. He'll work your ass off. Pretty soon it sounds like."

Grinning, he nodded, looking a little dazed. Then looked down at her with a frown. "This is moving us pretty fast. Are you okay with this? Should we look for two apartments?"

Frowning, she started toward the parking lot and their rental. "I'm not sure," she admitted. "I think if I'm willing to move across the country with you I should be able to live in the same apartment as well. Don't you think? We've practically been living together anyway for the past few weeks."

She paused to look up at him and was caught by his gleaming smile. "You know, if somebody had come up to me six months ago and told me what I was going to be doing and where I would be, I would have called them damn liars and beat the shit out of them."

Lacey laughed because the same applied to her. "Me neither. But I think we're doing what's good for both of us. I mean, Duncan's group probably doesn't get into the same intrigue you're used to, but it's better than floundering around looking for something that you have to settle for."

Max unlocked the car and handed her into the seat, then hurried around the front of the vehicle. It was hot outside today in Colorado, but a very different kind of heat from Virginia.

Once he dropped into the seat and turned the key in the ignition to start the AC he turned to her. "I don't know where to begin. I've got so much I need to do. I guess we need to know about your job though, first. I don't want to come out if you're not going to be here."

She waved a hand. "I'm actually not worried about the job. I think Colorado is a reciprocal state when it comes to my certifications and I'll need to file some papers, but once I do that, it's not normally very hard for a nurse to find a job. I suggest we look for an apartment right now, big enough to work for both of us."

The thought of officially living with somebody sent tingles

of alarm through her, but also gave her a warm, content feeling inside. Max had moved a lot of his stuff down to her apartment over the past couple of weeks anyway, so it wasn't a great stretch to have him there all the time.

"You may have to ride your bike out, or maybe haul it in a U-Haul with your stuff. I know I'll need one to get my stuff out here. But it sounds like we may be coming at different times. My paperwork will take at least a couple of weeks, but it sounds like Duncan needs you as soon as you can get here."

Making an odd face, he shook his head. "Things are changing, Angel, but I have to tell you, I'm okay with every bit of it. You've given me a purpose several times over and I wake up every day with an eagerness I thought I had lost forever. I will do everything in my power to make sure you have the happiness you deserve."

Lacey blinked, so thankful she'd followed her crazy instincts and this man into the alley that day.

"I don't think you have to worry about that, Max. You've already made me happier than anyone else ever has. Seeing you this excited feeds my soul. I love you dearly."

She leaned forward to rest her lips on his.

THEY FOUND AN apartment complex they liked just a few blocks away and put down a deposit. If they didn't like it later they could find another, or perhaps a house.

All of Lacey's worry about the VA job faded as soon as she walked in the door. Good karma returned to her when the nursing recruiter sat her down and opened with, "Duncan Wilde says I would be a fool not to hire you."

Duncan was a long-time volunteer at the VA and had come to career counsel some of the men, then outright hired a few others she was told. He'd called Mrs. Hampton last night at home to let her know Lacey was coming.

The supervisor went over the hiring package and told Lacey the job was hers if she wanted it. With no hesitation she said yes. Lacey promised to file the transfer paperwork as soon as she got home and she would notify Mrs. Hampton as soon as she was confirmed to work in Colorado.

"I'll be glad to get you. We have more jobs than qualified people."

Lacey walked out of the VA almost dancing. Max had waited in the car in the parking lot and she climbed in, then almost lunged into his seat to wrap him in her arms. "It's mine," she gasped. "Duncan called in a favor and I have the job as soon as I can get out here."

Max laughed, drawing her tight into his arms. His lips covered hers and Lacey knew that both their lives were going through epic changes, but she had faith that they would be stronger for the trials.

The End…

If you would like to read more about the disabled veterans of the Lost and Found Investigative Service, check out these books:

The Embattled Road (FREE prequel)
Embattled Hearts – Book 1
Embattled Minds – Book 2
Embattled Home – Book 3

Books *related* to the Lost and Found Investigative Service, but not directly in the series line:

Her Forever Hero
SEAL's Lost Dream

Other books by J.M. Madden

Second Time Around
A Needful Heart
Wet Dream
Love On the Line – Book 1
Love On the Line – Book 2
The Awakening Society – FREE!
Tempt Me – Book 2 of the Awakening Society

Connect with J.M. Madden

If you'd like to connect with me on social media and keep updated on my releases, try these links:

Newsletter
http://www.jmmadden.com/newsletter.htm

Website
http://www.jmmadden.com/

Facebook
https://www.facebook.com/jmmaddenauthor

Twitter
https://twitter.com/authorjmmadden

And of course you can always email me at
authorjmmadden@gmail.com

About the Author

NY Times and USA Today Bestselling author J.M. Madden writes compelling romances between 'combat modified' military men and the women who love them. An eternal optimist, she believes there is a soul mate for everyone, no matter what the situation or physical challenge. She's written 18 romances in the past three years and has plans for many more.

www.ingramcontent.com/pod-product-compliance
Lightning Source LLC
Chambersburg PA
CBHW072122250626
47159CB00007B/2534